Brick and Marrow

Brian Hunter

Third Edition II_XX_MMXXV

dedicated in loving memory
of the unforgettable GRH

without whom,
none of this would be

~

Carter Machine

Monday, October 14th 1946

Amber-hued daylight peeked through the greasy, stained, cracked clerestory windows of the workshop roof. Daylight was all the light the workers had for most of the day; the lights wouldn't be turned on 'til it was almost too dark to read a gauge. Fifty industrious men flitted about the workflow between cumbersome machines, massive avocado-colored General Electric motors with their tin-shrouded belts wrapped tightly over whirring pulleys that moved those industrial presses with enough force to crush a Cadillac.

The rough-hewn wooden letters of 'Carter Machine Co.' sturdily mounted along the roof facing the harbor were outlined clear as day by the sunlight as they billboarded across the broad interior wall of the shop. They drew across the corrugated steel walls like some macabre movie advertisement. Men in gray leather smocks walked through the shadows cast by the name of their employer, seeming not to notice the branding across their faces as they carried fresh-pressed steel panels to the next workstation.

For a while, the droning of large machinery seemed an orchestra of brutal noises: *Clunk-swish-creak-clunk*, endless cycles of a song that was music to no man's ears.

Suddenly, a shrill sound pierced the air and echoed across the shop. In an instant, a hundred red STOP switches were pressed in panic, some so hard they broke those cheap bakelite-plastic buttons. Unfortunately, the sound that stopped all the ants from marching was the primal scream of a wounded man who had just lost something crucial.

The outcry was brief. It was even borne more of fear and

panic than of the soon-following pain. Scores of heavy levers were quickly left unattended as all those towering machines had fallen dead silent in the space of a few heartbeats. A dozen or more men gathered as one of their own was carried away to seek help for his wounds, a careless fool who learned his lesson around such treacherous metals in the harshest of ways.

Gabriel Marshall had gone pale. All the blood flushed from his face except perhaps his tired, red eyes. A cold chill stung his nerves. His trembling hand still held the emergency-stop lever of his hydraulic sheet metal stamping press as he watched his working partner Mark carted off by fellow shophands with Mark's right arm mangled and bleeding profusely. More than the gore, Gabe fixated on the wilted look on the young man's face as though he had just been betrayed, discarded. A trail of sticky red followed along the concrete floor as the fallen crewman was dragged away.

Gabe stood still in shock and dread, closing his eyes as he tried to replay the exact sequence in his mind; he remembered his partner shouting "clear" after placing a four-foot steel sheet to be formed by titanic forces into a simple industrial basin. Gabe had then depressed his override switch and yanked the machine's actuating lever, and in nearly no time, the air was pierced with a cry from Mark, a damned fool who had bent down to tie his shoe and leaned on the machine, right *into* the machine, to steady himself. Mark's arm was caught and crushed under the force of that hulking machine's hydraulic panel-stamping jaws. It was a horrific injury, career-ending, to be sure.

Standing silent for several minutes, wisps of blood still spattered across his gray smock from that poor bastard, Gabe hardly noticed as a shop foreman walked up behind him and placed a hand on Gabe's shoulder. At that moment, Gabe knew precisely what was going to happen.

Some of the boys in the breakroom would talk about the foreman who had no name, the man who'd overseen so many men that he stopped bothering to introduce himself. If you worked at Carter for long, you knew who he was. A short, hairy brute of a man with baseball mitts for hands. He always smelled of cheap, minty aftershave and a 5-cent cigar. *Probably lives alone, the miserable old mug...* Gabe had thought of him in the past.

While those boys' breakroom conversations about the boss flashed in Gabe's mind, he turned to face the foreman. The man tapped a stub of ash off his cheap cigar onto Gabe's boot in such a nonchalant manner that Gabe could take no offense.

"Kid, listen up. See, I served, just like you. I dealt my fair share of ugly on a lot o' those goddamn krauts, and if it weren't for the bullet in my hip I'da served up even more. I know you did good. But see, you're like a razor blade. We all are. You cut a million hairs in your life, sure, but now you're too dull to cut any more hairs without causin' a mess. I just can't afford to keep you on 'round here. This might'a been your first mistake, but it's also gotta be your last, son. For chrissakes, you look like you ain't slept in a week as it is. Get some rest and find work that ain't so dangerous, you listening?"

The man stuffed a small sheet of pastel pink paper in Gabe's hand before giving Gabe the grimmest, deeply disappointed glance Gabe had ever received. It was eerily reminiscent of the look of a loving father watching his son go hard against his upbringing or commit some mortal sin.

Gabe took a deep breath, pinching the bridge of his nose and wincing in embarrassment as he realized that without steady work, he'd be on the street in mere days unless he dipped into his meager pension savings.

He decided to protest his unfair dismissal; by the time Gabe was able to clear his throat and creak out a rebuttal, the foreman had already walked away, leaving him with nothing but a twisted-up gut and a small gaudy piece of paper chattering in the breeze of the shop's massive ducted fans. The walk home would be a long one today; there was no spare money for the train.

The rest of his day at Carter Machine was a haze. Gabe faintly recalled finding his way to the backrooms, changing out of his workman's clothes and into a serviceable pair of slacks and a shirt. He didn't even bother to shower as most of the boys in the shop would do after a hard day in the oily workshop. The locker room was a ghost town now. While it was usually a bustle of sweaty and foul-mouthed men talking about the coming night's conquest or how badly they wanted to see the next Cagney movie, it was past lunchtime now, and Gabe was given solace and quiet to collect his things.

As he packed, the only chore he took any real time on before departing was taking a moment to toothpick-clean the chain and intricate grooved details of his pocketwatch over a chipped and rusted white ceramic bathroom sink. It was a tenuous effort, as his hands were still shaking, and he hadn't really had the sense to wash off the day's grease and carbon silvering that laid itself deep into the scars and folds of well-worn palms.

That watch was as old as Gabriel himself. His father Gilbert's watch, in fact. Every man in the Marshall family had owned it; Gabe received it from his father by mail after he'd completed basic training, and it had been Gabe's gift to his uncle Robert after Gilbert had passed away in Gabe's absence. Gabe was always appreciative that Robert had stepped in and taken care of the Marshall estate while Gabe was away at war. So, in a short and very strained letter, Gabe had insisted Robert keep and care for the watch just as his father had done for as long as Gabe could remember. He'd written that letter succinctly thanking Robert for his assistance by the dim light of a GI battery lantern in a damp, crowded tent outside France not long after deployment. Gabe had insisted Robert sell what was left of the estate, save the watch and whatever else Robert had wanted for his parish. Gabe had no need for the home or the possessions inside, what little of it remained after the fire.

Now Robert was gone, and the watch had come back to Gabe. Such a watch was a relic of another time in which gentlemen wound theirs manually every day, set by the nearest church bell chimes: nine, ten, noon. A thousand little thumbscrews were plucked from their nests by a fingernail and spun a good dozen times, giving the springs life enough to keep time until perhaps the next day. A several-day winding could be wrung from a better watch. In New York, Gabe heard no reliable chimes with which to start his day. He was forced to stop at the desk of the small 'hotel' (in its prior iteration, a very well-attended brothel), where he had been lucky enough to find a room he could afford. Behind the dusty and cluttered desk of the hotel, there was a fancy electric clock with long sweeping hands hung high above a bookshelf. A silky red cloth-wrapped cord limply snaked down to the wall socket, where this clock drew its fair share of power and made an audible buzzing noise as it kept a perfect time. The young woman behind the desk would nod at Gabe as he paused to catch the hour, though she was usually on the phone chit-chatting about some raucous topic such as her recent dates with a black-haired, square-jawed sailor just stateside for the week (or sometimes just for a night).

Gabe reflected on the history of that watch as he cleaned its chain free of the dust and grit that seemed to permeate every crevice of the workshop, and he felt glad that he'd never have to so sodiligently clean that old and tired brass chain again. Its previous owners had cared for the watch for decades, carefully polishing the glass and using toothpicks to keep the knob's ridges shining to their minuscule depths. Robert's caring touch still showed in the gleam on that old brass watch. Gabe felt a pang of guilt, knowing he'd probably never be able to care for it quite so well as either Gilbert or Uncle Robert had.

Hanging his head a bit, Gabe tucked the small and heavy watch back into his shirt pocket next to a pair of cheap cigars that were crumbling at the ends. He stopped near the exit to see Carter's payroll clerk whereupon he showed his little slip to receive his final pay of a few dozen dollars. That clerk said next to nothing, counting the dollars and coins as though it were a mundane chore. Even more disheartened about his expendability, Gabe trudged out of the building into the streets that cut between a hundred similar warehouses and workshops. The alternating brick and corrugated metal walls still rumbled and echoed with the sounds of industrious men building, making, and earning their wages.

Having passed a few of his coworkers on the way out, he saw not one of them dare catch his eye... it was almost as though they avoided him, lest they might be seen as someone 'like him' and receive a small slip of paper themselves. Around the corner, down an alley, a few blocks' walk further passed before Gabe got his feet back on a nicer neighborhood's pavement. He slipped between passersby, chin near his chest and brow furrowed in concern with hands shoved deep into his pockets. A few shop windows caught his eye; he scanned them as he passed for the oft-seen crudely hand-written 'help desired' or 'labor needed' signs, but Gabe saw none. He grumbled over how common they had seemed when he arrived months prior. How easily he'd gotten the job at Carter, now how quickly that was taken.

A simple question resonated in his head. *Why am I here?*

The question was New York City, specifically. More truthfully, in this context, his question could have meant anywhere. Anywhere but home. Anywhere but his bedroom. Any time before he shipped out with ten thousand fresh-faced patriots and took up killing in the name of serving Uncle Sam. Any time before misfortune stole his mother and before morbid despair claimed his father.

He came upon a bench in a small clearing, not far from a market he'd frequented in times past. The cement space had once been a wye, where train tracks met from three directions, but now was just some unused plot a short walk from the docks.

Sitting down on that bench, Gabriel lit one of those cigars he'd received from a friendly coworker the week prior. It had been gathering dust in a shirt pocket in Gabe's locker, but the shirt belonged to Carter Machine Co., and Gabe took only what he could fit in his own pockets. He'd even left behind the boots he wore. The heels had worn out long ago, so Gabe abandoned them for the next sap to take the job—the thought of anyone needing those size thirteen tugboats of his amused him just a bit.

He sat there struggling to answer that question and justify to himself why he was sticking around. His mind drifted to what brought him to New York: Robert Marshall. His too-recently deceased uncle. The last vestige of a family he'd had, the only reason he would ever want to be in such a dirty and depressing city. The only other reason? Well, she had come along about the same time Robert departed. Gabe wondered to himself if that one gorgeous glimmer of hope in a diner smock was what had kept him sallowing in the Bowery for so long.

Smoking that cigar, Gabe recounted to himself the story of Robert's demise. Mulled over what was holding him to New York City with such a tenuous grasp. His recollection mainly was images and few words. In his upset state, Gabe was unable to recall anything but heartache and loss.

Some six months earlier in April, Gabriel had flown back from France; his part in the war being thoroughly over and done due to a medical discharge, though he'd seen some time in hospital before he walked free of that old life. Robert had taken up boarding in New York City, looking for a fresh start from all the pain and loss back home. Gabe had no intention of going home, so he took a train to see Robert and take in a bit of the city life.

For half a decade, Robert had been writing to Gabe regularly throughout the young man's paid-in-full tour of Europe, as his uncle had referred to it. The letters would be received in bundles every few months; Gabe's unit moved around too frequently. Nevertheless, Gabe had enjoyed each letter. Well, *nearly* every letter. The one short and somber note that Robert had written to inform Gabe that his father, Robert's brother Gil, had passed... *that* letter was not so welcome.

In truth, that letter was more an apology than anything. An apology for not being stronger, an apology for leaving Gabe and

Gil to their own devices after they'd lost Gabriel's mother, Patricia, to that raging fire that had torn their town asunder. The same fire which had claimed Robert's church and, in no small way, Robert's faith along with it. Robert had never found his forgiveness, and even in Gil's passing, there was no closure for the man. Robert had continued to blame himself, which was no surprise as the fire itself had begun in his church. It was something any man of conscience would be hard-pressed to forget.

The cigar embers burned and spiraled; the cigar disappeared slowly. Gabe recalled the quiet hospital room where he held Robert's frail hand, which shivered a bit in Gabe's firm grasp as the old man's kidneys failed. Gabe tried to warm and ease him, but no medicine could fully subdue the symptoms. Gabe could see clearly that dusty apartment that his uncle had been inhabiting, covered in stained clothes and empty bottles, and the stench of sick soaked into the mattress. He could still hear that clatter of the old Crosley record player he'd brought to Robert's bedside, dropped in shock as he saw Robert's cold form draped in a stained white sheet. That unforgettable sound of shrapnel from that record player crunching under his heavy feet as Gabe stormed out of that godforsaken death ward.

Gabe hoped to forget the smell of that musty old room where Robert had been hiding from the world for too many years, living off a pittance. Gabe's mind forced forward the memory of the last time he saw this feeble and bedridden man alive, a gaunt figure who perplexingly shared the eyes and smile of the young and fearless Uncle Robert who'd helped raise Gabriel from a rugrat to a soldier.

Both of those iterations of this man were now gone, ashes and detritus in a simple urn alongside those of Gabe's mother and father. Urns, which now occupied a small wooden fruit crate under Gabe's bed, in a sad, tiny room where he could hardly sleep. Gabe was alone here in this city of decaying stone monoliths, and the cigar was now bitter and short.

The sunset was slow as molasses over the distant spires as the foul air of the harbor drove Gabriel to stomp out the stogie and trudge away home.

Bad Neigbors

The rest of the walk home was long, but Gabe didn't curse it, considering he could hardly afford bus fare now. He was looking down at the little map of the city he'd been carrying around, a slight tan booklet stamped 'The New York City Pocket Visitors' guide, 1945 edition'. They'd been set out free-to-take at the Rexall Drugs he'd shopped in the day he arrived in New York, now a good bit worn from being toted around in his pocket for so long.

He recalled a conversation he'd had with a bartender in a dingy pub one of those first few days in the city. Sleeping in flophouses to save dimes, Gabe spent most of his first days in New York bellied up to a bar or sleeping on beer-stained benches, the occasional pitiful night hung over a rope. He'd been chatting with the barman and offered his opinion based on his travels during the war, "They sure did a good job putting this city together. Everything lines up. You go over to Europe, those big cities, it's all jumbled. No sense to it; every street points in a new direction!"

The bartender oozed cynicism.

"Sure pal, but the difference is, they have some history over there, and they didn't have boats and trains and technology when those places were built' the paunchy barman had quipped, 'there was nothing here but marshland and natives maybe a hundred years ago. I'm not sure what this city might look like in another hundred... but it sure couldn't get much uglier!"

With that, Gabe had toasted the notion and bought the bartender a whiskey; he agreed, even to this bleak day. *Ugly damned city.*

He had only a half-dozen blocks to go when he realized he'd made the last portion of the trek without looking up from his feet as he navigated the sidewalks of the Bowery, a rough and dirty stretch of New York that had earned a reputation for fast talk and loose women.

Only some of the locals still called this place the Bowery; its name had been synonymous with crime and vice for more years than many men lived. Some civic-minded folks had, a few years after WWI, made a real public stink about changing the name of the place. It was an attempt at washing away the past. Those peoples' voices were drowned out by the raucous sounds of the bars, flophouses, and men's clubs lining the streets. Countless reasons a man could lose his shirt, and lately, lose much more.

The streets were teeming with rough and frustrated men. Men who worked hard for a living, men who would rather spend their extra dimes at those sinful businesses than go home after a day's labor to an empty room. The Bowery was often conspicuously absent of women, especially after the sun had set.

The stories of violence and vice were now, after the war, almost glamorized. The recent trends in entertainment after the war had movies and stories showcasing a criminal protagonist as some sort of dark hero, which bothered Gabe more than it should. He hated the neighborhood, hated it with every bit of passion he'd ever been able to muster. The glorification of it all was something he felt born to despise, not as a pious man, just as a gentleman.

Gabe kept walking, ruminating. Thoughts idled in his mind like quiet spirits, memories of his father Gil sitting on a weatherbeaten split-log bench under their backyard trees.

Gilbert Marshall had spent countless hours with Gabe on their property tending to chickens and fixing whatever tools and equipment Gil could find for free, talking to him about the values he held close—the non-Christian morals of good men versus the imposed morals of most men, the way to live right in a world going wrong. He shared stories of his father's struggles against the darker temptations of the world. Gil had been sure to instill in Gabriel a need to do right by those who had done no wrong and to live humbly. His pride was built upon respect for others, his family reared on that same tenet.

In truth, Gabe had struggled with that agnostic righteousness being his learned nature but not always his primal instinct. His memory wandered to vignettes of times he was abroad when he was paid to fight that ugly war against what he was told was *true* evil. Some sort of immense conglomerate force looking to burn away the American life after having nearly succeeded with other cultures and peoples. Gabe's brow softened a bit as he thought of the more heroic moments he'd spent out there, given a clear enemy and the means to do the right thing without judgment. Moreso, he was proud of the men he served with than his actions, but the thoughts of war he quickly shut away.

The closer he got to his building, the more he focused on his surroundings and his feelings about them. Sure, there were days he'd actually miss being that infantryman, facing death and hunger and occasionally trench-foot... but never, ever would Gabriel Marshall miss the stink of the Bowery. That place had an oily, humid air that told tales of secrets hidden away in the sewer grates, of alleys echoing midnight screams, and of corner curbs worn bare from the cheap wooden soles of the vile men waiting there for another opportunity to cheat or steal.

For a moment, a bright marquee cleared his mind... the theater near Bowery Street, a short walk away under the elevated tracks of the railcars that lined many streets, was advertising one of Gabe's favorite movies. Gabe paused for a moment on the sidewalk, staring under the beautiful, ornately lit marquee as it stood against a gray and grimy street. Black block-lettering silently shouted MILLION DOLLAR KID, a comedy. Seeing it the year prior, the film had Gabe belly-laughing at the antics of a handful of sharp-tongued youths always looking for a way up in the world. He thought about how much he'd *love* a good laugh, but his right hand resting inside his pocket was wrapped around damn near the only money he had to his name, and he couldn't spare even the dirty dime to see that silly movie again. Heaving a sigh of disappointment in himself, he turned back to the sidewalk, back to the walk home.

Another few blocks passed, and he could feel the eyes of the people in the shops and restaurants... He felt them gazing upon him as though they knew innately his quiet disdain for their home, and their eyes squinted in disgust as if they took it personally. He shook his shoulders a bit, almost trying to shake off their gaze (which he was half-certain he was imagining, anyway). As the dim light of a familiar hotel sign cast his shadow, Gabriel knew he was 'home'... a thought that disappointed him even more than losing his job.

Gabe opened the front door and heard the familiar chime of a small brass bell; the charming little accessory shopkeepers and business owners relied upon to lift the chins of weary clerks, reminding them to greet everyone the same. A brunette head lifted behind a large desk, and the dowdy little girl behind that desk nodded and smiled,

"Good evening, Mr. Marshall!"

Before Gabe could reply with his customary hello, she continued.

"You're a day late on your upkeep. Shall we settle your bill?" and she tapped her finger on the counter as if it were a mercantile barrelhead in the old west.

Gabe nodded back and wearily handed her the crumpled papers in his pocket. The bills were loosely wrapped in the pink slip unceremoniously given by that nameless foreman, and she unfurled it along with the dollars, looking at it inquisitively.

She brought her eyes back up to Gabe and offered, "I sure didn't realize your name was so nice, Mr. Marshall. Gabriel... Isn't that from the Bible? I only know most folks here by their last, and those are usually phony..."

Gabe smiled a bit; she was being sweet in an honest way.

"Not so much; it's an old name, a family sort. Just call me Gabe."

He looked down past her dimpled chin and saw a small gold cross tangled in her sweater.

"You a Christian?" he inquired.

She smiled and clasped the cross.

"Well, *raised* Catholic, and it sure makes my poppa happy to see me wear it. How about you?"

"No, not really. I read that book a dozen times over the years, but it didn't say a damned thing I needed when I was, ah... when I was *away*."

As he paused, he looked down from her eyes to the pile of dollars on the counter.

His words hung in the air for a moment, and the girl fidgeted with the chain on her cross necklace. Gabe saw his entry on the ledger in front of her and recalled filling in that check-in box on the night he arrived; he'd scrawled US ARMY under the 'references' column as though he had no family or friends to speak well of him. At the time, it had made Gabe more at ease with the place, feeling like he could sleep a little better in a joint that required references. It hadn't taken him too long to realize that they simply wanted to know whom to contact in case you died or couldn't pay up.

The girl knew what Gabe meant by being 'away'; she'd lost her brother in the damnable war, but nobody ever asked her or seemed to care. She still kept a picture of him as a reminder, as a bookmark. Sadly, it usually ended up between the pages of a magazine; she wasn't much for reading.

She said, "Well, I like your full name. Why doesn't nobody call you that?"

Her grammatical error told Gabe of the girl's humble upbringing.

"Short name from my youth, and it just stuck around, don't you know? I joined up right after my school years."

Gabe was hesitant to be forthright with the girl; in reality, he begrudged his Christian name and the tones it carried—tones of high chapels and old men telling people how to live, whom to love, and whom to hate. The name had been his cross to bear, an ironic thought he'd had once or twice.

The girl smiled again at him, counted out his owe, and gave him a few dollars back that she likely shouldn't have.

"I'm sorry you lost your job, Mr. Marshall. I betcha something'll come along."

Gabe smiled back and collected his papers off the counter. As much as he hated it, the little gal had just done him a kindness more than anyone in this big, awful city had yet.

I don't even know her name.

Guilt scratched at the back of his brain on that. Still, he didn't have the energy to ask her. He nodded as he stepped away.

Grabbing a newspaper off the wooden rack by the desk, the near-penniless man dragged his feet up the narrow Victorian stairs to his little forlorn room and that damned squeaky Murphy bed. As he made his way up, he glanced down at the paper, a local print:

TRAGEDY HASTENS HUNT FOR MURDEROUS MUGGER

New victim renews fears of unseen threat in the streets!

Chrissakes... he thought to himself as he opened the door to his room. *That's got to be ten or twelve people now. This goddamned city!*

Mumbling to himself, he carelessly untucked his shirt and set his shoes aside, eyes still on the article. He recalled moments in past years of sitting in a tent or a mess hall trying to make out the news in the European papers, stacks of them having been trucked in and shared amongst a hundred GIs.

He sat on the edge of his bed and pored over the news. Horribly vivid and ghastly images flashed in Gabe's mind as he read the paragraphs of the article describing the terrible scene that played out the prior night in his very neighborhood. The reporter certainly seemed not to care for the delicate sensibilities of innocent readers.

In a hushed tone, Gabe read to himself the reporter's firsthand account of the scene aloud to himself as he perched his behind on the edge of the bed.

"A grisly scene unfolded here in a small alley off Rivington Street. Another apparent attack in a string of recent, gruesome muggings-become-murders in an otherwise safe neighborhood. This reporter has seen tragedy and evil, yet this awful perpetrator seems to be bent on more atrocious acts as the tally in this unfurling horror steadily climbs. Several detectives are on the scene, where a chalk outline of a man alive just yesterday is smeared with evidence of what was, indeed, an unjust and agonizing end. The barricades put up by police have been nearly inadequate in keeping away the flock of frustrated and angered locals trying to make sense of such tragic, needless violence. Last night's victim was a respected longtime resident of Sixth Street. Though we cannot yet publish his name, he is survived by a justifiably distraught wife and two now-fatherless sons. One Sergeant Mullally from our Police precinct had this information for our readers:

"Today, we are all in shock at this terrible scene. In what appears to be another hold-up, the victim was beaten to death with a blunt instrument, and it is unclear whether belongings were taken. With the victim having no known connection to nearby establishments, our department is ruling out theories that this might be collateral damage from a barfight or other vice activity. As with prior assaults, no witnesses came forward. Anyone with information as to what may have happened or where we can find our suspect will be rewarded.' Contact Sgt. Mullally with the NYPD in person or by telephone switchboard at CI 7-6007. Until we find this dangerous perpetrator, local women and children are advised to stay indoors after dusk and only travel in vehicles or when necessary."

Gabe stood up, undressed to his undershirt and shorts, swallowed the lump in his throat, and read on. The article continued,

"This reporter interviewed local citizens who had witnessed suspects of prior murders leaving the scene. One possible suspect is a male, about five and a half feet tall, with dark hair and a pronounced step. Other accounts place the assailant at over six feet. When questioned by The Herald, the Sgt. had no comment regarding the fact that all known victims of this spate of robberies-turned-killings have been male. More details forthcoming;

be sure to catch tomorrow's edition!"

There was a brightly lit flashbulb photo of two policemen 'holding the line' behind a wooden barricade. No gore could be seen, but a few men in the photo were grimacing over something awful just out of frame.

Gabe felt a bit sick in his stomach. He had read many such articles in the dailies, usually alone in his room or over a coffee in the lobby parlor, and each time, it made him sick. Still, he couldn't help but read the articles. Through all the descriptions, through all the awful words and photos... there was something different about it. Something struck a chord with Gabe and made him more curious than upset. He'd felt this unease plenty of times, usually when he was around death and violence.

Sitting down again on the corner of the tired old Murphy bed, Gabe gazed down at the quilt adorning his uncomfortable mattress. It was a rosy red and blue tapestry of flowers and finials, vestiges of a short period when someone had truly put an effort into renovating the old brothel. The quilt hung limply, tattered around the edges, and underneath it was a pauper's mattress.

Bet these old walls have seen some salacious nights. Hell, I couldn't ask a gal back here... I'd seem a damn fool or a cad. I couldn't ask a proper lady, anyway...

He pondered for a moment the sorts of folk who may have perched on the same bed, in the same place, in years past... staring across the small room at a weary pine armoire, the crown molding cracked and broken where people had carelessly hung their garments and handbags causing so much strain on the thin, unnecessarily ornate wood mantle along its top edge.

To be honest, Gabe had been responsible for at least one of those cracks. He recalled the first night he had the room the previous spring, hanging his heavy coat off the top edge of the armoire to dry after a surprise rain shower.

He recalled that evening, attempting to find some shelter under the L-train tracks perched on iron columns above the street. His problems had only multiplied as he discovered that the rain came down through the open framework of the elevated tracks and brought down with it a direct, filthy, oily-black water that had for decades been staining the sidewalks and streets below. He'd only realized after a few drops of it found its way past his teeth, the grime and filth raining down from his ill-conceived 'shelter.'

On that recent rainy night, an acrid and dirty taste in his mouth vividly brought back the memories of hazy air dense with diesel tank exhaust on a nameless battlefield in war-torn Germany. Taste is a powerful sense, strongly tied to so many wonderful and terrible moments in life. Under that steelwork, he had spit profusely and cursed his carelessness and stupidity with blue words. He'd never forget that damn stain on his tongue.

As Gabe stood up to finish getting ready for bed, he tossed the newspaper onto the foot of the bed, hoping thoughts of alleyway murders and the bitter flavors of his past would fade away. His tired hands gently hung the gleaming brass pocketwatch on a short wall peg that had likely been there for decades. He was exhausted mentally, physically, and even more emotionally. The burden of losing yet another job was a burden he could handle begrudgingly.

Gabe laid his head down, hoping for sleep.

I sure could use a whisky... the good stuff... not the crap in the nightstand. Maybe tomorrow. Probably not... maybe.

As the bed groaned underneath him, he mumbled some blue words into his pillow about that foreman, about fairness. At the same time, his jaw relaxed... his breathing slowed... a night of peace and comfort. Exhaustion overtook him as the streets remained quiet outside, a rather unusual atmosphere for any night in the Bowery. Maybe the city owed it to him on this night.

Smoldering City

Tuesday, October 15th

Gabe woke to a raucous bang from the window. The sharp sound set off the man's nerves; despite being groggy, his years of battle and honed instincts had overtaken him instantaneously and jolted him awake. He rubbed his eyes clear as he sprang to the window, both frightened and excited at the sound. Peering out the window to the street not far below, he saw a simple scene of slow cars and barren sidewalks. Dawn gave a warm glow to the sky in the East, and the streets were golden red and glistening with morning dew. Not a soul traversed the sidewalk adjacent; looking down, all he could see were dozens of awnings flittering in a breeze; he saw not a thing worthy of his nerves. His heart relaxed from a wild fervor to a calmed pace as he let out a sigh of relief, stretching his arms wide and still scanning the street below for anything else of interest.

Probably just a backfire from some old jalopy, he assured himself. *I just can't catch a good night's rest here.*

Gabe hadn't been sleeping well since arriving in New York, unsure if it was the bed or the smell of the place or perhaps the too-frequent noise coming from neighboring rooms when someone had brought home a guest for a bit of debauchery. In the moments after waking, some folks can recall their dreams with such clarity that it feels like sheer memory. Gabe was one of those poor bastards.

As he wiped the dusting of sleep from his eyes, he felt echoing feelings of fear and loss. Sitting back onto the bed half undressed, recollections of the night's dream overcame him quickly, and his imagination still gripped his mind as it does in slumber.

A scene of serenity, his dreaming self standing near the railing

16

of a porch. A fine country home or perhaps some small business. Somewhere inviting, a house with rough-hewn wood banisters. The railings were painted a crisp white and showed a bit of wear. His one true love (whoever she was) had just driven away in a stylish dark-blue convertible from the 1930s; he looked at his shoes and saw them clean and shined. He and that girl had been talking in hushed tones to avoid a spectacle outside. Something about their home, about wealth: she was unhappy with her place in the world. Clearly upset, her face was still so beautiful and kind...

In an instant, still in the dream, Gabe found himself standing high atop a green knoll, looking down upon a coastal urban sprawl. A clustered and suffocating city built of gray columns slowly racing to touch the sky, the place was dimly lit, as though there were no power or electricity. Murky waters surrounded the entire city and stretched off to infinity, their waves tearing at the edges of the mute metropolis.

The dream worsened. A massive cell of gray-purple clouds rumbled forth and reached down from the heavens, touching the top of the towers like an ominous and unnatural handshake. The clouds were gathered unnaturally; smaller cells combined to form something of a funnel that thrust downward in fury toward the heart of a modern Gomorrah. That was one of the Bible's tales that had terrified Gabriel as a child.

Gabriel's dreaming self stood atop the hill, bearing witness as the clouds drew down in a pattern to perfectly mate with the eaves of the skyscrapers like the teeth of a vicious animal. Then, in an instant, flashes of immense and crackling red fireballs shot down from the clouds into the city; he could clearly see the flares of what must have been pure hellfire flickering their brief light across the walls of those wicked buildings until reaching the streets below, where they exploded and burned the city to its core. He looked away in terror, realizing that he was now alone on the hilltop, and thought back to that anonymous love, a lithe, blue-eyed woman whom he had never known.

The ground beneath his feet shifted with a wail. The lush hilltop slowly dissipated, folding inward on him as the green pastures became leaden grey walls. He was now within that smoldering city. He tilted his head up, witnessing the celestial and thunderous assembly of wicked clouds above, their purple light richly casting down over his frame. His body was in light, but his eyes were in shadow.

Standing before him, a faceless man clad in a black cloak was moving ever closer but taking no steps. A spectre, an apparition. This creature howled out like a hurricane gale in the night, and the cold, dead walls of the street echoed that otherworldly cry. Gabe was frozen in panic and fear, his body stiff and his eyes still cast in shadow. He could see now that the ghostly silhouette in its tattered cloak had reached out to him, its knurling fingers slipping around his throat.

A flash of electric purple certain doom from above, its smoke creeping down the walls themselves to surround him and this new foe. After the blinding light and a blink of blackness, Gabe's vision was clear as day as the hellstorm subsided. Only now, he was facing himself. It was like looking into a mirror but feeling only the pain of that other self in a reflection, a shadowy copy who was choking nearly to death. Gabe's strength was now his demise, his powerful grip capturing the last of that familiar body's life and drawing a blackness all around. Confusion. Scorched and dissolving sky, as wisps of ash and smoke became all that could be seen. Purple, then grey, then a swirling red-black. The stench was vile.

Once again, he sat at the edge of a creaky bed in his small room. Gabe pressed his palms to his eyes, almost as if to exorcise those images from his mind. He looked down at his shoes.

Who was that girl? Was it... Christ, dreams don't matter, he reminded himself, *and I've got problems to solve.*

This was true. He needed work.

Standing up and collecting his sundries off the dresser, he looked over the newspaper scattered across his floor where it had fallen from the bed the night prior. He sneered, trying hard to ignore how much the story had bothered him. He shuffled down the hallway toward the baths, past the closed doors of other residents. There was nary a sound from a single room, except a faint snoring escaping room three-oh-three.

As Gabe shaved and showered in the restroom at the end of his hall, he looked around at the other men readying themselves for another day of work. A vestige of the old brothel life of the building, the group bath was perhaps the only aspect he rather enjoyed. Not for some perverse reason, no; it reminded him of the mornings in the barracks when the men in his unit would ready themselves for the day's duties. They would take turns at the two sinks with their hazy, silvered mirrors. The men would shower and shave, dressing meticulously with one foot upon the old wooden benches while talking crudely. They all made a hobby of taking verbal jabs at each other, and it was a nice distraction.

For a fleeting moment, Gabriel Marshall felt a bit less alone. As he readied his shirt and tie, he thought fondly of the day his father taught him a proper shave. A faded, glorified memory of his childhood that often carried him through his morning routine. The face in the mirror was smooth, pink from the steamy water, and reminded him of his father's face when Gil was younger. He was sure what stock he came from every time he looked in a mirror. He noticed a nick from the razor and put a little bit of tissue on his chin, just like his father had taught him.

He returned to his room and donned charcoal slacks and coat, his only proper suit. Looking at the shiny pocket watch dangling off the wall hook, he saw that he'd have just enough time for a cup of joe up the street before heading to the work & labor agency uptown. He thought about the little corner cafe he'd visited dozens of times in the six or so months he'd been a resident of this New York City neighborhood. He thought about Lindy, the girl who worked there and served him on most of those visits. The watch slipped into his vest pocket smoothly and with a satisfying tug on the fabric. Its chain end was fastened behind a button midway down his vest.

I wonder if that Lindy gal might be there. What a doll. Probably waiting for some lanky young GI to come home. Lucky bastard!

He snickered to himself at the thought of being jealous of an imaginary man. He'd only ever been a customer to this girl, and it was silly to be jealous or even envious. He'd known her long enough to make an advance, but it had never felt like the right moment to ask her for anything but decent service. Burying the thought and finishing his dressing, Gabriel Marshall felt almost dapper as he snatched his wool hat off the corner bedpost and headed out the door, hat-in-hand.

Can't risk mussing up the hair just yet.

Luck and Charm

The air was clear; a breeze had blown away the usual gutter smell of the Bowery. Gabe felt the warm sunshine on his face as he made his way up toward Sixth. Art's Diner, one of the local establishments, had been there for decades, and its age was starting to show on the counters. It didn't bother Gabe; they had the best coffee in the neighborhood.

He hadn't appreciated coffee until he joined the service. Gabe had been temporarily stationed at the Thompson-Robbins AAF outside Helena, Montana, a newly dedicated Army airfield not too far from home. Everyone knew it as 'Helena AAF' for the sake of saving ink and confusion. One typically dreary morning, he'd been offered a cup of coffee from a staffer's plaid-printed thermos and, seeing the hot steam arising, decided to try his first sip. Gabe had almost spit out the brew; it was intense and oily, tasting of earth and leather. Regardless, once he swallowed it and felt it warm his guts to the pit of his belly, he figured he'd better not waste the drink that might help him through a cold shift. Three piping-hot cups later, he was humming old show tunes on-post at the front gates and had volunteered for a double shift so his booth buddy Nicholson could take an evening off. He'd *never* had that much energy! "Yep... point of no return, I'd say!" he had mused with a smile to the Lieu who'd given him the coffee.

The smile drawn across his face at that memory was all it took to carry Gabe all the way to Art's on light feet. He felt confident about today, standing tall as he walked through the old wooden doorway on the corner at Art's. He hung his hat and turned toward the counter to see the sweetest sight; little miss Lindy was already standing at his corner of the counter, a glass carafe in one hand and a steaming cup of joe in the other. She smiled at Gabe warmly as though she had been waiting for him to arrive.

"Good morning, big guy! How long has it been... a week?" She gave him the most disapproving look, but he took it well as she was still wearing half a smile.

"Sorry, Lindy. You know I have to catch the early train to the shops. Well... I did," he grumbled with a frown as he glanced toward the floor.

"Oh, NO! What happened, Gab?" she asked, using the silly nickname she'd come up with for him one Saturday afternoon over a slice of pie. It was her way of poking fun at him for not being talkative enough for her taste.

"Nothing I can't get past. Seems they just didn't have any work for me anymore."

He spared her the honest, gory details of Mark's accident the day prior. She wanted to lighten the mood.

"I *thought* you looked a little bedraggled. This city is rough around the edges! Not like your midwest..."

He knew the dark circles under his eyes were a telltale.

"Lindy, I had the *strangest* dream. It's hard to sleep in this town... Listen, don't you worry about me. I'll find another job like I always do. How've you been? I sure hope you're staying safe. What with the awful things that have been going on around here?"

She watched him take a sip of coffee, counting her words, and did not want to discuss the recent ugly stories in the papers.

"My days all sort of... blend, if you know what I mean, sleep or no sleep. I've been cooped up in New York for too long. It's Tuesday if I'm not crazy."

He nodded to affirm himself, smiling through a swig of coffee.

"Listen, Gab, let me ask you. Have you ever worked in a kitchen?"

"Oh yeah, dozens of times. I was a K-P on rotation when I first joined the service. That's short for 'kitchen personnel.' I've done it all, miss."

Lindy giggled at him, explaining 'K-P' to her. She relished in Gabe's chatty demeanor today, and she wasn't going to say anything to quiet him.

"Well, listen. Art's been away a more lately, and there's next to nobody to pick up the slack here when I get a little busy. Maybe you could help out for a while, I mean if you're interested?

You're a big guy, probably got enough pep to get through a day of this grind."

She thumbed back toward old man Art in the kitchen, behind the serving window, over the massive iron grill.

Gabe smiled and nodded to Art, scratching his chin in thought. Then, he gazed out the window for a moment, watching the morning traffic pass by. "It's not exactly my forte…"

"…and there'd be plenty of coffee on the house…" she offered further, hoping to sweeten the deal.

"Ha! You drive a hard bargain, little lady; I just might take you up on that. Let me head up to the employment agency up the road and check in with them for work that's a bit more my speed. And maybe I'll come by afterward, and we can talk a little more."

She beamed at his promise to return. "Tell you what, since you're almost done with that coffee, I'll give you another cup to go. Breakfast is my treat today, I insist. You just think it over, and I'll tell Art I might've found us a real hard worker to help out around here!"

She poured him a full white paper cup, black and strong, *just* how Gabe liked it.

"Lindy, I sure appreciate you being so generous with me," he commented before downing the rest of his mug and grabbing the lidded paper cup. She smiled warmly and went to check on her other tables.

He grabbed his hat, waved it toward Lindy, and was out the door. As he walked past the hand-painted signs in the broad glass windows, he could see her smiling face from the corner of his eye as she watched him depart.

That girl sure is somethin' else.

His firm-soled dress shoes hit the pavement with a bit of spring. Something at the core of a man, no matter how hardened he may be, softens with the attention of a kind woman. His long strides carried him quickly up the street, the sidewalks now peppered with bleary-eyed locals who had been up a little too late in front of the RCA or spent too many hours leaning on some lacquered oak in a flophouse bar.

He felt the breeze in his hair tugging gently at the wave he'd carefully set in pomade, but not tugging enough to make him worry or stop at a reflection; he still held his hat in his hand to keep from messing up his little pompadour before the pomade set. He knew exactly where he was headed; a few blocks north, he knew of one employment agency, gilded lettering in the window and holding a good reputation at Carter Machine.

He'd heard from a coworker a story of men being sent to new worksites for days or weeks, then receiving zero pay, then being laughed out of the building at the agency that had sent the poor bastard. "Damn thieves own so much of this town they get to have offices!" he recalled Andy Kelley bellowing in the locker rooms back at Carter Machine.

I hope this place is on the up-and-up; I don't want to dig into savings just to pay my damn rent...

Gabe turned a corner and saw the office of Davis General Employment. With nice, clean steps and freshly painted windowsills, he felt he'd found the right place. He walked up and swung the door open wide, stepping in with confidence. The man behind the desk looked up from a newspaper he'd been squinting at, his eyes belying his years more than his full head of dark hair let on from a streetside view.

"Mornin' son, how can I help ya?"

The old man was smiling broadly as he set down his paper. His genial demeanor was reassuring.

"I'm here for work, sir. I was just, ah... let go from a machine shop by the south docks, and, well, I just can't be without work, you see..."

Gabe squeezed the brim of the hat he was holding over his belt buckle. He was carrying on a bit, as he tended to do when he was nervous.

"Well, hang yer hat and have a seat. Let's look at ya!" Gabe took the only seat adjacent to the desk and settled into its comfortable cushion and narrow arms as he tried (unsuccessfully) to cross his legs. The old man chuckled, as did Gabe through his embarrassment.

"Sorry 'bout the chair, young man, I don't quite fit right either; it was a bit more accommodating when I bought it twenty pounds ago! It wasn't made for a man of your, ah... midwest frame. What's your name, son?"

As Gabe shuffled about a bit more in the chair, coming to rest somewhere in the comfort spectrum between a church pew and a school desk, he replied, "Gabe... Gabriel, sir. Gabriel Marshall, sir."

Gabe chewed his tongue a bit along the edge every time he said his Christian name. It was a nervous tick, a 'tell' of his feelings toward his first name, but he kept it to himself.

"Well, Gabriel, relax a bit. I can tell you're probably a serviceman. Army?"

Man's got a keen eye!

"Yes, sir, I was infantry. Served on the front. Had a couple of decorations and a little responsibility before the end." He didn't mention his early discharge.

"Well, then, you're in luck. I can see you're strong, and I can see you've got a good upbringing. Half the mooks walk in here don't even take off their hat!"

Gabe chuckled a bit, feeling already at ease with the old man. "I was brought up well, sir. Thank you. Might I ask your name?"

"Hell, it's on the building, son! Rick Davis. Richard, but that doesn't matter any. Just call me Davis. I have been here thirty years; come next spring. Put a lot of good men to work after *both* wars. I've got a reputation in the community. You planning to do right by my name if I send you for honest work?"

"That's the only sort of work I'm looking for, sir."

This was the smoothest interview Gabe had ever had.

Davis reached out and clasped Gabe's bigger hand, shaking it with the vice-like grip of an ironworker. Then, he slid a clipboard across to Gabe, attaching a single-sheet questionnaire that asked Gabe for details of all sorts.

"Listen, Gabriel, I'll be back in a handful of minutes. Go ahead and write this thing out, and when you're done, just hand it to Donna in there."

Davis motioned toward the next room, where a young woman sat behind the most enormous damn typewriter Gabe had ever seen. Gabe nodded at her and then stood, shaking Davis' hand once more. Davis left the room after motioning toward a couch behind Gabe.

Gabe went to the sofa, which was far more inviting than the narrow chair. He took a seat, leaned back, and crossed his legs to use his knee to support the clipboard. It was quiet; all Gabe could hear was his pen scratching along the paper and the faint rustle of whatever broadsheet Donna was lost behind across the room.

In another room, he heard Davis making a phone call. It sounded like a friendly conversation. A few laughs echoed, a few dirty jokes half-heard, and then finally, the soft clang of the phone receiver set back on its brass hooks. Gabe smiled to himself; he could tell it was good news. He wasn't a college man, but he knew people well enough. He knew when a person was being genuine. He scribbled his slanted signature across the clipboard just as Mr. Davis walked back into the room.

"Just now finishing? Heck, I hope I didn't talk long."

Davis took the clipboard from Gabe as he stood, glancing over it. His brow furrowed, he looked up from the board.

"I see here you're from that little spot back in Montana that had some trouble a few years ago... I remember reading about that."

Gabe looked at his shoes, thinking of how to respond.

Seeing he had caused Gabe some concern, Davis carried on.

"Oh, it's not my business, just my old memory workin' faster than my manners. Sorry, son, everything looks just fine here."

Gabe let out a bit of breath and smiled a half-smile, clearly less off-put than moments prior.

"No apology warranted, Mister Davis. I don't think about back home much these days."

That was a lie, however well-intentioned.

Davis nodded, walking the clipboard to Donna behind that typewriter. He then withdrew a notepad from his pocket and leaned on the desk to scratch some information on it. Tearing off the little sheet, he handed it to Gabe, who looked down at the perfect cursive—it was just an address and a single name.

"Washington?" Gabe inquired aloud.

"Yep, that's the man you'll go see right now if you're up to it. He's waiting for you. Washington's an old friend of mine, and he runs a dockside yard down there for the New York Central Railroad. He's been looking for some reliable men lately; I know you'll do the Davis agency proud, son. Anyway, there's no honest work on this side of town this week!"

Gabe smiled and felt warm. This man had just done him a kindness. Gabe was almost overcome with relief at the prospect of having work again.

"Thank you. I appreciate this more than I can say, sir. I'll give them the best I've got."

They shook hands yet again, leaving Gabe's mitt almost sore this time.

Hell of a grip for a desk man! Gabe had thought. He donned his wool hat, tipped the brim to Donna, and turned out the front door even more confident than he had entered. Heading southeast, he walked quickly through the neighborhoods and warehouses, headed for a ferry to Brooklyn, where he'd make his way to Bush Terminal, New York Central's yard on the piers south of Governors' Island.

Gabe could be shoveling coal or polishing toilets for all he cared; he just wanted to *work*. A strong work ethic was something he had always tried to maintain since he was just an ornery youth helping on weekends at his uncle's church or the neighbor's little hardware store seated between the grain silos and the railroad's mile-long icehouse.

Nearing the harbor, he could see steam locomotive smoke rising in the sky, his anticipation building. His dress shoes clacked loudly as he walked with purpose; he figured he would arrive sometime after the lunch whistle sounded, but he made haste, knowing Mr. Washington was waiting. He spent the walk and the ferry ride, damn excited about whatever work they'd give him.

The Yard

The sun was high as the late morning passed, nearly lunchtime. After the ferry trip and a bit of walking on either side, Gabe was aware his feet hurt from those hard-soled leather shoes. He didn't care, just was aware. He wiped the sweat from his brow, still wearing his suit with confidence in the noontime sun and warmth. His excitement was electric as he neared the last blocks before the railyard; he could smell the harbor water in the sunshine, a salty smell that was far stronger in the sunshine. It permeated this place.

As Gabe arrived at the principal office of the yard, he took a few minutes on the stoop of the building without his coat, trying to cool off from the walk and wipe away a bit more perspiration from his brow and neck with a pale blue handkerchief. He stood close to the building, trying not to be noticed as he observed the men coming and going from all corners of the busy industrial avenue. Men in overalls carrying swinging lunch pails, men in suits with sizable cigars swatting each other on the shoulder and motioning grandly as they told some story or anecdote.

Nice to see people chummy, better than Carter...

Gabe hoped this job was a bit more social than the last, industrious men bantering amidst the work, making the day go faster with crude humor and chatting about their loved ones. Gabe had often lamented the absence of friendliness and conversation at Carter Machine, the workshop feeling acutely stern and sterile: just those damn machines and clanking tools.

Maybe, Gabe mused, *this is just what I need. Some honest work in a place where I could make a friend or two.* He folded his handkerchief and tucked it away, slipped his coat back on with a flourish, and stepped into the aging but beautifully ornate stone archway of the NYC railyard offices.

He noted the old wooden flooring of the hall had worn bare in the middle of the hall and moreso directly in front of the offices. Many working men's shoes had graced those floors before Gabe's. He stopped at the first open office, leaned in (now again hat-in-hand), and politely asked the first person he saw about 'where to find a Mr. Washington?'

The woman looked up from her desk, smiled warmly, and called out "Harold!" across the small office. Another man stood up from his desk, nodding at Gabe.

"Yessir! How can I be of service?" he called out from the desk.

Gabe waved across the office to him and began to say, "I'm here to see," but the woman at the desk interrupted emphatically, "New guy for WASH-ington!"

The slight-framed man sprung out from behind that cluttered desk and made his way to the front of the room and through the banister gates to Gabe. The man extended a hand to Gabe and introduced himself excitedly as "Harold Burton, Clerical Administrator, my pleasure!" and Gabe returned his handshake with enthusiasm and offered his name. Harold then deftly stepped past Gabe into the hall and made a 'come along' motion as he started his way down the hall. Gabe followed quickly behind him. He sized up this Harold Burton as they walked down the deceptively long corridor.

Christ, this hall's longer than the building! Maybe that's what keeps him so skinny! Gabe snickered.

Their heels made a very uneven clacking due to the difference in stride. Gabe saw Harold was a wiry man who moved with emphasis: short, quick movements, lots of energy. A cheap suit draped off Harold almost as a toga might; Gabe remembered seeing togas in schoolbooks with charcoal illustrations from European history. Harold's bony shoulders looked practically sharp enough to cut through the thin fabric.

A few dozen hallway doors passed, and Gabe realized that the building must follow along the tracks of the railroad, all length, no width, much like a train station. He glanced through some of the glass hallway doors and caught a glimpse of the railyard through an outside window. There were puffs of steam and smoke rising scattered about the railyard.

I think I'm going to like it here.

Harold led Gabe down to the last door at the end of the hall. They stepped out into the sunshine into a small courtyard with benches (likely for the employees' breaks), and Gabe found himself following Harold across paved railroad tracks. Both men were careful not to misstep between the railhead and the cement. Gabe strode across both tracks while Harold took a little hop-step between them, bounding off the wooden sleepers that lay under the rails.

After a break in the lineup of boxcars, they found themselves at the business end (the open-sided observation platform) of an aging New York Central passenger car. Its wooden siding was a faded olive green, the handrails and massive iron knuckle coupler showing enough rust to make you wonder if this car might have been abandoned at some point. Little flakes of paint came away from the handrails into Gabe's hand as he followed Harold up the sidesteps of the railcar, and they both came to a stop before opening the door into the car. Harold turned to Gabe and shook his hand briefly.

"Here we go! Wash is a heck of a guy, just a *heck* of a guy. Good luck, buddy!"

With that, Harold swiftly stepped off the platform down the steps, around a boxcar where he disappeared from view.

Gabe once again wiped his brow with the handkerchief, straightened his tie with its plain gold-tone clip, and stepped inside the car with a smile on his face. In an instant, he was hit with the sweet smell of pipe tobacco burning. Its blue trails writhed in the closed air of the old passenger car. His eyes adjusted to the dimmer inside light; there was a table at the end of the almost empty car. He walked past a row of red velvet passenger car seats, an old-style seat of cast-brass frame. He recognized these seats in style, having ridden a few older train cars as a child, and then remembered how he used to flip the seatback forward to make the seat rear-facing. That used to drive his mother crazy; she'd furrow her brow and shake a finger at Gabe but say nothing for propriety's sake. Father would simply chuckle at his mother's frustration and encourage Gabe just to *settle down now. Gabriel, leave it as you found it!*

And little Gabe would.

Seeing the outline of a man at a far table with a small electric lamp at his side, he thought, *That must be Washington!* And approached the table.

"Hello, sir; I suppose you've been expecting me. Gabe Marshall, sir."

The man looked up at Gabe with a smirk, nodded at him, and spoke with a deep voice.

"Take a seat, Gabe. My name's Ward Washington, but you and everyone else just call me Wash. How are you? Hell of a trip to make in that suit in this heat; you were only at Davis' place an hour ago, must've been like walking through a swamp!" Wash laughed a bit at Gabe's yet again gleaming forehead.

Gabe took a seat in the old wooden chair after slipping off his coat to adjust to the humid car. He sized up Wash rather quickly, a stern-faced man about his father's age, with a silk vest on and a build like a pack mule... short, wide, and strong.

"It was sure a bit of a hike, sir, but worth every step. Thank you for seeing me on such short notice."

"Hell, don't thank me, son. I haven't given you the job yet!' Wash joked, 'But I'm in damn dire need of good strong help around here. Tell me, what do you know about trains?"

Gabe thought back over his years and gave a very measured response: "Sir, I haven't spent any time working on trains, to tell the truth. But see, I've ridden on trains, tanks, even planes... damn near every machine the Army owns, and I can make quick sense of anything you point me in the direction of. If there's a manual, I'll read it at home."

Wash sat back in his chair and chewed on the end of his pipe for nearly an eternity before speaking again.

"Well, listen, Gabe. I've been doing this job for years, and I learn something every damn day. They put me in charge of moving these train cars, cleaning them, and caring for them. I have two dozen men working for me, but it should be forty. Plenty of my men came here wet behind the ears, but they all had two things."

Wash raised his hand with two fingers up, lowering them as he spoke.

"I need an honest man, and I need a careful man. If you're honest, you'll work as hard as you can. If you're careful, you'll earn a good keep and survive this job. Can you do those two things?"

"Yes, Sir, absolutely. I've got those attributes and a few good others."

Gabe bobbed his head in honest affirmation of his own words, his gaze locked with Wash as they spoke. He thought about Mark and that bloody mess of an arm but had to remind himself that it was Mark's fault.

He gave me the 'go-ahead'; how would I have known?

Wash stood, shook Gabe's hand enthusiastically, and patted him on the back. Gabe stood as Wash led him out through the nearest end of the car.

"C'mon, Gabe, you can't work in that damned monkey suit any more than I can smoke in the gas room! Let's get you some proper attire?"

Gabe smiled and nodded, following him out the back-end door of the aging railcar and back toward the offices he'd just come from. The rest of the morning was a blur; Gabe hardly said another word besides yes and thank you. Nodding to seemingly a hundred questions by the staff in the office, he gave them his sizes. One woman had commented across the desks, "he's built like our engine house! Bring out the heavy stuff, Harry," and she sat Gabe on a hallway bench while a stack of work attire was assembled for him.

While Gabe sat there happily, considering all the ways in which he hadn't screwed anything up, he heard a quick click-clack of heels approaching in the hall. It was Harold once again. Gabe was delighted to see the quirky little man. Harold was shuffling down the hallway carrying two heavy blue coveralls and a set of boots half as large as Harold himself.

Harold reached the bench, dropping the footwear to the ground with a resounding THUD and letting out an audible sigh of relief.

"Harold, thank you! I coulda helped..." Gabe lifted a boot and saw they were just about his size.

"Aww, no, it keeps me strong!"

Harold jokingly flexed his stringy arm, which elicited a good chuckle from Gabe.

"Let's get you a locker and let you go about your day, Gabriel!"

It was the first Harold had said Gabe's name. There was something familiar, something very comfortable about it. It felt like it came from a friend.

"Thank you, Harold. I'm excited to get to work! Just *Gabe* is fine if it's all the same to you. When do I report?"

"...report?' Harold asked with an eyebrow raised, 'Don't tell me... you're an army man? Where'd you serve?"

Gabe shrugged. "I put in a few years, mostly overseas, but I suppose I'm just asking when I should show up for my first shift."

"Tomorrow morning, if you're up to it. Wash says we've sure got a lot to show you 'round here. There is no shame in being a little wet behind the ears, right? That's what Wash calls it."

Gabe snatched up the boots and bale of denim coveralls and followed Harold down a hall to the locker room. Harold prattled on about how best to navigate the yard, who to avoid, and who should be helpful. Gabe was assigned his locker and received a freshly typed employee card and a little stack of tokens for the ferry. It was a great kindness, and Gabe felt very wanted just then. The two parted ways, and Harold sent him home with a farewell.

"Be sure to rest up, Gabe, you're gonna love it here! Just think of me as your guide."

Gabe beamed with pride as he held his NYCRR employee card in his hand. He was nearly at the ferry terminal when he looked over his little paper employee identification card with its misaligned block lettering.

GABRIEL TUCKER MARSHALL

NYCRR - EMPLOYEE # 3751 - 10/46 - S YARD

He slipped the card away into his wallet, boarded the ferry, and made his way west across the river toward home. He stood on the front deck of the gently bobbing ferry in the cool fall air, the sun setting richly golden behind so many towers and spires. It was then, this moment, that his weary eyes first saw beauty in this grey and vast city. He smiled widely and thought of Lindy.

Dreams Abound

The dock approached silently, the ferry slowed, and the bobbing rhythm became a mild undulation. Gabe made his way back to the loading ramp, standing tall in the line of weary commuters. His face still half-plastered with a smile at his day's good fortune, he disembarked over the ferry planks and began his trek home. He considered taking a bus, but it seemed like such a short walk at the time. Misting rain had started to fall, but not enough to bother. He made it through the warehouses and industrial streets that stood between the ferry and neighborhoods.

By the time he'd cleared the last dockside buildings, a steadier rain had begun to fall, and he knew it was only a matter of time until his suit was drenched.

I'd give my last dollar for a trench coat right now... he mumbled to himself. The bale of coveralls and boots in his hand was feeling heavyish with the rain working its way in. As he walked north on a narrow avenue lined with walk-ups, Gabe remembered a few cut-throughs that might help shorten his trip home.

Need to cut this damn walk short or I'll get waterlogged!

He counted the blocks, passing a few familiar structures. On his left, a small alley looking somewhat derelict sliced through a swath of tenements. Gabe pivoted into the alley, and after a few steps, he found himself treading on greasy and damp cement. His hard-soled dress shoes failed him now as both of his feet slipped out from under him. Dropping the bale of clothing, he flailed for a grip on something, *anything,* but his hand met only air as the back of his skull met the corner of a shipping crate.

WHUMP

The sound itself was dull and short, but it was the last

thing he heard before landing askew in a puddle of discarded food scraps and collecting raindrops.

Succumbing to darkness and deafness, he slipped into unconsciousness. A deep dream took over now, wherein Gabriel was just a youth. The memory was vivid, clear as day.

He found himself seated at the dinner table with his uncle and his darling mother, Patricia. The table had been set, Robert was bowing his head in prayer, and his mother was serving a casserole from a glass dish to their plates. She stood next to Gabriel and heaped a pile of food onto his plate. He felt warm, safe.

"Young man, you get started. Your father won't be home from his deliveries until late; I promise we can celebrate your birthday tomorrow. Is that all right, sweet child?"

Little Gabriel nodded his head in agreement, mouth already filled with food. He looked to Robert, who reached over and patted him on the head.

"Gabe, you better slow down, or you'll finish before your mother gets her first bite!"

Robert was poking fun, and Gabe laughed cheerily with a full mouth.

His mother, with her patience of a saint and doting nature, scooped a bit more casserole onto Gabriel's plate before sitting down in front of her dinner. Gabriel looked past her to the kitchen sideboard, where his birthday gift sat. It was a perfectly bound green box with a white ribbon and a tidy bow on top.

"Do you think Poppa would mind if I opened my present?"

Robert shook his head and wagged a finger.

"Gil searched high and low to find you that gift, and I want to see the look on his face when you open it. Just because your father isn't home tonight doesn't mean he isn't trying to do the best for you. And we cannot stay up and wait for him, as I've got some business at the church tonight."

Gabe let out a sigh. He was disappointed, more about poppa missing his birthday dinner than about his gift. His mother reached over and clasped his hand with hers.

"Gabriel, you know how hard your father works to make sure we have everything we need. I promise if he could be here for dinner, he would. Twelve years old, you'll be a working man yourself soon enough!" she opines with a broad smile.

That was true, and Gabriel knew it well. He knew how hard his mother worked to take care of the household while his father worked to provide. He set his mind to ignore the brightly papered gift for the night, and the three enjoyed a delicious dinner followed by a perfect sugar-crusted apple pie for dessert. Even without his father present, it was a wonderful family meal—the last Gabe could remember.

The evening had ended, and Gabriel was sound asleep in his bed, dreaming about the endless possibilities of what might be in that shiny green box. Was it a toy train? An erector set? Perhaps a new electric toy car... so many possibilities!

Childish dreams comforted him under his warm blanket as the hours ticked by.

He awoke with fright to the sound of his father bellowing his name so loud it nearly shook the walls. Gabe drew back his covers and began coughing immediately; his bedroom was filled with smoke! He could hardly see the door as his father kicked it open with tremendous force.

"GABRIEL!"His father shouted in a panic.

"Poppa?" Gabriel choked out as he tried to sit up in his bed. His stomach was clenched; he was heaving and spitting from the smoke sickness. His eyes stung harshly.

Without another word, Gilbert snatched Gabriel out of his bed and sprinted down the hallway with him to the front door. They fell onto the lawn before Gilbert jumped back onto his feet. His father was coughing as well but trying to say something.

"Ga... GABE, You st..." Gilbert coughed so violently that his glasses fell off his face.

"Gabe, STAY HERE. Dear God, your mother..."

Tears streamed down young Gabriel's face as he coughed into the sleeve of his nightshirt. He could hardly see, but Gabriel watched as Gilbert sprinted back in through the front door to rescue his love from the smoke and flames. Wiping tears away and gagging on smoke, Gabriel could see that the porch and rear of the house were engulfed in licking, frantically climbing flames from a charred and smoky lawn.

It was hard to hear over all the shouting, but Gabe heard screams. Victims. Neighbors. What felt like eons passed as this child tried to regain his senses and clear the smoke from his eyes. One neighbor came sprinting across the lawn and stooped down, wrapping her arms around Gabriel. She was distraught, but her eyes were keen.

"Gabe! The fire... my husband rescued your uncle; he's alive, but the church is ablaze! Where are your parents? Where is Gil? Patty?"

Squinting, Gabe replied as he watched his home ablaze.

"He's inside, miss Rosewood; he went back in for Ma!" Gabriel

clutched the arm of the woman tightly, hardly able to move out of sheer fright. He lifted one trembling finger toward the house.

Moments later, his father stumbled out through the front door through putrid, billowing smoke. Over his shoulder, Gilbert carried Patricia out onto the lawn next to Gabriel. He laid her down gently just before he collapsed aside her, wheezing for air.

Gabriel jumped up and ran to his mother, falling to his knees as he clutched her hand. Gil was coughing and gagging, gasping for breath. Gabe's mother was still and silent, her face and arms covered in black ash and soot, which clung to her sweat.

"Mama? MAMA!" Gabriel shouted with a hoarse throat. His cries went unanswered.

Before long, Robert had found his way back to the Marshall home, which was now engulfed in flame. Gilbert found his feet, dragging Gabriel and Patricia back nearly to the street, away from the fire. Robert stood back, hands over his mouth in terror. Neighbors up and down the nearby streets were battling their fires, mostly in futility. The wail of a single fire truck's siren was like a banshee trying to roar over the din of the flames. From the lawn, every home Gabe could see was succumbing to the aggressive inferno.

The Marshall family huddled close on the grass in the cold night air. Radiant heat from their home burning in effigy reddened their faces while Gabriel's father clutched his wife, pleading in vain for respite from God above. Robert fell apart and sat away, alone, in the grass. His head lolled in his hands, and in the flickering firelight, his shoulders shook as he sobbed. It was as though he knew there would be no salvation, no miracles this night.

The violent memory faded to black, leaving as swiftly as it had come.

Thump

Gabriel's hearing returned first. He heard the muffled voices of men and the shuffle of feet. Soon after that, he began to feel his limbs against the hard ground. He felt cold—not a simple chill, but a cold that soaked to his bones and permeated his soul—a deathly chill, as his father would have called it.

He could see the beam of flashlights moving about. As his vision cleared, he looked up into the eyes and weary face of a beat cop. Two uniformed police officers in square-cornered hats and wool uniforms were leaning over him.

"Hey pal, you okay? You really took a whack there, y'know."

"What, ah...' Gabe pressed his palm to his head and winced, '...what happened?"

He could feel a knot forming on the back of his head, and his fingers were slick with blood.

"You took a fall and knocked your lights out, pal. Seems that way, anyway. We've got a wagon coming. Don't you move, now?"

The voice was calm but insistent. Gabe's vision was still bleary and dark. He realized he was lying on the ground, soaked through his clothes in chilly rainwater. His head was throbbing yet numb. Someone had put something soft under the back of his head. It was Gabe's own bundle of work clothes sans boots.

He reached for any grip to stand up, but one officer grabbed his shoulders and held him down.

"Pal, just lay there, see? We'll fix you up. Thought we had some sorta tragedy out here, but come to find you here dressed to the nines, pal. You're sure lucky you didn't get rolled or worse!"

Gabe thought about it for a moment and patted his hip, feeling the small wad of bills and papers still shoved to the bottom of the pocket. His pocketwatch chain slunk coldly against his tummy. He thought about what the officer said; getting 'rolled' was usually a mugging enforced by a billy club.

"Help me up. I want to get up," Gabe grunted.

Gabe reached out for a hand. The officer looked down at Gabe, sized him up again, and, with a click of his tongue, said, "Okay, pal. You got it; just take it easy."

The nearby officer motioned for his partner to come and assist. They hoisted Gabe to help him get his legs under himself. Gabe grasped a corner of a trash pail, got on his knees, and stood up, still woozy from the blow.

"I'm sure I slipped, but oh-boy, my head just aches like a bastard. How did you find me?"

The older officer looked at his partner with pursed lips and then looked back at Gabe.

"Well, to be honest, pal, we didn't know you were alive. See, we had one of those damned muggings right here just last month. This is our beat; it's a big beat, so we lean on the neighbors for a watchful eye. The Commissioner has us patrolling the worst blocks; we're trying to keep up vigilance, see? But Murphy, here, Murphy spotted you first. Damn near gave me a heart attack thinking we found another one."

Gabe's recollection overcame his disorientation. *Another one? Shit, he must be talking about the murders.*

He tried his best to lighten the mood, offering, "Oh hell, I'm no stiff... I just feel that way!"

The coppers let out a relieved laugh. Gabe continued chatting as his vision cleared further, wiping mucky rainwater from his face and eyes with his sopping-wet handkerchief.

"So one of those victims was found right here, you say?"

The cop looked at the ground, "It was a mess, yeah. See, it was right up the way. Not twenty feet from right where you were layin'. An awful scene, just awful. 'Bout five weeks ago, I seem to recall."

Gabe looked down the alley and saw trash pails and abandoned wooden crates. Not a sign of a killer anywhere. Just brick and mortar and a few bits of clutter. That, and his blood. A chill shot down his spine.

"Well, officers, listen... I really appreciate the help. I think I'm fine to get home and try and clean up my head. I don't need a medic. I've had worse thumps. Even been shot once!" Gabe patted his thigh where a Luger bullet had taken a bite a few years prior.

The second policeman, Murphy, speaking for the first time, replied, "Well, sir, all right. We will let you go on your way. Just let me get your information for our diligence."

Gabe smiled a bit and leaned against the same crate that had earlier been his near-demise.

"Sure, no problem. I'm up in that firetrap by the laundry and that penny theater, the old cathouse. 3rd floor. Name's Gabe Marshall."

He reached up and felt the lump on the back of his head again... his fingers grazed the edge of it, and, with a sharp wince, he knew he'd be hurting tomorrow. He reached into his pocket and handed the cop his freshly-minted NYCRR employee card and his Army Identification, which he'd carried for the new job, which Murphy went to copying down in his notepad.

"All right, sir. Thanks a bunch. Be safe getting home tonight, yeah? Oh, and I see here your job, new hire?"

Gabe smiled through the pain at the thought of it, "Just today, sir."

"Congratulations, certainly, pal... but... sort of a piss-rotten way to celebrate!"

The cop was chuckling, and Gabe was embarrassed but still laughed at himself.

"Thanks, Officer... Murphy? I sure appreciate you guys finding me out here. Listen... do I need to do anything here? A report or some such?"

Murphy looked to his partner and then back to Gabe.

"Sure, pal. In fact, I'd appreciate that. Considering you declined any care, it might look good on us if you went into the precinct just south of here and gave a statement tomorrow or Thursday. The brass is encouraging everyone to write out a bushel of paperwork these days with all the mess that's been going on, you know. Makes for good records, makes people feel better."

His partner chimed in, "And give us a good talking-up!"

"Sure thing, as soon as I get the chance. I'll do just that, Officer. Thank you."

Looking back over his shoulder once more, Gabe pictured

the scene in its prior state, a gory mess replete with gumshoes leaning in close, flashbulbs firing.

The officers each tapped the brim of their hats a bit, almost in unison, to offer their polite goodbyes.

"G'night, sir."

"Yeah, G'night, pal. Take more care gettin' home, wouldja?"

They'd clearly been on the beat together for a while.

The three men had walked back out of the alleyway onto the sidewalk, parting ways. Gabe walked North while the officers walked South. The rain was gone, but the streets were glistening wet. Not a single automobile passed; it was a stark and quiet night. The sky was pitch black, save a few wisps of the clouds which had brought a brief and fervent rain that caused so much calamity for Gabe. His hat was crushed flat, a flop of waterlogged wool. With the bushel of wet and bloody clothes tucked under his arm and boots draped over his neck by the laces, he stuffed both hands in his wet pockets and hunched over the rest of the trek home. He was soaked, chilled to the core.

As he walked, he mulled over the vivid dream he had experienced back there in the alley. He thought about the memories that filled his heart with lead. That terrible fire, the victims. His mother. His *family* after that night.

Three blocks and two dozen buildings were charred to ash that night. Too many folks, including his mother, had succumbed to smoke inhalation, the fire brigade chief had later stated in the town's only newspaper. After the smoke cleared and an account was made, 17 people had lost their lives. Gabe only *really* cared about one of those people, but the enormity of it still made him gut-sick. He knew that not everyone was dead before the flames got to them.

Smoke inhalation, my behind...

For a number of years, Gabe had been successful in avoiding thinking about that night. Perhaps Mr. Davis's earlier allusion to it had brought up those old, painful memories. He thought about how his uncle had dedicated most of his life to being a 'man of the cloth,' and in one fell swoop, Robert's faith was shaken, and his church became ash. Some years later, when he was older yet still in school, Gabe's father took Gabe aside and explained it better.

Apparently, Robert had been butting heads with some local fundamentalists; they didn't like that Robert had an open-door policy to folks from *all* walks, every color and faith. In fact, they insisted he turn away anybody who didn't meet their narrow definition of "Christian". Robert refused, and the argument came to blows. In the scuffle, a rack of prayer candles got knocked over. Once the drapes caught fire, there was simply no stopping it. A little mishap cost so many families so much.

Aside from discussing his feelings with his father, Gabe had never shared with anyone how deeply it had affected his beliefs. Such awful consequences for such 'righteous' actions. He felt like Robert's lessons were all bullshit and that Gil *must* have been right in his non-belief. Gabe never again looked to the sky with any sliver of faith and never wished to hear his full biblical name. That family dinner was the last day Uncle Robert ever spoke about God or faith without spitting, and neither Gil nor Gabe had seen the inside of a church since.

Ironically, the story spread like wildfire in Montana. It was a tragedy with a positive outcome; the fires' devastation and the poor response caused some notable changes in the firefighting community. Over time, it would save lives—little comfort, of course.

Gil had comforted Gabe many times with the platitude, "Perhaps, son, this will eventually save more lives than it cost." Gabe didn't care; there wasn't an excuse in the world that could ever make him feel better about all of it. Gil's turning to the bottle put little confidence in Gabe. The fire had been talked about statewide, even country-wide. It was the only real news ever to leave his hometown; next to nobody knew the town of Oakdale, Montana, for anything more than death and tragedy. People still remember it.

Davis certainly remembered.

Thinking of Davis, Gabe's mind quickly found its way back to his new job. Setting his mind to it, he imagined all the bustle of a railyard, the noise and steam and smoke of the engines. He thought about that beautiful ferry trip and looked forward to being on the water every day.

I'm gonna do the Davis Agency proud. I'll show them hard work. I'll be the best worker they ever had! Headwound be damned...

He clenched his fist in affirmation, still damp with blood from his accident.

I'm not going to let some headache ruin my first day at work.

As he walked, his stomach growled; he hadn't eaten all day. His willpower took hold, and he pushed that thought away, knowing it was too late to eat and get any proper sleep.

Hell, I told Lindy I would stop in again. Art's had been closed for three hours now. Dammit.

In short order, Gabe arrived home to peel off his soaking clothes. Without a shower, he crept under the covers to warm up. Due to his wet wound, he spread a clean washcloth across the pillowcase, gingerly lying on his flank and belly so the back of his head could heal.

With the little alarm clock on the nightstand now key-wound tightly, he settled into the musty pillow and felt sleep coming swiftly. He was exhausted. The muffled chatting and laughing (of a rather flirtatious nature) emanating through the walls from a neighboring room set a grimace across his stubbly face as he put a second flat, lumpy pillow over his head.

This city had been a poor choice for a small-town boy; Gabe rarely woke without feeling wholly burned out these days. He was determined to rest this night.

No more nutty dreams tonight, no sir.

Wet behind the ears

Wednesday, October 16th

His wash-up routine required a bit of extra care due to his noggin; Gabe donned his warm knit-cotton robe and night attire, sore as hell and waiting patiently for a shower and a sink to shave. In the meantime, he made some small talk in the hall with another resident. Gabe had spoken with this man many a morning, the both of them half-dazed from sleep. Gabe had never managed to catch a name for this kind older man from some nameless town in the southeast, traveling between labor jobs. At this point, asking the man's name would be rude... a simple 'pal' would suffice (Gabe supposed the man probably didn't know his name either).

They discussed the local food and some choice coffee spots. Gabe was always happy to talk about a cup of joe, be it the best or the worst, and they discussed what the streetcars must be like after the rush, sharing a laugh that 'only the tourists know about that.' They had a chuckle at how damned tedious the streetcars could be; everyone cramped up in a rickety tin box, passing the time reading advertisements for Burma-Shave and Camel Cigarettes plastered to the painted ceilings of those electric trolley cars.

They leaned on the banister to the main hall and stairway, letting a rather plump woman walk past without a word. The nameless old man tipped his invisible hat at her when she passed, her nose in the air at their morning banter. After she passed, Gabe's pal wrinkled up his nose and sort of penguin-walked away to the washroom, mocking the rotund woman and giving Gabe a bellyache in stifled chuckles.

What a way to start the day! I need to get a place where I don't wait in line for the head...

A short while later, clean and feeling refreshed despite the throbbing behind his ears, Gabe stepped a light foot onto the pavement to make his way in haste toward the steam ferry. He strode fast and darted between people along the streets.

His eyes caught a few shiny new cars among the usual black fords and dull taxis, including a gleaming new '46 Packard rolling down the street. *WOW! What a grill!* He thought, eyes fixed on the two tons of blue lacquer paint and a half-ton of chrome that thundered past. Its long hood line and sweeping rear deck had it looking something like a Hollywood star, just shine and curves. His best buddy Cam had often said that about those shiny new Detroit automobiles... "Those cars are all chrome and curves, Gabe. Too showy. I just want my lil' Studebaker truck, you know... rusty but trusty."

I bet Cam would change his tune if he rode in one of those land yachts...

After the ferry and a bit more walking, Gabe arrived at the yard. He ignored his stiff, sore body; he was determined to establish himself today and begin anew. He walked into the main entrance and through the corridor of the freight offices while the morning yellow sun refracted through some of the windows. The smell of oiled leather and stacks of yellowing paper permeated the place. It felt welcoming, like an old home. He made his way out the back and toward where he would earn his keep this day.

The day started quickly with a number of different yard men showing him various aspects of maintaining the equipment. Grease gun here, oil rag there, lantern fuel always last and always carefully. He hitched couplers and set brake wheels; he helped haul new parts up onto the tender decks of hot and noisy steam locomotives shunting around the cars. One of the foremen had told him about the new diesel-electric locomotives they'd been seeing, the new breed of engines that (as the foreman put it) "could never replace these old mules we run here," referring to the aging coal-fired steam locomotives.

Those diesel-electrics (lazily referred to as simply diesel) were more straightforward to maintain. They had a far better economy, though they were years away from being used in mainline passenger service. They weren't yet built to be pushed hard like the giant, seemingly mile-long snarling, snorting, and elegantly streamlined coal-fired steamers that motivated the fastest, most luxurious passenger trains. Those were the engines that built America; those were the flagship of the New York Central Railroad. Half the movies coming out of Hollywood had some scene on a swiftly moving, streamlined passenger train, and Gabe loved being a part of it now.

Gabe was rightfully impressed by the way these men fawned over the steam locomotives. It amused him how simplistic and ill-conceived the American railroads were compared to his travels in Europe; over there, everyone preferred trains to cars. Not here in New York, no sir. Not since perhaps the nineteen-twenties. Cars outnumbered trains a hundred to one, maybe even a thousand.

As the day wore on, Gabe was given further training on servicing and cleaning the switchers (a terminology for car-switching locomotives that only carried enough coal and water for local work), which the yard men took great care to maintain.

Half-past three, Harold Burton came hurrying through the tracks of the yard with a smile on his face. Gabe was just finishing loading some service tools up into a cupola caboose. The caboose stood stately with its little windowed cupola housing jutting up from the roof, from which railroad workers could see out above the other railcars. Gabe found himself pleased to see this man come shuffling up the yard to greet him. Stepping down off the platform of the caboose, Gabe pulled off his stiff cowhide work gloves so he could greet Harold with a firm, nearly jaunting handshake. Harold shook like a truckload of lumber on a bumpy back road.

"Mister Burton, how the heck are you? It's a muggy day to be wearing such a suit. Have you been hiding in the office all day? Let me grab you a pair of gloves! I could use a hand!" he joked, giving Harry a firm pat on the shoulder.

"Gabe, I tell ya, I would love to... but I have a condition!"

"Oh? What's that?"

"I have a deadly serious case of the *no-thank-you's*!"

Harold winked at his cheeky joke, and both men burst into laughter. Forgetting all the work and the trains, this was the highlight of Gabe's day.

"Besides, I just came out to see if you'd quit or died yet. No such luck?"

Gabe could see this man was looking to make pals, and that was good news. Gabe had barely a friend to speak of in New York, and he figured Harold was as good a guy as any to pal around with.

"The day's young, and I might just take a dip in the harbor to cool off!"

Harold pretend-gagged and squinted toward the water's edge.

"Listen, you stay out of that muck. Do you see any toilets around here for the guys working the end of the yard? That harbor water is probably twenty percent piss and three percent dead bodies!"

Harold motioned up the gravel path toward Gabe's co-workers, two of whom were napping in the shade of a flatcar loaded with lumber as the others played cards on a big wooden cable spool repurposed as a table.

The dark humor caught Gabe off guard. Harold wasn't joking about the restroom situation, either.

Harold shielded his eyes from the sun and peered at his slumbering subordinates, muttering, "Those guys wouldn't know hard work if hard work bit them in their behinds..."

Feigning an offended face, Gabe retorted, "Now Harry, that's... well, probably true! Hell, I'll skip the swim if you let me take a nap like Jones up there."

"Nap? A little piss never killed anyone, Gabe; hop in and then get back to work!"

Both men nearly doubled over in a fit of laughter. As Harold wiped away tears at the corners of his eyes, a steam switcher engine ambled past and soaked both of them in two side-sweeping chuffs of steam. Harold tried to jump out of the way but was too late.

"Well, sir, you just got a free suit pressing. You look dandy! Honest, though, what can I do for you?"

"Oh, it's my job to check on you, didn't I tell ya? I heard you're already picking up on the intricacies of our work. Foreman says you're not a buffoon... so far."

Harry dusted his suit off with his palms, leering at the still-passing steam locomotive and its train of boxcars.

"That's good to hear, real good. I tell you honestly, sir, I needed this job. I know it's my first day, but I sure like the sort of work, and I don't mind the management much either!" he prodded at Harold.

"Say, just call me Harry, would ya? I'll let you know if I need to be 'sir'd' someday. Today is not the day. Say, Gabe, you should join me at the Crown'N Dagger later after work. It's a decent little pub up the street. See, I like a cold beer before I head home. They got some new refrigeration there; no more icebox!"

"Harry, I can't join you. I need to be somewhere after work. How about tomorrow? Friday?"

His new friend shrugged and stuffed his hands in his suit pockets.

"I'm there most nights. We can figure out a good day, pal. Have fun with your plans!"

With a ridiculous wink and smile, Harry implied Gabe's plans must be of a 'dame nature.' Gabe let him believe it.

The last few hours passed, and the five o'clock whistle blew. Offices cleared of workers, docks cleared of longshoremen as all the gritty and overworked men in the yard packed up their lunch pails and headed toward wherever they called home. Dozens of men, dressed chiefly alike in their railroad-issued overalls, headed for home or toward a cold drink.

As he gathered his belongings from the workshop bench, Gabe realized how damned tired he was from a day of hard labor. Still, he'd promised those police he would go and file that report on his accident.

Get to it, old man, sleep when you're dead! He chided himself.

White Globes

After a ferry trip and a few pauses interspersed in his walk to rest his feet and watch the sunset, Gabe's weary legs led him to the local precinct on the edge of the Bowery. A tired old granite building with massive and brightly glowing white globes posted out front on cast-iron posts. Finding his way inside, past a few uniforms heading out for patrols, Gabe reached the counter and rapt the lacquered wood with his knuckles. The uniformed desk officer who'd been facing away turned around on his heel, seeing this large man in dirty coveralls looking exhausted.

"Yessir, can I help you?"

"Likely so, Officer. I came in to file a report. Had a little accident yesterday, and the patrolmen I spoke to said it'd be a good idea if I came by."

The Officer brought out a form and stuck it to a wooden clipboard, handing it across the podium.

"Tell your story here, and we'll discuss it when you're finished, okay pal?"

Gabe took about ten minutes to explain his accident. His account simply described his walk home, his unfortunate fall, and the brief but pleasant experience he'd had with the officers who found him. He left out the part about his unsettling dreams, as nobody needed to hear that nonsense. The report was accurate and perhaps fluffed up a bit for the officers; they'd been so helpful that Gabe felt the need to make them look good for their commanding officer.

After completing the statement form, Gabe returned to the desk but saw nobody there. Some ten feet past the desk and banisters, though, was a nicely suited older man at a water cooler, scowling and clutching a thick file under his arm.

"Excuse me, sir, I have a report here I'd like to leave with you."

"You could set it down there; that'll do," the man in the suit responded.

A pang of familiarity struck Gabe just then. He knew this man's face.

"Say, hadn't I seen you in the newspaper, sir? The articles about those muggings?"

The man turned to him, finished the little paper water cup, and tossed it into the garbage without looking. Striding up to the desk with a very hitched gait, he set his folder down and extended a hand.

"Sarn't Dermot Mullally, son. I've been in the papers too damn much lately. What brought you into our precinct tonight?"

Gabe handed over the clipboard and the one-page statement he'd written, not really expecting Mullally to read the whole thing.

"I had a bad slip in an alley yesterday, that's all. Took a good knock on the head,' he turned to show his injury to the sergeant, 'and the men of yours who found me were so helpful, I supposed I oughta give them a good report. They mentioned it's been pandemonium here with all this bad activity, Sergeant Mullally."

The old man set the report down on the desk, barely reading past the name up top.

"Well, Mister Marshall, you're in good hands here in the city. No matter *what* those papers tell you."

Gabe smiled, pleased to hear such reassurance.

"I can usually take care of myself, sir. I fought worse things not too long ago."

"Oh, you're a tough guy, huh?' the sergeant joked with him, 'good to know. We won't find you arse-out in any more alleys, then?"

"Oh, I don't know sir, best nap I've had in a while!"

The two laughed, and Mullally started to walk away with his file. A photograph slipped out of the folder and fluttered to the floor under the banisters. It landed at Gabe's feet, face-up. Upon reaching down to pick up the photograph, Gabe felt a rush of blood on his face. It was an innate reaction, pure revulsion. Gabe was holding a brightly lit silver-tone picture of a white room; in the center of the photo was a long metal table holding up a man's body nearly torn apart, a body disemboweled. It was laid out for autopsy. The man's face was caved in, unidentifiable. Featureless.

Such a grisly sight was familiar. Too familiar. Gabe held out the photo.

"Sarge, uh... you should take this."

Mullally pivoted around and stormed back to the hip-height banisters.

"That's not for public consumption, son. Not for civilian stomachs!" He reached an impatient hand out to take the photo back.

Gabe slowly handed the photo back, apologizing.

"Not my intention, Sarge. To be honest? Feels as though I've seen this stuff before."

"Jesus Christ, *that* photo? Which paper? They're not supposed to publish that stuff. Blasted rags!"

Mullally's tone was sharp and angry, and he started to turn back toward the far cluster of desks where a handful of uniformed officers were clacking away at typewriters.

"No, sir. Not like that, not in print. I've seen this sort of thing *in person*... during the war."

His emphasis, and perhaps his honest face, were what set Gabe on a new path at that moment. Mullally had stopped in his tracks, gripping the photo and nearly crumpling it as he sized up this pillar of a man in front of him, from the grimy boots to the sandy stubble on his strong jaw to the sadness in his eyes, recalling such horror. Mullally could see this man was not bullshitting.

"Come with me, son. We need to have words."

The police sergeant grabbed the folder and stepped down back behind the wooden banisters. He beckoned Gabe to follow, and the two men made their way to a small, well-lit back room with frosted glass windows. The old cop slid the file across the desk at Gabe but placed a hand on top and looked Gabe squarely in the eye.

"Son, have you been reading the papers?"

Gabe looked back with pure respect and nodded. "Yes, sir, every day I'm able."

"You were a serviceman. When did you get back?"

"Sir, I've been back stateside some six months or so. Came to New York for family, but... well, it's just myself now."

"Tell me what you meant by *you've seen this before*, son. Be clear about it."

Gabriel opened his thin, tired wallet and pulled out a

small black-and-white photograph from the back folds. He slid the photograph across the counter and Mullally tilted his gaze downward.

A small clip of newspaper print, perhaps 3 inches across and under two inches tall. It was amazing the detail those prints and cameras could capture... even with his old eyes, Mullally could clearly make out a background of rubble and half-destroyed statues depicting a stoic bird... in the foreground, a squad of men in front of a bullet-riddled black limousine with wire wheels and chrome aplenty. A menacing eagle insignia was emblazoned on the perforated door.

With a raised brow, Mullally muttered, "Hold on now, this is that Nazi's car. The special one they used in their pamphlets, chrissakes, I saw this photo in the papers last year."

Mullally's eyes focused to look a little harder. There, in the foreground, was the face of a man sullied by dirt and blood with hands clenched across a GI rifle, and clearly the face of the man who at this moment stood arm's length from the Sergeant. Gabe cleared his throat a bit, stood up tall, and spoke clearly.

"Sir, Staff Sergeant Gabriel Tucker Marshall, commander of the platoon that took that damnable city in that photo, sir... Didn't do it for the press, but here we are."

His hand twitched, yearning to salute, but he repressed the instinct and stood firmly still.

"Marshall, explain to me what you meant. Where did you see this sort of trauma before? In the war?" as he waved the gory photo in question.

Gabe took a seat there next to Mullally's desk and leaned back a bit. Mullally did the same, mirroring Gabe's body language.

"Okay, sir, it might be a bit complicated... let me tell you a story. I saw some things, sure. A lot of what we came up against never made it past the red tape. They never print the whole truth. Here's what I *know*. My boys and I had spent months at a time out on the front. Armed and ruck-sacked and totally detached from our company. Always a little east, a little south, a little west. Our mission objective was to wait until there was a conflict, and we would pierce their ranks from a flank and clear it from the middle out. A small group of men, qualified men, we did that more times than I counted. Myself and maybe a half-dozen of the best soldiers I've ever known."

"So you were in a specialized unit?" Mullally inquired.

"Never officially. Too much accountability there. We were just a small detachment from the battalion: Mason, Rich, Parker, Irish, the lot of us. We would get into the stink, and we'd never leave anyone wearing swastikas standing or breathing."

Mullally leaned forward in his chair, eyes locked with Gabe's. "Tell me more." He started taking notes on a small pad he'd withdrawn from his coat.

Gabe cleared his throat and continued.

"How it was explained to me by my LT, he said we moved like a surgeon's knife, making a narrow entry and touching nothing vital. That way, we could move into some given pin-point, a small target like a building or a city block. Wherever our intel said, we would find the bastards, the worst of those goose-stepping fanatics. My boys got pretty hardened, see. We trained for six months as the worst of 'em... we had to be sharpshooters, all the best knife and pistol training, hell... Cameron Mason could shoot a bottle off a fencepost at forty yards with a waterlogged revolver."

He could see he had Mullally's complete and focused attention.

"So, we go ahead, and we make small advances or clean up the occasional mess. We move in with a few backup units in the big cities, laying down fire from over their shoulders and helping clear roads and buildings. But that wasn't the crazy stuff. See, in a few cities we made it to, we found talk or markings of smaller SS units, smaller clusters of Germans who themselves stayed off the front. Held back as they needed to keep working without being in the crossfire. So, my unit, we made our way up into a few small areas, and we'd burn down whatever they were up to as quickly and quietly as we'd arrived."

Mullally shuffled in his seat a bit. "I've heard some things about their special projects, their experiments. Hoover wrote a hell of an argument on it, about how they've given up on the Geneva Convention."

"From what I saw, that's the truth of it, sir. They were zealots, the lot of 'em. All the higher ranks were either too scared to defect... or true believers. Those SS were true blue to their cause, but some of them were brainwashed. Minds warped, I don't know. It was wild, unpredictable. Their men could be caught without a weapon, and they'd pick up any goddamn object like it was Reich-issued! One of them picked up a *teakettle* and charged us! Charged six goddamned soldiers armed to their teeth, with hellfire in his eyes. He wasn't scared, and he wasn't in his right mind. He was unhinged, fearless... just vitriol and fangs."

"What flavor was it?" Mullally interrupted.

Gabe paused, not understanding the question.

"...flavor, sir?"

"The *tea*, Marshall. In the kettle. What flavor was it? I'm an Earl Grey man myself..."

Gabe chuckled as he realized Mullally was trying to lighten the mood. Gabe took a deep breath and leaned back in his chair a bit.

"Pretty sure it would have been *asshole* flavored, knowing those nancies..."

Mullally let out a snort and leaned back himself, taking out and lighting a cigarillo. "Sounds about right, son. Go on, then!"

"Well, we put him to ground, but it took more bullets than it should. Parker counted twenty-two holes in that man by the time he quit. Commander said they'd been giving some powerful concoctions to their soldiers, but this felt like more than that."

"So what does this photo have to do with all *that*?"

"Well, maybe a month after that, we'd made our way to a small farm north of Küstrin hunting a mobile command detachment while Irish and Parker scouted and came back, said it looked clear. We got close and took our time. Nobody was around, which was a good thing, but no vehicles. Almost no sounds. Parker and Gary Delaney swept around the dells and came up behind the farm while myself and Cam took point with the others watching our six and flanks."

He paused, looking out the little window in the door. He needed a breath.

Mullally nodded to say 'continue.'

On the table, Gabe used a bladed hand and a fist to indicate their attack pattern.

"Well, we get up close, and we hear this godawful scream. We assumed Gary and Parker had just taken a combatant down, so we proceeded with caution. I came around the barn, looking down on the dell, and there was Gary sprawled out unconscious. A fully uniformed SS Officer, an older man, was knelt over Parker and just *covered* in blood. I could tell from twenty yards that Parker was wrecked, Sarge. Just... just absolutely wrecked. The SS was shouting something I couldn't really hear. I just lifted my barrel and sent one clean shot his way. Might've seen daylight through the hole my bullet punched... he fell off Parker..."

Gabe's story trailed off, and Mullally leaned into the desk

and rested his temples on his fingertips without breaking eye contact. The smoke from his cigarillo encircled his head like a halo.

"Well, son, what happened?"

"Sir, Parker was... he was just brutalized, crushed his face and his chest. That bastard did more damage without a pistol than I'd ever seen. Cameron called it... 'animalistic.' Just like in your goddamned picture. Just like that stiff... this lunatic had reached into Parker's body and been pulling his ribs apart with his bare goddamned *hands*. Broke his fingernails off in the process. Like a panicked animal... in a matter of seconds, almost no time. Almost no time at all, and he gored that kid Parker. Shit..."

His eyes welled up a bit, but he stayed steady.

"Sorry to hear. I'd like to know how it ended, son. If you're able...?" Mullally had a tone, something calming in it. Gabe swallowed hard and continued.

"Well, Gary came to, and he was... he was just bawling. His best pal was in pieces, and he was right there. I had to help the man up and hold him back. Gary fell apart for a while there... Never seen such a mess, not—"

Mullally cut in, "Well, not until now." They glanced toward the folder in unison.

With a heavy sigh, the old detective leaned back and shook his head solemnly.

"That's the worst goddamned thing I've heard in a while, son. I'm sorry about all of that. War is ugly, no doubt."

"It's been almost two years, I haven't...' Gabe leaned into his chair and shrugged as he looked at the ceiling, 'I haven't really talked about it since I got back stateside."

Both men were silent for an awkward amount of time before Mullally picked his folder up, dusting off the cover. Gabe sat and stared at the desk, which was covered in closed files.

"Did they ever sort out why that happened? Why would that soldier go to that length just to take down your man, Parker?"

Gabe shrugged as he gazed toward his shoes. He hadn't thought about any of this in two years, and he didn't want to talk about it anymore.

"My C/O insisted it was mania, a reaction to the drugs they force on their soldiers. It's lightning in a pill. I'm sure you read about how they use amphetamines on the front. Some of those bastards don't sleep for days. Suppose it could drive a man mad...

Sure, some allied troops took 'em, mostly long-range pilots, but I kept the boys in my unit away from that crap. Not worth the risk."

Mullally was scratching some notes on a pad in front of him, not looking up as Gabe spoke. He had an expression on his face that bordered on disbelief. Hesitantly, he passed Gabe the folder he'd been holding earlier.

In silence, Gabe opened it and found more photos clipped together, preceding some reports. In each image, the scene was the same. That autopsy room, the metal table. In each photo was a different man, all three appearing to meet a similar fate as the first. It was a bloody, awful mess. Gabe was relieved not to see the photos in color; he saw enough of that in his dreams. Behind the pictures of the victims were four photographs of personal belongings. Wallets, watches, dollars, and rings. It was indeed a standard thing to inventory possessions after a crime, but this was nagging at Gabriel. Why were there so many valuables if these were victims of muggings?

He didn't ask, and the sergeant didn't offer.

"Marshall, this isn't the sort of thing they prepare policemen for, I'm sure you can imagine. There should be a difference between what happens in a civilized city and what happens in battle, don't you think?"

Gabe closed that folder filled with pain and handed it back.

"Yes, sir. I've been reading the paper every day since I got here. This is my neighborhood now, and I know some of these folks are my neighbors. They *were* my neighbors. The papers didn't say... they didn't really detail how bad these attacks were. I don't suppose you caught the guy yet; I would have read about it. I saw there was another just a couple of days ago..."

Mullally counted his words before responding. "We deal with the usual bullshit here, robbery and burglary, bar fights, and a bit of the oldest profession. They just don't train officers for this sort of thing. We don't even take on racketeer or mobster cases; there are special units for that. Top men. Right now, these files tell a different story than what the papers are printing. So we double-up beat patrols and canvas the neighborhood, but I'm not sure it'll be enough. What do you think, Marshall?"

"I think you've got your work cut out for you, Sergeant, that's for sure."

They sat and discussed the service a bit more. Mullally

seemed to have been a Navy man, but only for a few years and not during wartime. He mentioned how very few of his boys in the precinct were servicemen. He welcomed Gabe back if there were any more revelations. Gabe promised to stay in touch but wasn't sure he cared to be involved in such gruesome matters again.

"Well, you've been a help and given me some things to think on. Can I just ask you one more question before you get outta here?"

"Sure, Sergeant, sure."

"What did he use?"

Gabe was confused. "What do you mean, sir?"

"Well, what did that Nazi use against your boy Parker? What was it that did all the damage? Don't tell me it was another *teapot*..."

"Oh, right... he had a brick, sir. Just a broken red brick from the crumbled-down chimney. Bashed him to pulp and kept going."

"Right. Listen, you head out and leave your information with the desk. I'll think about what you said. Thank you, Mister Marshall. And keep this mess to *yourself* for the time being."

Shaking the sergeant's hand and departing, Gabe made his way out, exhausted and upset from those old memories.

Wanting to wind down a bit, Gabe stopped for a cold beer on the walk home. He didn't want to go to sleep just yet, but he knew doing so with all the lousy thoughts in his head might bring him dreams he didn't want anymore. Luckily, he didn't have to walk more than two blocks before he found a little hole-in-the-wall bar with a glowing COLD BEER neon in the window. This was the part of New York City known for its drunkards, after all.

Dead Tired

Thursday, October 17th

RINGGGG

The alarm clock clanged. Gabe's weary hand slapped it off the nightstand, hearing it chipping the floorboard as it landed. He didn't care in the least. He swung one tired, hairy leg out of bed, then another. Slowly, he lumbered off the creaky old Murphy bed and left it where it sat, unmade and always in his way.

I could fold it up, but I don't really need the space. Who would I tidy up for?

On this morning, Gabe was feeling just drained. He was so groggy he couldn't even remember arriving home the prior night after stopping at the bar for that cold pint. It seemed that he had more than just a pint, to be sure. He hadn't slept enough hours, whatever the cause; in fact, he'd been so beat the night before he hadn't even remembered to shut his door all the way.

I hope none of the neighbors were peeking in during the night...

Not too bothered, he slept decently with shorts or briefs on. Usually.

It was another cool October morning, and Halloween was fast approaching. The sounds of the street called to Gabe through his rough-edged curtains. He had set the alarm a bit earlier than usual to allow time for a morning visit with Lindy and to tell her the great news about the new job.

He showered like it was a race, strapped on his boots and coveralls, and made way for the diner. He said a brief hello to the desk attendant on his way out, seeing this morning it was an older man looking pale and frayed.

Looks like my damn curtains... Gabe mused as he hustled past the newspaper rack and out the door.

In his haste, he'd forgotten two things: firstly, his pocket watch. He had left it on his dresser and didn't notice until he nearly reached Art's diner. The second small thing he'd forgotten, he hadn't noticed as he walked into the diner. He had felt fatigued that morning, but upon seeing Lindy, he forgot all about that.

"Gab, come *over* here!" she chided Gabe sternly as he walked in. You look like you've been sleeping on a bench!" She brushed her hand on his cheek, finding a rough day of stubble on his chin.

He stammered out, "Oh, no... I missed a shave, did I? Must have been excited about *work*!" implying that she should ask about his new job.

"Well, Mister Marshall, spit it out! Tell me some good news. You must be working if you couldn't stop and see me just as you'd promised. Two days... You had me worried, you know that?" Her words left her mouth with a bit of disappointment, and her hands on her hips spoke of the same.

Oh boy, she really did miss me? he thought, *I better make nice.*

"Oh, it's all good news, Lindy!" he cheerfully replied, sliding into a booth.

"You gonna make me interrogate you, ya big lug?" she teased.

"I found solid work down at the railyard on the south end. You wouldn't believe it; it's really a great time over there!"

Lindy patted him on the shoulder and set a menu in front of him.

"Tell you what, mister, if you sit and wait for a spell, you can tell me all about it after I clean up the counter, O-Kay?"

She liked to enunciate the O and the K crisply, almost drawing them out. Gabe figured she might've seen some starlet do the same on the big screen, and he loved the sounds it made in the air now that she had adopted it. Gabe didn't mind a little eccentricity; every sound from her mouth was music to his ears.

"O-kaaaay, little lady, I'll set a spell and wait for you." She winked over her shoulder at him.

He did just that, patiently watching her whisk away dishes and messes from the counter with a grace that looked almost stolen from the celluloid of a Walt Disney film. Just then, he recalled the first night he'd been to Art's. It was the first time he had ever laid eyes on her. He remembered that ember she lit in his chest. At this moment, Gabe was having a real tough time ignoring that little flame.

In a fly-by, Lindy dropped a hot cup of joe in front of him with a side of thick buttered toast, precisely what he wanted without him needing to ask. He felt pretty special just then.

Her clean-up finally finished, she returned to the table, bringing him a plate of eggs and potatoes as she sat in the booth somewhat side-saddle; she had always felt that Art wouldn't want her sitting and ignoring her duties, but a little lean into the booth to chat with the customers wasn't so frowned upon. She'd assumed that Art, the old man with a blind eye, had no real idea how the pair felt about each other.

She leaned in close across the table and rested her chin on her hand, elbow propping her up. Gabe wondered if she could smell the mechanical grease in his coveralls or the pomade in his hair. He was transfixed by the smell of coffee and the bright blue jewels that set in her interested gaze.

Gabe ate while they chatted, rude as it may be. His story was truncated a bit. He told her about the two days before and how crazy it all seemed, as though it was all meant to be. The way he took a spill and ended up sitting across from that leathery old sergeant. Hamming it up with a wince, he showed her the bump on the back of his head.

"You could have been really hurt, or worse! If a big boy like you isn't safe, what about little old *me*?" She was half-joking.

"Oh, the only danger to me 'round these parts is my own self. No reason to worry!"

Lindy poked him in the arm and frowned, but only for show. "As if that's going to stop me!"

He finished telling her about the yard, about how friendly Harry Burton was, about how beautiful the sunset had been, and the ferry's charm in its bobbing and sputtering past fishing trawlers and piers. He wrapped up his story by mentioning that he was a bit weary that morning but damn excited about the job. Lindy offered a kind word on his turn of good luck.

"Kismet!" She said with a wide smile.

"Uh... kiss *what*?" His cheeks very nearly turned red just then.

She giggled at his mild ignorance.

"*Kismet*, silly! It's when things happen that are meant to be!"

"Oh, well then... it must've been kismet, yeah, that's the ticket... I'm one lucky fella, I tell you."

She smiled and pushed his plate toward him.

"You big goon, you haven't even finished your toast! Listen, eat up, and get outta here. You're gonna be late!"

Gabe glanced at the clock on the wall, standing up and stuffing a triangle of buttered rye toast in his mouth. He reached for his pocket to pay; Lindy stood up next to him and grasped his forearm, stopping his hand in his pocket. Her touch was gentle and warm.

"Hey now, this one's on me too, Gab. Breakfast is my treat, my way of saying congratulations. You keep talking my ear off, and I'm gonna have to start calling you *Gabriel*; I won't be able to tease you anymore!"

In a dozen or more years, he had not heard his full biblical name without feeling a pang of disdain; he'd chosen *Gabe*, and it was important to him.

This moment, the first time in his life, this was different. On every day before, he disdained his proper name spoken, but now it whispered into his ears like a vesper... like a goodnight kiss. The word left her lips and sounded heavenly, as though she were the one who was meant to speak it after all these years.

There and then, Gabe decided that he would stop beating around the bush with her. He withdrew his hand from his pocket and slowly, gently took her hand into his.

"Lindy, I'm sure I've been a drag these past months. You've been so friendly, nicer than any man could ask for. You are the sweetest girl I know in this damned city. Maybe in the world. Can I come and talk some more with you tonight? I'd love a piece of cobbler and a bit more of your time."

Awaiting her response, he recalled how awfully bad her cobbler had been the first time he'd tried it, and he prayed to some higher power now that she'd been improving on her recipe.

"Why, mister Marshall, I would absolutely love that. Say, meet me here at six tonight, O-Kay?" she replied with a cherubic smile.

"Sure thing, little miss. I'll be here with bells on!"

Waving goodbye, he strode the two steps out the door after he snagged the final piece of toast from the plate.

Lindy's smile wouldn't fade from his mind for the rest of

the day.

An hour later, the man walked into work nearly late. No lunch, save the week-old apple he'd grabbed off his dresser. It tasted like dust; he tossed it into the harbor and went without. His work was slow today; he moved with a pace and diligence that he hoped would ensure his safety through tired eyes. The tower clock's small hand swung around at a glacial pace, pointing once at the noon sun and eventually at the skyline to the east. His second day on the job, and he liked the work plenty well, but this sort of work was brutal without enough rest.

Five o'clock came at last, departure time when the toot of the steam whistle startled a grease can out of Gabe's loose grip.

You survived the day, old man.

Leaving the grease can where it lay on the gravel, the scruffy man dragged his feet to the punch-clock and left the yard without lifting his gaze. On his way out to the ferry, he stopped at a small deli and grabbed a paper-wrapped mystery sandwich, which he ate slowly on the boat ride. He tossed a few fallen crumbs out to the gulls and chuckled a bit at his exhaustion, knowing he was deliriously tired. The food helped a bit, recharging him a bit for the trek home.

You need to lose some pounds, old man. This is young man's work.

He knew as he fought to stay awake on the ferry that he hadn't the energy to visit Lindy, to make good on his promise. He thought about calling her when he got to the lobby.

Walking into his building, he nodded to an old man hunched over a paper behind the counter, and it struck Gabe as odd. He realized he'd hardly ever seen anyone but the young girl there before. *The little lady must have a day off,* he reasoned. Past the desk, Gabe reached around the banister and grabbed the day's paper. He walked over to the lounge in the lobby where the phone booth door was closed, and someone inside was chatting away, so he sat down, intending to read until they finished so he could call over to Art's to apologize to Lindy and reschedule.

The old man who'd been minding the place came shuffling over to Gabe and set a bill in front of him over the newspaper.

"Looks like you still owe for a week back in August. Can you settle up?"

Gabe's eyes locked on the ledger for a moment.

"What? That can't be right, sir; I pay every week!"

The man replied with a stern look, "No sir, not every week. You didn't pay back on that first week of August. It's not in the ledger. Marked late an' everything."

Gabe knew he'd never taken a free week; he paid like clockwork after payday from Carter Machine for nearly the last six months. He took offense at the insinuation he wasn't honest.

"Sir, I am *certain* I paid. I paid cash to the girl who worked here, same as always. I'd have noticed an extra third of my pay padding my pocket... say, you can ask her! I'm no damn freeloader. I just paid up with her a few nights ago."

His frustration was genuine, but he kept his composure.

"Dammit. Sorry, Mr. Marshall. Sure, I trust you, it's... You're not the only resident this has, ah... I'm sorry. Seems that my employee and bookkeeper, Alice.' the man cleared his throat a bit. 'It seems she wasn't as keen on keeping books as I had hoped. A few of the residents claim to have paid for weeks that never got entered and for the life of me? I can't find their money or receipts anywhere. Damndest thing, but... I hate to infer Alice was anything but a good person."

Confused, Gabe asked, "Did she quit on you? Common for a larcenist to scram before getting caught!"

The old man shrugged defeatedly. "She didn't show up this morning. I called her parents on the telephone, and they gave me the runaround. Perhaps she got sick of the dull work, or perhaps you're on the nose, and she felt guilty about her... ah... poor bookkeeping. Sorry for bothering you, Mr. Marshall. Suppose I'll just have to chalk this up to the cost of business."

"Sounds like you might've got yourself stiffed, sorry to hear. I'll keep up on my rent, as I always do. Hope you find better help, pal." Gabe tried not to sound curt in his reply.

The landlord shuffled away to the back office, leaving Gabe with a perturbed feeling in his gut about the young girl. Now, those heavy eyelids and weary feet were really taking hold as Gabe went to stand up and made a distinct grunt in his effort. He had a sour taste in his mouth from the earlier accusation that he was a freeloader.

That slumlord knows the books are bad, and he gives me a hard time? And that's nearly two months old; maybe he should be checking his books more often. Suppose he's got it bad enough. No harm done.

Still aiming to use the phone, he peeked into the glass

pane of the phone booth door in the corner of the lobby. It was more of a phone closet, to be sure. The sizable woman from the hallway was still using the phone, and Gabe just didn't have any more patience to sit around and wait for the line to free up. He felt defeated as he tucked the paper under his arm.

Without the energy to make his date, he used the last of it to trudge upstairs in his heavy boots and clothes. Then, Gabe set his mind to see Lindy again in the morning for another early meal and apologize for standing her up like she didn't matter. She mattered plenty. He felt poorly about it but couldn't protest a good night's sleep.

Within moments of walking into his musty and meager room, Gabe was out like a lamp. It was a dead, absolute slumber... dreamless and warm.

Cobbler

Friday, October 18th

RING

The little alarm clock chided him for sleeping so long; Gabe grumbled a blue word or two, pawing it to the floor. It landed pretty nearly in the same dent it had made precisely 24 hours prior. He slid out of bed, feeling less like a dead man than he had the prior day. Still, he hadn't slept nearly well enough.

Nevertheless, Gabriel still felt a small jolt of excitement at the prospect of a weekend despite the pangs of guilt that he'd stood Lindy up twice in just one week. He grimaced at the tongue-lashing he was about to receive if he made enough time for coffee. He figured he'd better get ready with haste, telling himself *just make the time, you lazy bum!*

After a fast shower and a thorough shave, he was ready to face the day. Coveralls and a pair of boots sure made for quick dressing, something he was thankful for as he rushed out the door. He hurried out of the place, not even turning his head to say hello to the old man behind the desk.

A short jaunt up a few blocks, over steamy potholes and patchwork cement curbs, and Art's was just across the street. Usually, the Dutch doors in front only had the top half open. Today, the whole door was wide open, and from a quarter-block away, he could smell the breakfast meats sizzling and hear the clatter of patrons' silverware amid happy conversation. He steadied his hand and checked his hair in a nearby reflection. *Good enough, I hope...* he assured himself as he stepped across the street to the diner.

He entered and sat in the only seat free at the counter. A

well-dressed man to his right nodded at him and made a little extra elbow room for Gabe's burly frame. In a flash, little Lindy was standing in front of him across the counter, trying her best to look disappointed.

"Oh, *you* again, huh?"

She glared at Gabe, her fists planted on her hips. She was giving him a hard time, and he hoped it was just for show.

"Listen, Lindy, I'm damn sorry I missed you. It's not an excuse, but it's been a rough week. I just wasn't able to come through. I aimed to call over, honest, but there was this... anyway, I wouldn't have been good company."

Gabe grimaced at the embarrassment, wringing his hands under the counter.

"Well, must have been something *serious* to keep you away from my peach cobbler!"

She chuckled at her comment, and at that moment, Gabe realized that Lindy must've known *exactly* how mediocre her 'family recipe' cobbler was on the lone occasion he'd ordered it.

Gabe often thought of that morning some five months ago, not long after he arrived in the city. Lindy had been testing Gabe with a slice of that cobbler. She'd watched him eat the burned (yet somehow also undercooked) cobbler down to a clean plate, trying to keep a straight face. He'd done it to be polite, but he figured it must've made a good impression on Lindy.

Without hesitation, she winked at him and smiled warmly. Gabe replied as honestly as he knew how.

"I've been burning the candle at both ends, I think. I could use some rest, that's all. I must be getting old, or damn foolish, to miss out on plans with you."

She blushed, turning away toward the kitchen to hide it from him. There were orders up and ready for her customers. The well-dressed man one seat down looked toward Gabe with a nod as if to say, 'Nice going, pal!'

Most of the men at the counter were wrapped up in the newspaper or the quiet radio in the corner, retelling sports scores over the din of Art's noisy kitchen.

Gabe unfurled a fresh newspaper from the counter and took stock of the day's events. An article on Wall Street was easy to skip. Two pieces on elections, no big news. He folded the paper. On the underside, it hit him in the gut. Another murder. Another mugging. He scowled at the small print and read it to himself.

ALLEYWAY KILLER STRIKES AGAIN - FIRST FEMALE VICTIM FOUND

The headline ran across the lower front page in bold ink. The photograph was not of the crime scene. Instead, it showed the face of a young lady looking prim and proper. The missing girl's Christian name, Alice Miriam Moretti, was etched in respectful script underneath the grey image.

It was Gabe's friendly little clerk.

"Oh, for Chrissake..."

Lindy was standing nearby and turned on a dime to face him.

"Everything all right?"

Gabe slid the newspaper across the counter and tapped a finger on the portrait of the deceased girl, mumbling, "I knew her."

Lindy took the paper and turned it around to herself, reading only a brief snippet of the obituary, and much of the color left her cheeks. Lindy dropped the paper and took Gabe's hand with both of hers.

"Oh dear, I am *so* sorry! That's terrible... were you close?"

He heaved a breath, took a sip of coffee, and shook his head, 'No,' as his words failed him from the surprise.

Far more flustering to Gabe than the lack of words were Lindy's soft hands resting on the counter, clasped around his right hand. The touch sent the warmest sensation up his spine and flushed his cheeks. He spoke up, talking to his chest, his head hung a bit low.

"Sure, I knew the girl in passing. Oh, that's poor wording there. Just *casually*. She worked the desk in my building, the room I rent. I saw her there almost every day. Decent kid, lots of life. I just saw her a few days ago."

"Oh, Gab, my gosh... if I had known the day would be like this, I would have spared you the ribbing. I'm not mad at all anymore, honest. I'm glad you had time for me. Listen, have you still got time to eat?"

"Sure, I do, Lindy. I made the time today, but I couldn't have forseen the bad news. Sorry about that."

He lifted his gaze to hers and gave her a quarter-of-a-smile, all he could manage; she smiled warmly back, but her eyes belied empathy. His heart was heavy. He felt guilty about the young girl's passing and about speaking poorly about her the night before.

Lindy's soft grasp on his hand drew away as she turned toward the service window and told Art to "get a big plate on that grill!"

Gabe missed her touch already, but she had work to attend to.

Breakfast went by quickly; Gabe barely spoke more as Lindy was busy with serving and cleaning while many more well-dressed folks entered and took the tables around the windows. For a Bowery diner, this place drew a clean crowd. That's how Gabe had known on his first meal at that counter that it was likely the best food in the area, seeing people coming from outside the neighborhood to eat there. He mindlessly watched the passersby; it was a nice distraction from the news. Most of them didn't turn their heads or glance inside.

Maybe they tried the cobbler...

Eating his meal in silence, Gabe made plans to speak with Mullally about Alice. This was a sudden turn of events, and Gabe's morbid curiosity struck him; he wanted to know more about how Alice met her end. With a full stomach and more curiosity than disgust, Gabe read on. The article was short and almost disrespectful compared to other dense, provocative articles about these goddamned murders.

"Of tragedy and consequence, a young lady was found on the outskirts of the bowery at 3 o'clock this morning. The discovery, the grisly fate of one Alice Miriam Moretti, was made by a janitor cleaning up after the late shift at the Manhattan School for the Deaf and Blind. The victim had no association with the school. The injuries of the girl were reported to be extensive, but details have not been released to this reporter. Police refuse to comment as to the validity of this reporter's theory; the proximity and timing of this tragedy indicate that it may have something to do with the string of residents found robbed and brutally attacked over the last many months. Public outcry has yet to take effect, and this reporter, in his experience, believes that only when people see the true scope of the crimes in the form of a full press release from the local precinct will this tragedy be taken seriously. Alice is survived by her parents, Paolo and Corrinne Moretti, who, at this time, could not be reached for comment. Though police would not corroborate, there is a quiet rumor circulating that there is a witness to this heinous act. More information to follow. For now, this find newspapers prayers are with the family of the souls taken so senselessly."

Seeing Lindy was hard at work at the other end of the

diner, Gabe put his dollars on the counter and headed out toward work. The flurry of concern and skepticism about all of this crowded his mind like a cluster headache. He imagined little Alice lying bloodied in an alley, just like he had been. Just like the other victims. Like that poor bastard torn apart in Mullally's photograph. It took him the walk and the ferry ride and nearly the entire walk on the other side to clear his head of that young girl's face.

Pints with Harry

Friday's here, old man. Just nine hours until you can rest...

Standing on the prow of the ferry boat Gabe assured himself that he could make it through this day. He had survived a rocky week, but this day was cheerfully sunny. The air was warm and fresh, and he felt guilty about being in such a foul mood on such a lovely morning. He could not stop mulling over that article about poor little Alice. He set his mind to it with the problem-solving he learned in primary school, his six months of college, and the years of harsh wartime that followed. They used to tell him to 'consider all sides' as a ranking officer, the same line as he'd heard in his tedious Sociology classes back in high school. But they were right.

There is something really unusual about all of this. How could it take so long for a solid witness? I wonder what they saw. Maybe Mullally will be up to talking about it. Hell, they've found nearly a dozen of those grisly scenes, and it took all this time for anyone to see a thing. He must be skilled. This city gets quiet, sure, but damn near every wall and window has a person inside. Not one witness? Not one scream?

He trudged into work punching his card, starting the day's assignment stripping paint from a fat-bellied 6,000-gallon tank car. He spent an hour mindlessly scraping away the old oil-and-dirt varnish caked on the handrails and steps as he continued to deliberate on the situation. All he could think about, what *excited* him, was the prospect of a witness as the newspaper had implied there may be.

People turn up dead every day in this city, but this isn't just street crime. It's not sloppy, and it's no string of muggings... those poor souls had their valuables when they were found. Can't see it as a crime of lust, at least not with the male victims. Unless...

The sun rose overhead and warmed him, reddening his

neck through dirt and beads of sweat. His rail car was looking better by the minute; he took little notice.

Nobody saw a thing until now, or none of those poor souls had cause to make a noise?

Just then, he had an epiphany. It was something familiar; he was reminded of a Hitchcock movie he'd seen at a dirty little theater while on a weekend leave in old London.

They must have either known the bastard... or hadn't seen their killer as a threat. Nobody's that lucky; you can't sneak up on so many men in dark places without a mistake or two. Moreover, you don't find a dozen well-dressed folks lurking in alleys at night in the damn Bowery. Hell, I see people walking around clutching their bags, looking over their shoulders... those folk went quietly and got lured into those alleys. Didn't know what they had comin' until they got it. So maybe they either knew this sonofabitch, or maybe he dresses ritzy? Offers them money? What if he's dressed up like someone they could trust? Perhaps a police uniform... No, not those rough sorts. They fight cops, not follow 'em into dark alleys...

His labor continued, sanding and scraping away with a steady hand and scowling at the ideas in his head. He answered a question nobody asked, words echoing in his mind as he toiled on that train car.

Maybe a dame lured 'em in with perfume and fishnet stockings or... no, must be a man. No woman I've seen has the strength to hold folk down and make them silent, commit that sort of malice... those bodies, their faces... Christ's sake, no. It must be a man. Men commit the evil in that goddamned folder.

Picturing those photos had his stomach churn a bit. He stood up and stretched, ate a bit of nuts and jerky from his pail, then got back up on the car to focus his hands back on the work. He aimed to keep his mind on the job, fixing some grab rungs. It was no use; against his better judgment, Gabe's mind swirled with memories of folks meeting their end. Things he'd come to terms with, even if it still knotted his guts.

People meeting their end either freeze up, staring death in the face, or they shriek their bloody heads off. Saw enough of that in combat. Heard too many cries. Even soldiers make a ruckus in their last moments, even hard men. I wonder if Alice...

Hours had passed as he rolled through scenarios.

Who would that poor girl have been meeting so late? How did she know the man?

Gabe recalled her phone conversations he hadn't intended to hear, whispers about handsome new acquaintances and late nights. He considered bringing that up to the Sergeant, but then he thought better of it.

No sense in sullying her name, making her out as a harlot without cause. For all I know, she only met those boys for bible study, not my business. I'll keep that idea to myself for now.

As the lunch whistle blew, Gabe took a short walk over to the pier and hung his weary arms over the ropes, half-leaning on a post. He was getting tired, but those handrails on that tank car were looking clean and ready for painting. He knew he'd have to let Marco or one of the paint shop boys take the job of getting them finished. He hadn't had time or training in the paint shop, and it was hard to get those handrails painted smooth with any old brush. He knew enough about painting from his youth, spending summers as a neighborhood handyman and helper. All those days working his palms raw had bought him the finest bicycle they sold in the Sears Roebuck catalog, and it taught him honest hard work. He'd made Gil damned proud, which his father let him know on many occasions.

Thinking about those summer jobs, his mind finally let go of the nasty thoughts about alleys and pale, drawn-out faces frozen in terror. Instead, his mind played a nice montage of picturesque little row houses, quiet yards, and gently falling oak leaves across acres of perfectly trimmed grass. The town's edge, rolling hills. Behind the barns on the south side of town were all the places he used to love to sneak about after school. His favorite hideouts were old barns; he'd find some nifty dugout under some old car fenders or a pile of rusted-shut tools discarded when farming was more manual than machine-driven. The smell of yellow weeds and fresh-cut grass was in his nostrils, and his hands could almost feel the tired and worn-smooth wooden handles of those old rusty tools. His father's modest workshed was full of them.

Damn, good memories. I wonder if I'll end up back home, not that Oakdale has much to offer. I don't think I could be happy there alone...

He wished he could simply step back from this smelly pier and the noises of tugboat horns and step back into the cool shade of the barns or the trees that lined the hillsides. He wanted to take a nap among hay bales and dusty farm trucks. His eyes were closed, and his nose was in the air, feeling the sun and ignoring the world around him. He was deep in thought, almost in a trance, until his mind was snapped back to the moment by a toot of a steam whistle in the yard. One short toot, then one longer. He knew the sound meant it was time to head back to work. Though he had skipped a meal, he wasn't hungry; he had plenty of grit left to get through to the 5pm whistle.

During his last hour, Harold came through the yard and rolled his sleeves, small old tattoos showing. Harold had come by to say hello and inquire about Gabe's weekend plans. Gabe figured Harold was looking for some gossip on that little lady whom he knew had Gabe's attention. They fell into conversation, and Gabe set down his brushes and scrapers, leaning back onto the railings of the car.

"Harry, honest! No plans! I need to rest up. Maybe I'll catch a show! One of those greats like the long Egyptian movie or that one about the drunk detectives... who knows, buddy? How about yourself?"

He was lying. He'd be going to see the Sarge again.

Harold looked at him with a skeptical eye as he picked up a sheet of sandpaper and helped knock some paint chips off a ladder rung. It was a funny thing; Gabe could sense that Harry saw right through the bullshit.

"Well, buddy, you see, I'm a boring sap, so I need stories from guys like you to have something to live up to! Gosh, I'm liable to just sit around the room and read a few books. Though, a movie sounds pretty nice... say, pal, how about we bachelors go out and rustle up a little action, yeah?"

Gabe stifled a laugh at the idea of Harold being some dazzling ladies' man.

Harold's eyes fixed on the ladder rung he was stripping, and Gabe thought he might have hurt Harry's feelings with the chuckle at his expense.

Suppose one drink wouldn't hurt...

"Sure thing, Harry, sure thing. I can't say no to that. I'm more of a scotch whisky man myself, but if you're buying, I'll drink anything! I gotta run an errand afterward, so I can't stay too long."

Harold beamed with pride at his newly acquired drinking pal.

"Well, that settles it. See you on the steps at five sharp, big guy! Let's make this a real famous night, okay?"

Harold gave two thumbs-ups and rolled down his shirt sleeves before walking away to attend to the rest of the day's work back in the office.

Gabe replied with a cheerful grunt and a wave goodbye, then turned back to his dirty work.

A cold beer with a new friend. Hell, I could use a real friend in this dirty old city...

Gabe knew he'd need to find his way to the precinct after a couple of pints with Harry so he could share his thoughts with the Sergeant if the old man were still on duty.

The four-thirty shift change whistle blew, and it was time to head out. He changed into denim pants and a cotton shirt he'd left in his locker. He felt refreshed. His shirt was casual and far more comfortable than the coveralls he'd usually wear to and from work.

Two minutes after five, Harold was already waiting on the stoop of the long office, just as he had promised. His shirt now untucked, tie loosened, and looking oddly like a silk noose, Harold had a clearly more casual demeanor when he was off the clock. The two men exchanged a few pleasantries and gripes about the day as they set off for the Crown 'N Dagger.

A short walk from the yard, the men were entering the heavy pub doors, Harry first and Gabe in tow. As Gabe's eyes adjusted to the dimly lit bar, Harry stepped in and cleared the way through the modest crowd of men, motioning Gabe to a circular chest-high table near the back. Harry stopped at the bar to order a round, then joined Gabe at a high table. Harry was fiddling with his tie, impatient for his drink.

They barely had taken off their hats when the barmaid brought their beers to the table. Gabe's eyes lit up at the sight! Perfectly frosted, brimming with golden ale, and they were the biggest damn glass steins Gabe had seen.

"Harry, those must be thirty ounces! This is just what the doctor ordered!" Gabe exclaimed, clinking glasses with him.

Harry let out a bit of a long sigh, relieved to be off the clock.

"Gabe, I tell ya... it's these moments that keep me going. There's nothing like a real drink after a day in that dusty freight house. Did I tell you they used to keep pigs in that building? PIGS!"

He blurted out the word excitedly and loudly, but Gabe saw the other folks around paid him no mind. Harry chuckled a bit to himself, raised his glass to Gabe's, and gave it a clinking 'cheers' at their accomplishment of surviving the week. Gabe held his glass with both hands, feeling the cold soak into his weary mitts and take away the day's ache.

"Harry, I tell ya, again, thank you. Thank Wash when you see him next. What a job! I don't think I earned my pay so hard since I slung a rifle and wore down fresh recruits! Thanks again for helping me get acquainted."

Gabe proceeded to take a swig of the stein, which must have been half the mug in a gulp.

"Boy, I get ya. Did you know I started work in the yards? I know the work, Gabe. I sure don't miss it. I'm not... I'm just not built for it, ya know? The service neither, that's not the road for me. I'm lucky I have math skills and a decent suit, or I'd be out on a street corner *selling* myself! Think I could make a dime?"

Gabe spit a little beer into his mug, stifling a laugh.

"Chrissakes, Harry, you've got to wait until I've taken a drink to say that sort of thing?!?"

"Gabe, buddy, I have to say... you seem like an honest man, a good man. What's with all the cursing? I'm not offended, but... you sure do take the Lord's name in vain more than any sailor I've met."

Mouth full of beer, Gabe simply raised an eyebrow as if to say, 'Yeah, so?'

"It's no bother; I'm just wondering, is all."

"Sure, I suppose you're right, pal. I'm no sinner, Harry, not often anyway... you would never guess it, but I was raised with a man of the cloth in the house. My father's brother, Uncle Robert. He was a good man, but my pop didn't much believe that old book, and neither do I. Sure, I respect churchgoing folks, but let me tell you, I can't follow any book that's got a page with instructions on keeping slaves or stories of god himself murdering firstborns. It's just a bunch of hooey to me. I don't know, Harry. I can try and stop if it's bothersome to you."

"No sir, don't worry about that, just wondering was all. Suppose I feel the same in most ways. Like I said, you're welcome to say what you feel; it just seemed odd from someone who clearly came from good stock. Oh, hell, that sounds mean-spirited. I'm sorry, Gabe, it's this damn beer talking. I'm not really one to judge."

Gabe chewed his tongue for a moment and thought over what he might say to get past all of it. Before he could respond, Harry stepped in again and changed the subject.

"Hey, do you know much about cars? I've been thinking

about buying a car someday; I sure want to get outta the city some weekends, so... do you know much about them?"

Gabe was relieved at the question and wasn't going to point out that Harry was *terrible* at changing the subject.

"Suppose I do. My father always had real working-man-type cars, Dodges and Studebakers mostly. He knew a farmer who also owned a dealership not far from home, and Pop always demanded a simple budget car. Hell, a Studebaker would suit you nicely, Harry. I like their style well enough. They even offer those smooth automatic transmissions in case you want to drive without interrupting... uh... the *attentions* of a nice young lady in the passenger seat!"

Harold's cheeks reddened, and he looked sheepish. Gabe knew an inexperienced man when he saw one, and Harold sure showed the signs.

"Gabe, I tell ya, it's like you're reading my mind! All my dames will certainly appreciate the advice!" he joked, a little tipsy at this point.

Gabe grinned and kept at his mug of refreshment as he took a good look around. He saw a mix of old walls and tired ceiling tiles, new floors, and shiny brass on the bar. Along the walls, there were photos of celebrities.

"It's a good place, Harry. Glad I took you up on the invitation." he offered, finishing the last of his mug.

Harry raised a hand and ordered two more beers as he leaned into the table a bit.

"Say, Gabe, you were a serviceman. What's it like, you know... what was the *fight* like?"

The hard left turn had Gabe searching for answers for a bit. Luckily, the next round arrived quickly, and he had time to take a few sips before he found the words.

"It's no good, Harry. It's a special kind of hell. There's good cause for war, sure. We can't go letting lunatics take over the world and murder good folks in zealotry, can we? But it's deeper than that, and it's... not always so black and white. You have to judge a man by his uniform on the battlefield, and you pull that trigger knowing the guy on the receiving end of your barrel has a family. A mother, a father. Babies awaiting their return. Just like our boys. You do the best you can to do the right thing, but nobody got out of the war with their old self intact. That's just not the way it is."

"Did you kill a lot of Nazis?" Harry was rocking on his barstool, something almost childlike about his excitement at the conversation.

This man has never been in a fight, Gabe thought. *I'd likely have his back if he ever did...*

"Sure, it was part of the job—a necessary evil. I had a small unit of some very hard men, and we did everything we could to cut their ranks down and save Allied soldiers. We saw some real nasty stuff, crazy stuff. Those people are fanatics and damn cruel."

He took a swig of his beer, hoping that Harry had run out of questions on the subject.

"I can't even imagine what you saw, but I've seen enough movies to know that it's not the place for a guy like me!" Harry exclaimed, thumb aimed at himself.

Gabe shrugged and set his now empty mug on the table, grinning at his friend.

"Don't worry, they wouldn't put you out on the frontlines anyway. You're smart, and that counts for more than brawn. They would've had you in some comfortable tent commanding supply line, but I think you would get bored waiting months between those USO shows!"

"Maybe, plus I like the freedom here. I like doing what I please, and I guess I should say thanks for serving, Gabe. Can I get us another round?"

"I'd love another, but say... I'm pretty bushed, and I still have that errand to run. See you Monday?"

Gabe was lying; he wasn't tired, but he didn't want to talk about the goddamn war any further this evening. He wanted to see Mullally.

Harry shrugged, offering, "I'll be in your neighborhood Sunday, tryin' to find a new suit. Wanna take me to that little diner you told me about? I haven't had a good breakfast in a while!"

Gabe relented and waved him goodnight. "Sure, pal, I'll see you Sunday. Say ten sharp, meet me at Art's. Easy enough to find, only one in the Bowery. Check your phone book for the address."

Harry gave a thumbs-up and turned back to face the table of women sitting nearby, though he didn't chat them up.

As Gabe took up his hat and headed for the door, Harry turned back and broke out into a little song from the movies; channeling his best inner Hollywood crooner, Harry sang Gabe off with "Happy traaaaails to youuuu..." which faded off into a gulp of another beer that had appeared at Harry's table.

Gabe nodded to the barmaid in appreciation and set a dollar on the end of the bar on his way out.

It's All Bad News

A breeze blew in from the east, and Gabe was thankful the ferry had inside seating on this chilly evening. The walk after the ferry was brisk enough to keep him warm despite being without a coat. His walk stopped in front of the old precinct's large frosted globes in front of the building. It was quarter-to-seven, and the white lamps were glowing brightly, casting their shadow across the street and up the building fronts. He ran his hand down their cast-iron bases, which were rather ornate but somewhat rough-hewn. The claw feet seemed like roots, writhing unevenly down before embedding into the granite ledges. He made his ascent on the steps to those heavy, weatherbeaten blue doors. As he reached for a handle, the doors swung open.

A small group of reporters were deserting the building, easy to tell since most of them kept their press credentials tucked into the band on their hats. It was an old tradition, some inside joke that maybe only the press boys 'got.'

Upon his entry and to his dismay, the same clerk from before waved Gabriel away. He'd been kind but firm.

"Mullally ain't here, sorry pal... man's gotta rest sometime, ya know? He's off duty until tomorrow, roundabout ten. Come back then if it can wait."

I guess I have a memorable face... "Thanks, officer!" Gabe offered with a wave.

Leaning in the door with cool night air blowing against the back of his neck, Gabe walked his dismay right back outside as he headed home. *Got to clean up and get a coat before I do anything else,* he figured. Those heavy work boots were killing his feet by now, but luckily, the walk home wasn't too far.

As he walked through the door of his building and

headed for the rickety staircase, he noticed the old man was sitting at the desk, looking defeated, hands on the counter limply. Gabe felt the urge to apologize.

"I see you're still here. I'm sorry, sir, I read about Alice in today's paper. I had no idea the other morning, and I'm sorry if I was short with you."

The man's shoulders slumped a bit more, and he motioned out the door toward that rough neighborhood. He vacantly spit out a reply as he gazed down at the desktop.

"They found her in a terrible state. I own this old firetrap. The station called me after seeing my name on the payslip she had in her purse. Alice was a good kid, she... she was... just torn apart, I tell ya. They asked me to identify her. I had to call her father and ask him to join me. I knew her just well enough the officers told me to call her father... but I figured that poor man couldn't handle seeing her like that. His little girl, she..."

The old man's sputtering words broke down into a quiet, heaving breath; he was irreconcilably upset. Tears welled up in his eyes as he stared down at the cluttered desk.

"He came in a cab while we waited over the white sheet. I stood there while the detectives told him his little baby girl was murdered, Mr. Marshall. I don't think I should have been there. And to think, I was sure she was just a thief... Have you ever seen a terrible thing like that?"

Gabe's gut went cold.

"In a way, I have. Many unfortunate folks, and it's *never* easy." He commiserated, thinking of his own time in the service. He was rattled yet again by the thought of it, by the idea of that little girl lying on a cold table somewhere for no good cause.

The old man behind the counter sunk his face into his hands, seemingly not wanting to talk anymore. Gabe lurched up the steps to his room and felt that knot in his stomach yet again. Closing his eyes, he could almost see Alice lying in a terrible way, ruined and left broken on some dirty floor. His insides felt that chill of nervousness, of danger. He couldn't simply let it go; this was his home, and a piece of it felt tainted now. He double-stepped back down the stairs and reached the front desk again. Gabe tapped the man on his shoulder a bit, as he hadn't moved and still had his face buried in his palms.

"Listen, I'm sorry, pal. Tell me one thing. Do they know

anything useful? Maybe you overheard something useful? The papers... well, they glossed over it."

The man shook his head slightly but then replied in a hushed tone. "One of the officers, I overheard him talking. They were saying it was a German in the alley, outside their apartment. They heard it, and they didn't do a thing to intervene; that's what the policemen said... good lord, I can't imagine the guilt they must carry."

That knot in Gabe's throat turned to a shot of lead, heavy and firm. Images of trenches filled with dead soldiers flashed in his mind, Reich uniforms and evil weaponry. Railcar-mounted heavy guns, indistinct screams of anger and terror echoing through city streets that were wholly torn asunder from both artillery and incendiary, all such ruinous things.

Without another word, he made his way upstairs.

No use in prying further, he told himself; *Mullally will tell me plenty if I ask right.*

After a hot shower, he made a run across the street to grab a cheap bottle of rye whiskey from the corner market. Returning to his room eager to open the bottle, he set his mind to plan how he would confront the topic with Mullally. Finding a pencil in the old corner hutch, he turned to the newspapers he'd been stacking in his bedroom. He had been collecting the papers out of sheer laziness or occasionally to save a movie advert or classified. Now Gabe was thankful for being less tidy than usual. He pulled out the papers with headlines about the ugly murders or any possibly related crimes. He simply tossed the rest under the bed, not caring to tidy up just now.

Gabe sat back in his bed with a dozen-or-so broadsheets and began re-reading those depressing articles fervently. As he'd opened the bottle, the cork had broken apart, the pieces of it still clinging wetly to the bottle's insides. Some cork was in his drink; he'd spit it out and continued drinking. Pencil in hand and brow furrowed, his notes and annotations began coherently but quickly trailed off into angry circles and highlights. He was both focused and frustrated; it was one thing to know that there were terrible folk in the world, but it was another to have this violence happen so close to home. That made him mad as hell.

It wasn't long before he finished the booze, more than ten ounces of cheap rye. The evening passed him in the blink of an eye. When the grandfather clock downstairs chimed midnight, Gabe realized it was time to get some rest—hours of deliberation had passed as he pored over those somber newspaper articles, over that gray photo of the girl. He felt helpless, almost violated, and he hated that feeling. He knew what he had to do.

"Seems it's time *soldier* Gabriel Marshall got involved..." he grumbled aloud.

He leaned back in bed, feeling his pulse in his neck and chest throbbing from the sugary booze. He felt hot and uncomfortable.

I'm not gonna get any sleep like this. Maybe I'll just snag one more bottle across the street before they close up for the night.

He slipped on dirty denim pants and a trench coat, hiding his night-shirt by buttoning the coat all the way up. The boots went on easily without socks, but the leather inside was cold. With three dollars in his hand, he gingerly crept out of the building as a courtesy to the folks who might be sleeping.

Not that they ever gave him the same.

Station Stop

Saturday, October 19th

The morning started with light rainfall; Gabriel could hear the raindrops before he opened his eyes.

Goddamn cold in here... Shit. Head is killing me. Left the window open...

With his knuckles, he rubbed away the sleep as he tried to sit up, his back stiff and aching. As he drew back the blanket, he could feel that it was, in fact, his trench coat. Simultaneously sitting up and letting the coat drop to the floor, he came to realize why he was so cold.

He was sitting shoes-off and partly drenched in vomit, slouching half-upright on a wooden bench in a gazebo smack dab in the middle of a grassy promenade park he recognized to be some five blocks away from his walk-up. It was so early that the sun had not yet risen.

"Oh, for chrissakes, Gabe. God-DAMN-it!" he shouted from a hoarse throat.

The weary man cursed himself further as he stood up, picking up his trench coat. Then, a cheap glass whiskey bottle fell out of its furls and smashed into countless pieces on the cement. He spit dry, awful spit onto the pile, and he could taste stomach acid. His breath was putrid.

Got to learn to handle my liquor, I'm too old to be a god-damned park bum!

He chastised himself further, clenching his fists and wheezing a heavy breath. He could hear the sounds of the city beginning for the day and realized that he'd better not be seen looking like a railcar hobo. Boots now on his feet but as yet untied, he swung the coat around his shoulders and buttoned it up to the neck before stumbling and catching himself on one of the white-painted beams that made up the frame of the gazebo.

The rainfall continued. It was gentle, but he knew he would get drenched on the walk home. He fumbled and found nothing in his pockets but his key and the wrinkled-up remnants of his termination slip from Carter Machine.

Shit.

He flipped up the collar of his coat and gritted his teeth. His feet chafed because he had no socks. The walk home was his punishment, not that he had the money for a taxi anyway.

His stiff back had him hunched over and grumbling most of the walk home, short as it was.

What do you think Lindy would say if she saw you like this, you horse's ass? What do you think your father would say?

Berating himself, he trudged through the damp morning air and wiped his brow and face free of tangy raindrops frequently. Eventually, he returned home and got up to his room without seeing another soul. He was relieved that he wouldn't have to explain himself nor suffer the dour glances surely forthcoming from his gossipy neighbors if they knew where he'd been.

The only thing greater than his embarrassment at his stupidity was his disappointment; this was the third time in as many months he had woken up somewhere a man shouldn't be sleeping. The stoop of a church once and the bench of a flophouse twice after that. He knew perfectly well that if he had been spotted on that bench by any police, he'd be hauled away to sleep it off in a cell, risking his job and whatever chance he had with Lindy. Sauced up, he tended to forget that fact.

Get yourself together, Gabe. The last place you need to end up is the drunk tank.

After taking the time for a hot shower, no shave, he slipped on his still-damp coat and made his way toward the precinct. No coffee, no food. His hangover was mild for now; he'd had plenty of them and knew how to ignore it. For now, there was work to be done.

As he stepped inside the Bowery Precinct, Gabe caught the eye of old Sergeant Mullally across the open bullpen, which contained over a dozen desks and steel filing cabinets. Mullally beckoned him to come through, and the young desk cop with a ruddy complexion waved him through.

"Thanks, Officer... ?"

The young officer tipped his hat a bit, cheerfully responding, "It's Harris, sir."

"Harris, it is." Gabe rapt his knuckles on the barrister-style rails, walking through the swinging gate.

Arriving at Mullally's cramped corner desk, Gabe sat and leaned back a bit to where his shoulder rested on a column behind him.

"So, what have you got for me today, Marshall?"

The Sergeant had jumped right in. He hadn't offered a greeting nor a handshake, as most courteous folks might. This man was all business. Gabe leaned forward and clasped his hands.

"Well, Sarge, I heard some queer things about that unfortunate young woman your boys discovered two nights ago, Alice Moretti."

"What sort of things did you hear, and from whom?" Mullally seemed on edge.

Gabe wanted to tread lightly so as not to catch the ire of the old copper. "Firsthand information, sir. I came to find that girl was the desk clerk at my residence. Nice girl, never deserved that sort of end."

"Our latest victim worked... in your tenement?" Mullally asked with an eyebrow arched.

Gabe nodded, shrugging, "She was at the desk most mornings, sir. Just a nice young lady. She didn't deserve this."

"So what was so queer that you had to come down and see me?" Mullally chided him.

"The owner of my building said the man you're looking for is German."

Mullally scratched his chin and sat back into his seat, trying for a poker face.

"That might be one theory, sure. How does that involve you, Gabe?"

Gabe cleared his throat and began to speak in a frank, fast cadence that he had been known for in the service. Every man in his unit knew that you'd need a cup of joe and a keen ear if you were going to speak with Gabe Marshall.

"I'll explain, sir. First, there's this nonsense in the papers stating the bastard has been sneaking up on folk. Sure, I could see the first couple folks being surprised, maybe... but after three or four or a near-dozen murders in under a year, well... just look around, Sarge! People nearly never go out late around here these days. Folks are scared, not even knowing these are all related crimes. You hardly see anyone walking alone, big or small, man or woman. Hell, that theory's damned silly. The victims knew the bastard. They must have. That, or they felt safe with him. It doesn't add up otherwise."

Mullally fumbled in his desk drawer. He picked up a small cherrywood tobacco pipe and chewed the end of it, his teeth nestling into the chewed-up resin like a sleepy dog in a fireside bed. He nodded solemnly, not looking up to Gabe.

"Okay, Sarge, then you've got this witness stating it was a German."

Mullally dropped the pipe from his mouth and looked up with a glare.

"That's not in the files, son. Careful with whose company you repeat that."

"I supposed it wouldn't be, sir. Are you saying it's an unfounded rumor?"

Mullally continued nibbling on the stem of his pipe as he drew out one long cedar match and struck it to light on his linked watchband. Gabe thought, at the moment, it must have been the keenest trick this fellow knew.

I've got to practice that with some matches when I get home. Maybe with a cigar instead. The thought escaped him briskly.

Mullally puffed out some musty tobacco smoke and half barked, "Say it is, what then? What's the angle?"

"Well, Sarge, what I don't get is this; how in the blazes any German-speaking man, after this terrible war, would get anyone to follow him into an alleyway in the dead of night? I read that even the damn Dutch farm folk out in Pennsylvania are taking English dialect classes because of the hostility towards their native Deutsch these days."

"Sounds fishy, sure. Perhaps they were coerced... *if* that's the case." Mullally quipped, smoking the pipe and staring off at a far wall.

"Well, not to mention, these folks were found with belongings, right? Watches, wallets, a purse? That's no robbery like I've ever seen, sir. And the brutality... I don't think it's a perversion, is it? There's something rotten about all of it."

Gabe was trying to lead the Sergeant to admit that the attacks weren't muggings at all. It was so damned *obvious*.

"Marshall, that's... I can't really have an opinion on that. Not yet. Every precinct in New York has a copy of this case file, redacted in places to ensure we don't have any...' Mullally sneered at the word, 'leaks."

He withdrew a folder from his desk drawer, taking half its contents out and handing the rest to Gabe. As Gabe grabbed the folder, Mullally held onto the corners tight as if to intone, 'This is important.' Gabe nodded his head in understanding.

Mullally released the folder, and Gabe opened it deftly. The first page was simple: a Coroner's report with a block-printed header. The girl's name bannered the top of the first-page report, Alice Miriam Moretti. Gabe scanned the page and saw that the "cause of death" section appeared to be a damned novel.

He read that portion, skimming words and whispering to himself, 'unknown object... blunt force... lacerations... no incision. Multiple ruptured arteries... fractures... Separation of issue caused by... fatal trauma caused by manual object unidentified'.

He thumbed to the following page, a freshly developed page-sized photograph of the poor girl. He scanned it from top to bottom, his eyes recognizing the hair, the little cross necklace Gabe had mentioned to Alice, just making conversation.

"Oh, Christ. This poor girl, look what happened to her face..." Gabe muttered.

The photo was hued in black and white, but the extent of her injuries was clear. She had been brutally gored in the chest and neck, almost ripped apart in the process. Below her crushed jaw, broken and crooked, it was hard to make out what was really left of the girl in that dark photograph. Her eyes were clear as day and wide open, rolled back into her head. She looked like a ghoul, laid out in a final shriek on wet cement.

Gabe turned the photo over in the folder, hoping for some reprieve, but the next photo was nearly as bad; it was taken from a few feet back, and the gloss of spattered blood reflected off the walls of the place where she met her end. Gabe's face went soft and still as his training took over and shut out his emotional response, his hands calming and his lower lip pursing. His face felt cold with adrenaline, and he sat down in the chair, still clutching the files.

Keep it together, Gabe! He steeled his resolve not to react with disgust.

Mullally's pipe smoke was sour-sweet, smelling of oak and something like bourbon. It swirled around the desk where they sat. He was silent, watching Gabe.

"So we have a mystery on our hands, son. You've seen sadistic men at their worst. You think this might be related, or it might just be plain old bad luck. Nobody's making that call yet, son. So, that leaves me one question."

Gabe didn't know where this was leading, so with an open palm beckoned Mullally to pose his question.

"Marshall, If New York City had a genuine Nazi out there killing folks on our streets, how would we find and stop him without raising a panic? From reading about what happened in Nuremberg through the start of this month, it seems to me that a majority of the Nazi soldiers and sympathizers who escaped were wise enough to lay low or start fresh somewhere. They're dragging these sumbitches out of hiding around the globe, matter of fact."

Mullally sat quietly for a few minutes while Gabriel read more of the file and considered the question. Leaning back into his chair, the sergeant smoked his pipe, watching the wisps rise.

"You couldn't put it in the papers. The war has barely ended, and a lot of folks are still scared. German immigrants are everywhere in the city; they helped build the country. As you said, they didn't catch all of Hitler's scoundrels, and people remember that. Christ, look what they did to the Japanese! The war is over, but they're still in cages and work camps! No, you'd have to solve it without making anything public if you want to prevent panic. But you'd have to admit, at least to yourselves, that you're not chasing some small-time mugger. It's far more serious than that, and you know it, sir."

Mullally nodded with a grimace on his face. He took a long draw on the pipe before responding.

"So you understand that... *hypothetically*... we'd have to prop it up that way, blame it on simple robbery. Try and prevent public panic; try and prevent some lunatic from picking up a hammer and doing his best impression. See, folks have a way of getting squirrely when the news gets bad enough. Simply put, it would need to be kept quiet."

Gabe counted his words very closely before responding. He knew the Sergeant wasn't going to confirm anything, but he didn't need to.

"Sir... If you admitted these were violent murders and not muggings, that's all it might take to get folks paying attention to the streets without mentioning it might've been a German..."

Puffs of smoke crept across the desk as Mullally raised an eyebrow, working out his measured response.

"You might be right, but of course, we've considered that. It would cost us more in public faith than the commissioner is willing to lose. So it stays quiet."

He's clearly bullshitting, with no conviction in his voice. A street cop, brass or not, dealing with this? He must be out of his depth. I know I am.

Gabe knew Mullally would want to stay in charge of the conversation, but his faith in the Police was dwindling.

"I don't agree, but I'm no politician, sarge."

The sergeant peered over his shoulders, hushing his voice a bit as he continued. A keen look was in his eye.

"If this department blew a cover story to root out a killer, we risk a panic. If they don't, we may never find this bastard and just keep stumbling over dead civilians. I'm well aware of what we're risking, son, and you better be mindful of that as well. I'll talk to the Commissioner about what you told me of Parker and your experiences, and the Commissioner will decide. Until then, don't say a damned word. How's that sit with you, Marshall?"

"I can work with that. I'm not looking to interfere. Just tell me... you have a witness who heard German. Was it a German accent or German words?"

Mullally was tired of the hypothetical. With a grumble, he sat forward in his seat and opened up to Gabe.

"Off the record? And I'll tan your ass if you say a word of this past our steps."

Gabe nodded solemnly, "Off the record, sir."

"We found a neighbor who said he heard cursing, some shouting in German tongue. He's a schoolteacher, he ought to know. So we canvassed. Nobody in that block speaks or knows a soul who speaks any decent German. I suspect that has something to do with the last three years of war this country has been fighting; people are afraid, and rightfully so, to be seen as one of *them*. Now, maybe it was a load of horse puckey, but in my eyes, the man seemed credible and even repeated a few of the words he heard. Schoolteacher, smart man. His story stayed consistent through three detectives' thorough questionings, so we have a lead there."

"Okay, but what did the killer *say*?"

"It was a bit unclear due to the jarring nature of such an eyewitness account; the witness wasn't entirely sure. Something about 'blood and bones'... strange stuff, son. That's all we got from it save for a few little fibers and a dress shoe print in the blood spatter. Damn thin leads to follow if you ask my boys. The only solid lead I have is that every victim seems to be a bad apple of some sort. Every one of them has a record of criminal conduct, or close to it."

Gabe chose not to mention Alice's possible history of pilfering, especially now.

"That doesn't sound like anything I've heard, sir. Not specifically. But, I took point on a few missions behind the red lines, and I've seen some damned strange things, sir—evil things. I've heard some arcane and biblical stuff come out of their mouths in battle. Some of my enemies were just soldiers doing what they must, but some of them were... they seemed brainwashed. Violent to their core. I believe some of their soldiers enjoyed all the killing."

"And you think the allied boys didn't?" Mullally shot back.

Gabe fought the flood of imagery from his time fighting the Axis. Trenches rife with the remains of brutally slaughtered ally soldiers, the civilians' bodies he'd found dismembered or shot to hell sitting in their homes. It still made him terribly uncomfortable.

"Well, listen, it's gonna be a busy day, son. What say you think about it for a couple of days? I respect your service, and perhaps there's a way you can help with all this. Check in with me first part of next week. Can you do that?"

"Absolutely will, sir. I'll take a little time, even talk to my old unit about it. Maybe I'll come up with something more for you."

"Okay, son. Check out with Harris at the desk when you leave, and give him your contact information. Phone, address, all of that, in case I need it. If something comes to mind, call me. *Only* me. None of those ideas about this case goes to the papers or your friends, understood?"

Mullally's stern warning was understood. Gabe shook the old man's hand and departed with a nod. He stopped at the desk on his way out, and while he wrote down his information for Harris at the desk, he started to feel a bit flushed. A lightheaded feeling hit him harder as he walked outside and down the big staircase.

His tongue had planted in his mouth, and he now felt sick, not just in his stomach but feverish. It was a slightly familiar feeling of unease. After the adrenaline subsided, his body was calm and cool, but his heart and mind were racing, and fire blazed in his temples. It was a short walk home from the precinct, and he knew he wasn't going to make it far.

Hope I don't lose my lunch.

As he leaned over a filthy gutter with twinging spasms in his belly, he remembered something crucial.

I didn't have any goddamn lunch...

He spent ten minutes heaving and spitting stomach bile over that curb, trying to make himself sick and clear the cheap booze out of his stomach. To no avail, but he tried. By the time he gave up on his effort, he was even sicker than before, and his eyes hurt from straining. His guts were made of a sailor's knot.

It wasn't the photo that had upset him. It might've been the whisky and four hours of sleep out in the elements, but more than likely, it was adrenaline. Gabriel had a sensation in his chest that he hadn't felt in a long time. His heartbeat was up, and his blood felt hot.

He was *excited*, and he had a call to make.

Mason

A black Bell telephone rang out three times before its owner lifted the receiver.

"Yeah?" A gruff voice answered.

"Cam, is that you?"

Cameron Mason was the all too familiar voice on the other end of the line.

"My favorite punching bag! How's New York treating you?"

"Honestly? Like a damn punching bag. You promised you'd teach me to box like you. I'm *still* waiting!"

Cam's grumbling laughter carried over the line.

"Gabe, I'm just teasing you. How are you, man? I haven't heard from you since, well... It's been a year or so. What's goin' on? You talk to any of the brasswatch boys lately?"

"Just you, and I'm starting to regret it!" Gabe teased.

Gabe chortled at the word. "Brasswatch. Hell, I haven't thought about that in a good while... where did that come from again?"

"You know damn well, Gabe. We used to assign that dead-weight Oliver and sometimes Darby to stay on the lookout for brass and ranks whenever Shamus would get us wrapped up in his... shenanigans. Ain't that the word he used? Made causing trouble sound classy. Damn Irish. He could sniff out a good wager in a pile of rubble, think I still owe him five bucks!"

"Yeah, but that nickname?" Gabe prodded.

"C'mon Marshall, remember that night our lanky Captain found out? He started callin' us the 'Brasswatch Boys' like it was a damn musical! Made Darby do pushups until he chucked. Gave you that ass-chewing right before he grabbed a stool and downed the last of our bottle."

"That man was a terror," Gabe replied.

"Good times, yeah."

"Suppose it coulda been worse, Cam. If you hadn't saved the man from certain death no less than twice as I recall, he might've named us the 'latrine scrub boys'!"

His friend's voice rang out with honest laughter through the receiver, and Gabe realized how much he missed the man.

"Cam, I tell ya... I've been out here in New York this whole time. It's a beautiful mess. You'd love it here. Utter goddamned chaos."

Cam sighed, but Gabe could hear the smile in it.

"I bet I would, all those shows and games! California's not too bad, but Richmond is the pits unless you're building ships. I'm too old for that heavy lifting shit. Maybe I *do* need a change of scenery. You stayin' out there with family how you planned?"

Gabe could feel a little catch in his throat, delaying the somber answer to that question.

"Uncle Robert passed. Hell, I barely got here, and he just... passed. Bad kidneys."

Cam clucked his tongue in disappointment. "That's a shame, Gabe. I'm sorry. I know how close you were."

"He was a good man, hard life got him,' Gabe paused, not wanting to dwell on bad news, 'say now I, uh... met a gal, Cam. She's really tops. Just an amazing gal. About to ask her to a proper dinner... How about you? How's the lady doing?"

"Ginny? Virginia. Oh boy, she's a handful, Gabe. The girl doesn't know how to cook! I've been teaching her when I have the time. It's a real scene. My kitchen is a war zone right now. Light of my life, you know how it goes."

"A man's gotta eat, you know. Say, how's her other... uh... attributes? You can always make *yourself* a sandwich if there are other things to appreciate."

Cam was in stitches again, holding the bridge of his nose and laughing into his chest.

"Dammit, Gabe, you really have a way with words, you know it. She's lovely, and that's all you need to know. Anyway, I think she's gonna marry me if I ask soon enough. Second Time's a charm, ain't it?"

"Well, then ask her somewhere *special*, Cam! Bring her out to New York and get her to the top of one of these fancy buildings! But... well, maybe don't bring her just yet..." Gabe sighed a bit into the receiver.

"Why is that?"

"Well, to be honest, Cam, I need your ear for a minute."

"Sure, but I got a cigar going outside and..."

Gabe cut him off, "I'll mail you another, Cam. This is important."

The tone of the call was starting to match the subject matter.

"Sure, Gabe, I have plenty of smokes. What's weighing on you now?"

Gabriel leaned his shoulder into the booth of the payphone, standing there in the lobby of his building. He didn't want anybody overhearing the conversation, and he didn't know a better place to make the call. With a long breath, he rested his head on the wall and relayed to Cameron the whole sad story. He explained how the Bowery was a poor neighborhood known for crime and vice. He explained how he had been reading about a string of murders in the newspaper and how, for a while, it seemed that's just the way things were there in the rough part of town. He told Cameron about how he bumped his head and wound up falling into the thick of it with Mullally.

"Sounds like you stepped in the shit, Gabe."

"It's crazy, but it feels like I'm meant to be involved. Just a couple of days ago, the cops had their first female victim in all of this, and wouldn't you guess, she worked in the building where I live? I didn't hardly know her, but it still hits close to home... It's not right, Cam. Someone's got to *do* something."

Cameron was listening intently and looked out his window to the cigar he'd left resting in a crystal ashtray in the sun. Its ember had gone cold.

"Gabe, I don't think you should be getting involved in all of this. The way you left the service, I gotta tell you I think it would be better if you stayed away."

Without acknowledging Cameron's comment on his discharge, Gabe kept on by describing what he had learned from Mullally. Informing Cam about the police files, Gabe commented that he didn't think the police were in a position to get very far with their investigation. Gabe described the horrible state of the bodies they'd found, the gory details, while Cam tapped his fingers nervously on the wall near the phone.

"Worst of it is, they finally had a witness the other night. Nobody saw anything, but they overheard some yelling. Cam... the witness said it was German."

Silence on the line for a bit now. Gabe's receiver dinged, signifying he needed to pay up for more time on the phone. He dropped another nickel in with a hollow clatter as it fell into the belly of the phone.

"You know what that sounds like, don't you, Gabe?"

"I don't want to think it, Cam."

"But it does, Gabe. It sounds just like when we... when we lost Parker. It sounds the damn same, man."

"I know, but... how do you figure it's possible? Why the same attacks? Do you think it's those drugs they were all taking? Some sick tribute?"

Cam thought on the question for a few moments.

"Gabe... d'ya remember all that weird shit we went through in that bunker in the spring of '44? Remember all that devilish writing, that ritualistic stuff? You know, that dead sonofabitch with the baby mustache was heavy into the bad religion, man. Voodoo. Occult. Whatever you want to call it, his cronies played with that stuff in their higher ranks. They believed it gave them some kinda power, some crazy connection to all the ambition and all the willpower in a man."

Gabe butted in, "A bunch of *hooey*, all of it."

Cam grunted in agreement at the comment. "When you went into the infirmary for a while when our unit was disbanded... I was assigned with Irish to research that mess for the intelligence unit we got attached to, Gabe. We weren't allowed to speak of it, but I know you got briefed on it while you were layed up. Colonel Kemper, right?"

Gabe was hesitant to talk about his time in the hospital, even with Cam.

"Yeah, they spent some bedside time with me, went down that road. They tried to find some answers about what we saw out there. Not that I believed it, Cam."

"Hey, you remember that day that bastard took down Parker? Remember how his uniform was a little different... like he had some special rank? We hadn't seen it before, man, and we never saw it again."

"Hell, of course I remember that, Cam. I took him down. Not that it did Parker any good. I took those little pins off his collars. They seemed like gold. I don't know, maybe they are. I have them sitting around somewhere, it doesn't matter... He's a dead sonofabitch, and he got his reward, and we lost Parker to those lunatics, and now I'm losing neighbors to something maybe just as evil, and I don't know if I can sit back and let it happen again."

Cam's line was quiet for a few moments before he piped up, "Gabe, don't mess with this, man. You're out, so stay out. Seriously, this ain't gonna end well. Listen, what did you say was the name of that police Sergeant?"

"Cam, I appreciate your help. It's Mullally; he's out of the Bowery precinct. Why do you ask?"

"Just wanna know who to talk to if ya get yourself in a pinch, that's all, Gabe. You're just one guy, and you're a goddamn civilian now."

Gabe knew he wasn't going to receive the encouragement he hoped for from this old friend.

"O-kay, Cam, you made your point. When things quiet down a bit, I'd really like you to come visit, bring that lovely girl with you, yeah?"

"Yeah, sure, man... sure. Shit, you owe me a cigar. Send me a postcard with your spot, where to reach you. And watch your behind, man."

Gabe laughed and agreed before he hung up the phone and returned to his room, where he sat at the small writing desk near the open window.

A cool breeze was coming into the room as he sat thumbing through the deck of cards that he kept on the little desk, listening to the small fluttering sounds the corners made when he rowed down the stack with his thumb. In the corner of his eye under the bed, the metal ammo box he'd kept under his bed caught his attention. It held nearly everything he'd brought home from the service, which wasn't much.

He knew that there might be a small clue in there, including those rank pins from the dead SS officer, but he recalled how he always felt a bit uncomfortable holding those awful keepsakes.

Probably a crime to have them.

Gabe knelt to pick up the box. Sitting back down on the

bed, he opened the creaky lid and lifted out a German revolver he'd brought home; it was still wrapped in a soft rabbit pelt, which he had bought in an Idaho gift shop along his train trip toward New York City once he was discharged. They'd sent him through an army clinic in Washington to see a specialist before they gave him his discharge papers. Now, that soft golden hide carried the distinct smell of gun oil. He set it aside without unwrapping it.

Digging into the box to the bottom, various brass and copper medals and badges rattled around between his fingers until he found the matchbox that held the Nazi pins. He slowly slid open the tiny cardboard box, dumping the pins into his palm. As the room's light glinted off them, he realized that they were merely gold-plated; the edge had worn down to the cheaper metal underneath.

They're just plated, that's all. I can't melt them down and sell the slugs. Maybe I could make them into something. One of those boys back at Carter could recommend a place for that. Gotta give 'em a ring. Hell, I might be giving Lindy a ring, too.... I sure hope Mom's ring is still safe back home. Robert said the bank box was paid for a dozen years. Shit.

He pushed thoughts of Lindy to the back of his mind while he inspected the Nazi trophies under a beam of dwindling sunlight.

They were etched among the back with some sort of old letters, familiar like Greek or Cyrillic. Those little gold pins were shaped like swastikas but with jagged edges and what almost looked like two eyes inset. He recalled how nobody in the unit was able to identify the symbol when Gabe had discreetly shown them around... it was just so goddamn *strange*. He had never seen these symbols before or since, and he had never brought it up to his COs. Something in his gut had told him back then that mentioning the pins would cause more problems, and he didn't want anything interfering with his discharge or keeping him in the service a single day longer.

Gabe was disappointed that those engravings still made no sense, but he figured it would be good to keep them handy in case he needed a talking point with Mullally. Strangely, he felt more uneasy now than ever before. He slipped the pins in the pocket of his trench coat hanging nearby.

He turned back to the bed, picking up the soft rabbit hide wrapped around the gun, which he dusted off with the fur as he unwrapped it. He sat on the bed and rested the unloaded gun on his leg, his finger away from the trigger, contemplating the whole situation for an hour or more.

The sound of a car horn outside startled Gabe back to reality from his daydream. His stomach growled, and his eyes felt weary, so he tossed the ammo tin onto the floor and dropped the gun into the other pocket of his trench coat. He then walked out the door to find some food up the street, knowing that after a meal, he'd catch a very well-earned night of sleep.

When Gabe returned home, dusk was setting. The now full-bellied man tossed back the blankets on his bed, finding the cool pillows perfectly inviting as he lay his head down.

Wonder what Lindy does for fun? I've got to see her in the morning... Oh, hell. Harry. Breakfast with Harry. That's right...

He promptly fell asleep with a smile on his face.

Lazy Sunday

Sunday, October 20th

RINGGG

The alarm clock performed its duty, and Gabe reached over to palm it to the floor. Thinking better of it, he curled his mitt around the little clock and wound it up a bit. He tucked it behind his pillow and prayed it would wake him again.

ringgg

The muffled bell sounded again. His eyes opened, one at a time. About an hour had passed, and Gabe felt a little less like a boot heel than he had thought at the first chime. He placed the clock gently back on the nightstand with a pat on its little bell. He genuinely felt a bit guilty for swatting it to the floor not once but twice the prior week. As he sat up and half-blindly felt his slippers, he saw his reflection in the corner mirror. Hell, I might as well stay scruffy and see if she likes it! I'll need to shave tomorrow for work, anyway...

He cleaned up and made small talk in the washroom with a neighbor, another man whose name escaped him, but his face he could pick out in a crowd. They discussed the weather and the chill moving into the city. The kind fellow warned him wisely about the seasons after hearing Gabe hadn't spent a winter in New York before.

"It's gonna get colder, buddy; just wait! It's only October. This is nothing. November will be here soon and probably bring snow. It's rough here in the winter, so buy a good coat and stay in!"

Gabe thanked him for the advice and made a mental note to buy some heavier shirts.

Now scrubbed up but the scruff still showing on his face, Gabe made the familiar walk to the diner.

When he arrived, he saw Lindy just then setting a fresh table near the door, facing away. He extended a hand to her shoulder, and she spun around in surprise, spilling some coffee out of the glass pot she'd been holding. Avoiding the tide of hot black brew, he lurched back and nearly doubled over off-balance. Luckily, he caught himself on a booth seat corner, and she caught her balance by grasping his arm.

"Hello, beautiful!" Gabe offered with a smile.

The embarrassment on her face washed away as she stood up and straightened her apron, giving Gabe a smile that started in her eyes. The sunlight coming through the large glass window shone across her face like a stage lamp. It seemed like an eternity she held onto his arm until she slowly released her grasp and stepped back, leaning one hip on the booth nonchalantly. She set the coffee pot down and poked him in the chest.

"How was your Saturday, you big lug?"

The big lug shrugged and slid into the booth as he blotted up a puddle of someone else's spilled coffee with a napkin.

"Didn't do much, to be honest. I ran an errand and spent some time catching up with an old friend on the phone. Rest, mostly."

"As long as you had fun. All I did was pick up Karen's shift; I have hardly had a day off in two weeks, Gab! I could have used a day like yours."

"Well, perhaps we should spend a Saturday relaxing together..." he blurted out.

Gabe had never planned on being so forward. He'd wanted to set the scene a bit or do something more romantic, but now he felt as though he was being too casual about it.

She tapped her fingers on the table for a moment, rolling her tongue in her mouth and looking out the window. Just before Gabe could offer an apologetic withdrawal, she turned her gaze toward his and shot him down.

"No, I don't think so, Gabriel..."

His heart absolutely sank to his stomach.

"I'd rather you show me where you like to go on Sundays. I'm free at three." She offered with a wry smile.

In all his life, Gabriel Marshall had never felt so thoroughly duped yet so elated. In his reddening cheeks, Lindy saw exactly what she wanted: a man who was simply happy to have her attention. Not her affection, her love, her looks... just her attention.

"You know, Lindy, I think I just maybe can make that work! I'll see you at three!" He said cheerfully as he slid out of the booth.

As he got up, she pouted at him with a protruding bottom lip.

"You're not going to stay for breakfast, then?"

He turned to her and smiled, replying, "No, miss, I've got preparations to make! Say, if a slight man with bright blue eyes comes through here lookin' for me? Tell him I owe him a meal."

She cocked her head to the side and smirked, "Oh, so I'm not the *only* person who gets stood up by Gabriel Marshal?"

He let out a deep sigh and shrugged, "I've almost got my feet under me, Lindy. Don't give up on me?"

She poked him in the chest and said, "Get outta here, Gab, I'll feed your friend and forgive you just this one last time."

Gabe took her hand and kissed her knuckles before departing with a spring in his step. Lindy stood there speechless, watching Gabe leave.

Art had been observing from the kitchen, and other than a wide grin, he kept his thoughts to himself.

Vino

Three O'Clock rolled around, and Gabe was due any moment. Lindy sat on the corner stool, having changed her clothes for the occasion. Wringing her hands, she was impatient and a bit worried Gabe might not show up yet again. She sat there for what probably felt like an eternity but really was perhaps about three minutes.

Her gaze had turned to the floor. As she sat there counting the tiles under her feet, Lindy heard the beeping of a sedan horn outside. She lifted her head, and outside at the curb was a black DeSoto sedan gleaming in the sunlight.

Gabe stood one foot up on the running board, holding the rear door open wide. Dressed more casually in a button-up shirt and slacks, he motioned for her to 'come here.' Lindy leaped off the stool and out the door, not stopping to say goodbye to Art, who took no offense. As she bounded out and reached the sedan, Gabe took her hand and squeezed it ever-so-gently.

"Lindy, doll, you look absolutely stunning."

She rolled her eyes sarcastically, "You big liar! I smell like coffee, and I've got mashed potato in my hair. I can smell it!"

He tried and failed to stifle a belly laugh, retorting, "Sure, but I really like coffee," as he helped her into the seat. Lindy cozied up to Gabe while the cab headed up the road.

As the DeSoto weaved through traffic toward downtown, they chatted about the neighborhood. Lindy pointed out a few interesting shops and buildings along the way, places she intended to visit someday. Gabe commented on how the older portions of New York had so much history in their architecture and so many little surprises.

While the sleek sedan made its way, Lindy was running

her hand in the cool air outside through an open window. The fluttering breeze sent the edges of her dress tossing about. Gabe tried his best not to notice her legs, nearly ghost-white pallor in stockings that rose well above her knee. She was a classic kind of dame, and he didn't want to seem like a cad and ruin the moment with a hanging jaw. His gaze stayed on her soft cheeks, the smile she had.

"Nice day for a drive, Gabe. I hardly go anywhere, but when I do, I always walk or take the train. This is nice."

He took her hand as they watched the city rush by from the warm comfort of the DeSoto's spacious rear seat. A few more blocks passed, and they were almost to their destination. Lindy hadn't asked where they were headed, and Gabe figured she deserved a pleasant surprise, so he hadn't offered so much as a hint.

The cab rolled to a stop on a side street in a nicer neighborhood outside the Bowery. Gabe had paid in advance, so the driver simply tipped his cap and nodded, waiting quietly as they exited. Gabe opened his door wide onto the clean curbs of this ritzy stretch of town. He stepped out, standing tall over the car, offering a hand to Lindy for a polite egress. She was slightly taller than usual, wearing heels as he had never seen her do; she stood a couple of inches closer to Gabe's face, but more than that, he noticed how those heels shaped her legs so perfectly.

A pang of guilt struck again as he thought he might be ogling, and he brought his gaze back up to meet hers. In the waning daylight, Lindy was a sight. She belonged in a frame from a movie or a still photo from a magazine advertisement. The notion struck Gabriel that she was more demure and radiant than any starlet that had ever been on-screen. He was so *very* smitten.

Waving away the cab, Gabe placed his arm gently around her shoulder and nodded toward the opposite side of the street. She turned and saw the most breathtakingly ornate theater. Its peaked roofline rose like a gold-leafed cathedral over the city block. The colors of the marquee shone onto the street brightly, with chasing lights blinking around the edges as the red neon lettering lit up sequentially. It reminded Gabe of theaters he had seen in some charming places around Europe, and he recognized he'd made a good choice of venues. They stood there for a few moments, admiring the sign. Finally, he broke the silence with a whisper in her ear.

"If I'm not careful, they'll ask you to sign autographs!"

She blushed both at the sweet words and at the warmth of

his breath on her cheek. They stepped briskly across the quiet street into the shadow of the building, the sun setting behind the concrete and glass.

She turned to him and remarked, "Well, you big lug, it's nearly four o'clock, and you probably haven't eaten!"

He smirked and touched his thumb to her chin. He moved her head and gaze gently just to the left of the theater, and her eyes met with the most charming little Italian restaurant. A young man in a white apron over a starched shirt was outside, watering vivid purple flowers that were hanging in baskets from the cast-iron awning corners. The awning itself was made up of red and white stripes.

"It's just like the cafes in Italy!' she exclaimed, 'I've never been, but you can hardly find a LIFE magazine without some ad for a getaway taking up the beauty of Italy…"

Gabe nodded, and they walked toward the entry hand-in-hand as he remarked, "I'd rather be here than Italy."

The host met them with a polite smile, holding the stiff cardstock menus with both hands and offering a little bow as they walked in. He raised one hand, palm open, toward a little table just inside the door. She looked up at Gabe, and he knew instantly what she desired.

"No sir, we'd prefer the patio, if we may."

The host nodded, "Yes, sir, of course! Lovely day in the sun for a lovely couple!" and winked at Gabe.

The pair chuckled, neither protesting the statement. They took their seats, scooted in after the host had helped them into each, and then unfurled lovely, stark-white linen napkins onto their laps. Gabe was thankful that his mother had given him so many lessons on etiquette. She was a stern woman, but only because she cared, and he knew that.

Sitting under the nearby heaters, Gabe couldn't help but notice how close in hue those linen napkins were to Lindy's legs—at least what wasn't covered by her stockings. He silently counted his blessings for that breeze back in the DeSoto.

Lindy sat across from Gabriel, holding her menu up but staring intently at him. He couldn't help but smile at the idea that he was more interesting to her than fine dining. He decided to offer, as a gentleman should, to order them the best of the menu.

"I don't know if anything has caught your eye just yet, but I know a few of these dishes that look particularly special."

Lindy took the cue and set her menu down gently.

"Gabriel, I know you have good taste. I trust whatever you choose will be delicious!"

Her enthusiasm was refreshing.

"Well, I promise you won't hate it. But if you do, more for me!" He said with a wink.

She giggled and placed her hand on his, turning his palm upward on the table as she looked over his calloused and weatherbeaten hand.

"I would never have imagined such a hard-working man might take an interest in fine dining. Look at your mitts! You sure must earn your keep. What other surprises have you got in store for me tonight, mister?"

He clasped his fingers around hers without breaking eye contact.

"Well, if I told you they wouldn't be surprises! Wine?"

"Red!" Lindy offered with a nod.

"Aperitif?"

"Whatever sounds good to you, Gabriel, I'm famished. I had a mind to eat before I left work, but that wouldn't have been fair to you now, would it?"

"Only if you'd brought me *half*!" he joked, beckoning their server to their table.

The waiter came toting a decanter of house red, and Gabriel motioned for him to fill their glasses. Then, he proceeded to order an appetizer, dinner, and dessert. Much to Lindy's surprise, he ordered their meal in what sounded to Lindy like rather fluent Italian.

"Surprises. I knew it! Did you have to practice that?"

"Sure, a few years ago back in Venice. Pretty place, but I'd rather be right here... better view."

A grin spread across her face as she shyly turned her eyes toward the street as she answered.

"Say, I might have to take you with me if I ever travel the world, Gabriel."

"I'd enjoy that, depending on where you go." His grip gently tightened on her hand, and her smile grew ever-slightly more.

Feeling his warm hand and missing his smile already, she turned back to face him and leaned forward with her elbows on the tables. Resting her cheeks in her palms, she changed the subject.

"I'm not much for small talk, not when I'm hungry. So, I

want to know… if you're game… just exactly why it took you so long to ask me out."

Gabe nearly spat out the sip of wine he'd just taken. Politely dabbing the corners of his mouth, he settled back into his chair and took a deep breath, followed by an exasperated sigh.

"Little lady, it took me a lot of courage to get you here, and you're going to bust my chops about it?" he teased.

She sat back, scowling comically and mimicking his tough demeanor. She crossed her arms for dramatic effect. Through a smile, she poked at him even further.

"No, you know I don't mean it like *that*. I'm honestly just curious. I'm a smart girl, Gabriel. You can keep your reasons to yourself, sure, but… suppose I'm only asking as a way to say how glad I am that it finally happened."

He crossed his arms to mimic her and tilted his head to one side quizzically. They looked at odds, but both were simply having fun. Winking at her again, he shot back.

"Say, how about you? After all, these days, women have just as much say in things like that. I'm a staunch supporter of women's rights! How come you took so long to ask me?"

She laughed out loud, her head thrown slightly back. Gabe watched her hair waterfall down her shoulders a bit.

"Well, I suppose that's fair. You should know that Art told me *months* ago that I could ask for any shift off if I made some plans. I'm certain he was talking about *you*."

"So the old man knows, huh? I suppose I have a terrible poker face. Say, maybe you could give me lessons."

She shrugged and leaned forward once again, reaching out for his hand. He obliged with a gentle touch, and she squeezed his fingers tightly.

"The *last* thing I need to do with my time is to try and change a man. So far, I like you just the way you are. I can see right through you; it makes things easy!"

He nodded and took another sip of wine; she followed suit. They held hands for quite some time before the food was brought out.

"I can tell you come from good stock, Gabriel. Why don't you tell me a little about them? I don't think I've ever heard you mention your family, except for your uncle Robert. Where did you grow up?"

He held back a grimace, never being the sort to talk about such things without prompting.

"Robert was the last family I had, to be honest. My father, Gilbert, passed while I was deployed, but he was a great man and a good role model. He was a simple man, too. I don't know if I'm so simple, but I'd like to think he set the right example. It's funny; he was a serviceman just like me, though he never saw any combat. I think when he encouraged me to sign up, he didn't really know what that would mean for me. Still, he was the most honest man I've known, and that was likely what kept me on the right track. Midwestern boys have a good reputation for good reason, so I'm told."

She squeezed his hand again and softened her tone.

"...And your mother?"

He looked away for a moment, wistfully. It was brief, but Lindy could see that it was something Gabriel struggled with.

"My mother was a rare sort. Kind as can be, never doting. Stern at times, sure, but I was a handful. She took care of the homestead while Pop worked long hours. She held us together, kept the home happy every moment."

Lindy interjected, "She sounds like a wonderful woman; I'd have liked to know her."

"Yeah, she was. Passed away when I was younger, still in school. It was a... it was a bad accident. We had a fire. Small town, they never really recovered.' He paused for a sip of wine; Lindy just sat and listened. '...Pops never really recovered."

He could see from her expression that he needed to lighten the mood a bit, so he changed the subject swiftly.

"I know you grew up around here. How about you, your parents are still locals? Do they approve of you gallivanting around with some cad like me?"

She smiled again, which let him know he was on the right track. The soft music emanating from a record player in the restaurant carried on with Italian crooning, and the sunset reddened the sky as they spoke.

"My family? Oh, we're rather boring, I'm afraid. My father is Swedish; his family came here when he was just knee-high. The rest of them moved back to Sweden after the depression. I don't know anyone but my mother's side, most of them live up in the Northside of town. She's Irish-Italian, sort of an unusual pairing, I'm told. She's all fire and fury, father has a cool head. It's funny; whenever they bicker, it's really just her goading him on. In fact, Art has known my father for decades. He says I'm just like my father... I suppose that's a good thing?"

"Irish-Italian, you say? I would bet that's where those lovely bright eyes of yours come from."

"Oh, come on, you can't just turn everything into a compliment! Sure, people tell me I look just like my mother except for my blonde locks. I suppose I'm lucky. Papa is a great man, but he's not much to look at!"

She giggled, and Gabriel followed suit.

"Well, if they're around, perhaps sometime I'll be lucky enough to meet them..."

"Oh, don't you worry; I don't think we could get away with more than a few dinners before they either insisted on meeting you or my father had a bounty put on your head!"

"Oh! Protective sort, huh?" He asked with a raised eyebrow.

"Maybe a bit. Actually, quite a bit. It's tough being an only child, great expectations to live up to."

"I know the feeling. Well, I'm sure you're everything they hoped for and more, sweet girl."

Just then, their server appeared with several plates of aperitifs, resting them gently on the table.

Three bowls of piping hot pasta, each in a smallish dish and each with a different sauce. One bowl was piled with long, thin noodles and a thin red sauce that smelled of red wine and mushrooms. The next was a similar, thicker pasta with butter and fresh, dry cheese sprinkled on top. Lastly, a small dish of short noodles rested in a creamy white sauce that looked to be garlic and little else. The steam rising from the table smelled heavenly, and Lindy tapped a fork on the closest dish.

"You're going to fatten me up, Gab!" She teased.

"I'm sure it's okay to treat yourself once in a while, Lindy. I've got things to celebrate!"

Dying to eat, their conversation turned to food. As they ate and sipped their wine, the two of them discussed the best and worst foods they had eaten. Gabe had to lie a bit so as not to spoil her meal. He'd been in some strange places and eaten some even stranger things. He told her about the canned food in the trenches, which wasn't all that bad. "Sticks with you until it doesn't." Lindy described a ghastly Swedish dish her father adored, made of spoiled pickled fish. Gabe mockingly gagged, and she swatted him with her napkin for his antics.

"Be careful, big guy, or I'll have Art put that mess on the menu!"

Gabriel could feel that the night was unfolding to be a success. They laughed, they teased; this little lady kept up with him and truly cared to know him better. That was a refreshing change for a man who had spent the last six months in the city alone and most of the six months before that in military hospitals, no good place to socialize.

Lindy was clearly having a great time, and he did his best to keep the conversation light. Finally, they reached the last course, a delightful dessert.

The server brought two espressos while Gabe stacked their dishes to lighten the busboy's load. They each downed the thimble of stiff coffee in a sip and sat back just as their waiter brought out one final dish, a frozen dessert.

"Oh, I love ice cream! Perfect choice, Gabriel." Lindy commented.

"They call it gelato; it's a real treat! Over there, they don't serve ice cream. This is a bit lighter; I think you'll like it! I heard it's popular in both France and Italy..."

He handed her a spoon and insisted she take the first bite.

Just as he did, she picked up another spoon, scooped a sizable bite, and stuffed it into Gabe's mouth.

"You first!" She exclaimed.

Lindy then let him feed her a bite. As the smooth sweetness saturated her palate, her eyes widened, and she jokingly snatched the dish to her side of the table.

"This is amazing, Gabe! Are you going to order one for yourself?" she said, still chewing a bite.

Gabe pouted and shrugged in defeat until she fed him another spoonful. This went on back and forth until the dish was gone, at which point Gabriel glanced at his pocket watch and realized the time.

"Lindy, we had better not order another, or we might not make the show!"

She nodded, sipping the last of her red wine. Gabriel took care of the bill, gently placed her soft sweater over her shoulders, and took her hand as he led her just up the block to the movie theater. She had taken note that Gabriel left a very generous gratuity for the bill, something he was known for at the diner as well.

Her quick strides kept up with his long steps for the short walk to the theater doors. Gabriel stepped to the will-call window, where he picked up the tickets he had reserved earlier in the day. The school-age attendant tipped her pill-box hat toward Lindy, who was marveling at the marquee's chasing lights shining through wisps of evening fog.

Gabe, clutching her shoulders from behind, whispered in her ear, "Well, beautiful, I'm going to take you into this movie now, O-Kay? But you've got to promise me one thing."

"Oh, sure, Gab, anything!"

He motioned toward the brightly lit poster box near the door, which fancifully displayed a lovely color promotional for a popular Clark Gable film. He took her hand and wiggled his fingers between hers before answering.

"Well, you've got to promise me you won't go falling for that lead man. He's a measure more handsome than me, y'see. Can I trust you?"

In his warm smile and feeling his gentle hold on her, Lindy knew no other man was taking her sights off Gabriel Marshall, but she wasn't going to give him that ego boost just yet.

"I'm not going to make any promises, you big goof! You'd better catch me if I faint!"

She poked him in the shoulder. Her best attempt at a serious face was laughable. He knew she was just ribbing him, so he clasped her hand firmer and gently led her into the plush theater lobby to grab popcorn before finding their seats.

The chairs were crushed red velvet with ornate brass armrests. Lindy lifted the armrest between them and found her place nestled against Gabe's broad chest. They held hands and watched their movie in content near-silence, only the crunch of popcorn and the shuffle of feet coming and going in the dark.

Shortly after the movie ended with its predictable heroic line and passionate kiss, as did many of this particular mustachioed star's films, the couple found their way outside to a familiar sight: the sleek black DeSoto. The same driver awaited his fare with the rear door open, tipping his cap as the pair stepped into the cab.

The drive back to their neighborhood was as smooth as a

flight on a new jet plane. Cozied up in the back of the cab, they laughed and joked about silly things. Lindy turned the conversation back to Gabe's family as she mentioned hers.

"I'm going to insist mother and father see that film; I'm certain they'll love it. Say, you mentioned your uncle to me a long time ago, but I think we got sidetracked earlier, and you never finished telling me about him. Is he...?"

Gabe hesitated for a beat but decided against sugarcoating things. His guard was down; he had consumed too much red wine and comfort this night.

"Robert was all the family I had left, but I lost him not long after I moved here. Not long after I met you. He was up at the invalid hospital on the north side. He was a bit frail even before his kidneys failed, and it seems there was nothing they could do."

Lindy immediately regretted asking; Gabe could read her expression. She put her hand on his arm.

"I worked there for a while. You know, or perhaps I never mentioned? I was a nurse some years back. That place was filled with sadness and decay. I only worked in the central ward, but they've got a panopticon where they keep the folks they think are high-risk. Quite a few shell-shocked men just wasting away down there... drugged out of their heads and staring out the windows. I worked there for a few months, but I simply had to leave.

"That bad, huh?" He remarked.

"No, it was all right, I suppose, but... I just couldn't stomach all that sadness and ache. So, I went back to the job at Art's place, and I had worked for him during summers while I was a schoolgirl. It's not much compared to medicine, but I never walk home with a heavy heart. I'm sorry for your loss, Gabriel. You've had so much of it."

With a soft smile, he placed his hand on her knee and turned back to sugarcoat things.

"Everybody has a past, sweet girl. There are far less fortunate people than myself; I'm just thankful for the times I've had. In fact, I'm quite thankful for the time I've had just tonight. That dinner sure was something!"

Lindy took the hint and placed her hand over his, still warm on her knee.

"Oh, isn't that true? I've had Italian before, but never like that. You sure know how to eat!"

He patted his stomach, which made her giggle. They sat back into the seat, cozied up together, and made a pact to try some other new types of food. There were so many strange and wonderful offerings all over New York City. She also insisted that next time, she would be allowed to pay.

"Lindy, I've never heard of such a thing! I'd be no gentleman at all if I were to pass a check across the table!"

He was genuinely surprised.

"Well, it sure would mean a lot to me. And besides, I pay for my food when I eat alone! What's the difference? Don't be so stodgy, Gabriel!"

At that moment, the cab softly rumbled to a stop in front of her building. Gabe helped Lindy out of the back of the cab, and they stood on the stoop of her building. Realizing he was only a medium walk from home, Gabe sent the car and its politely quiet driver on their way.

The evening had gotten slightly cold, and now she stood on the first step of her building. Gabe stepped to her, placing his hands on her waist. She was closer to meeting his gaze but still lacking a few inches. He could feel her trembling slightly in the night air.

"Gabriel, I had simply the bes—"

Gabe cut her sentence off with a kiss that silenced her entire world for a few moments. She closed her eyes and draped her arms limply around his neck and his broad shoulders. They lingered, embracing like this for a profound moment, then gently broke away with her softly exhaling and opening her eyes. Their breath was a fog in the cool night air, swirling away in the breeze. He held her close as though he feared that the faintest wind might carry her away. She nuzzled her chin into the nook of his collar.

After a minute of somber embrace, Gabriel gently removed one of her arms from his shoulder, took her hand by the fingertips, and kissed the top of her hand softly.

"Again, soon."

Standing on her toes and leaning in close, she whispered back.

"*Very* soon." She replied in a velvety tone.

She drew away and sauntered through the door into her building. In the reflection of her building's doors, he could see her steal a last glance at him.

What a woman...

Subterfuge

Monday, October 21st

Monday morning came, and Gabriel quickly arose to a fresh breeze waltzing through his window, which was slightly ajar. He didn't mind the cool air at night, and he rather enjoyed the way it cleared out much of the dust and that musty, dirty boots smell in the room. He showered, shaved, dressed quickly, and departed for work. He chose to cut through the markets a few blocks up and stock his lunchbox, at the same time pausing at a dime cafe and filling the red plaid-printed coffee thermos he'd bought at Grand Central Station the day he'd arrived in New York City. The girl behind the counter looked a bit like Miss Alice, though certainly not on a slab. He tried not to think about it.

Some fruit today, yeah, that'll be nice.

After picking out a few pieces of fresh fruit, he considered his paunch while perusing the streetside merchants' tables for hard bread and some soft cheese. An old habit he picked up in his tours around France, Gabe tended to eat simple most of the time, dried nuts and cured meats and anything that would keep for a day or three. He would avoid heavier foods and anything too sweet. A few minutes later and a good handful of coins lighter, Gabe made his way toward his ferry with a heavy tin lunchbox and the thought of Alice still ringing in his head. The sun warmed away the morning harbor mist on the streets as he walked; it would be a beautiful day.

He spent the ferry trip and the entire walk mulling over the quandary that lay before him—Mullally wanted him to keep quiet about the little girl, sure. He could do that. There were plenty of folks who might not mind a bit of Wild West action if the possible identity of this killer got out, but it could also cause some collateral damage, and Gabe wasn't willing to be the cause of any lives lost. He'd seen plenty of that in the aggressive bombing campaigns he and many of his brothers-in-arms had survived.

What bugged Gabe most of all was what Mullally had said about the victims being a bad sort. The sergeant's tone had implied perhaps they deserved it. Who would know well enough about these different folks for that to have been a motivation? No, that didn't sit right with Gabe, and he wanted to dig *deeper*.

Shortly after two o'clock, Gabe was knee-deep in a pile of lumber intended for re-decking a flatcar. He heard clanging from behind and turned to find Harry lazily swinging a wrench and striking the rung of the ladder at the car's end. Gabe immediately remembered he had stood Harry up at the diner on Sunday.

"Oh jeez, pal. I am so sorry!" Gabe pleaded, dropping the lumber he was holding.

"Sorry for *what*? I had a great meal!" Harry said with a broad smile on his face.

"I'm a horse's ass! I told you to meet me, then I asked Lindy out, and she said yes, and then I checked my watch, and I had to —"

Harry stepped over some beams and patted Gabe on the shoulder.

"Stop, stop! I missed you by two minutes! I was late anyway. Got held up at the tailors. But yeah, Lindy served me. I didn't bother her, just cleaned my plate and hit the pavement. She sure looks swell! "

"You're tellin' me, Harry, you're tellin' me..."

"Well, it's no big deal, Gabe, but now you owe me a pint and some conversation, yeah?"

Gabe acquiesced. "Sure, hell, I need to use the men's... I got a good one for you right now!" and he walked with Harry back to the offices, all the while telling a tale of the kindest little French girl he'd met in a hotel a few years back. She was a flutist, and Gabe made sure Harry's imagination ran wild with that. In reality, she was just a friendly girl who served the boys a pitcher of lemonade on a hot day. But Harry wanted *stories*. Gabe delivered.

"She had lace in places I didn't know existed; they don't teach you that stuff in Montana, y'know..." Gabe motioned with his hands, cutting the imaginary shape of the girl into the air.

By the end of the salacious story, Harry was jokingly pleading with him to stop.

"C'mon pal, you're *killing* me! You'll have me falling in love with a gal I never met! Maybe France would be a nice place to retire..."

Gabe shrugged, melancholy memories of wartorn cities now in his head. "Well, they'll need a few years to clean up after the war, but... good people, great scenery. Most of their food is for the dogs, but what do I know?"

Harry laughed all the way down the hall as Gabe ducked into the restroom to splash some cool water on his face and lighten his load.

A few hours more work passed, and Gabe was working slowly, knowing he'd be up late. He finished decking the flatcar after a while, then found himself tinkering with some broken lanterns on a caboose until the shift-end whistle tooted across the yard.

Making haste in his commute, Gabe arrived home and changed out of his filthy coveralls. He dropped his dirty work garments on the fire escape just outside his window so as not to stink up the room before he could launder his clothes properly. He put on some slacks and a decent shirt, almost bounding for the door in excitement. His trench coat would suffice against the evening chill. On his way out, he saw his pocket watch, Robert's pocket watch, laying on the dresser. It glinted with the light from his corner lamp. Gabe felt a pang of sadness, wishing his Pop and Uncle Robby could see him now, out there doing some good again.

He left the watch behind.

<center>~~~</center>

"I told you, I don't want anything to do with it!"

Yet another door slammed in his face.

Dammit. Third time lucky, I hope...

Gabe slowly paced down the hallway to another door, knocking gently. He could hear some movement inside but it took ages for the person to unlatch the bolt of the door. It opened with a rusty and grinding creak.

"Hello there, do I know you?"

The little octogenarian lady at the door was hunched over, leaning on a cheap wooden cane that creaked against the floor. The rubber cap on the end had worn through, and the floor was scuffed to hell under her feet.

Oh, hell. Don't get another door shut in your face, Gabe.

"Ma'am, I'm... I am here on behalf of the neighborhood benevolent coalition."

She lifted her head a bit, hunched over as she was in her old age.

"We have a coalition?" She asked incredulously.

"Yes, ma'am. Gabe Marshall, pleased to meet you!"

She extended her hand to meet his and clasped his hand.

"Madge Baker, young man. It's quite late. Are you here on official business?" Her raspy voice was pointed but not stern.

"Oh, in a way. I was...' he paused for a moment before he had the most brilliant idea and continued, 'I was tasked to ensure the seasoned folks in our neighborhood had the mobility aids they require. It's a city initiative, don't you know."

She raised one eyebrow as though she were about to swat him with a wooden spoon. "Mobility aids?"

Gabe smiled and gestured toward her cane. "Yes, ma'am. And I can see that yours is in dire need of repair!"

She stepped back and grasped the doorframe, holding her weight as she handed Gabriel her cane. "You can fix this?"

For a moment, Gabe felt a pang of guilt about how deceitful he was acting. Still, moreso, he was struck by relief that he'd finally found someone in this building to speak to, as this tenement overlooked the alley where Alice's life was taken so recently. He had to forge ahead; this was the only address he remembered from Mullally's files.

"Yes, ma'am. Certainly. Simple repair, don't you know? We can furnish you with a replacement rubber foot and a fresh wrap on the grip, and it'll be as good as new!"

He handed the cane back to Madge, and her tense demeanor immediately relaxed.

"Oh, won't you come in? I won't look a gift horse in the mouth, young man. Surprised as I am."

A few minutes later, Gabe was sitting on the sofa with Madge Baker, measuring her cane for a replacement rubber foot. She looked enthralled at the process but was likely simply excited at the prospect of some free help. This was a poor building in a poor neighborhood.

"Now, Madge, may I call you Madge?" She nodded that he may. "It's a simple repair, and we'll have a replacement in your mailbox within a day or two; you just pull off the old cap and pop the new one on. Simple as can be!"

She patted his arm, beaming with cheer. "You're quite a nice young man. You spend your time helping others?"

Gabe leaned back a bit into the rickety old sofa.

"I try, ma'am. I do what I can with the faculties I was given. Say, speaking of help... I heard one of your neighbors is a teacher. I know they aren't paid much... perhaps the coalition can assist in some way?"

Madge shifted excitedly in her seat. Her eyes flashed brightly, and for a moment, she bounced in her seat like a child.

"Oh, that would be Mister Crawford on the third floor. Apartment three-bee, like a little bumblebee. That is how I remember! He is a kind soul. We have tea... oh my, every Tuesday evening! That's tomorrow!" She clasped her hands excitedly, thinking of her plans.

Gabe took her hand and squeezed it gently.

"Shall I check on mister Crawford, then?"

"Oh my, yes. Please do, young man!" After walking him to the door and giving him a kindly peck on the cheek, Madge sent Gabe on his way.

In no time, Gabe was knocking on a door that had no numbers nailed to it as the other units had. The silhouette of where the '3' and 'B' once hung was stained into the tired paint by cigarette smoke and edges of varnish.

A voice came from within the unit. "Help you, stranger?"

Gabe saw the light shifting through the little brass peephole.

"No, sir. Unless you have a free moment, perhaps I can offer you help... Madge sent me down. Gabe Marshall."

There was a pregnant pause and a muffled cough. Then, the rattling of a door chain being unlocked. The door opened wide, with a rail-thin man in a sweater vest standing there staring holes through Gabe.

"How do you know Madge? You don't live here, I would *know*." He pointed at Gabe, with a lit brown cigarette hanging limply between his pointing fingers.

"I'm just a local volunteer with the neighborhood coalition. Madge said I should check and see if there's any assistance we can provide you."

The man stood there for a time, looking Gabe up and down and sizing him up. Gabe noticed Crawford' weight shift on his heels and his hand gripping the doorknob tightly. He looked like a mongoose coiling back in defense. Gabe knew he'd been made.

"Bullshit. If this rotten neighborhood had a coalition, I'd know about it. I've been here two decades, and the only thing these city blocks have in unity is a rat infestation. What are you doing bothering Madge with your stories? Are you some kind of... *confidence* man?"

Gabe had one chance to redeem himself. He stepped back a half-step, relaxed his posture, and let out a long sigh.

"You've got me. There's no coalition, but there *should* be. I wanted to speak to you, but I didn't know your name. I hope to ask a few questions, but it's for the good of the place. For the good of you, Madge, *everyone*. I'll show you my identification; I'm a good sort, no trouble. You'll see."

Crawford took a drag of his cigarette, pondering Gabe as he exhaled into the hallway.

"Well, you're a big guy, and I'm in no position to fight you off, so I might as well have you in for tea. C'mon."

The slender man's posture relaxed as he shuffled back into the apartment, leaving the door wide open for Gabe. Gabe followed him to the kitchen and sat down across the table, where there was an ashtray filled with stale cigarette butts piled the size of a man's fist.

"Mister Crawford, I'm not with the police."

Crawford chuckled and tamped out his smoke just to light another.

"I could tell. They can't go five seconds without flashing a shiny badge. I had a shiny badge once and acquired it from a box of cereal and some stamps. What a *joke*."

Gabe motioned to the pack of cigarettes, and Crawford handed him a cigarette and a lit match with a swiftness that was downright artful. Gabe took a light drag, wincing at the burn in his throat.

"Sounds like you're not too pleased with the way they're handling things around here lately. I'm not with any coalition, but I do live here. Just a few blocks down, in the... you know, the old brothel."

"That place is a mess. I had a... I had a friend who lived

there for a while. Creaky beds, creaky neighbors, just the *worst*. Sorry that you're so hard up."

"Mister Crawford, I wanted to—"

Gabe was cut off.

"Keith. That's fine. Gabe?"

"Yeah, that part is true."

Okay, Gabe, you have until I finish this cigarette to ask what you want. I'm tired, and I'm not making you tea."

He smiled wryly, and Gabe patted the table as he took a drag of his own cigarette.

"Brass tacks it is. I came back from the war with a little fight left in me. Somebody's sneaking around these parts at night making slaughter of our neighbors, of decent folk, and I'm not going to sit around and let it happen if I can do something about it."

"Oh, you're a hero, eh? I have known my fair share of heroes. None of *them* were police, either. What could I possibly have to offer the new sheriff in town?" He tapped his ashes onto the table.

"Seems to me you were likely the witness who overheard that murder in the back alley not too long ago."

"It was late. I don't sleep well. Sometimes, I nap at work, between classes... but here, I barely sleep. It was late, and I was tired. I heard a bit, sure."

Gabe watched as Keith tamped out his smoke and lit another but made no mention of the conversation stopping there.

"You heard German?"

"Yeah, German. Rang out like a shot, which is ironic because he didn't kill that poor child with a gun." Keith chortled, and smoke puffed from one of his nostrils.

"What did he say?"

"Something akin to 'my blood, I will take blood and bones'... hard to tell for sure because he was more growling it than speaking it. Full of rage. He sounded like...' Keith paused, gazing out the alley-side window, 'like a Viking going into battle. A war cry."

"Doesn't sound like this guy is a sane sort. Not after what..." Gabe trailed off.

Keith rested his head in his palm, elbow on the table. He was bedraggled, his eyes sallow and surrendering.

"After what he did to the girl. I *saw* the body. They made me look at it."

Gabe felt awful for dragging this waif of a man through

those dark memories. He looked *so* frail to Gabe.

"I can go if—" but Gabe was cut off again.

"Shall I put on tea?"

Gabe nodded, smiled, and lit another cigarette from the box Keith had left open.

Making Sense

Gabe murmured to himself as he arrived under those white globes.

"The precinct seems quiet... hell, it's a Monday night. All those troublemakers might get juiced later, but quiet is good... Hope Mullally's around."

As he entered past those heavy blue NYPD-lettered doors, Gabriel got a wave-in from the usual desk officer, Harris, to head back into the precinct toward Mullally's desk as though Gabe belonged there. That made the very civilian Gabriel feel a bit like he had in his days wearing a uniform.

Arriving at the desk, just as Mullally returned to the pit with a cup of joe, Gabe quipped, "Hey, chief, did you save some for me?"

Almost without pause, Mullally raised a hand from his other side, which had been facing away from Gabe, and held out another piping-hot cup of black coffee as they sat down.

"Saw you come in. Old cops, we see everything. Don't ya know, son? Any man that can down this precinct's swill deserves a cup and an ear."

With a smirk, Gabe got comfortable in the chair, and the fleeting thought crossed his mind as to whether he should take up being a policeman.

Free coffee and a good pension! He mused silently. He took a short sip of the black brew as he tucked the thought away in the back of his mind for later consideration.

Gabe wore a wry smile, which Sergeant mistook for simple pleasure with a decent cup of coffee.

"Well, Marshall, what have ya got? Anything new?"

Gabe chose his words wisely and trod lightly. He didn't want Mullally asking many questions in return. He'd had enough back-and-forth earlier in the evening with Keith Crawford, who was sharp as a scalpel even through all the rundown of his body.

"Why yes, sir, in a way. Say, before I go on, I have a question. You had implied, when last we spoke, that the folks who'd been victim to this man before the little gal... you implied they had been unsavory types. How so? I mean to say, what specifically made them so? Each of them?"

Mullally chewed on the question for a few moments.

"Well, that's the consensus, son. I might as well lay the cards out since you're likely asking a question to which you know an answer.' He paused for a sip of coffee and sighed a bit before setting it down and continuing, 'Y'see, all these ugly scenes, each one of those folks... each one of them had been a real piece of work. Here, let's take a look."

Mullally opened his desk drawer and pulled out a four-inch-thick binding of files, which he slid across the desk to Gabe.

"Okay, take a gander at the notes attached to the back of each of those files. The one that's tabbed in yellow. There you go."

Gabe thumbed through the first file, Christopher Mays. Thirty-six years old, one hundred thirty-three pounds on the table.

"Mays," Gabe murmured over the file.

"Christopher J, yes sir,' the sergeant replied, 'That kid was a compulsive gambler and two-time guest of the North Station's drunk tank after brawling. Had a mouth on him, a real unpleasant cus when he drank if you ask the locals."

Gabe flipped to the following file, offering the name Perkins.

"Martin M., that's a winner. It took two men to bring him for petty theft last year; he still had the wallet of the man he'd just rolled; the word is, he spent his free time selling stolen goods on the avenues. Bastard could box, that's for sure. Gave one of my detectives a black eye last spring! He met his match, not to say he deserved that end..."

Gabe nodded, looking at the photo of the man with a neck thicker than his head and a sneer like a mangy dog. That man looked like a true villain. Gabe thumbed further, the following file.

"Cleary." The man in the photo was gangly, his collar loose and his ears lopsided. He looked like a slow-witted farmer Gabe had known back home, but rougher... swarthy.

"Jasper Lawrence Cleary. Do you know that the son of a dog made the paper *twice* before? He sent three bullets through a police sedan. It didn't hit any vitals, but that Dodge sedan was two weeks old. Released on bail, and a month later, he was nabbed burgling a jeweler off Cooper Square. It's hard to miss that man. A bystander gave him a wallop, pinned him until the uniforms arrived. He was squealing like a pig!"

Gabe had a bit of a laugh at the image in his head.

"You could go down the list, Marshall, but it all reads the same."

"Even Alice.' Gabe offered solemnly. 'That's why I'm here, to clear the air on that."

"Yes, sir, even that little girl. Since we last spoke, my boys have done a little digging. Theft from at least three employers that we know of. Including that cathouse you stay in, it seems she was cooking the books and stealing cash right under that old sap's nose. Surprisingly, she comes from good stock. Not needy folk."

Swirling coffee in his mouth, Gabe said nothing as Mullally rambled.

"Every man was either convicted or suspected of some dirty deeds at some point... I don't mean to speak ill of the dead, but the fact is that each one of them was a bad apple. The list goes on; it's right there in the files. Black-and-white. A few murders we couldn't prove, a history of problems with women or a local clique of Irish, Italian... not good church-going folk, you know. One of them, the man, was an Army deserter, and when he came back, we collared him for robbing elderly folk. He'd follow them from the bank downtown! Broke one woman's leg... a real bad cus. Hell, I can't say we've had anyone stop in and vouch for a single one of them; not a one seems to be missed. It's the strangest damn thing because..."

Mullally's tone was hushed, and he shifted much closer in his seat, halfway nose to nose with Gabe. Gabe thought this was odd, especially for the usually more stoic Sergeant. Mullally's voice was hushed as he continued.

"See, at first, some people thought it might've been one of our own—maybe an officer, maybe a clerk... but someone who had access to records. When we started to put it all together, though, see... we had to hunt, dig deep to figure some of these out. It took a while because a lot of petty stuff doesn't make the records, but yessir... each and every one of them was some kind of devil in their own right. That's how I knew it wasn't a uniform because it took us months to figure all this out. Nobody's got that gypsy third-eye around here, pal, no way. We'd have a better arrest rate!" he joked with a somewhat sinister chuckle as he leaned back from the more secretive portion of the conversation.

Gabe went back to thumbing through files as he responded, not looking up from those pages as he spoke.

"Well, in all honesty, Sarge, that's why I came. I heard about that recently, the same account from a different perspective. Someone knew somebody, as it goes."

Mullally nodded and gazed into his own rapidly cooling coffee.

"Well, listen, now we have the conundrum, Mister Marshall."

"Yes sir, what's that?"

Mullally swilled more coffee and smacked his lips before continuing, "Well, I'm here with over a dozen case files, and I can't find a damned single thread to tie a German into any of it. Not a bit, not a peep save the one witness who really didn't *see* a thing. What do I do with that? We've exhausted contacts in every neighborhood and nobody has a thread to tie onto. And if it's true, what is a lunatic kraut doing cleaning up our streets?"

Gabriel leaned just slightly closer and said, "Well, Sarge, that's why I'm here. That's why you need me. That's something I can help with. I think you have your only credible lead with the teacher. He's got quite a brain."

"So you met Mister... Crawford, wasn't it? What did he have to say to another civilian, Gabe?"

"Enough to have me convinced that his account is worth more than a dozen paper-pushers' theories, sarge. He told me what he heard, how Alice was alive for a few minutes, how the poor child cried out like a child. The killer was *laughing*."

Mullally deflected.

"Mr. Marshall, you have some brass balls, I tell ya. You know, I did some digging on *you*."

"Oh? Well, what did you find?" Gabe was intrigued at the prospect of being investigated. He had little to hide, in his own opinion.

"Suffice it to say that your C/O Captain Briggs has some

pretty kind things to say, son. Lavished on the praise. Seems you were quite the hound out there on the front; you know your way around a bad situation. He was a Lieutenant in Chicago before he joined the service; he knows the work. I spent a solid hour on the phone with him, and he told me about his fishing trips. Briggs told me you'd be an asset and said you were one of his best. I told him a bit about the cases and told him the newspaper version of what happened to the girl. Maybe a detail or two on top. As it goes, he's interested, but he's not of the detective mindset, so to speak. But you, Marshall, he said you would be my ticket if there ever was one. And hell, I could use a break in the case, son. I haven't hardly been home in months."

Gabe nodded, affirming the dire situation, and asked, "What can I do to help?"

Mullally stooping up, he paced near his desk a bit. Gabe could see his suit was worn nearly through at the elbows, and his shoes were scuffed and sallow.

"All I need from you is an idea, Marshall. What do we look for? How do we flush out a foreigner without raising panic? We've got the NYPD's best men working on it quietly, but most of the folks in the neighborhood won't talk to a badge. I want to hear your ideas before we do anything. Due to your experience with... you *know* with what. Just think about it, okay, son?"

"Sir, I'm going to do what I can to help and not get in the way. I can't abide something like this in my backyard, not when I've got people I care about living here. I'll think on it a bit, and I'll be in touch. I have a few ears to bend first."

With the last sip of warm coffee, Gabe shook the Sergeant's hand and departed. Mullally was nose-deep in a case folder before Gabe got to the banisters.

That old dog needs a vacation. Hell, so do I... Gabe thought as he breached the heavy doors back into the evening air. *Maybe I'll get in the way just a little...*

Take A Walk

Gabe glanced at the clock mounted high on the precinct lobby wall as he departed. It was about 8:15. He was out in the night, the city sounds echoing through the streets and steam rising from the gutter grates. His mind was wide awake.

Christ, it's late already, but I'm not tired in the least... I could do a little walking around and check out a few things... That's the last time I let Mullally dose me with a cup of joe after dusk. I bet that's what he wants, tryin' to get me wound up like a clock and set me loose on the street to sniff out some clues! I'd better get moving. There are too many damned dark corners in this city...

A crisp breeze on his skin and a belly of hot coffee had Gabe feeling quite invigorated. A fog had rolled into town the past hour as though a cloud had settled down to earth. Yet it was heavy and acrid fog, carrying the scent and tinge of the harbor with it. Now, Gabe was quite thankful he'd grabbed his trench coat and a wool cap.

No need to go home; let's put some boots on the ground!

He made his way toward the south-end streets where now, at this hour, all the hustle and bustle were starting up for the evening. Gabe passed bar after bar after bar. Dark, closed storefronts littered the blocks but he paid them little mind. The lights and music coming from the bars seemed to fill most of the streets around these parts. It occurred to Gabe that *maybe all folks do in this town is drink!* He passed no judgment, no sir, he enjoyed a good pint himself... he was merely amazed at the variety (and at the same time, lack thereof) in the rough town's drinking establishments. He puckered at the foul air in his nose coming from those places as he passed; it smelled like hot sewers and sweat.

Gabe considered the contents of those police reports,

which were stained and tattered on the edges and corners by dozens of hands.

There's no formula, no precise method that had been used to take the lives of those unfortunate people. No, there's only a theme. An idea. This sonofabitch lures people into quiet, dark places. Unpopulated spaces, warehouse loading docks, and alleyways. Not much light in those corners of town... seems that in this part of town, everybody is pinching pennies and leaving light bulbs missing from their fixtures. Those photos... some of the victims had cuts and slashes, and some of them were strangled. All of them were beaten to a pulp. Why never a gun?

He passed a bar full of patrons, neon lights in the window, and three bright bulbs warming their shades over the doorway.

Streets are plenty well-lit wherever there's vice to be sold! It's when they go take a walk that they're in danger.

Eventually, Gabe came across a narrow alley, perhaps the twentieth he'd scouted this evening; this particular one seemed familiar. While walking its length, he realized this was the specific alley in which he'd slipped and cracked his noggin. He recalled those two cops, a couple of hardworking types, and how cool-headed they were in helping Gabe back to his feet that night. Standing there in that wet and cold space now, an eerie feeling swept over him. In his mind, he recalled their warning and what they said about him lying there nearly in the same spot in which some sad fool had met his maker. The thought sent a chill up his spine, and he hurried out of that damned alley with an incredible feeling of unease.

Be a man, Gabe. You're no coward. Bad things happen all over. You've stepped over plenty of stiffs.

The self-chiding brought him a bit of comfort as he hastened to continue his patrol with a scowl on his face and his hands swinging half-clenched, not stuffed into his pockets as before.

Since he'd been a child, Gabe was always amazed at how a thick fog could muffle and mute noises. Where usually he'd expect to hear the click-clack of his heels across the hard streets and walls, only a dull thud for an echo rebounded with each step. The air absorbed the sound like a pillow. As he walked along, he tapped his knuckles on various objects: mailboxes, Police callboxes, signboards, lampposts. He enjoyed the way the different metallic and wooden sounds made various soft echoes within, but almost no echo found its way out into the street.

He'd been walking for over an hour now with no real direction, just crisscrossing the short blocks and thinking. Finding himself on a rather crowded street near the docks, he wished silently that he'd brought his pocket watch but estimated it was at least ten at night. Noting the folks passing by, it seemed to him that some event or show had just released its patrons into the street. Folks smaller than him (some rather notably wider but still no match to Gabe's stature) moved politely out of his way. With each passing patron, he'd tip the brim of his shepherd-style wool cap toward them and greet them for the evening. "Ma'am, sir", "Pardon me". "Thanks, pal!"

It was all rather polite, unusual for the time of night and the location of the courtesy; he was walking across from a burlesque theater, which indeed also functioned as a brothel. It had caught his eye with all the chase lights blinking in sequence around the marquee, typical for many theaters from vaudeville to the operas in France (which he had seen whilst he was traveling, in GI green, of course).

Passing a sturdily built man, Gabe felt a sleeve brush against his own. "G'night, pal," he cheerfully offered.

"Güten Abend!" replied the stranger, who continued away down the sidewalk. It was some of the first German words Gabriel had heard since his arrival in New York, considering the times it was almost impossible to get a German to speak their tongue due to the stigma of the war. Gabe swiveled about to get a better look at the man, but all he saw was the tails of a heavy wool coat flitting around a corner.

Gabe called out again, "Hey, pal! Hold on a second!" But the man had already gone.

Gabe's heart started beating steadily faster, much as it would when he knew danger was near during his service. Not a panic, no, this was pure excitement. Gabe looked up and down this street and saw no persons about. The street was nearly vacant; no more passersby. The knot in his gut told him he had to follow!

He took to a quick place, striding in the direction the German-speaking man had gone. Only seconds had passed, but as Gabe turned the corner, the man was nowhere to be seen. Gabe's throat tightened, as it seemed almost evasive in how quickly this man disappeared. He could hear the soft thudding of comfortable shoes on cobblestone, a sound he knew well. He glanced down the street and saw a railroad access right-of-way between buildings. He hadn't noticed any railroad runs through this part of town; he now realized how he had walked out to the more industrial edge of his neighborhood.

His gait took him swiftly over to the railroad right-of-way, a narrow path between buildings for trains to move and often to deliver freight. The paths were frequently too narrow for anything more than the trains themselves, and the paper would usually run stories about drunks and hobos being struck and killed by freight cars or locomotives moving around blind curves in those areas. Knowing this but not really caring, Gabriel walked right past the brightly painted cast-iron NO ENTRY and DANGER KEEP OUT signs clearly posted right into the alleyway as he walked along the tracks inlaid throughout the very rough cobblestone. He could hear his breath, but his footsteps made almost no noise; he could still hear the soft rubber thudding of someone else's soles on similar ground.

He ran his hand along the wall to keep his footing, feeling the rough brick scraping under his fingernails and a few small callouses he had earned at work. The roadway curved, as railways do, and he was in a narrow space between two old warehouse buildings. The curved walls were lined with high-set freight doors nearly waist-high, massive ten-foot-tall wooden frame-hung doors opened sideways to meet the boxcar doors as freight trains parked to conduct their business in the district. His hands now grazed the edges of the wooden doors, some smooth and others splintered and rough from mistreatment or perhaps simply age and weathering.

He followed the footsteps, but they were muted now and hard to hear. They became a shuffling sound, like feet dragging on cement.

That's damn odd, Gabe thought, *what the hell could he be dragging out here?*

With that, the shuffling sound grew louder. Gabriel realized it was not a shuffling sound; it was more of a chuffing! His heart sank as he looked back and realized he had walked perhaps a hundred yards into this service passage when he realized his mistake.

Christ, that's a steam loco!

He spun so quickly on his heel that he slipped and fell. He'd caught his grip on the bottom of a massive freight door, but as he fell, he yanked on the door so hard that the wooden slab pulled off its tired hinges and clattered to the cobblestone, breaking apart all around him. Ten feet of wood plank door lay across the tracks embedded in the ground.

Stumbling to his feet, Gabe began to run the way he'd come, back to the street where he could get out of the way of that oncoming train. As he passed several more freight doors in the corridor, he heard the sickening crush of the massive wooden door being obliterated by the immense iron driving wheels of the steam locomotive. He dared not look back; he had but a precious few moments to save his hide!

As he neared the end of the service way, he could see his freedom breaking through the permeating fog as the narrow walls opened to the street. The locomotive engineer must have spotted him as well; a deafening whistle from perhaps a dozen feet behind blasted through the air, nearly causing Gabe to lose his footing in surprise. The metallic squeal of emergency brakes being applied caused the entire train to shudder and scream in protest of the hastily made stop. Gabe stumbled out into the street, stumbling past the sidewalk as the deadly locomotive came to a grinding halt, blowing off its steam valves and still sounding the shrill steam whistle.

The brakeman leaped off the front of the steamer and toward Gabriel, shaking his fist furiously in the air.

"YOU GODDAMNED LUNATIC! What were you doing back there? You coulda been killed! You nearly gave us a heart attack, and we ain't ever run over a man on the tracks! Christ's sake, man, what were you thinking?"

The man was still shaking his fist while his partner wiped a sweaty brow with a red rag, appearing somewhat relieved.

Gabriel, still breathing heavily as he stood up to dust himself off, stammered out, "I... I'm sorry, following... I was following someone. I'm sorry, fellas!" He waved up at the man, who was now climbing back up the loco's front steps, fists clenched and scowling.

Gabe wheezed out, "I.. did you see anyone back there? I was following..."

"No, pal, there wasn't anyone back there! Just you and that pile of goddamn lumber! Why would you drop a door on the tracks? You tryin' to derail my consist?"

His chest heaving with foggy breath, Gabe shot back, "That was an *accident,* and I'm sure I saw a man run that way! Maybe you weren't paying attention?"

The old man sneered and grumbled, leaning far over the safety rail of the locomotive, retorting, "You don't know your ass from your elbow, son! Listen, I'm gonna tell you this once. Don't ever play chicken with no god-damn train, or you'll lose... big-time!" His words echoed across the street, fading into the dense fog.

"Oh no, sir, never again. It was an honest mistake. I work for the railroad, south-dock yard hand... I work for Wash. I'd *never* risk that!" Gabe didn't want to arouse too much attention.

The engineer scowled, spit a mouth of tobacco juice on the railhead, and nodded. That seemed to placate the brakeman. "Washington? Huh. Well, see that you don't, son. Now get the hell outta here while we clean up this mess!"

The old man paused and turned back to Gabe with a comforting tone, "Suppose those doors must be worn out, to just fall on those tracks out here. Good thing there weren't no people around..." and he turned away as Gabe finally caught his breath.

As the crew fired the steam blowoffs and reversed the grimy black steam engine a few dozen yards back into the alley, Gabe walked around the corner and collected his thoughts.

Christ, I haven't been that close to a goner since they lit up Leipzig! I better get my head right. I'm lucky those gents were watching it for me tonight...

With that, he decided to make his way home. The clock was nearing midnight, and Gabe had work in the morning, not to mention he'd had plenty of action for the night.

He counted street signs, consulting the little map at a nearby bus stop. He spent the long walk home recounting the events in his mind. The fright of nearly being flattened and the excitement of the night not only seemed to cloud his memory of exactly what the hell happened but also whether he'd seen someone at all.

I wonder if I'm losing my marbles here. What if I was just seeing things? No, that's... I don't have those problems. Hell. What if I was following some nobody? What if I got my mitts on him? What then?

The thought disturbed him as it brought up images of some of the things he'd been forced to do in battle, the ways in which he was trained to hurt or kill a man.

I'd better make a promise to myself here and now. Chrissakes Gabe... You'd be strung up quick if you caught the wrong man and put him in a hurt. No, sir, you'd better be sure. Better be certain.

Arriving home, a brief hot shower put his mind back to ease enough to get some sleep. His only reprieve was the knowledge that in the morning, he would make time to see Lindy and thank her for such a fantastic evening the prior night. As he tossed and turned, he could swear he almost smelled her perfume... and he realized then that he was lonely. Damned lonely.

I shouldn't get ahead of myself. She's a doll, and I don't know how much competition I've got. If I play my hand right, maybe... just maybe, there's something special in the cards for us.

Those images of shadowy men, cantankerous trains, and the smell of New York's foggy streets all faded. Only echoes of Lindy's honeyed voice permeated Gabe's restless dreams.

Idle Talk

Tuesday, October 22nd

Dawn arrived, and the scruffy-faced man prepared himself as usual. He arrived hungry for both food and attention. Just his luck; Lindy was game for both. She set him up with a sizable breakfast and a little peck on his cheek when nobody was looking. Lindy's demeanor with Gabe was so kind and warm that he thought he might just melt into the seat right there like a chocolate bar left in the sun.

As she stood over him to refill his mug, he leaned in and jokingly asked, "If I just stay here, just stay right here... would you ever make me leave?"

She threw her head back in brief but genuine laughter. "Why, Mister Marshall, if you stay and never leave, soon enough, you won't be able to get out of the darned booth!' She poked his ribs playfully, 'And then what would I do? Who would take me to the cinema? You'd be here crammed in this booth *all alone*, stuffed with bacon and pie, and the lights turned out. I'd have to throw a dust cover on you!" She poked him again, and he laughed into his coffee mug mid-sip.

"Well, sweet girl, I suppose I'll have to settle for a less occasional meal and a more occasional trip to the cinema... with you, of course." He winked at her.

With a shy smile, Lindy blushed and topped off his coffee. "Why that sounds like a proper compromise, doesn't it?" She shook his big mitt with her comparably diminutive hand, sealing the imaginary contract and scrunching her face like a dour old businessman. Gabe chortled at the face. After a facetious curtsy, she went back to organizing the next table after clearing it.

"Anyway, I bet Harry would come and visit me stuck in my booth. He said you served him quite a fine meal!"

She smiled and pointed toward the kitchen. "Then he can marry Art! Now that man can *cook*! I think he snores, though..."

They burst out in laughter as Art looked at them through the service window, shrugging and going right back to his cooking.

Lindy topped off Gabe's coffee and offered, "I remember seeing him, as you described. He was a bit quiet. I suppose that's not so bad."

"Get a couple of pints in him; he gets louder than his size!" Gabe remarked, sipping and watching Lindy attend to her other customers.

Gabe quickly ate the rest of the chow and hugged her around her shoulder on his way out the door. Her little fingers-only wave goodbye gave him a warm feeling. He'd wanted to ask her out but chose not to rush things just yet.

This girl's sweeter than her cobbler, he mused as he finished his food and waved goodbye.

The commute went by quickly. When Gabe arrived at work, he found Harold Burton scowling and tapping his fingers on his elbow, leaning against the hallway punchcard machine.

"You, sir, are almost late!" Harry chided him.

Gabe paused, shoulders tense. "Who, me? Wait... *almost*?"

"If you're not early, you're late! But honest, I just wanna hear how it's going with the dame?" he let out a little laugh. Gabe realized he wasn't in trouble, so he relaxed a bit.

"Okay, Harry, fine. I'll tell you over lunch. Nutty days, lately."

"Hey, nutty is okay! I'm about to go sit in my office for three hours poring over chicken-scratch work orders and paint budgets so I could use a little nutty."

"All right, Harry, I've got your nutty stories. Meet me at that yellow transfer caboose at lunch, the one with the broken glass."

"You got it, pal!" Harry made guns with his fingers, as children do when they play Cowboys.

Work passed quickly; another coal hopper needed service, but it was just maintenance. Gabe was mostly oiling bearings and replacing seals—simple work made for a quiet morning. The lunch whistle called out, and Harold met Gabe at the caboose they'd agreed upon. Some youths had broken the caboose's bathroom window with a large rock, which was found resting in the toilet along with half the fallen glass. Old wood-paned windows were no fun to glass, but luckily, Gabe wasn't trained on that job. Not officially, anyway, despite how his father had taught him to replace panes on the barn windows as a young man.

The men waved hello to each other and climbed up into the creaky wood-side caboose from opposite ends. As they took a seat, Harold munched on a meager-looking salami-on-rye that was clearly brought from home; Gabe was still full from breakfast. The pair sat down and ate together, not in silence but not actively conversing. Harry made a few comments about one of their old-timer workers over in the paint shed, and Gabe didn't take offense because the man really was terrible to deal with. Always screwing around, never finishing jobs on time, and being generally unlikable during the lunch hour.

"I'd give John a piece of my mind sometime if I wasn't the boss..."

Gabe nodded and chewed the last of his sandwich.

"Say, how about you? What's news in your world?"

"Oh, I'm dull as can be. I don't know what I'd tell you about. I went and got my shoes resoled last week; good work, too. Look!"

Gabe watched as Harry lifted both his feet off the ground, kicking his feet like a child.

"Looks sharp. Nice boots! Look almost army-issued, you know that?" Gabe offered an honest compliment.

"Yeah, with the weather changing, I figured I'd get some better footwear for the cold. These were used, just a dollar. Bought a sharp peacoat, too!"

"Navy style?" Gabe raised an eyebrow.

"You know it! Surplus store up on 20th had a sale. It seems they can't handle all the supply they're getting. You service boys sure get some quality duds! I always liked a sharp uniform. Just never got to wear one!"

Gabe smiled and handed Harry back the pop.

"So tell me, where'd you grow up, Harry? Around these parts?"

"Not here, but close. A little town upstate, Monroe. Pretty sleepy, glad I got out."

"Oh? Have you always liked the city? There's good work

upstate, I hear."

"It's all manual labor, farm work unless you know someone. Honest, Gabe, you see me picking apples and mending fences?"

Gabe chuckled as Harry shrugged his slender shoulders.

"No way, Harry, you're a brainy type. I'm the brawn.' Gabe offered, looking around the caboose, 'But I'm doing just what I can, and so are you, I reckon."

Harry scowled, appearing dejected. "I should have been a man of action, like you. How's the action over at that diner?"

"You're a cad, Harry. Everything's fine. Like I told you, I took her out Sunday and saw her again this morning. She's a real special gal, Harry."

"I agree. Maybe she's got a sister! Say, what's the craziest thing you ever saw on base? Any good stories about the barracks? Ever see anything wild in the war?"

Gabe knew that the *honest* answer would be a long story, so he decided to shorten it a bit. It was good to change the subject from Lindy, anyway.

"Oh, nothing too odd. Out on the front, it was all grind and grit, mud and marching. A lot of waiting around for action, then some odd day you rest your head for two seconds, and then bullets start flying... but after a while, after enough of that, you don't panic anymore. The best stories come from the base camp anyway. One evening, Cam caught a fish in the river we were posted near with his *bare hands*! It must've been twenty pounds! He stood in that river for an hour, waiting to spring on one of those monsters. He was so proud... Captain told us to throw it back and get to bunks. Cam was having none of that! He tossed it to the Captain, and that fish slapping its tail caught our Cap across the face. I swear, I've never seen a grown man run as fast as Cam did that night. He was MIA til dawn! It's a shame, too, because Cap got his revenge on the fish by flaying and scaling it on Cam's blankets with a Ka-Bar knife and serving it over a barrel fire. Best fish I've ever had! The fucking stink in that tent, though..."

Harry was in stitches. "Cam sounds like a character! What's he like?"

"He's my brother, as close as blood... just a different shade. He's a colored fellow, about a decade older than us. Joined up late, but after seeing him in action, I always looked up to him for guidance. He was a hell of a soldier—just a sharp, capable sort. Cam must've saved my skin on a dozen occasions and saved his a few times, and he insists I didn't owe him. Yessir, he's great people."

"Oh, I see! Where's he at now?" Harry asked, finishing off the soda pop.

"Cam's in California, enjoying the sunshine. I think he'll be coming to visit soon. Say, have you got any brothers, Harry? Any family around?"

Harry looked down into the empty can for a moment, still and quiet. Gabe could see that Harry was down about it.

"I had two brothers, yeah, they were in the Army. Lost them both. It was a-' he paused with a sigh, '...it was hard to lose them right near the end of it all. That damned war took a lot from me."

Gabe stood up and patted Harry on the shoulder, "Hey pal, I didn't know. I'm sure they were doing the right thing. Chances are, we got the fuckers responsible."

Harry stood up and shook it off. "I don't think the right people paid for it, but time will tell, I suppose." He motioned to the door.

Gabe walked him out to the caboose platform, and Harry tugged his shirt to stop him.

"Hey Harry, just... let's talk a little less about the war, yeah?"

With a dour look on his face, Harry faked a smile and hopped off the steps, "Okay, you got it!"

And with that, Harold strode off to beat the end-of-lunch whistle, leaving Gabe in the shade with an empty pop can.

As the day drew on, Gabe labored on some minor projects and shared a few dirty jokes with the yard hands who were tooling on nearby cars. Gabe silently chided himself for being so crude.

I never used to swear like this. Suppose I never really talked much at Carter Machine. These fellas aren't so bad; they are good stock. Who cares about a few blue words?

That afternoon, while he finished work on the coal car, Gabe decided that it would be in his best interest to lay off the investigations for the week, get his act together, and spend some real quality time with Lindy if she'd have him. Just before the end of the day, he ran to the yard administrator's desk and requested a late start the following day so he could savor his breakfast at Art's and ask Lindy to have a night out with him again. There was humility in his hoping she'd be keen to go out again; deep down, he knew the girl was enamored with him.

He had *every* intention of keeping it that way.

Pins and Needles

Wednesday - Thursday

Breakfast came and went quickly. Art's diner was busier than usual for midweek. Lindy had taken care of Gabriel's food and drink as best she could, but the kitchen was slow, so she was as busy as could be. Gabe supposed the food was slow owing to Art taking a day off and the young fill-in cook not quite having the knack for keeping up with all those orders. Gabe didn't mind; just seeing Lindy was enough to keep a smile on his face.

I'll ask her when I ask her. I don't want to be pushy when she's already going full tilt. It's not as though I won't be here tomorrow or someday soon anyway. It can wait.

He finished his chow and made way for the door while giving Lindy a wink and a tip of his hat goodbye. As he was stepping out the door, she called out, "Cold days really bring them in! Tomorrow, big guy?" To which he simply gave her an O-Kay with his thumb and forefinger; she winked and blew him a small kiss as he left.

Gabe spent most of the day learning some service techniques on one of the steam switcher locomotives there in the yard. It looked just like the locomotive that almost squashed him just a few days prior; it might have even been the same, but his amusement at that was something he couldn't share with anyone at work. Harold had been swamped at the office, and Gabe was missing his friend by the time the 5 o'clock whistles blew. With no plans and the yard foreman offering up a few hours of overtime to help with fixing up an icebox car that had been busted up in a switching accident that morning, Gabriel jumped at the opportunity to make some extra money. He finished up by about seven o'clock and found his way home.

That evening, Gabe went directly home after work and picked up the day's newspaper from the lobby downstairs. One of his neighbors had already unfurled the paper and made a mess of it, but he didn't care. He had grabbed a cheap little glass bottle of bourbon from the corner market and was glad for the opportunity to sit down and relax with the paper quietly.

No murders, no grisly business. That's a damn relief!

Plenty of the news was disheartening, of course. Newspapers were filled with facts but one must filter through all of the dramatic articles about socialites and goings-on downtown, typical city life. Still, Gabriel could recall reading the newspaper back home once a week and catching up on nearly every single thing a person would need to know about their hometown. Gabe missed the simplicity, but he knew that it would be a long while before he could think about returning home to Montana or finding his way back to a simpler life.

Skimming through the section for work, the bold title of 'HELP REQUESTED,' he didn't see anything that would be a better fit than what he was doing now. Longshoreman, wall setter, bus driver... the starting pays were meager, and none of those jobs would be a step upward. Sure, he wished the railroad could pay a bit better, but it was honest work, and he would have a few extra bucks in his pocket with the new job. He'd been squirreling away what little he could at Carter, with his Army pension depositing directly into his bank account and a bit of savings in a rolled-up tobacco pouch in his bottom drawer, he had a nest egg if hard times hit... but being a thrifty minded sort (aside from the booze), Gabe never wanted to dip far into savings if at all. The idea of reaching into that pouch or walking into a bank perturbed him. It made him feel like he was failing at this new life.

Gabe's father had taught him how to ledger his money and plan for hard times, but it was Cam Mason who'd given him something to think about one night in their cots. Earlier in the day, while patrolling a small village under Allied occupation, he and Cam had found a coin purse with a folded-up fifty Francs on the street; Cam had nicked the cash and dropped the coin purse in a dustbin. Later that night, Gabe was teasing Cam for his half of the spoils, as he was the one who spotted the purse. "Cam, I could use my half and get us some good smokes and a bottle, maybe two... we don't have anything decent in the mess tent lately, anyway." Gabe had spent the last of his month's loose wages already on some nice warm hand-knitted socks a week prior in a dry goods store near a train station where their troop train had stopped to take water. Cam chuckled at Gabe's daydreaming and leaned over the rail of his bunk to set Gabe straight.

"No, sir. I'm puttin' my half in my boot and puttin' yours in my special hiding spot. You can have it when we're on our way home. Every dollar counts, son. Every dime. Settlin' down money, Gabe, you're gonna want that."

Gabe phooeyed that thought, sighing, "I don't think I'll ever settle down, Cam. Small-town life is for suckers. I want to travel and eat every meal in every place. See the world where there's no artillery flying overhead. Maybe I'll write about all this, too."

"Shit, Gabe, you ain't the worldly type. You want a soft bed an' a chubby wife with a nice yard; you just don't know it yet. I bought my house for a song after the crash in '28 when everybody went flat. But me? I was *ready*. Sold my pop's Ford to buy that house. You gotta plan for a life. And a little mess tent gruel ain't gonna kill you, big boy." Then he'd reached across and poked Gabe in the tummy. It was a warm memory. Cam had been something of a father figure to Gabe nearly as much as he was a friend.

Hmmph. Settling down money. Not that I want to settle down here, but someday sure. I can't be starting a family in a walk-up...

With a glance at the clock and seeing it was nearly ten at night, Gabe laid the now half-empty bottle of bourbon on his nightstand and hit the hay.

~~~

Thursday morning was a rainy mess. Gabriel hadn't slept well because of the wind and rain pattering his window all night, but he supposed it was better than an alley-side window where he would likely be woken up by folks rummaging through the trash roundabout five in the morning. That was one small thing he was thankful for compared to his neighbors, who griped about the ruckus often. There were enough needy folks in the bowery that such pitiful scavenging was a daily occurrence; Gabe tried hard to pay no mind.

As he walked to Art's, the cold air made Gabe wish for a scarf. Fortunately, Lindy had help today and was far less busy, allowing her to sit down for a couple of minutes and catch up with Gabriel.

"So, you big lug, what do you say we get together again
~~~

soon and check out one of those hot little spots we saw on the drive last week?"

He loved how forward-thinking she was. It was absolutely modern for a woman to be in charge of making a date.

"I've got all the time for you, sweet girl. What do you have in mind?" He looked around, and seeing that nobody was paying them any mind, he leaned forward a bit and clasped her hand, cradling it softly.

"Sweet, huh? Now, that sounds like an idea. There's an ice cream parlor three blocks from here that I heard has quite the root beer float!" Lindy was beaming at her idea.

"I'm in. Tonight any good for you, Babydoll?"

"No can do, Gab. I've got dinner plans with a school friend. Belinda's in town for a trade show today, and I haven't seen her in a number of years. Her company is selling these beautiful new typewriters, she can type nearly a hundred words a minute! Not to mention she's easy on the eyes, or so the boys say...' Gabe responded with a chuckle, and she squeezed his hand, continuing, 'Is tomorrow good for you? I've got the day off, we could meet here at six when you get back from the ferry!"

"I'm sure Miss Belinda couldn't be any easier on my eyes than you are. And I don't need anything typed up! Six o'clock is perfect, and I'll eat light."

She gave him a little peck on the cheek as she got up to return to her other tables, and Gabe finished up his breakfast with gusto. He waved goodbye to her just as three more tables sat.

That little lady sure works hard...

Gabe put up his trench coat collar and pulled down the brim of his hat as he made his way to work through a cold, steady rain. He was damn thankful for the seemingly waterproof coat, stuffing his hands into the deep pockets for warmth, but when he felt that old revolver in the front pocket, he set to mind that he would be wise to put it away once he got home. He had to wear his trench coat in the rain while he worked as the yard's loaner rain slickers were a tattered mess, and most didn't fit his broad shoulders anyway.

I have to be careful not to muck it up; my best coat as it is.

Gabe spent the morning toiling away on another flat car, simple work replacing wood planks on the platform that had broken down over a few years of heavy use. He was thankful for the plank roof he was working under, paying little mind to how leaky it was in a few places. When the lunch whistle blew, he hurried to the end of the yard, where he found most of the yard crew eating in a small service shed; it was good cover from the drizzle that had been pelting the men all morning.

Harold arrived quickly, sitting on the empty bench next to Gabe and unpacking another dry sandwich he had brought under his coat. Gabe was working on his usual bread, cured meat, and aged cheese. They were alone in that corner of the workshop.

"C'mon Gabe, don't tell me there's no new stories? What've you been up to all week? I've been itching to get a drink, but I could use more adventure than that... what say we go uptown sometime?"

"Oh Harry, honest, I've been so busy, I'm making some plans for time with Lindy. I need to step up my living situation as well, to be frank. Perhaps down the road a bit..."

Harold Burton gave him the saddest look, like a scorned puppy.

"You're not looking for a better job, are you?"

Gabe remembered that he had something nifty he could show his buddy. He reached into his pocket and exclaimed, "Say, have I got a surprise for you... Close your eyes, yeah?"

His pal grinned eagerly like a child and held out his hands, eyes shut tight. Gabe gingerly placed the cold metal object into his buddy's hand. Harold felt around with his fingers for a bit, a determined scowl on his face as he tried to discern what he was holding.

"Come on, Harry, give me a guess."

"It's... is it... a million smackaroos?" Harold replied, fingers still fumbling.

"Close enough, pal. Open your peepers and tell me what you think!"

A wry smile came across Harry's face, and he opened his eyes and looked down into his palm. Gabriel was sure that his pal was going to be blown away by what he was holding.

Harry's smile faded immediately. His eyes locked on his surprise. His brow furrowed, and a frown replaced his usual cheerful countenance.

"It's... Gabe, this is a... *Christ*, are you supposed to have this?"

"Harry, it's just an old keepsake, if you want to call it that.

What's the big deal? I thought you'd be more impressed?"

He looked down at Harry's open palm, and one of the two little Nazi rank pins was gleaming in the bright shop lights. In a hurried clap, Harry cupped his palm and shoved the pin back into Gabe's hand. Harry's body language was immediately tense and uneasy.

"I don't want to be seen holding that thing. You shouldn't have that!" Harry whispered, upset as could be.

"Look here, it's our secret, okay Harry?' Gabe consoled him, 'I'll put it away. I thought you wanted a taste of adventure. Was I off base there, pal?"

Harry's posture relaxed a bit, and he shrugged, shaking his head side to side just slightly.

"Sorry, big guy, I swear I don't spook easy, but some of that stuff just makes me nervous. Besides, I thought you said we were gonna stop talking about the war!" He let out a chuckle and swatted Gabriel in the arm.

"Hell, I thought I had really upset you! I suppose not everybody is keen on holding plundered Nazi regalia in their hand. I completely understand; don't worry about it. But hell, did you see that thing? Isn't it just damn strange?"

Harold stood up and adjusted his trousers, scanning the room. "Not like anything I've ever seen, that's for sure.' His shoulders relaxed a bit, and he raised an eyebrow over his next question, 'So what do you think it means, Gabe? Where you even find such a thing?"

"I'll spare you the details, but let's just say it belonged to somebody who hurt one of my men, and I hurt him back."

Harold pondered the comment a bit before replying.

"I'm sure you did what you had to do. Say, I've got to get back to the desk, a darn stack of paperwork calling my name. Why don't we have a drink this weekend, can we? Maybe Saturday?"

Gabriel was so relieved that he hadn't offended Harold beyond recovery, and he didn't want to disappoint him now.

"Sure thing, give me a ring Saturday morning at my place, and we can figure it out. I could sure use a drink myself!"

With a wave, Harold made his way out and back toward his duties. Gabe finished lunch and powered through the day, just looking forward to Friday, looking forward to Lindy. He picked up another couple hours of time-and-a-half after the five o'clock whistles just to help pad the wallet a bit. He reminded himself of his goals as he labored on a several-hundred-pound knuckle coupler replacement with Doug from the paint shop, who was also keen on extra hours. They worked in the rain with a lantern on the platform over their shoulders.

Can't say no to a few extra dollars in my pocket. Need to keep earning if I'm going to take this girl anywhere nicer than an ice cream parlor! Why do they always save the heaviest bastard jobs for end-of-shift?

The thought of being *anywhere* with Lindy took his mind to warm places... beautiful respite from the aches of the day.

Sweets

Friday, October 25th

Five minutes to six on Friday evening, and the pair were already holding hands, walking the few blocks from Art's to the ice cream parlor. Their walk had gone by in a flash as she filled Gabe in about her 'night on the town' with Belinda. Apparently, the poor girl had too much wine. She fell asleep on Lindy's couch not long after dinner, whereupon Lindy spent the rest of the evening with the latest issue of Good Housekeeping courtesy of her mother's coffee table.

Gabe poked her in the arm and declared, "You should have phoned me up! I make a good cup of Joe. I could have saved the evening!"

"Oh, I didn't mind. Belinda was a bit of a drag anyway; all she wanted to talk about was typewriters... I would almost rather read about Electrolux vacuums or some silly new soap! Honest, Gabe, *anything* is more exciting than sitting around a typing machine all day! Droll housekeeping talk makes me a dullard, but at the very least, those recipes in that magazine gave me some ideas..."

"Cobbler?" He teased her, and she snickered. Gabe kissed her cheek. Just then, they arrived at the brightly lit sweets shop, and Lindy stopped Gabe and pointed to the sign over the doorway. The hand-painted wooden sign hanging over the door, SERGIO'S, was a bit weatherbeaten but still plenty inviting. It was beautifully colorful.

"See?', Lindy exclaimed, 'I *told* you this place looked charming!"

She had a little hop in her step; she was so excited about dessert. She swung the door open, and Gabe followed her in.

"Now, I never doubted you, Babydoll. I've never met an

ice cream I didn't like!"

She giggled and sat him down in the corner booth before she went to the counter to order the biggest ice cream sundae the towering man behind the counter was willing to make. Lindy returned to the table to wait impatiently for their dessert.

She took Gabe's hand and watched cars passing by.

"Lindy, I've been thinking about this all week."

"What's that?" She cooed.

"You know what I mean, spending time with you. It's become quite a pastime for me! If I didn't have to work, I think I might just hang around the diner all day and watch you twirl around the way you do. Like a crisp oak leaf loose in a breeze."

She blushed, turning to him and leaning close with her shoulders rolled forward.

"What if I were busy? What if I gave you the cold shoulder?"

He smiled and nodded toward the man carrying a foot-long crystal canoe toward their table. Ice cream, whipped cream, cherries, and fudge—it looked more like a buffet than a sundae.

"Cold shoulder, huh? Easy... I'd warm you up!" Gabe retorted with a grin, leaning back to make way for the incoming dessert.

Gabe turned to the man in the white apron, a towering man with olive skin and bear paws for hands. "Thanks, pal, best service I've had in a while!' while giving a little sideways wink to Lindy as he asked the man, 'Might you be the proprietor?"

The man grinned widely and set spoons on the table in front of them, replying, "Last I checked! Good to meet you both. Sergio, never *sir*." He reached out and shook Gabe's hand.

"Gabe, and my good friend Lindy, and it's a pleasure to meet you. Say, not much business on a Friday night?" Gabe asked, craning his neck around and mainly seeing empty seats. Two men in coveralls were quietly drinking coffee in a side booth, and that was it.

"Sure, I get plenty; you've just got to wait 'til later. All the youngsters come out and spend their allowance, sometimes the school's baseball team ends up here after a game in the season, a few kids come here for a cheap date... To be frank, I don't get a lot of folks your age, much less mine, on a Friday evening. Still, it's sure nice to see!"

Not missing a beat, Lindy chimed in, "If that sundae's half

as tasty as it looks, you'll be seeing the two of us plenty often!"

With a hearty laugh, Sergio pointed to the dish. "You're gonna love it, but it's melting!"

Gabe picked up a spoon and shoveled a scoop into Lindy's mouth, and she could hardly swallow from laughter.

Sergio waited for her to finish the bite, and the thumbs-up she gave him was all he needed. He gave her a thumbs-up in return and mentioned, "Funny, you two remind me of me and my little lady, Debra. Would you believe I proposed to her in that very booth you're keeping warm right now?"

Gabe looked down at his paunch, pressed up against the table in the small booth, and then looked up at Sergio, who was easily twice Gabriel's size in stature and personality. He let out a little chuckle, and Sergio knew precisely what had Gabe in a stitch.

"Okay, sure, it was a while ago. I used to be this big!' Sergio motioned with his hands in the silhouette of a lean, trim former self. He waved the thought away as he turned and went back behind the counter, loudly offering up, 'Sport Boxer, don't you know. I was *good*, too! I fit just fine in those booths, just fine!" Laughing heartily, he walked a carafe toward the back for the two men with their coffees.

Lindy squeezed Gabe's hand tightly and picked up her spoon. "Do you make friends everywhere you go?" she asked as she fed him a heaping spoonful of ice cream in return.

Mouth still half-full of frozen goodness, he snickered and shrugged. "It's not hard when you're happy!"

He fed her an equally large scoop, and she rested her elbows on the table, beaming at him as she ate. There was whipped cream and one chipped peanut stuck to her chin; Gabe didn't say anything. He just looked at her soft skin and warm smile, which started in her eyes, and he felt smitten. At that moment, he could think of a million questions about her but didn't know where to start without feeling like a quiz show host.

"Say, tell me something I'd never guess about you!" Gabe inquired as she fed him another spoonful.

"Oh, let's see... say, I was a nurse for a time. I was in the newspapers once."

"Oh, *this* I gotta hear!" He said with a laugh.

"It's not much, really. I was fresh out of grade school. There was a terrible rain, and the streets were practically canals.

Flooding all around the city, and the Bowery is a bad place to be with all the disrepair they leave these streets in..."

He was listening intently, breaking up her story with small bites as she talked.

"A young boy, Lawrence, from down my block... as a girl, I would nanny for his family, and little goofy Larry was stomping about in the rain like a dolt and got pulled right down a storm drain that had unclogged from the sheer pressure of that water. Would you believe it?"

"I'd believe it! What did you do?"

She fed him a melting scoop, the sundae rapidly disappearing.

"I was the only person there slim enough to fit down there after him. So, *whoop*, down I went! Soaked to the bone and looking like a drowned rat, but the little guy was just fine... I lifted him far enough so they could pull him out!"

He was on the edge of his seat. "How did you get out?"

She pointed at his belt buckle, "Hoisted up by one of the men's belts! He pulled me out like a mineshaft rescue. It was simply terrifying! I nearly drowned myself, all that mucky water! I can still taste it."

Yeah, this city seems to tinge everything, even the rain...

He sat back and let out a whoosh of breath he'd been holding. His mouth puckered, remembering the taste of that damned dirty water in his mouth from the elevated railway. "That's amazing. You saved the little guy! Bet it felt good, must've felt like Superman getting out of there unscathed!"

She looked away for a few moments, then down at the ice cream.

"Well, there was a jagged edge down there. Who could have known? I was cut badly when they pulled me out... I still have a scar..." She placed her hand instinctively on her thigh. "The nurses and doctors stitched me up, and that's when I decided to be a nurse! I wish I'd had better stitches; it's not pretty..."

Gabe lifted her chin with his thumb and offered her another bite of ice cream, which she sheepishly took.

"We've all got scars, Babydoll. It adds character if you ask me. I got shot once myself, didn't I tell you? I'll show you the scar sometime!"

She took a bite and smirked a bit. "Save that for another

date, you absolute brute!"

Gabe glanced out the window and saw it had started raining.

"Say, if we don't want to get washed away ourselves, I think I should take you home." He reached for a napkin and wiped a dash of whipped cream from her chin.

He motioned out the window to the glistening streets, and she nodded in agreement as she fed him the last bite of ice cream and chocolate sauce. They grabbed their coats and waved goodbye to Sergio, who was now engrossed in a newspaper behind the counter.

They caught a cab, and the drive was short, and soon found themselves standing once again on the steps of her building. Gabriel couldn't help but think about the last time he stood there... that heart-stopping kiss. Before he could say anything, Lindy grabbed the collars of his trenchcoat and pulled him in close.

"Do you know how much I'm going to miss you after I walk up these steps?" She spoke the words softly in his ear. Gabriel turned his head and kissed her gently on the nape of her neck. It was Dewey and cold from a dozen gentle raindrops.

"I'd say half as much as I'll miss you, sweet girl." He could feel her pull him in even closer, and she draped her arms around his neck.

He leaned back just enough so he could kiss her, and she closed her eyes as he did. Her embrace tightened as they kissed a long, intense kiss. The sort of kiss he'd never had, the kind that had him wondering if he'd fall over dead just then.

After a while, she drew away a few inches and took a deep breath, placing her warm palm on his cheek.

"How about a picnic on Sunday? Weather should be nice; Papa said it might be our last sunny day before winter..." she asked softly.

Gabe placed his hand over hers on his cheek, pressing firmly. He could feel the stubble on his chin rustle against the cuff of her coat. With his index finger, he stopped a rolling raindrop on the tip of her nose.

"I'll be right here on these steps at noon, Babydoll."

From the step, she rose on her toes and kissed Gabe on the forehead before turning and going inside, waving goodnight through the stained-glass window.

Gabe waved back with a grin, and after watching the

lights to her home turn on up above the street he turned to head home with a spring in his step yet again. He knew just the place for a fine picnic. He'd wished the night hadn't ended, but he could hardly wait for Sunday.

He let out a full-chested sigh and started down the street. From behind, a soft voice called out.

"Hey, don't leave just yet!"

Gabe turned back and saw Lindy leaning over the railing of her balcony, beckoning to him.

"Lindy, everything O-kay?"

"Seems the old folks left for the night; Papa left a note saying they went for a show and a hotel uptown tonight, so... I suppose... care to come up for a nightcap?"

Gabe paused under the dim glow of the streetlamp, and he doffed his hat, smiling broadly as his heart skipped a beat or three. His speechless gaze was all the answer she needed.

Family

Gabe's taxi left him on the stoop of the cathouse half-after seven in the morning. He took a quick, steaming shower and tossed on some fresh clothes, hardly paying any mind to anything but memories of the night before. Sitting on the edge of the rickety bed, he took a moment and closed his eyes, his imagination running wild. He could still feel Lindy's skin against his. It was like a dream he wanted to dream forever, and Saturday morning went by in a blur. Gabe knew he'd have trouble collecting picnic supplies on Sunday, as half the small shops would be closed in consideration of church. Italian, Irish, Presbyterian... most of the folks in this neighborhood would spend their Sunday focused on church, and he had little interest in joining them.

After a few hours, he'd been all across the neighborhood. He stopped into the Greek-owned dime store for a sweet little set of traveling dishes in a wicker case, which he'd seen some weeks prior, and even found a nice burgundy gingham tablecloth for the spread. He crossed the east side of the neighborhood to get to a Rexall, where he bought a few sundries for getting sharp, including a new pomade and some cologne that the Seaforth Company advertised in TIME magazine, which Gabe often kept as a nightstand coaster but opened on occasion.

The girl in the ad sure seemed to like the scent... he remembered the ad clearly, a fresh-faced woman holding forth a variety of men's shaving sundries and scents. *No bikini, no fawning. Just simple, clean advertising. It must be worth a try!*

Near the entry, Gabe spotted something else he needed: a

rubber cane foot for Madge Baker. He requested the store deliver it to her building across the neighborhood. After explaining the old lady's situation, the clerk promised it would be done 'first thing Monday morning, sir!'

Gabe felt far better now about how he'd fibbed his way into her good graces. *She'll appreciate it, I'm sure!*

After the last stop at the small grocers near the corner liquor store to grab some bread, wine, and cheese, he knew he was all set. Just as he arrived home and was placing the perishables in the shared icebox, the desk man called him over and handed him a note that was comprised of Harry's name and phone number, nothing else. It was all he needed. Making his way to the little phone closet in the lobby, he cheerfully rang Harry, who answered in no time. They made plans to meet at four o'clock sharp, right there in Gabe's lobby.

After getting his shower kit rearranged, including those new scents and that little jar of Brylcreem pomade, he changed into a festive luau shirt he'd won in a Bingo raffle on-base a few months before his tour ended. Gabe remembered that snarky little fucker Ernie Hawthorne had stolen the shirt from backstage at a USO show in '43, but it was too big, so he'd tossed it in the prize pot the men had cobbled together instead of cash or smokes as most men did. Slipping on a decent set of slacks and his wingtip shoes, he trotted down the stairs and settled down in the only comfortable chair in that lobby. Feeling cool and relaxed, he cracked open a beer he'd picked up alongside the picnic groceries. Sitting there in silence, except for the traffic passing by, he found himself deeply bored after a few minutes of watching the disheveled old man from room #405 slowly placing cards in a round of solitaire near the window.

Hell, if Harry's gonna be an hour and Lindy's nearly a day away, I might as well catch the news.

He went and grabbed a shabby-looking newspaper from near the door, unfurling it after settling back down into the plush leather armchair. Swigging the beer, he couldn't help but sigh at the headline plastered across mid-page.

CRIES OF VICTIMS' FAMILIES IN MANHATTAN ATTACKS FALL ON DEAF EARS

With another swig, which finished the bottle, he read on.

"Citizens of Central and Lower Manhattan continue to seek answers from what appears to be a deaf and dumb Department of Police. This reporter could find no ranking Officer, Sergeant, or Detective to make a

statement further than the boilerplate promise of impending apprehension coming out of the Mayor's office. To date, no persons have been publicly apprehended in the ghastly and vicious muggings, nor have the Police given any solid assurances that the attacks that have taken the lives of more than one dozen citizens might soon be over.

Corrinne Moretti, the mother of the youngest known victim of this senseless crime spree the likes our city has never seen, shared the following sentiments in a recent interview with reporting staff-

"They released the remains of our only child but not her possessions nor her case file. My husband is strongly considering legal action against such an incompetent Police force, perhaps even the Mayor himself. My little angel will be put to rest with no justice, and it breaks my heart that maybe if we weren't from a struggling part of town, those robber barons and landlords at City Hall might get off their duffs and do something!"

One officer, who declined to go on record, acknowledged the increase in patrol man-hours between dusk and dawn despite our Mayor's statement that no such increase in vigilance was warranted. Each citizen is advised to consider their own safety when traveling alone and to avoid strange places and unknown persons. Persons with information regarding the tragedies are urged to step forward to provide any information that might lead to closure for these victims' loved ones. Call the newsroom at BAR 5435, day or night. Reporting staff is awaiting your call."

As he finished reading the article, he felt a weary pain in his temples from scowling. Looking up from the paper, he could feel fresh tension in his shoulders and a grimace set upon his face.

Chrissake, that poor woman. She must be beside herself over this mess. I haven't heard from the sergeant, and by the looks of things, they aren't any closer to putting a cork in it. The newspaper isn't doing the police any kindness, that's for sure, but I don't think they're as incompetent as all of that. I guess I'd better check in with Mullally soon, anyway.

With a scowl still on his brow, he took a deep breath and rested his head on the cool leather headrest for a moment. Exhaling the stress as if it were smoke, he could feel himself relax into the cushions, and he knew he needed an upbeat distraction.

Say... this place suits me alone, all right, but what if I somehow convince that little doll to spend more than a couple of evenings a week with me? You can't build a life on a creaky old cathouse mattress, much less in the dumps of the Bowery... hell. I better start lookin' for something a little more upscale. That'd be the thing...

After some thirty minutes of hunting through the

minuscule print of classified advertisements, he'd found and circled at least a half-dozen possibilities for a new homestead for himself and one more very special gal. Some of those ads really up-sold the homes, promising the 'best views' and 'quietly retired neighbors', and Gabe was skeptical that anything in his price range would be halfway decent, but he knew he had to hope for a stroke of luck. Pondering the options, he remembered being given contact information for the New York Veterans Administration when he was discharged. He had no interest in going to the Brooklyn Army Depot lest it would help his pockets.

Luck and charm are what I need. Just a place with a couple of rooms and a damn kitchen! Maybe the V-A can help me find some new digs, but the paper's a good start. I'd rather do it myself...

Just as he flipped the broadsheet page to check through another hundred listings, a shadow at the front door broke his concentration. With a grin, Gabe set the newspaper down when Harold strutted in through the front door. With a wave, as he stood up, Gabe greeted his pal warmly.

"Harry, you look great, buddy!"

"Yessir, I got a haircut and bought myself a new set of spectacles! I saw them in a movie, and I knew I had to spiff up my image, aiming for something a bit more mysterious. You really like it?"

Gabe folded up the paper and stuffed it into his back pocket.

"Harry, you look like a whole new person. Well, at least...' Gabe rubbed his chin thoughtfully for a moment; 'at least now, you don't look like someone's musty uncle!"

Grabbing Gabe's shirt sleeve, Harry yanked him out the front door.

"You drive me to drink; ya know that, Gabe?" Harry retorted.

"I get that a lot..."

Harry socked Gabe on the shoulder, "Say, *you* look like someone's uncle in that silly shirt!"

"It's Hawaiian. Just trying to put a splash of color into this awful city." Gabe mockingly brushed off his lapels.

"You look like a splash, all right... a real big ugly puddle! I shoulda brought a mop!"

The duo laughed halfway to the bar, cracking wise at each other again and again.

In short order, they neared the edge of their neighborhood, arriving at a nice little wood-facade tavern cheaply decorated with a bright Irish flag draped inside the window. Its colors balanced brightly against the dark grain of the ornate wood window trimmings, and a streetlight reflecting off its silken threads made it shimmer in the dim city light. The sun had not yet set, but the city had a way of absorbing the light from the horizon and almost saturating the sky itself with the peaks and eaves of tall, looming buildings. As Gabriel opened the door to the tavern and politely motioned Harry to enter (despite grumbling, "Get your ass in there" through a half-smile), Gabe stole a glance at the sky. A prop jet made its way across the sky in a southwest direction, barely audible above the din coming from the doorway. Gabe wondered, for a moment, what it would be like from a seat on that plane... did anyone see him? He felt small, which was a rare thing for this stout midwestern man.

Harry had already bellied up to the bar and dished out a few very meek compliments to the barmaid before Gabe had even sat down. Her face was rosy, but her cheeks were taut with a sheepish grin; Harry was making progress! Gabe nodded toward the girl, grabbed his pint, and put it to his lips as he pondered his earlier comment and took a sizable swallow.

Is this city really so awful? I don't much care for cities, but if a place like this can raise a gal like Lindy, maybe it ain't so bad... And I'd bet she would want to stay near her folks, anyway. I'd be understanding.

He sat back a bit and watched Harry chat with the girl a bit more about mundane things like the window signs and which of the men stooped over the bar might be regulars. Gabe was amused watching the little guy chat. He realized Harry was a kind man, unassuming. People just seemed to take to him. In the bars, around the railyard. It was difficult not to like the guy. Clearly, the barmaid felt the same. Her shoulders shrugged a bit with Harry's gentle prodding, but she stood there, holding a glass and a rag, ignoring at least four parched and grumpy men at the other end of the long brass-railed bar.

After a bit of time, she was able to escape from Harry's attention and wander up to appease the scowling regulars. Harry turned back to Gabe and poked him sharply in the rib.

"Gabe, GABE!' He loudly whispered, 'Didja see that? I think I might have a shot with this girl!"

"Bourbon or whiskey?" Gabe couldn't resist teasing.

"No, you horse's ass, a shot... I mean, a *chance*!" Harry's brow showed his displeasure, probably feeling a bit underestimated.

"Sorry, pal, I'm just fooling about. She's got a sweet face. She's a bit Italian-looking in an Irish place, but she's a doll. Just remember to invite me to the wedding, okay?"

Harry looked down his nose for a second, chortled at the stupidity of his now-derailed train of thought, and clinked glasses with Gabe.

"You're right. You're always right, big guy. A girl like that would never go for a pencil-pusher like me. Right? Anyway, I wanna know something. You better not bull-shit me, either."

Gabe tried to figure out what was about to come next. *Oh hell, what does he know?*

Harry took a long, dramatic gulp of his drink, making hard eye contact with Gabe.

"I wanna know what you've been up to, Gabe. You look like hell most mornings. You have been drinking *without* me?" His furrowed brow relaxed into a nefarious wiggle, just like Groucho Marx.

Gabe was relieved as could be.

"Well shit, I didn't figure you for the lush type!"

Harry scowled at him, and Gabe pinched his shoulder.

"Brass tacks, yes... Almost every damn night... but I'm at home in that dusty old room with my pants off. I'm not social like you, Harry."

Harry slapped the table, exclaiming, "I *knew* it! I'm really trying to help you build a place here, you grumpy old so-and-so. If you're going to be up late getting sauced, you might as well have some company."

Last thing I need, fella. You've got no idea.

"I get that, Harry. Suppose if I were sleeping a little better, I wouldn't look so run-down in the mornings. That bed is a pain in the ass, not to mention I've had a spate of rough dreams since I got to the city."

Harold patted him on the arm reassuringly, offering, "Well, it's a good thing you found your dream girl to keep your head outta those nightmares!"

Gabe half-smiled at the thought of her. He raised his hand and called over the barmaid. "Anything Scottish?"

The woman nodded and glanced back at the mirrored shelves and all the colorful bottles of poison. Sure, I do. How's this?"

She then produced a caramel-colored square bottle with a tired old label for Gabriel. It had clearly been around for some time.

"Hey now, that's just fine! Just don't get any of that dust in the glass?"

The girl smirked at Gabe's joke and glanced at Harry, who was oblivious to her affections at the moment. He was busy cleaning his new spectacles with his shirttail.

"What, what's happening?"

Now untucked but not quite disheveled, Harry looked like the rest of the regulars, and Gabe got a good chuckle out of Harry's oblivious response while the girl brought Gabe a short glass tumbler with an inch of scotch whisky swirling around the bottom. Harry had, on several occasions, mentioned he didn't much care for scotch, so Gabe hadn't ordered him one.

Gabe tipped his small glass back sparingly, still finding his way through two more scotches, as Harry worked on another three beers. Gabe told Harry about his plans for a new place, about wanting to be closer to work and find a life with Lindy. He pulled out the newspaper with the rental classifieds, pointing out a few to Harry on the broadsheet spread out over their bar table.

"See, this one has a big bay window, but it's on the Northside, so maybe the view won't be much use. I think we'd like a bigger kitchen, and the ad down here says it's perfect for family meals! Isn't that swell?" He tapped his finger on the circled adverts as Harry squinted to read them in the dim light.

"Oh wow! You're really moving ahead with this, huh? Maybe you should think about an office job with a few more bucks attached, Gabe. Those prices look a little steep for me!"

"I tell ya, bud, it's not too bad with my little pension considered. I'm not crazy for wanting this, am I?"

Harry winked at Gabe and shook his head side to side, mouth full of drink.

"Harry, you're a good man. I wonder, when I tie the knot, will you come to be my witness?"

Harry leaned back and looked around the bar, a furrow in his brow.

"I, uh... you... a wedding?' he stuttered, shrugging his shoulders as he leaned back toward his drink, 'Sure, of course, I'd love to... I'd be honored." He hadn't thought about the fact that Harry could end up being a real pal for life. Now, he could see it clearly.

Harry's speech was a bit slurred, but his surprise made Gabe acutely aware that he'd not previously mentioned his plans to Harry, his long-term intentions with Lindy, and it caught Harry by surprise. In fact, it was the first time he had discussed his intentions with anyone, to any real extent. It just felt natural to him, and he also mused that the liquor might've had some involvement in his candor.

"You're not crazy, Gabe. She'd make a lovely wife. Who else will be coming? Friends, army buddies? Family?"

"I've got no family to speak of, Harry. My friends *are* my family. All I've got is this job and fewer close people than I've got toes, and that's *nine*. Goddamned trenchfoot..."

Surprisingly, Harry didn't respond. He was looking at the bottom of his mug. Gabe realized he might have struck a nerve yet again.

"Say, I know you lost your brothers to the war. I'm sorry about that, pal. I know how that can be."

Harry was quiet for a short time, then, in a flash, he snapped out of it and raised his chin with a smile on his face.

"I'd love to be at your wedding, Gabe. You know it. Of course, I gotta survive our nights out if I'm gonna be there, so let's tuck this one in and call it a night, okay? I've got somewhere to be later."

"Oh hell, Harry, if you don't give your phone number to that barmaid on the way out, I'll make you wear a salmon-pink tux to the ceremony!" He poked Harry in the shoulder, and Harry blushed.

"Maybe next time, big guy. I don't wanna spook her. You should be looking at those places soon, right? Find the best apartment? Can't hardly get married just to live in an old dusty brothel."

Musing at Harry's blunt truths, Gabe downed the last of the whisky as Harry leaned back and finished his pint. Harry was the first to get up, heading out the door with a wave and tip of his hat toward where he left some dollars on the bar for the barmaid.

Gabe knew Harry was right and set his mind; he would talk to Lindy's father to seek approval on the matter. He knew he'd have to meet Lindy's parents first, which would be a hurdle to jump before proposing. There was warm contentment in his heart and his belly as he sipped the last of his scotch whisky. He glanced at the pocket watch, seeing it was only half-past eight.

Yeah, I had better take a look at some of these places while I've got any legs under me... Gotta see them both at night and during the day; I don't wanna end up stuck somewhere scummy!

Brownstone

Tonight was the first night Gabriel could feel the stinging air of the winter coming on. Fall was losing its annual battle with the slushy, sharply cold winter. It had been a bit of an Indian summer through most of September, sunny days of summertime dragging into the abrupt fall and giving plenty of people cause to stay out later and enjoy some decent weather while it was still around. New York was famously unforgiving in the winters; more locals had told Gabe than he could count.

The cold would keep people inside. Of course, the Bowery was near-empty after dusk, unlike some other parts of the city, lately due to the fear of death and dismemberment coursing through the collective consciousness of arguably the grimiest neighborhood in the city.

A slightly inebriated Gabriel Marshall walked toward the little part of town not far from the skirts of the Bowery, which he had been focusing on in his hunt for a new dwelling; Gabe could see little Halloween decorations in many of the windows looming above the street: little paper bats, small gourds and pumpkins. The occasional cheap plastic decorative light, glowing orange as if to whisper *All Hallows Eve approaches, ye be ready!*

As a child, Gabe had loved Halloween far more than other holidays. It was so exciting to dress up and try and be something else, whatever ghoul or goblin that may be. His mother had crafted him a pretty fancy costume at one point, using burlap bags and tattered coveralls to transform him into something of a scarecrow. One particularly stormy October thirty-first, when he was still in grade school and doing quite well in his studies, Gabe's mother let him choose his costume; he insisted on being a frightful and gory spirit from the beyond. She argued that ghosts are never bloodied, but Gabe held her to her promise. Begrudgingly, Mother had applied a cake of five-and-dime women's makeup on his face to give him a ghastly pallor, then finished the look with some raspberry preserves dutifully applied. His pals from school had been left awestruck when they saw his impressive costume compared to theirs.

Now, as he walked in the cold October air, he smiled, recalling how silly those schoolboys looked in little white ghostly sheets and sailor uniforms and that one quiet boy named Theodore who insisted he was dressed as President Woodrow Wilson. Teddy was just wearing his church clothes, but who was Gabe to judge much less care? He was a *ghoul,* and he haunted his school admirably that day. That was until the homeroom teacher shrieked at seeing Gabe's raspberry-bloodied mouth and shouted, "Go wash it off immediately, Gabriel!"

He felt nostalgic at the thought of seeing children wandering around, knocking on the doors of their neighbors in hopes of getting some sort of candy or sweet, though just as often, it was a little cheap plastic toy. In the better neighborhoods, folks might hand out lithographed tin wind-ups of robots and cars, but not here. The windchill bit at his face and neck as he walked, but his long coat was plenty warm, and the booze he had been enjoying with Harold certainly helped.

Planning his route was straightforward. All of the apartment ads he was interested in were within about eight blocks of each other, so he knew he would start with the closest and his night at the furthest. Unless, of course, he fell in love with one along the way and had cause to stop the hunt.

The first building was quaint, six stories tall and half as wide. It looked like, at one point, it had been converted from an old warehouse, square-shouldered with plain windows. He walked up the steps and peered into the doorway, where the lobby was glowing and casting its light out onto the street. The floors of the place were relatively clean, but the paint was peeling off of the walls. As he surveyed the tired accouterments of the entryway, he saw a cockroach skitter across the floor inside and make its way between the elevator doors.

Absolutely not, no, thank you! I need a well-maintained place. Gonna draw the line at roaches and vermin!

And that was that. He turned on his heel and made his

way a block north to the following listing address. As he came to the cross street where he should find the address he was seeking, he noticed a stench wafting in the air. He peered down a narrow alley on the west side of the block and saw no less than twenty grimy, lidless garbage cans that were overflowing with bags of rubbish. He knew that stink. It was the backdoor of a restaurant, and the smell of rotting food was borderline nauseating. He walked away from the alley and rounded the corner, finding that the offending smell was following him. He stood in front of the double doors marked with a nicely polished bronze 9-2-6 above the doors, and while the building looked to be relatively clean and well-positioned in the neighborhood, he could still smell that stench.

Next time I'm around, I might check again, but for tonight, that's definitely off the list. I can't imagine nobody has complained about such a reek! He griped to himself, quickly heading down the street to the east in hopes that he could escape the smell. *Worse than the harbor at low tide, for chrissakes...*

Shoulders shrugged to keep his neck a bit warmer, and his hands stepped deeply into his pockets; he heard a commotion up the block that he recognized well. As he got closer, he saw a fellow step out the doorway and to the curb. The man lit a cigarette as he stretched his arm skyward, catching a bit of fresh air that couldn't be found inside the bar he had just exited. Closely overhead, a wrought iron frame held a hanging sign that was swaying gently in the cool night breeze. *Murphy's* was painted on the sign next to a cartoonish wooden barrel. Gabe knew he had found a little place to catch one last stiff drink before he continued his mission.

Thirty minutes and two dollars later, Gabe found himself standing on the same curb and stretching his arms to the sky in the same fashion as the man he had seen earlier. Now he understood why; that little bar had the most uncomfortable damn stools! No matter, Gabe was a trooper, and he wasn't going to let a sore ass stop him on this evening. As he stretched and yawned, Gabe leaned on a lamppost and nearly slipped off the curb. Catching himself from mid-stumble, he laughed aloud at the state he was in.

"Get a grip, you damn lush. There's work to do...' he chided himself, his words echoing from across the street as he continued, 'And you've already had too many."

"No such thing!" A voice offered from behind him. He turned to face whomever it was contradicting his commentary.

"What's your problem, pal? You don't know a man has limits?" He asked the chubby man leaning against the doorframe. The man had earlier been seated next to Gabe for a drink, and they'd been chatting about Gabe's hunt for a good place to live.

The man spat a toothpick on the ground and shrugged before folding his arms to stave off the chill.

"I don't like to put limits on myself. D'you?" He asked Gabe with a smirk.

"Suppose not." Gabe was half-serious.

"Well, man up and take a sip of this; it's damn cold out here. I'm half soused, and I can't feel my toes!" The younger man retorted as he handed Gabriel a flask.

"We're at a bar, and you bring that from home? You're a *true* professional!" Gabriel assured him, patting him on the shoulder and taking a swig of the man's flask. It was warm from having been in the man's pocket, a cheap bourbon with too much sweetness.

"What can I say? Not much else to do in this part of town, and nobody's waiting for me at home."

Gabriel handed back the flask and buttoned his collar up against the cold.

"I could say the same, but I'm aiming to fix that like I was telling you inside."

The man tucked away the flask and grabbed the door handle, leaving Gabe with the words, "Then go fix it, and come back and buy me a drink sometime, neighbor!" before ducking back inside the bar.

Gabe chortled at the idea of hunting down this lush and repaying his debt over a bar top. He pulled out the little folded newspaper broadsheet from his pocket and double-checked the following address. Now smiling and feeling plenty warm, he headed north, where he knew there was a brownstone offering a third-floor apartment with a fair rent, which might be just right for them.

Within a block, he could feel himself swaying just a bit. *Dammit, Gabe, you've gotta cut back a bit.* He regretted taking the drink from the flask, knowing that he had just about hit his limit.

You're gonna sleep like the dead tonight, old man.

As he arrived at the address circled in the paper, he could see that the building was a gem. A warm red brick facade with clean white windows and trim, planter boxes out front growing a thick ivy that crawled up the front of the building serenely. He stood there with his fists on his hips, looking up and surveying. He counted the floors upward, one-two-three. The third floor would be most likely split between two apartments judging by the balconies, and the streetside apartments had a lovely wooden-railed balcony that hung over the street. That was rare in this city owing to fire escapes becoming law, and he knew how much he would like having the balcony. He thought about how much Lindy might enjoy a balcony, a place where she could grow potted plants or hang the delicates after a wash… maybe even sit a spell on those warm summer nights and enjoy seeing the stars.

His fists still planted on his hips, he turned around and found himself facing a small park that had been built in the middle of this city block. Edged in rosebushes and picket fence, there was green grass covering much of the ground along with a small and very inviting gazebo. It looked very much like the gazebo he had woken up in recently. He shook the thought and focused on looking at the charming little street he was standing on, feeling a smile on his cheeks as he thought of how pleasant it would be to call a place like this home. It was clear this neighborhood was one of the nicer ones; he wondered if there would be children playing on the grass when the weather allowed.

This is it, Gabe. This is the place. I don't think Lindy could turn down living in such a beautiful spot.

He tucked his hands back in his pockets and nodded to himself, knowing that he would be calling the building's proprietor first thing in the morning. Inside his pocket and in his left hand, he could feel that folded-up newspaper sheet. He withdrew it and saw that he had only visited three of the five apartments circled. With a raised eyebrow, he looked around and saw that the streets were quiet. Up the block, he saw the taillights of a sedan puttering away but the neighborhood was still and calm, a mist in the air. He withdrew his pocket watch and saw that it was nearly eleven at night.

Gabe walked along in the dark, between streetlights, whistling to himself. A little trail of warm breath hung behind him.

He passed two more very well-manicured streets, one of which was a park similar to the one he had just been to. However, this block didn't have quite the same charm, and there were no balconies on it. He was sure he was already heading away from the most perfect place, but he soldiered on. He held a smirk on his chilly face, and he felt plenty tipsy.

This is the last place tonight, old man. You need your rest.

As he crossed the street and arrived at his fourth survey of the night, he stopped before he arrived at the adjacent sidewalk; Gabe knew immediately that this place would simply not be suitable. This particular apartment building was situated above a row of boutique shops and an inviting-looking liquor and tobacco shop. Behind him, a taxicab rumbled past and beeped its horn, telling him to get out of the street. He paid no mind.

Gabe had decided early on in his time in New York that he didn't want to end up in a building that was mixed-use as it wouldn't have the same homestead feel as a place that was strictly neighbors and families. Besides, this building had no balconies. Worse, the apartment was listed as a first-floor apartment, but he could tell that meant it was a basement apartment with high windows; he could see them peeking out at street level underneath the shops, which, in his opinion, should really be considered the first floor. He could also see up the street there was a good amount of neon signage and some chase lights, and he knew he was at the very edge of the neighborhood before it became blocks of businesses and bars again.

No thanks, I don't want to spend my days listening to the stomping feet of a thousand customers... and I'm not living in a damn basement like a bridge troll.

He grumbled to himself as he crossed out that ad on his folded newspaper with a small pencil. He stuffed the paper and pencil back into his coat pocket and brought out the little pocket guide map to find the quickest route home. The closest streetlamp gave him just enough light to see the little map. He put one foot up on the curb to steady himself. He could feel the booze taking its toll on him and making him mildly unsteady on his feet.

Just then, he heard a wail that startled him enough that he dropped his pocket guide. He turned, expecting to see a taxi cab 'laying on the horn' at him for foolishly standing in the streets. Behind him, the street was empty, and grumbling to himself, he picked up the little booklet from the street. It was damp and gritty from the water settled in the gutter.

"Shit!" He barked out loud, miffed that he would have to track down another pocket guide.

Noisy neighborhood...

Almost in reply to his cursing, he heard another shrill cry echo across the block. This time, not enthralled in his little map, he recognized the sound—a yelp, an outcry. It sounded like an animal in pain, like a coyote with its foot in a trap.

With gritted teeth, Gabe stuffed the wet booklet into his pocket and stepped onto the curb, looking around for some sign of where the sound had come from. His fists were clenched. He could feel his heartbeat quicken in his neck, and his face flushed with adrenaline from excitement.

Not tonight; I'm in no state to fight... He thought to himself, head still swiveling, hoping to suss out where the cries had originated. See no obvious answer, he knew what he had to do. He slipped his right hand into the pocket of his trench coat where the revolver still hung heavy. He started pacing down the left side of the street, walking as quietly as he could. He was almost on his tiptoes. The street was relatively narrow, an old neighborhood. He wasn't far from the edge of the neighborhood and only a few blocks from the water, so he knew that there might be unsavory sorts skulking around any corner at this time of night.

As he made his way around the far end of the building, he paused at the corner. He peeked around the brick wall and saw a clear street. There didn't appear to be anyone down that direction, and not a single sound to follow could be heard.

He turned around and began walking in the direction he came, wanting to check around the next corner. A blue pickup truck ambled down the road past him, but there was a commercial logo on the door and the driver looked to be a dour-faced old man who paid Gabe little mind. Gabe's right hand was still in his pocket, clutched around the cold metal of that damned Nazi firearm. He'd forgotten to pack it away when he arrived home, though he'd been meaning to for nearly a week.

Lucky for me, I guess.

There were several stairwells placed sparsely down the front of the building, walk-downs into the apartments set halfway below street level. As he passed them, he glanced down and saw nothing unusual at the bottom of any of the stairwells—old newspapers, trash bins, nothing suspicious.

In the air came the sound of a faint clattering echoed from nearby. He could hear it better in his right ear as he faced the building, and now he had a direction. It sounded like it had come from less than a block away!

Gabe hurried now, his footsteps louder and his breathing heavier. Reaching the end of the block, he paused with his back to the wall, the corner of the building just a foot to his left. He withdrew the revolver and clasped his hands around the butt of the gun, thumb on the hammer. He was perfectly prepared to use it. A little voice in his head reminded him *you haven't fired a weapon in a long time. Steady. Be steady.*

Taking a deep breath and trying his best to steel his nerves, he could smell the booze on his breath. He shut his eyes tightly for a moment to clear his vision, and when he opened them, he took one broad step left and swung around the corner, aiming the pistol down the street. He stopped there, perfectly still. There was nobody to be seen; the street was desolate. It was also relatively short; he could see the dead-end at a warehouse less than two blocks up. Flickering lights hanging over a loading dock, nothing moving.

Steel up, Gabe. You didn't imagine it!

Gabe reassured himself as he lowered the pistol, still gripping it with both hands. He paced down the side of the building, staying close and pausing at each doorway. Looking around and back over his shoulder, he hoped he was still alone on the street. His nerves were vibrating, and he felt his hands shaking ever so slightly.

When he reached nearly the end of the block, he could see he was utterly alone and in absolute silence—just a drunk wandering around the streets with a pistol.

Goddammit, Gabe, maybe you're just imagining things. Put the damn gun away before you make a fool of yourself.

He felt hot and sweated from sheer excitement. The cool night air was a reprieve, so he slipped off his trench coat and tossed it over the railing near where he stood.

Breathing heavily and feeling like a fool, he slipped the revolver into his pants pocket and turned around to face the building. With a deep sigh, Gabe leaned forward with his forearms on that stairwell railing, hanging his head and breathing deeply to help calm his nerves. Again, he closed his eyes tightly, trying to clear out the haze that had been left by too much whiskey.

When he opened them, he looked down into the concrete stairwell. Ten feet below, at the bottom of the stairs, he saw something that made his stomach tie itself into a Windsor knot. His hands clenched like vices on the railing where he had been leaning.

Below him lay a thin man in a dark suit, splayed out on his back with his coat wide open. The man's white dress shirt had become almost entirely drenched in red, mostly torn away where a mix of blood and flesh and gore pooled in his chest and neck. More minor wounds and gashes covered his stomach and face. The man's eyes were wide open and searching, the dim light of the doorway lamp shining amber across his terrified face and twinkling in the glistening blood that was flowing from his torso, pooling underneath him like the wings of some fallen seraphim.

Gabriel leaped over the railing and onto the stairs, scrambling down the remaining half-dozen steps where he reached the bottom and fell to his knees aside the fallen man. He grabbed the man's coat lapels and lifted this poor, broken soul off the cold cement, putting one arm underneath and bringing the man up onto his lap. His knees and shins were soaking in the blood this man had lost.

"Help!" Gabriel shouted as loud as he could. Not a soul answered his cries.

"HELP!" He shouted again, using every bit of power he had in his lungs and feeling his throat crack hoarse as he screamed.

Nobody heard, or nobody cared. Nobody came to aid.

The man's eyes were still wide open but unfocused, his head lolling back though he tried to raise it. Gabriel could see some life in them, so he put a hand behind the man's head and lifted it gently, bringing them face-to-face. Blood was flowing heavily from broken arteries, soaking into Gabe's shirtsleeves. The sounds of weak, wet breath bubbled out of the man's mouth. He was nearly still.

"You're okay, pal. You're okay... I'll get you some help..." he whispered to the man as a desperate and weak gurgle of breath found its way out of a mouth that was drawn tight in a silent shriek. This man was going to die, and Gabe knew it.

In those moments as he held this man, memories came clawing back to haunt Gabe. Memories of holding soldiers in their last breaths, memories of carrying the dead or sometimes just the pieces of them, to be identified and accounted for. Gabriel felt supremely helpless as he felt the cold overtaking the body of this man whose eyes flicked about in panic.

DO something! The voice in Gabriel's head shouted, *DO SOMETHING!*

With no other recourse, Gabriel reached into his pocket and withdrew the gun, his blood-soaked hand clenched tightly around its stock. He raised above his head and fired it into the air, three shots.

BANG

BANG

BANG

In that confined stairwell, the sound was deafening and set his ears ringing immediately. He didn't care.

He dropped the revolver and lifted the man's head once more, looking into those reddened and teary eyes, knowing that his efforts would be of little use. As he rocked the man's limp body back and forth gently, he could only promise the truth. His truth.

"I'm going to find him, don't you worry. I'm going to find the bastard, and I'm going to do him worse, pal. Just stay with me, help is coming..."

As the words left Gabe's lips and hung in the air, the gravely injured man's pupils dilated widely just as the last gurgle of breath squeaked out of his slack-open mouth. In seconds, the body became perfectly still as the spark in the eyes went out, and the husk violently shuddered once before voiding its filth onto the chilly cement.

In the distance, Gabriel heard panicked shouts of people out on the street and footsteps. In the distance, sirens. They would find him soon. He knew he had done the right thing, but now, as he lay in this pool of blood and flesh and pain, all he could think about was his man, Parker, lost to the same horrors as this unlucky sap going cold in his arms.

He hung his head as he closed his eyes and wept over the form of this man he never knew but deeply mourned.

Change of Pace

"Have you any idea what sort of trouble you could be in right now, buddy?"

Gabe looked at the face of his interrogator, but he did not respond. The clock on the wall behind the man said it was nearly five o'clock in the morning.

"You may not respect me enough to answer me, but you might end up answering to the courts if you stay clammed up. Is that what you want?"

Gabe sat there in the small and fitfully cold steel chair, his hands still cuffed behind his back. The man looming over him was sneering, agitated. He had introduced himself as Detective Ralph Kearney earlier, but Gabe saw not a hint of detecting occurring in the hour they had been sitting there together.

"It's not a question of respect, sir. It's just a question of you not understanding what I've been telling you. I want to speak to Mullally. That's all."

Gabe's retort seemed to raise Detective Kearney's ire further.

"There's *nothing* that old codger is going to do for you that I can't! I read the statement you gave to the patrolmen who brought you in here, and it just doesn't make any god-damned sense. So start making sense, or I'll toss you in a cell and lose the key!"

Gabe shuffled in his chair, trying to keep the chill off his spine. The tattered clothes they loaned him when they let him clean up were not worth much to stave off what must've been a measly fifty degrees in that room. Exhausted, Gabe had lost his patience with being treated as some sort of suspect for the crime of trying to help a dying man.

"Every word of it is true, whether you like it or not. I don't live my life to fit your narrative, Detective. And when you speak to Sergeant Mullally, you might see that you've been treating an ally like an enemy. So, out of respect, perhaps you'll take these cuffs off of me and, for Pete's sake, give me a blanket if I'm made to stay?"

Kearney scowled at him, storming out of the room carrying the folders he had brought in. Gabe stood up out of the chair, still handcuffed behind his back. He figured pacing around the room would get his circulation going and help stave off the cold for a while. He must've been alone in that room for thirty minutes or more, just pacing. Without any sleep and nearing exhaustion, it was hard to think clearly.

There's no evidence against you, can't be... you're innocent. They must be getting desperate over all of this. Hell, what are the odds a photographer would show up before those officers could clear people from the scene? Took a couple with me in 'em. It must look queer as hell. I sure hope they don't publish that crap in the paper; people are scared enough... but what if I mistook... no, there's nothing against me but the gunfire... drank too much, can still taste that goddamn flask of bottom-shelf booze...

He was in the far corner of the room, still pacing, when he heard the creak of the door behind him. He turned to see Detective Kearney throw a cheap woolen blanket across the room onto the table and slam the door, leaving Gabriel alone once again.

Christ, he looks worked up. How the hell am I supposed to put on a blanket with my hands behind my back? Shit. I should've asked for a cup of coffee.

Snickering at being waited on by such an inhospitable host, he walked over to the table and grabbed the blanket to drape over the chair, even though his wrists were cuffed. He sat down in the chair and leaned his head back, staring at the musty, stained ceiling plaster. He could see the duct that should have been blowing heat, but it was taped shut.

Better get out of here soon... I still have that picnic date... I'm absolutely beat.

The door creaked again, and Gabriel rolled his head to one side to meet his eyes with a man he respected—and, in this situation, a man he hoped would be a savior. Mullally stood there in the doorway, two cups of coffee balanced in one hand and a set of keys in the other.

"Good to see you, Sarge. I'm thinking I'd like the keys before the coffee?" Gabe offered, leaning forward and rattling the cold steel manacles on his wrists.

"I can oblige you with both, son, but in return, I'm going to need more cooperation than you gave my detective. Prick though he may be."

Gabe nodded solemnly and stood up, turning around so Mullally could reach his cuffs with those keys.

"I think we can oblige each other, sir. So long as you take me as an honest man, I've been telling the truth since the moment those patrolmen arrived and yanked me out of that stairwell."

Removing the shackles and patting Gabe on the shoulder, Mullally pointed at the coffees on the table and took a seat even before Gabe did. With a long, deep sigh, the Sergeant folded his arms and tilted his head slightly, his body language seeming more concerned parent than leathery old copper.

"You fired three rounds from a goddamn revolver, not caring who you struck?"

"The only thing I might've hit was a rooftop pigeon, sir. Besides, low-velocity munitions don't drop with enough force to do any real harm. I would've fired S-O-S like they trained us if I'd had nine rounds!"

Gabe was joking, and Mullally grunted at the stupidity.

"Glad you didn't, Gabriel; we can't lose that many pigeons."

Gabe nearly spit out a mouthful of coffee at that one.

"Did they tell you everything I said? Did they take my full statement? This is all just a case of..."

"Wrong place at the wrong time, I know, son. I don't doubt it, and I don't have any reason to. If you were the crazed lunatic running around making mincemeat of folks, you wouldn't be firing off emergency signals with what appears to be a German infantry-issued revolver. No, you're the crazed lunatic running around with the German infantry-issued revolver, trying to take on the criminal element in between house hunting and drinking what appears to be enough whiskey to kill your average farming mule."

He was deadpan and serious. Gabe wasn't sure how to respond, so he simply shrugged and took a sip of coffee.

"Gabriel, I want you to know two things. Firstly, I want

you to know that I am keenly aware that you are trying to help. Despite that, you're not helping. Not at this point. Secondly, I want you to know that I spoke to Cameron Mason a few days back, and he and I had a very candid conversation about what sort of man you are."

Christ. I don't want anybody else involved, much less Cam. He's been through enough...

Trying to be humble, Gabe asked, "What did Cam Mason have to say, Sarge?"

"Just what I thought he might. That you're a good man, that you were a hell of a soldier. But most importantly, you've had some troubles. He told me about the time you spent as a prisoner of the Germans over there, and he told me about the time you spent recuperating. Six months bedridden is no laughing matter, son. That's how much time he told me you spent getting your head back on straight. Is that true?"

The old man was leaning forward now, hands cupped around the hot coffee in that cold room. Gabriel formulated an answer as he slipped the blanket up over his shoulders, swigging the last of his coffee. On an empty stomach, he could feel it going down to the pit of his belly. It was the only comfort he had right now.

"I won't lie to you, sir, and neither did Staff Sergeant Mason. Sure, I had a rough time over there; a lot of men came back worse off than me. Far more men *never* came back. I suppose I should count my blessings on that. But that's behind me; it's been behind me for a long time. I would hope that by now you can see that."

Mullally slowly sipped his coffee and ruminated over Gabe's response. Gabe stayed quiet, remembering that old saying: *never volunteer anything.*

"You know that I can't have a vigilante running around trying to solve murders. My superiors leaned on me to hang this goddamned case around your neck, but I told them what-for. It doesn't change the fact that I can't have a civilian wandering the streets looking for trouble. Sure, that works for Jimmy Cagney, but that's not real life. Real life is knowing that if I let you carry on the way you have been, I might as well be sending you to an early grave. This isn't the war, son. It's time to give that up. You understand?"

Gabe nodded but didn't say anything. *I wasn't looking for trouble, but I sure didn't run either...*

"This means you're going to go home, get some sleep, and when you wake up, you're going to put on your shoes and go see your lady friend so you can focus on that new life. You find that apartment, work your steady job, and build something for yourself, whether that be here or elsewhere. No more playing detective, not here and not anywhere. Tell me you understand, Marshall."

The old man's stern face informed Gabe he had better say yes. He glanced at the clock and saw that it was getting past six in the morning, and all he could think of was counting sheep and seeing that wonderful girl. He looked down at his hands and saw there was blood caked underneath his fingernails.

"Sir, I understand. It was never my intention to get in the way, and it's certainly not my intention to get killed. You've seen the last of me, not that I didn't enjoy helping... but I understand the situation, and you are absolutely right: I've got too much to lose. I'm sorry for causing so much trouble."

Mullally's face relaxed from a grimace into what could almost be described as a smile.

"Oh hell, Marshall... I *know* you were just trying to help. If you weren't so keen, that man might have died alone down there. Instead, you gave the poor sap some comfort in his final moments. In my opinion, that counts for something. I've seen enough death in this godforsaken city to be able to value kindness. Of course, these murders leaving the boundaries of Bowery is bad news for the Mayor, but... that's not your concern now, Gabe. You'll be a damn fine *civilian*. Let us do our *jobs*."

"So I'm free to go to?" Gabe asked, shivers running down his spine as the warmth of the coffee wore off.

"Mister Marshall, you are free to go. I only have one question."

Gabe raised an eyebrow, pensive as to what the question may be.

"That revolver, you brought that back from the war? Those collar pins. I assume it all means something to you?"

Gabe was relieved at the simple question, an easy answer.

"Yes, sir. Just... I suppose they are just reminders of a different life. Things I left behind."

"Different life. Good. Not the *civilian* life. I'm going to give it all back to you on one condition. You've got to promise me you will pack that crap away. It's not appropriate for you to be carrying that weapon around; I *should* confiscate it and have it crushed. You file down the firing pin and put it in a cigar box or toss it in the goddamned Hudson River. Are we clear?"

Gabe knew that Mullally was right, though, for some reason, he felt a strange connection to that pistol he'd picked up out of the grass where Parker took his last breath. It was born from one of his darkest memories, but it also reminded him of the power he had. Of the war he'd helped win. Of taking the power of an enemy and turning it against them. It was quite a gesture on Mullally's part, and Gabe wasn't going to look this gift horse in the mouth.

"I've got a place for it, sir, somewhere safe."

"Good, then it's settled. Get out of this damn icebox. Go home, put your head down. Don't think I haven't enjoyed our conversations, Gabriel. Perhaps we'll meet again under better circumstances. I would see you out, but I've got a lot of work on my plate. Check with Harris out front; he's got your belongings. Turn left, end of the hall, and make the last right. Take care of yourself, young man."

Mullally stood up halfway to shake Gabe's hand before sitting down and opening up the folder he had brought in.

Gabe shook his hand vigorously, offering, "Sure, Sarge, another time..." before draping the blanket over the back of the chair and heading out into the hallway.

He's right, whether I like it or not. Too much to lose. I can't see getting involved further than I already have. I have priorities, and my top priority is waiting for me to take her on a perfect picnic. Hell, I need some sleep.

In short order, Officer Harris had retrieved Gabe's trench coat and wallet from an evidence locker. Gabriel slipped on the coat and found in the left front pocket a still-damp pocket guide. In the right front were the revolver and the pins. Gabe looked to Harris, who gave him a knowing look and tipped the brim of his uniform hat before returning to his post at the lobby podium.

Gabe took the hint and headed out the front doors, exhausted but not really minding the walk home. He felt a bit foolish in the spare clothes they had given him, but he didn't care if he never saw his other slacks and shirt again. Those stains might wash out, but the memories never would.

I'm not going to get enough rest to make that date. Better call the little lady and let her know I can't make it. Not how I wanted to spend my weekend... I should be having a cup of joe and heading out to sign a rental—damned idiot.

His tired mind churned up the image of that pale, stricken face of the man he had tried to save.

That poor bastard. What was he doing out in that part of town? He didn't look like the sort who could handle himself in a scrap. Sure, it ruined my night, but somebody ruined his worse. Dammit, Gabe! Shut that out of your head. You did everything you could, and the only person to blame is whoever was wielding that knife. Whoever tore him open like a butcher. That's not your business anymore, you heard Mullally. You gave your word.

He was serious, now fully intent on moving on with things.

Hell, you should have asked one of those patrolmen for a ride home.

He brooded over the whole ugly situation as he fought off the morning chill. Fifteen minutes later, he had made the walk home, his feet aching in wet shoes with no socks. Having washed the blood and mess off his shoes in the sink at the precinct after booking, there had been no good way to dry them. As he practically limped into his building, he saw the lobby was empty; he was thankful for that. He went to the corner booth and picked up the phone, dialing Lindy's home number, which he had memorized. It rang four times before it was answered.

"Eklund residence?" the voice of what Gabe assumed to be Lindy's father came across, the underlying tone asking, "Why are you ringing this early?"

"It's Gabe Marshall, sir. Let me apologize for calling this early; I know it's an inconvenience, to say the least. I assume this is Lindy's father speaking?"

"It certainly is, yes. Philip Ecklund speaking. You sound tired, young man. Is everything all right?" her father asked with genuine concern.

"I'm going to be just fine, sir, but it seems... I had plans with your daughter for a picnic today, and I'm afraid I won't be in any condition to make that date. Would you give her my apologies?"

Her father chuckled into the receiver, and his tone softened.

"Gabe, the little ladies are still asleep, and there's no hurry. I'm happy to pass along your message when my daughter is awake... will you be recovered by this evening?"

"I can't imagine I wouldn't be, sir; I just need some shuteye. Had a bit of bad news last night, and I won't be good company in this state."

"Well, now, you rest up, but I expect to see you here at six sharp. Pearl has a fine meal planned, and I would like you to join us if you're up to it."

Taken by surprise, Gabe had no choice but to accept the invitation.

"That would be nice, sir. I haven't had a home-cooked meal in a while. I'll see you this evening. Shall I bring anything?"

"Flowers. Women love apologies, Gabe, but they prefer apologies with flowers."

"Thank you, and please give Lindy my regards?"

"You can be sure that I will, young man."

With that, Lindy's father had set the receiver down. Exhausted and feeling a bit bemused, Gabe shuffled up to his room, mumbling to himself about it.

"Well, how do you like that? Stood up his daughter, and he asks me over for supper..."

With a scoff, he hung his trench coat on the rack and kicked off his shoes. He was asleep before the cool side of the pillow warmed to his face.

Petunias

"Ma'am, I apologize for the ignorance, but I have no idea what I'm looking for. I'm not much for plants..."

Gabe leaned forward, hands on his hips, trying to make out tiny handwritten words.

"You're not familiar with arrangements? If I had a nickel for every time I heard that, why... I'd have enough money to stop selling flowers! And *then* where would you be?"

The clerk at the florist shop was rosy-cheeked and zoftig, with the smile of a longtime friend. Her demeanor was warm and upbeat.

"I haven't bought flowers since I was a twig of a boy asking the red-headed girl down the block to the square dance, ma'am. It cost me a week's allowance, and that was a dime. Familiar, I am *not*!" He replied with a sheepish grin.

Handing Gabe a delicate white flower to smell, the clerk waved away the invisible notion of his embarrassment.

"I know that look. I see it often. Fresh flowers and live plants make a wonderful addition to your home... unless this is for a special someone?"

She winked, and Gabe thought of that red-pigtailed girl whose name he couldn't recall so many years later. However, he did remember getting his toes stepped on during the dance and the distinct image of the girl up-chucking spaghetti on the hayride on account of too much apple cider. Her parents had picked her up early, whereupon Gabe went to play baseball in his dress attire, ruining what his mother called 'your second-best pair of trousers!'... quite the memorable evening.

"They're for the only person in my life who deserves

flowers. I was a real mook and canceled plans. I figure I need something sweet, not like funeral or wedding flowers."

Empathizing with his situation, nodding with one hand over her heart, she clucked her tongue and looked over a number of bouquets. In little time, Gabe was holding a lovely arrangement of satin-bulbed pastel blossoms wrapped at the stems in crepe paper.

"Life happens, sweetie. You just stay kind and do your best. I know she'll love them! Any lady would."

Gabe paid her and left the change she gave him lying on the counter. With a reassuring and gentle grasp of his forearm, the woman bid him farewell, slipped him a business card for the next occasion, and sent him on his way just as the sunset turned golden-orange behind the city skyline.

Petunias and gardenias, huh? Smells like sunshine...

Gabe couldn't stop himself sniffing the bouquet as he walked toward Lindy's neighborhood. He'd had just enough rest and stale afternoon corner-store coffee to get on his feet. He hadn't shaved but hoped he'd be forgiven.

I sure hope this isn't an ambush, but maybe I deserve a berating for being so irresponsible. No, her pops sounded like a kind sort, and from Lindy's stories, her mother might be a saint. I think I'll be just fine.

~~~

Feeling confident as he arrived at the door to the Eklund home in the somewhat colonial-style apartment building, Gabe paused and ran a comb through his hair before tucking his shirt in a bit better than it had been. Wearing a genuine smile, he rapt the doorframe with his knuckles, *knock... knock-knock... knock.* It was the way his father used to knock on his bedroom door at dinnertime, playful and upbeat.

In short order, the door swung open wide, and standing before him was his favorite girl.

"Babydoll, I..." he lost his words as he held up the flowers for her, still standing out in the hallway.

Lindy was poised with her hip to one side, folding her arms across the white apron and yellow dress. In her hand was a spatula. The steamy smell of salted pasta at a boil was in the air. She grimaced at him, raising an eyebrow. Gabe handed her the flowers.

"I know I mussed it up..."

She relented with her grimace as an adorable smirk
~~~

tugged at her cheek; he had to refrain from reaching out and pinching it.

"Those are *beautiful*, Gabe. You look like a cat dragged you in!" Lindy insisted as she grabbed him by the lapel and gently pulled him forward into the foyer.

"It's a new fashion, don't you know? Boxcar hobo, it's all the rage in Hollywood..." he joked as she set the flowers on the little side table near the door.

"We're not in Hollywood, but I'll forgive you if you stir that pot."

He slipped off his coat and hung it on the hall tree, following her into the kitchen past the foyer. She kissed him on the cheek and handed him her spatula.

"Where are your folks?" Gabe asked as he stirred the noodles. Lindy stood beside him, tending to the sauce and seasoning it as it simmered.

"They're on the balcony with a glass of wine, and I think they're discussing my father's retirement."

"Oh? That's fine news, I suppose."

"You would think so, but they want to move to Florida!' she grumbled, 'It's too hot there. Nothing but orange groves and fishing."

"I didn't know your father fished; that sounds relaxing!"

Lindy stopped stirring her pot and turned to Gabe, poking him in the ribs.

"He doesn't fish. That's the silliest part. He's never fished a day in his life! I think he'll die of boredom before old age gets him."

Gabe rested his spatula on the oven and turned to her.

"What if I want to retire someday, somewhere quiet? I could teach you to fish, we could get a little boat and-"

She cut him off with a soft kiss, much more warm and lingering than in the foyer, before reminding him tonight was a challenge in itself.

"Let's worry about tonight before we make any plans to grow old together. How about that? You've got *two* people to impress, and you didn't even shave?"

He was embracing her around her waist and holding her closely, chuckling at her teasing.

"Not three people? Does that mean you really forgive me?" He prodded back.

Lindy ran her palms delicately across his stubble, then draped her arms around his neck.

"Oh, there's really nothing to forgive, big guy. I've gotten stood up before, but you calling at dawn and pestering my father was sweet of you. The flowers are worth a few points to boot..."

The pasta began to boil over.

"I'd better get back to stirring, and I can't make a good impression with burned pasta. I'll cash in those points later, Babydoll." He said with a wink.

Gabe set the table as Lindy cooked, and as food neared perfection, he went and retrieved her parents from the balcony.

"Enjoying the night air, folks? You'll have to forgive me; I should have come and greeted you when I arrived!"

Lindy's father, a silver-haired, very wise-looking man, snickered audibly. He reached out and grasped Gabe's hand with a stout grip.

"Philip Ecklund, Gabriel. My wife, Pearl. You've got your priorities straight, and we don't stand on tradition. Is Lindy all set in the kitchen?"

Gabe shrugged and nodded, thumbing toward the dining room, "She's a natural, and everything in that kitchen smells fan-*tastic!*"

"Gabriel, you're too kind!' Pearl exclaimed as she clasped Gabe's hand; 'nice to finally meet you. I suppose you'd better get used to good eating; my daughter knows every recipe I've ever tried and *then* some!"

Gabe took Pearl by the hand and walked her to the table, replying, "Honest, that's not the only reason I came tonight..."

Philip, sipping his wine to the last while still leaning back on the balcony railing, nodded and chided him, "Better keep those reasons *decent*, young man!"

Gabe laughed at the ribbing and excused himself to check on Lindy in the kitchen. She sent him back with wine glasses for the table. After Gabe set the fresh stemware down, Pearl side-hugged him and sized him up.

"You look like an ironworker! Now you fix trains, is that right?"

"Funny, you're nearly spot on! I worked in steel stamping when I got to the city, in fact, until very recently—heavy work, back-breaking if you're not careful. Suppose I do play with trains now, even made a few pals in the railyard. Good folks there, decent pay."

She nodded and glanced toward her daughter. "Honest work for an honest man; my Lindy has a keen eye for good stock. I noticed the flowers, by the by. A lovely choice!"

"You're too kind, ma'am!" He blushed a shade just as Lindy's father came in from the balcony and joined them near the dinner table.

"I'm certainly glad you could join us, Gabriel, all things considered..."

Something was hiding behind what Philip said, an intonation in his words, but Gabe couldn't place it.

"I appreciate the invitation more than I can say. Lindy has told me plenty about you both, and I've been looking forward to making your acquaintance."

Pearl smacked her husband on the arm playfully. "You hear that? He *wanted* to meet us! Now that's a gentleman. Gabriel, you're in luck. My little Belinda really has done wonders with the family recipes, you'll see. I'm practically embarrassed to cook at this point!"

"Can't wait! Anyway, I am sure I'd love your cooking just fine. I'm not much use in the kitchen." Gabe reassured Pearl as he pulled out her chair.

Lindy called out in retort from the kitchen, "Lies! Now sit yourselves down and pour me a glass of red; dinner is served!" as she sauntered out, balancing a piping-hot basket of bread and a large bowl of pasta.

The three took their seats as Lindy set the dishes down in the center of the table, returning to the kitchen for the sauce that Gabe had earlier poured into a porcelain serving dish.

Lindy filled each plate with pasta, bread, and freshly grated cheese. Philip filled each glass nearly to the brim with chianti before Pearl asked them all to bow their heads in thanks for the meal. It wasn't religious, but it felt spiritual to Gabe; the prayer was silent, and Gabe was thankful for that.

Philip broke the silence first. "All right, kids, eat up. The weather is going cold, and we could all use a little more insulation!" As he patted his stomach.

Pearl chimed in, "Save room for cake! Betty Crocker, don't you know. Wait until you try my frosting!"

Lindy had a mouthful of pasta already, but she locked

eyes with Gabe, so he gave her a subtle look as if to say *I love them already*. She smiled and nodded and placed a second piece of butter- and garlic-smattered bread onto his plate.

"Now, Gabe, tell us a bit more about yourself?" Pearl asked, raising her glass toward him and spilling a bit on the tablecloth with little concern.

"Oh, I'm a short story myself, ma'am. My father, a builder and a farm supply man, settled in a quiet spot back in Montana to stake our claim after the first war. He was an east-coast expatriate and always talked about Philadelphia and Chicago, but we rarely left Montana for more than a long drive. It was a small town, and I loved it, but I was mighty restless to see more. Ended up in the service."

Laughing, Philip butted in. "I've been to Montana; I remember that. It took me two days to cross that state, but that was before they paved the main roads... bruised my tailbone in that rickety Henry Ford clunker."

Gabe nodded with a grin and took a swig of wine before continuing.

"Well, I took a flight out of there as soon as I was old enough... I heard the war drums beating. Made my way to Europe after not too long. Heck of a mess over there; I served four years. I only came home because we beat the bast-... I mean to say, the *Axis*."

Pearl chuckled at his catching himself. "Oh, you can say it, Gabriel. Bastards, the lot of them!"

"*Mother*!' Lindy chided in disbelief, 'We have company!" She was feigning offense, only teasing.

Gabe continued, "Well, there's a lot of words we could use, but they're just losers anyway. I heard New York had a heck of a parade to celebrate the victory... thirteen thousand soldiers and every sort of festive float they could muster, up and down the length of the city. I missed the festivities, but I caught the radio broadcast while I was away."

In a graying memory, Gabe recalled lying in a hospital gurney and staring at the ceiling, the punchy radio announcer talking listeners through what a spectacle New York's victory parade was. He could recall the weight of a book tented on his chest. A tattered, well-worn print of Margaret Mitchell's 'Gone with the Wind'. He'd always hated how that book ended. Right now, he wondered if anyone felt the same after reading it.

Damn stubborn southerners...

Lindy's father chimed in, "Say, I took the ladies to that parade, Gabe! They threw more confetti on that day than I don't know what. Such a celebration. Shut half the city down, and the troops were parading tanks down the boulevards. Tanks!"

"I believe it. Bread?" Gabe offered the basket, and everyone took more for their plate.

"I never served. It seems you're a brave soul. It's men like you who saved the American way of life. I truly believe that." Philip raised his glass now, and Gabe joined in.

"Thank you, sir, just doing my part same as the rest of 'em. I'm glad to be home, anyway. New York isn't so bad." Gabe said, eyes on Lindy.

"Well, whatever you do, don't leave for greener pastures before you try my cake!" Pearl joked with a wagging finger.

Gabe changed the subject, "Speaking of a change of scenery, I heard the two of you might be looking toward Florida."

He ate more pasta while Philip and Pearl told their sides of it. The spaghetti was perfect, the noodles soft but slightly chewy. The red sauce was thick and not vinegary, not like those cheap restaurants that cut it with too much. Lindy had taken the time to season each plate as she had served, a fresh sprig of green herb sitting on top like the star on a Christmas tree.

Philip set in with a candid tone, "My wife tells me she would be happier someplace warm. I love this city, but it certainly has changed over time. Not what it used to be, and I don't think I like where it's headed."

"Philip retired at just the right time, and we could go just about anywhere. I simply can't see heading to the West Coast; we don't know anybody there. I've been to Boston once before; that place is awful! The streets are confusing!"

Gabe nodded and agreed, "I can't think of anything Boston might offer better than New York."

Pearl swigged some wine and continued, "Of course, we have several friends in Florida between Tampa and Daytona... they're really doing quite a lot of construction out that way. I hear they don't get snow! I can live with the rain, but I would love to get out of the snow. How about your family, Gabriel? Are they still in Montana?"

"Only in spirit, ma'am. I'm the last of my family."

Philip engaged the somber moment to ask after them.

"Tell me about your family, Gabriel. Do you take after

your father?"

Gabe had just eaten a bite of bread spread thick with butter and sprinkled with salt. He smiled as he chewed through it, which gave him a moment to compose the words.

"I suppose I do, in work ethic and backbone. He was a good man, a great father. Kind and compassionate but honest above all else. My mother would say how he was a bit of a ruffian in his youth, but I know she was embellishing a bit. Mom was delightful, herself. She did her best to keep me in line when Pop was away... patience of a saint. Not that I was a ruffian myself, but strong-willed. That's what she called me.' He looked down at his dish before smirking and continuing, 'Great cook, for the most part. There was one incident with chicken seasoned with anise seed... I'm thankful to this day Uncle Robert had potatoes and meatloaf in the icebox when none of us could take more than two bites! I swear..."

Pearl blurted out, "Anise? Like a *licorice candy*? Tsk... licorice chicken... I suppose I could try it with one of my recipes..." Philip pantomimed, gagging. Lindy smacked her father mockingly on the arm for being crude.

Lindy stood up and served another heap of pasta on everyone's near-empty plates, replete with that perfectly tangy red sauce and another sprig of garnish. "You all need to eat up. I made too much spaghetti, and there's simply no room in the refrigerator! Gabe, why don't you tell us about your travels in Europe? Had you seen anything strange and wonderful over there?"

Little lady, you have no idea... Gabe mused to himself.

Her father butted in, "We would love to hear about that, Gabriel. I've got plans to take this lovely lady on a vacation there,' he patted Pearl's arm and winked to her, 'once things have settled down a bit and they fix all the bridges. From what I hear, it's quite affordable to travel there right now. Not that I'm a cheapskate, but I've got to start saving if I want to buy my boat!"

"You deserve a boat, sir!' Gabe assured him, "though there are plenty of places across the pond, as they say, which were unaffected by the destruction. To be honest, even during the war and right up until the end, I saw some awe-inspiring things. Rolling hills covered in bright green moss and grass, forests older than Camelot. Mountains in Italy that seemed to jut up from the earth and scrape the belly of the clouds, the sheerest and most jaw-dropping formations. A friend of mine, a good friend, was deployed for a brief time near

Istanbul. He told me they have a natural splendor to those places that simply can't be described. And the trains, they sound like just about the best trains in the world. The Orient Express... *that's* the one."

Pearl was enthralled, exclaiming, "Philip, if you go back to teaching, perhaps you could find work over there! We could live in luxury—yes, I think that's a fine plan!"

Lindy butted in, "Well if you move across the world, you might never see your daughter again!"

Smirking, Pearl shot back, "Oh, I think you'll have your hands busy, my dear. I don't think you would even notice we were gone!" and she nodded to Gabriel, causing Lindy to blush and sink into her chair a noticeable amount.

It was all so much fun; Gabe had never seen such love in a family, let alone such a sense of humor. His face was nearly sore from smiling and laughing for the better part of an hour. The half-after-seven chimes sounded on the grandfather clock in the living room, and Pearl stood up with a flourish.

"Well, it's time for cake! Lindy, would you help me layer the cake and get the frosting just so?"

Lindy stood up with her mother, squeezed Gabe on the shoulder, and began clearing the plates. Philip was mulling over the wine swirling around the bottom of his glass.

"The ladies will be a few minutes, and they do a real number on cake decorating. Pearl won a prize for it once, in fact. I waited three days to eat that cake, and by then, it was bone *dry*! Tragedy, to be sure. Care to join me on the balcony for a bit, Gabriel?"

Gabe finished the last sip in his glass and stood with the old man.

"I'd love a little fresh air. Haven't laughed this much in a while, sir."

They went out and closed the door behind them. Philip had a newspaper tucked under his arm.

Lindy's father leaned over the railing a bit, looking out over the quiet street. Gabe leaned on the railing, peeking back to watch the ladies work in the kitchen through the little serving window that faced the dining and living rooms.

Family dinners are going to put some pounds on me...

"Gabriel, may I ask a difficult question and insist you give me an honest answer? Seeing as I've got a bit invested in you, what with Lindy... ah, you know."

"Certainly, sir, anything less would be disrespectful." Gabe was a bit off-put, not knowing what Lindy's father had in mind. Regardless, being in this man's home and having pure intentions with the man's daughter, Gabe intended to give an earnest answer no matter the question.

Philip sighed and turned to Gabe as he unfurled the newspaper. He handed it over with a dour expression.

Looking down at that newspaper in the dim light, Gabe squinted to make out the photo and text. A pit sank into his stomach like a punch in the gut.

The photo was a reporter's flash photo of the stairwell where Gabe had been less than a day before. In the center frame, under a white cloth drape, was a form of the man Gabe had held, gurgling and spasming as his last breaths were taken in that dank cement pit.

The bastards didn't even have the sense to put a black bar over the poor guy...

Gabe looked up to Philip, and his mouth opened to speak, but no words came out.

"Son, there's a mention of the only witness being a Bowery resident, reported as anonymous...' Philip pointed to a line in the newspaper article, 'so long as you don't know anyone with the initials G.M."

Gabe was silent, wholly unprepared to have such a conversation.

"Perhaps someone named G.M. who had a keenly bad night, bad enough to cancel a date with the woman he loves. But a good enough man to call, a good enough man to make good on his appointments and bring some damn pretty flowers. But a man wrapped up in a tragedy, nonetheless."

There was a silence between the two of them, and Philip's eyes were clear and piercing as he spoke to Gabe.

"Lindy told me you've been talking to the police about those murders in the papers, that you had known one of the victims. We strive to be understanding parents, and for that, our daughter tells us damn near everything."

"Sir, please let me-" Gabe stammered.

"Gabriel, I'm old enough to be a little wise. I know how you care for my daughter. I can see the way you look at each other. She comes home every night and tells us about her day, but the only time she smiles is when your name is part of it. She's keen on you, Gabriel, like her mother and I haven't seen before. Heaven knows this city is a mess. It'll chew you up and spit you out, and I well know that sometimes bad things happen to good folk. Lindy told us about your little lobby attendant, all of this sadness."

With a heavy breath, Gabe looked to the horizon and saw only concrete and dim lights. He couldn't leave all the talking to the old man.

"They certainly do, sir. I've no intention of being any further part of that mess, no matter how poor my luck has been. I was only speaking to the police because I wanted to help, and in a way, perhaps I did. But that's done; I'm out of it."

He glanced back inside where laughter and sweet voices carried on in the kitchen. Lindy's joyous laughter was unmistakable.

"I've got more important things to care for, and I recognize it, sir."

"Then I'm going to make a suggestion, young man. And you'd better heed my advice on experience alone."

Gabe nodded, saying nothing.

"Get the hell out of town for a couple of days. Take that whip-smart little daughter of mine somewhere nice and work on building something. I made the mistake of gallivanting around in my youth, taking too long to get serious with Lindy's mother. She wouldn't tell you this, but the first time I asked her to marry me?"

Philip paused, and Gabe nodded as if to ask what happened next.

"She turned me away, and she was *right* to. I wasn't ready. Too much boozing around and tussling with a bad sort. I was on the wrong course, and I nearly missed out on everything I have now."

"What changed her mind, sir?"

"I had to show her I gave all that up, *all* of it."

Gabe swallowed the lump in his throat. The interrogation wasn't the cause, no. It was the idea of losing Lindy.

"I was in the wrong place at the wrong time, mister Eklund. A few times. I didn't know what else to do." The words were true, despite the fact that Gabe had become involved so profoundly by his actions and will.

"You turn around, Gabriel, and you walk away from

trouble. You can be a man of action, or you can build something greater with someone who deserves your full attention."

"I want that, sir. I want to make a good life, and Lindy is the best thing that's happened to me."

"Hell, I know that Gabriel! She's one of a kind, much like her mother. All I want is for her to have safety, kindness, and comfort. She needs a *good* man, not a dead man. Not a soldier."

Taking his time to answer, Gabe leaned over the railing and breathed deeply. The cold, wet air coming off the water stung his lungs a bit, but it cleared the mist from his eyes.

He's gonna think me soft if I carry on like this. Smart old sonofa...

"You're right, sir... in every way. I intend to show you and Lindy that I'm committed to that."

"Good, because you may be built like a damn brick chimney, but I'll kick your ass from here to New Jersey if you don't, Gabriel Marshall. That's a promise."

Chuckling at his own words, Philip patted Gabe on the shoulder. Gabe turned to see he was grinning. It was reassuring.

"I keep my promises as well, sir.' Gabe reached out and shook his hand, clasping it firmly, '...always."

"Then we understand each other. Get rid of that paper, and let's get some damn cake... and call me Phil if you like."

As they made their way inside, Pearl had just set clean plates and forks at each seat. Lindy was right behind her, carrying a perfectly frosted cake that looked like it had come from a catalog. The white sugar frosting was smooth as satin and perfectly trimmed with little chocolate florets. The whole thing rested on a white lace paper doily.

Now, all Gabriel could see was this vision of beauty standing there, holding a silken frosted cake that could have been drawn down from the sweet dreams of a chubby child. His heart wished somehow he could save this very moment, not just as a memory but *tangibly*. He forgot the weight of the conversation he'd been having with Philip. He knew that living a moment in perpetuity wasn't possible, but he also felt that if he weren't a complete fool, he would do whatever it takes to have more moments like this in the future. There was only one way that would work.

"Say, aren't you a sight?" he asked her sweetly.

She winked at him as she set the cake down on the table,

"You're talking to the dessert, aren't you?"

"You could bake a thousand cakes, and none of them could ever be sweeter than you, Babydoll."

She gave him a sharp look as if to say, *"My parents are right here; don't be so sappy!"*

Gabriel would not be dissuaded. "Hard as you work, I believe you could use a vacation."

"I have never met a person who couldn't use a vacation, Gab! Now get over here and help me cut this monstrosity."

She extended a hand and the butt of a serving knife, nodding toward the cake that must have been eight inches tall. Gabe took the knife but paused and used his free hand to clasp hers. He stepped closer to her, looking deep into her eyes.

"Now I'm serious, little lady. What do you say, just the two of us? Niagara Falls, while the weather holds out. A real getaway."

Sheepishly, she squeezed his hand and nodded yes.

"Well, I suppose that would be just perfect, Mister Marshall,' she half-whispered, 'I haven't been out of the city in far too long."

"Then it's settled!' He turned to the room, calling upon Pearl and Philip, 'Places, everybody, places. I'll handle the cake."

As Gabe cut and served the slice of soft, satiny white cake to each plate at the table, Philip nodded and raised his glass to Gabe ever-so-subtly.

The men spent most of the dessert listening intently as Pearl shared a few fun stories about her youth. Recalling wistfully, she told of the summer she spent at a family home outside of Buffalo, not far from Niagara Falls.

"It was the most enchanting place, provided you had a mild summer. A few years were sweltering, and a few years were nothing but storms. But in between, I enjoyed many summers that were simply to die for. My uncle and his daughters would join us. They were a year ahead and behind me. We found every little nook and cranny of the forest to the north of their cabin. There was the moonlight that would light the path *so* brightly, and we would wander through the brush and take little round stones out of the streams. I do wish the family had kept the property; I would have loved for Lindy to spend her summers in the same way. Fate and fortune did not allow, but I suppose that's just life, isn't it?"

Philip leaned over and gently kissed Lindy's mother on the cheek while Gabe nodded in agreement and shared his experience of being young in a very rural place.

"Nothing like spending time in nature. I'm not sure who came up with the idea of cities, but they must have been one surly cus!' Gabe chimed in, 'Not to say I haven't found things worth appreciating here, but there's nothing like grabbing a thermos of cocoa and taking a cool morning walk out to a watering hole where you just *know* you'll pull out something worth cooking. My father helped me build a tree fort once... those woods were eventually made Bureau of Forestry land, but back then, it was just *land*. We never really ran out of space the way they did here in New York. I remember my father having the damnedest time climbing up the ladder of that treehouse; it was just scraps of wood nailed into the side of a tree. He did his best."

"I'm so sorry they're not around anymore, your folks... it's never easy.' Pearl consoled him, 'My parents were wonderful people; sadly, they never had the opportunity to meet Philip, nor their beautiful granddaughter."

Lindy finished a sip of wine and sought to lighten the mood, "Beautiful? I didn't know I had a sister!"

"Hey now!" her father interrupted with a grin. You're the most beautiful daughter I've ever had!"

"If I keep eating this cake, I'm going to be the most *bountiful* daughter you've ever had!" Lindy exclaimed as she shoved her plate away, still smattered with morsels of cake and frosting. She patted her tummy and winked at Gabriel, who reached out and grabbed the plate.

"I might not get another desert like this for a while, so I'd better finish that!"

The teasing continued as the cake disappeared from all their plates, and glasses were refilled once or twice before the grandfather clock chimed ten. Lindy was the first to get up from the table, insisting, "I had better clean up and get to bed soon. The diner will be busy. Mondays are bad, and cold days are worse!"

Gabriel helped her round up dishes and took to washing them while Lindy put away the rest of the pasta into the refrigerator. The fridge was stout in shape and colored perfectly avocado-green, and Gabriel thought about his time at Carter machine and all of the massive machinery painted *that same damn color! Not in my kitchen, no sir!*

A kiss at the door signaled the end of the evening, and Lindy asked Gabriel to visit her in the morning.

"No time, little lady. I've got some overtime to work this week, and you might not see hide nor hair of me for a few days."

"Does this have something to do with our little getaway?" Lindy asked, tugging at his necktie.

"Sometimes, Lindy, I am reminded that you are too smart for me."

She kissed him once more and poked him in the chest. "You're a fool. I adore you."

After a lingering kiss on her forehead and a squeeze of her hand, Gabe departed.

Big Plans

Monday, October 28th

Gabe knew all the yard foremen had a standing policy: overtime was always available... but it was usually muck work. The smelliest, filthiest jobs included clearing caboose latrine blockages, unpacking sludge-filled axle bearings, and pressure-cleaning oily fats from a tank car being pulled out of dairy service. That was the penance for working overtime, and it kept many of the boys in the yard from abusing such an open policy.

Gabe had gone to work on this day off to pick up some of that work. He'd done so much overtime the prior week that the scheduling clerk took him off the schedule for Monday, but here he was. On this morning, so far, Gabe had been relatively lucky. One of the switching locomotives had run over a dog in the street days earlier. Blood and gore spattered up one of the running boards, and there was fur and gristle entangled in the siderods, twisted around it like a barber pole. With a grimace, Gabe blasted that mess with a high-pressure water hose until there was no more animal stuck to the locomotive's underpinnings. He had to wash it twenty feet down the gravel until it sloughed down into a gutter.

Damn cur! What sort of fool creature doesn't hear a locomotive coming? Gabe grumbled to himself ironically as he tried to avoid splashback from that hose and all the muck.

He had arrived at seven in the morning and planned on working till seven at night, so long as there was more muck work to be done.

Around nine o'clock, he took a short break and hoofed it back over to the office, where he used one of the phones to make a call over to Art's Diner. The phone rang once.

"Art! Gabe Marshall calling."

"My best customer! It's hot in here, Gabe, and the grill's loaded... need me to get Lindy?" he offered kindly but with a touch of straightforwardness that was common for Art. Gabe knew plenty well how busy the diner could be.

"No, sir, just need to bend your ear for a moment."

"S'long as you make it quick, young man."

"Hoping to take your best worker for a bit of a getaway. Friday to Sunday. I apologize for the short notice and all, but is there any way that could be arranged, sir?"

There was a long pause, and Gabriel worried that he had asked too large a favor as he heard the receiver set down. He could hear Art working the grill over the phone, that long metal spatula clanging against that giant iron cooktop. Food was sizzling audibly. Then he heard the sound of Lindy's voice, giving Art a new order, to which Art responded with "going down!" which meant he was putting the food on the grill. After a few moments, Art came back to the receiver.

"You're in luck, young man. My niece is in town for a few weeks before her next semester upstate, and I'm sure she can pick up the slack. You make your plans; just have her back for Monday's opening shift.

"It's a promise, Art. Thank you kindly!"

Art set the receiver on the hook. Quite satisfied, Gabe returned to the yard and got to work replacing some busted ladder rungs on a boxcar built to haul automobile parts.

When the lunch whistle blew, Gabe didn't bother changing out of his heavy boots and filthy coveralls. He had just enough time to make the four-block walk to a travel agency he had found in the office phonebook. As he arrived he found the place empty save for one smiling lady working behind the counter. She looked so professional standing in front of a six-foot-tall wall of brochures, pamphlets, and advertisements for all the latest getaways.

"Here to see about the weekend of Niagara Falls, miss. Have you got any literature?"

"We certainly do, sir. Take a look over here; I've got just what you need!"

She reached over and plucked a brochure off the shelf. It looked like an oil painting: a beautiful, massive log cabin-style lodge perched just atop the sweeping plumes of water and mist, a picture-perfect imagining of Niagara Falls. With a nod, Gabe unfurled it on the counter.

"Looks to be quite the destination, don't you think?" He asked the girl.

With a shrug, she answered honestly as he could have wanted.

"I think they all look enticing, but I've never left the city myself."

"Ma'am, you've got to take the opportunity if it ever arises. I've got any number of reasons to leave the city, and only one good reason to stay. She's the reason I'm planning this trip, in fact!"

The clerk looked Gabriel over, his grease-spattered clothes and gritty working man's hands.

"Well, I'm certain that's one trip you are bound to enjoy. My boss goes there frequently, on his way to Canada for hunting. In fact, he stays at that hotel so often that we have a special discount package. Two nights, train tickets, and a room for two, with a ferryboat tour at the base of the falls. I'm told it's breathtaking!"

Gabe looked over the brochure and saw no prices.

"Can I afford it?"

"I would imagine so; it's a bit off-season, which does wonders for the rates!" She seemed genuinely excited for him. Clicking a ballpoint pen, she leaned over and wrote the price right there on his brochure.

"Sixty-five dollars, that's not so bad!" He remarked, still looking over beautiful pictures in the brochure. It was steep, but travel was never cheap.

"I would imagine so, considering the prices of everything if you bought them separately. If you ask me, they make their money on all the additional things. Dining, show tickets, all of that. It's not more than a day trip anyway, as the sleeper cars tend to be a bit more costly..."

Gabe mulled over the cost as well as his plans for the week. As he folded the pamphlet back on its creases, he started to thank the young lady and head back to work.

"Aren't you going to book your trip, sir? You wouldn't want to miss out!"

"Quite the salesperson, I see...' he teased her politely, 'can you do any better for a working stiff?"

"I suppose I could take five dollars off if you were to book today, Mister..."

"Marshall. Gabe Marshall."

"Let me call ahead and check rooms?" She already had her hand on the phone.

This gal's a sales whiz! He mused, resting an elbow on the counter.

"Sure thing, miss, I've got a few minutes."

As she made her call, he looked over a few more of the brochures for the different railroads that could take a person from a cold, hard city out into the country, out into beauty and lush green landscapes: the Milwaukee Road, Pennsylvania Railroad. Great Northern Railway, The Union Pacific. Each of the trains sped toward some unknown adventure and off the cover of its respective pamphlet. The colors were bright, flashes of yellow and red everywhere. At that moment, Gabriel wished he had a job or some purpose that could allow him to take all of those wonderful passenger trains to their furthest destinations.

Maybe if I ever leave the city for good, I will find a way to pack a suitcase with the little lady and see more of this world.

"Sir, they have a small number of rooms available through next week. Just tell me the dates, and I will make your arrangements!"

In a short few minutes, she had everything handled. The train schedule, names for the tickets, and even helping Gabe pick out a room with the best view at the Chateau Niagara. The way this gal pronounced it was eloquent. He placed a deposit on the trip with the money he had in his pocket, and he was to return one of the next few days with the rest of the payment. It was all in order, and she even gave him a handwritten itinerary in a nice ticket envelope with the herald of the New York Central Railroad on the front. He was over the moon with excitement by the time he left office, finding himself striding down the sidewalk and back to work with his chin up.

Stopping to grab a paper-wrapped sandwich from the deli up the block as he rushed back to make the end of lunch whistle, all he could think was *she's going to have the time of her life. I'm going to make sure of it.*

The rest of the day, he barely paid attention to the time passing. Mindless work, such as boring out and replacing rivets and painting new steel grab irons, gave him plenty of time to imagine how he could make the trip more perfect.

* * *

~~~

Tuesday came and went in a blur. Gabe had spent the day stripping and repainting a short brown transfer caboose that had been flaking and peeling away in the sun for what looked like decades. Gabe's only reprieve was running up the street on lunch once again and giving that kind sales girl the remaining forty-seven dollars for the trip. He'd stashed almost four hundred dollars in his room at this point between overtime and a moderate withdrawal from his longtime savings; good money to get them started in a new place.

By the time 6 o'clock rolled around, he had put in a solid ten hours of hard work, and his arms felt like limp noodles. Before leaving he confirmed that he was blocked off the schedule for the weekend. The scheduler marked him 'unavailable' Friday through Sunday, and Cecilia at the lobby desk promised Gabe plenty more muck work time-and-a-half the following week if he'd take it. "Maybe, but I might be tied up with moving. Let's see how it looks come Tuesday?" It struck him that he hadn't yet followed up on that sweet apartment after the rough evening he'd had on Saturday. He made his way home past the corner store, buying two cold beers and some yellow cheese and bread. It wasn't much, but he wanted to save most of his dollars for the weekend.

~~~

Gabe awoke with a solid plan on Wednesday, getting to work at six-thirty in the morning so he could take his leave earlier. He hoped to view that brownstone apartment if it were still available. He'd worn a good suit with his aim set on making an impression after work, changing into his coveralls in the locker room. The job this morning was replacing a busted engineer-side window frame on a switcher locomotive, easy enough work. When the break whistle blew, he made his way back to the yard office and took to the hallway phone, thankful he had remembered to bring that little folded-up section of the newspaper with the advertisements for all of those apartments he had been checking. He rang up the phone number attached to the little rectangular blurb for that particular rental.

"Mack here." The voice at the other end of the phone offered.

"Hello, sir. My name is Gabriel Marshall. I'm interested in that apartment I saw listed last week."

"What, the little efficiency on fourth?"

"No sir, the Brownstone past the park, up on the third floor. I suppose you've got several to let?"

"You bet I do, too many. I still got the brownstone, too; the last couple of looky-lous couldn't find the deposit; one was shifty. You're not shifty, are ya, son?"

"No sir, straight-laced as can be. And I'm set to make that deposit if it's half as pretty inside as out. I would like to come and view the place... perhaps this evening?"

The voice on the phone paused, then answered. "Of course! Come on by. I've got some plans I can change. Six o'clock? Bring a deposit. It was one hundred and five dollars. A hundred and five, no less, and forty-eight every month after that. Utilities included, for now. The price could be lower, but there are furnishings there, and we ain't in a rough stretch like the Bowery. Lots of competition, prices going up everywhere but that shithole."

You have NO idea, Mack.

Not wanting to volunteer anything that might stifle his efforts, Gabe kept his current residency to himself.

"I'm square with all of that, sir. I'll be there at six without fail; thank you for making time for me!"

Gabe was nearly hopping with excitement, but he tried to remain calm on the phone.

"Sure, pal, it's a good place. I'll be on the stoop. I cut the hedges every week. See you then!"

Just as Gabe hung up the receiver, he felt a hand on his shoulder. He spun around and met Harold's gaze, who appeared rather worn.

"Hey pal, hope it's all right I used the phone?"

Harry chuckled and waved the idea away.

"Last I checked, you work here, don't you?"

Gabe shrugged and laughed at himself, offering, "Suppose I work a little, sure."

"Listen, big guy, let's grab a pint tonight. Hit the Dagger?"

Gabe missed his outings with his friend, but he knew he had more important things to attend to.

"Can't, sorry! Big week! I've got someplace to be tonight;

how about tomorrow? I'm outta here Friday, so I'll be okay for a night out! Five o'clock on the steps?"

Harry's face lit up at the proposition.

"You bet, Gabe!" With a wave goodbye, Harry headed back toward his office at the other end of the building.

The next few hours seemed to drag on. Tedious work, Gabe had been tasked to fix one of the roof hatches for the ice bunker on a refrigerator car. Somebody, either clumsy or careless, had dropped a several-hundred-pound chunk of ice onto an open hatch door, which smashed the hinge and ruined the sealing flange. It was practically flapping in the breeze, as much as a fifty-pound roof hatch could.

Gabe sat on the roof and hammered away at the sheet metal until it closed well enough to be sent to the shed. After that, a new hinge would be installed by one of the older yard workers, Kieran, whose specialty was hot-riveting. Gabe cursed having to wait so long to leave, but he was also a bit thankful for having something to keep him occupied until he could see what he was convinced may very well be his respectable new home.

A street that nice and a view like that, the place has got to be something. I wonder what sort of furnishings he meant? Old dresser? Lumpy bed? Hell, if it's got two chairs and a front door, I'm happy. Lindy can help me shop for anything else we need if she says yes...

Six o'clock, the sun was setting, and Gabe was walking up to the address he had already memorized. He'd been practically wringing his hands on the ferry, his feet aching from the hurried walk. As he approached, he saw an older man in loose, too-big slacks belted at the ribcage, just hacking away at the bushes in the planter box next to the entryway. The old garden shears made a squeaky snip-snip noise as he worked.

"Hello, Mack?" Gabe asked.

The old man turned around, stood up straight, and tossed the garden shears into the soft dirt.

"Sometimes, it depends on who's asking! Gabriel, I'd assume?"

"Yes, sir, but my friends call me Gabe. I'm sure glad you were able to meet. I've got some travel plans this weekend.

"Hope it's somewhere pleasant, son. This damn city continues to surprise me in a bad way."

Gabe knew it was better to play dumb, but an educated

guess was that Mack had been referring to the unfortunate business just a few blocks away the previous weekend—the business Gabe had promised to stay away from for good.

"I suppose maybe that's just the way the city is now, but I'm not going anywhere!"

"That's good to hear; my last renter was coming up on ten years in this place. Nice lady, real quiet. She went out west to retire with her grandkids, and she left a few pieces of furniture. Quality stuff, if you like antiques."

"I love them, sir. They don't sell anything at Sears Roebuck that's better than good old hardwood."

With a grin, Mack waved Gabriel to follow him, and they proceeded inside to view the apartment. As they continued up the stairs, Mack shared a little about the building.

"It's quiet here; I've got a few teachers and only one family. Schools in the area are said to be better than some. Oh, and Pritchard adjacent to you on the third floor has a piano, but he only plays on the weekends, and he's not half bad." Mack opened the front door, and they stepped into a slightly dusty but cheerfully well-lit little apartment. The sky outside was blue-purple, and Gabe went straight to the windows.

"Piano? Sounds relaxing!" Gabe quipped as he stepped out onto the small patio. Mack stood inside, arms folded, tilting his head back and inspecting some small paint cracks on the ceiling.

"Yessir, nice lady. She was here so long, didn't need to paint the place recently. I'd be sure to get on that this weekend, should I find the right tenant. Somebody stable."

Mack tapped his finger on his temple and went back to staring at the ceiling.

Gabe took a deep breath of the outside air and imagined soft piano music. From up here, he could see some dead spots on the grass of the park that spanned the middle of the block. It looked much smaller from above but still plenty lush and green, a charming reprieve from all the brick and mortar.

"Suppose I should see the rest of the place before I commit... but I can tell you stable is definitely what I intend, sir."

He walked down the narrow hallway, sunlight cheerfully beaming in through the windows of both of the bedrooms to the right. In between them was a small shared bathroom with a round stained-glass window, just enough sunlight shining through to splash the green- and yellow-tinted rays across a gleaming white tile wall. Gabe stood there for a moment, just in front of the sink, imagining his morning routine of shaving and setting his hair just right with a dash of pomade. Then he imagined looking in the mirror and seeing, in the reflection, his favorite girl behind the shower curtain in her morning routine. He wondered if she might sing in the shower; he once saw some movie starlet doing that, and he was smitten with the idea of it.

"Everything looking up to snuff, young man?" Mack called out.

As he peeked into the modest closet in the second bedroom after finding the first more than satisfactory, Gabe called back, "It's all looking fine, Mack. In fact, it's just what I'm looking for."

After he finished inspecting the little closets in the hallway and the radiators in each room, Gabe was satisfied that this place really would be just right for himself and all of his big plans. In his head, he was doing the math of the rent versus his monthly income of nearly a couple hundred dollars, muck-work overtime included.

I'm sure I can afford the place; it would sure be easier with a second income, but I'm not going to worry about that yet. I haven't even asked the girl. Maybe I need this for my sanity either way. Nice place...

"Mack, I'm your man. I've got good work down at the New York Central yard across the harbor, not to mention the modest benefits the Army still sends me. It would just be myself and my lady, although I can't attest to building a family just yet. Either way, I'm your man."

He reached out and offered his prospective landlord a folded stack of bills, five twenties, and a five-dollar bill. Mack reached into his pocket and withdrew a sheet of paper, handing it to Gabe as he took the money.

"Hundred and five. This covers the deposit, sure. Rent is due starting the second month on the first day, and it's late on the third; sign the lease here, and I've got a couple of keys for you. I'll need to see your identification as well. Can't be too careful, not these days!" He chuckled a bit, but he was right.

"Mack, I grew up in a small place out west... everybody knew everyone. I know what you mean about the way life is going in the city, and I want no part of that!" With a smile, Mack patted Gabe on the back and led him over to the counter, where there was a ballpoint pen to sign that lease.

After a few more minutes of banter and a quick tour of the

building's hallways and such, they parted ways with Gabe's coat pocket gently clanging the two keys therein. He headed home straightaway; he had a call to make when he got to the lobby.

"Hello?"

"Pearl! It's Gabe Marshall. Hope it's not too late to be calling?"

"Gabe, it's a quarter after eight. I have a glass of wine to finish, and the nine o'clock radio hour is *not* to be missed!" She wasn't joking; the best radio spots were usually on after bedtime for youngsters.

"Well, if it's no imposition, is Lindy-"

"She's right here, Gabriel. Goodnight!" Pearl volunteered sweetly as she handed the phone to Lindy.

"Babydoll?" he asked, talking low into the receiver so as not to disturb the folks playing cards nearby in the lobby.

"I missed you at the diner, Gabe... maybe I miss seeing you wedged into a booth. When will I see you again?"

Trying to hide his excitement, Gabe played it as cool as he could.

"How's Friday morning suit you?"

"You're in luck, Mister Marshall,' her voice coyly stern, 'I just *happen* to be free on Friday. I'm free the whole weekend, in fact! Art was insistent; he said I work too hard. So what have you got to say about that?"

"I'd say he's a wise old owl. I'd also say you should pack a suitcase..."

Anticipation

Thursday, October 31st

Harry stood in the cold sunshine, waiting on the steps at five o'clock sharp, just as promised. Gabe was two minutes late, but Harry didn't seem to care. As Gabe walked up the gravel footpath that followed the building, he could see Harry poised there in a sharp gray suit, fists on his hips. He was staring up into the sky, a smile on his face.

Gabe was wearing decent evening duds, plain slacks, and another Hawaiian shirt that he needed to launder but doubted anyone would notice. His grey windbreaker was neatly tucked under his arm for when the cold started nipping after dusk.

"Harry, what are you looking at?" Gabe asked incredulously.

The small, dapper man turned to Gabe, fists still on his hips. His collar was open, his tie was askew, and his undershirt showed. As Gabe approached, he was thoroughly amused by what he saw.

Harry's undershirt was a bright blue dime-store Superman costume, showing that herald just as in the comic books. Gabe had been so busy the whole week, he'd forgotten it was Halloween!

"Pal, you look like you could lift that locomotive over there!" Gabe clapped, applauding the silly costume. Harry's size had him looking more like a child in a Superman costume, but Gabe wasn't going to say it.

With a grin and the most vigorous handshake he could muster, Harry squeezed Gabe's sizable and rough mitt.

"I may just do that! Just imagine being so strong. *Nothing* could stop you. You could win wars single-handedly! Or maybe two-handedly. Double-fistedly, that's it! Heh. Hope you brought a thirst, big guy! Let's get going!"

They made their way up the street, walking past a few small groups of children and youths in masks and an assortment of silly costumes and capes. The cold breeze and silvery clouds in the sky meant the sun was ready to go into hiding for most of a season, and today the sun would set within the hour, forcing those kids to get home soon or face the popular punishment of a wooden spatula applied to the posterior.

Discussing work for most of the walk, Harry told Gabe that Mister Washington noticed his overtime among others, and there might be an opportunity for advancement when the yardhands' lead-man Jack Olsen retired in the coming year. Gabe listened; Harry was doing most of the talking. Really, Gabe was half-listening and imagining the trip he was about to take with Lindy. The thought put a smile on Gabe's face that Harry was responding to in kind, oblivious as yet to Gabe's getaway plans.

They reached the Crown 'N Dagger in short order, sunset falling behind the buildings across the street. The place was busy, almost packed, and noisy as hell. Harry sauntered up to the bar where the regular barmaid was working. She hardly glanced at Harry as he stood up on the foot railing, leaning over the bar close so he could be heard.

"Ma'am, I've been fighting crime all day, and I'm parched. Two pints of your darkest ale, and two of your cheapest whiskeys for me and my ugly-shirted friend!"

She looked to Gabe, shrugging nonchalantly in his gaudy Hawaiian luau shirt. She laughed and gave Harry the o-kay with her thumb and forefinger. Pints were coming. Gabe grabbed the last free table, and as he sat down, the table wobbled like a drunkard.

Guess that's why it was open.

Harry joined him with the drinks. Seeing the wobble, he folded one of the cheap cardboard Blatz Pilsner Beer coasters down to quarters, ducked down, and shoved it under the offending leg. Gabe nudged the table, and not a drop of their drinks spilled.

"Fine work, Harry!"

"Not as fine as yours, big guy. All that extra hard work? You'll be in the office with me someday if you keep it up!"

"Who says I wanna be in the office, Harry? I like my job, it suits me. Keeps me strong."

"Yeah, well, I push paperwork all day, and I'm SUPERMAN!" Harry shouted.

"That's fair,' Gabe concurred, 'I'll need a cape... a *big* one!"

Harry clinked mugs with Gabe's and took a swig.

"Say, I found myself a place, Harry. Just like I said I would!" Gabe shared, knowing Harry would be excited for him.

"What, you and Lindy gettin' hitched soon? Say it ain't so! She might not let you come out and drink with me, pal."

Harry scowled, poking Gabe in the arm.

"Harry, listen. I'm going away for the weekend, and I'm gonna ask her to be mine. Officially. I gotta make some changes, you know."

"Now that's a big step, Gabe. Yeah, you've got big stuff on the horizon. Who knows, maybe I'll be looking for a decent place myself if I can find a good reason on two legs... if you know what I mean?"

Harry motioned toward a group of pretty, clearly uninterested women sitting at a table some ten feet away, deep in discussion themselves. Gabe looked at them and thought, *I wonder if Lindy has the sort of friends for a pub night out...*

"Sure, I know what you mean, Harry. It's hard to go it alone for too long, especially in such a crazy town. I've got high hopes for you."

Just then, two more beers and two more whiskeys were set down on their tabletop, and the empty glasses cleared. Winking at the barmaid, Harry slammed his whiskey in one gulp. Gabe followed suit, not wanting to be outdone by a man half his size.

Harry excused himself to use the restroom while Gabe nursed his beer and let his shoulders relax, taking a deep breath at the thought of his girl. The notion of waking up to her face, her perfume. The warmth of sharing a bed. The comfort of sitting in a sunny room with someone, just living. Every little great thing that could come from taking such a leap... the trip seemed like a foothold into a new life. A perfect getaway weekend, new digs in a safer part of town... He had every reason to be excited.

After a few minutes of Gabe being lost in thought, his friend returned to the table, settling down with a groan.

"I tell ya, it may not seem like it, but I sure do a lot of

work there at the yard office. Not saying it's anything like the heavy stuff that you do, but that job sure does give me cause to want a good long sit at the end of every day. Say, if you got those keys and you're going to make it official with Lindy, what about a ring? Have you got a nice stone for her?"

"Matter of fact, I do. I would need to go home, back to Montana. It's a real nice ring..." The idea of going back to that little town made Gabriel a bit wistful, but he paid his feelings little mind due to the booze.

"I thought you told me everything was gone? The house, even your uncle's old church?" Harry asked, confused.

"That's all gone, sure. The only thing left of all that is the barn my pops and I built, and last I heard, that's falling over. Probably kindling by now. But the ring... After the fire, my pop couldn't stand to do anything with my mother's jewelry."

"Coulda sold it? Paid for a new DeSoto?"

"No way, Harry, that wasn't my father's way, and Robert respected that. Robert took the lot of it to be cleaned and then put it in a safe deposit box in our name. Said he paid a dozen years on it. I don't think it cost much. Small town bank, you know. I've got to go back and get it, but that's a worry for another day. If Lindy is the right gal for me, she will understand."

Harry got an amused, misplaced smile and laughed a bit to himself.

"What did I say, Harry?"

"Well, that's the perfect plan! If you take Lindy back to Montana and you get sick of her on the trip, just leave her there and come back! I'll bunk with ya, pal. That's what friends do! I bet that ring would fit me just fine."

Gabe spit up his beer while Harry gave him a silly, exaggerated wink before finishing his pint and waved over another round.

"Oh hell, you're a nut. Besides, I'm not sure if I could keep up with your drinking, Harold! Where do you keep it all?"

"Got a bladder the size of a hamster. You know that! Just goes right through. And if I'm buyin', who cares? You're a pack mule, and you'll be fine."

"Sure, sure, Harry. S'long as I get my winks, never met a bottle-ache I couldn't lick. Hell, you know what they call a hangover in Germany, Harry?"

"...Not the faintest idea, Gabe."

"A 'katzenjammer', Harry. It means *screaming cats*, as in that's what it sounds like when you're in the throes!"

"Well, I don't much care for cats, but I'll remember that! Just don't get ahead of me. Fair is fair!" Harry exclaimed as he took another break to relieve himself.

The boys continued this routine of drinks, banter, and stumbling to the porcelain for a good four hours. Harry told a few stories. He told Gabriel about how his brothers used to take him fishing in a lake not far from home. He wistfully recalled his mother's baking, how she could always find something in the cupboard, no matter how paltry, and make a meal out of it. Gabe chimed in about his own mother's baking experiments, and Harry guffawed at the idea of aniseed-seasoned chicken.

"Like licorice? That's atrocious, Gabe!"

"You're tellin' me! I swear, she ate a good bit of it with a grimace tryin' to rope us in, but she *knew* it was a swing and a miss."

"I'm sure she had some home runs, though?"

Gabe chortled, nodding his head. "Oh sure, sure. I ate well most days; maybe that's why I'm a pack mule, right?"

Harry nodded. "Glad you agree."

Harry asked about Gabe's childhood, wanting to hear every story Gabe could remember about schoolyard bullies and girls in pretty dresses at church. Gabe told a few tales, none too crude for a bar but a few that required a lean-in for propriety's sake. Harry seemed to be in great spirits by then, better than Gabe had ever seen. They'd gotten good and drunk, and it was grand.

"If I didn't know any better, Harry, I would guess that *you* were the one taking a vacation tomorrow!"

Gabe was teasing him, but it only put a bigger smile on Harold's face.

"I'm just excited for you! I made some big plans for the weekend, but I don't want to put a curse on it. I'll tell you all about it when you get back; I'm sure we will *both* have big news!"

Gabe glanced at the neon wall clock and realized he should pack it in for the night.

"Okay pal, but it's half after nine, and I'm a mess. What say we call it a night so I don't make a fool of myself on the train in the morning?"

Harry stood up and shook his hands and head like a wet

dog to clear the haze. It was ridiculous, but Harry had no shame.

"I'm not tired, big guy. How about I walk you home and we tie one more on before I get lost in your end of the city? I think I'll call out sick tomorrow and take myself a little vacation!"

Gabe had no reason to turn down the offer of one last round. He wanted to hear a bit more about Harry's weekend plans and reflected on how Harry was always just plain good company.

"Sure, that sounds like a fine idea!" Gabe offered, standing up and realizing only then that he'd had a few too many as it was.

"Great, just let me hit the pisser before we go!"

"O-kay, Superman, get at it!" Gabe ribbed him as he stepped outside.

One ferry boat ride later, the boys were walking up to Gabe's building. Harold had been hiding a glass flask of bourbon in his coat, which he'd produced a block after the bar. They'd finished the flask on the ferry ride. Gabe felt well and truly punchy, near exhausted.

"This is me, pal. Hope you find something warm to end the evening...' Gabe said, with a firm grasp on Harry's shoulder to keep from swaying, 'I shoulda quit while I was ahead!"

"Okay, Gabe. Mind if I use the loo before I wander off?" Harry pleaded, swaying a bit himself.

They went inside the dark building, creeping up the stairs quietly so as not to disturb the other folks already asleep. Gabe pointed Harry to the men's washroom and lurched back to his room. After a few minutes, Harry came knocking. Gabe's head was already on the pillow and his shoes on the floor. He grunted for Harry to come in.

"Hey pal, you sleep well, okay? Say, mind if I borrow your windbreaker? It's colder than a polar bear's left tit and it's Halloween... I don't mind if it's three sizes too big!"

Gabe didn't even open his eyes, just beckoned toward the door.

"Sure pal, on the rack under the trench coat. Don't get lost in it!"

Harry patted Gabe's shin and whispered, "G'night big guy, have a swell trip!"

Gabe didn't respond; he was out like the flicker of a Jack O'Lantern on a windy night.

Ferroequine

Friday, November 1st

Gabe's wake-up call was a neighbor tromping down the hallway stairs dragging a steamer trunk as they departed (he'd hoped they were leaving for good), was irksome enough to get him sitting upright at the edge of the bed. His alarm clock sat idly by his bed, having made no noise yet but passing the minutes with its near-imperceptible tick. It was half as silent as the pocketwatch nearby, though, and kept nowhere near as good a time. Gabe picked up that little watch by its chain, and it dangled in front of him with the morning rays bouncing off the crystal, reflecting its silvered dial and jewel-like roman numerals from within.

Dammit, Harry. I've gotta stop following you to the bottom of a bottle... he scolded himself in silence.

As the watch slowly spun on its chain, the light caught its little polished numerals, which reflected brightly across the wall, and then Gabe's roughly stubbled face. Gabe realized he'd not cleaned and polished that watch since the day he left Carter Machine, as he would leave it untouched and protected most of his day in the railyard. Nevertheless, it needed attention, and he set his mind to clean and polish it thoroughly as soon as he got back from this trip.

The moment he stood up, his head began throbbing, indeed attributed to the prior night's hours of sousing. The tautness in his legs departed after a hot shower at the end of the hall. Afterward, a few aspirin found their way into his stomach with a glass of lukewarm water from the tap in his diminutive in-room sink. He packed his bags, dressed for travel, and headed curbside for a cab.

A yellow cab came by after a short time. The motor under

the hood of the little Studebaker purred as the cab made its way to the Eklunds' building. The shades were drawn back tightly, and as Gabriel looked out the window, he could see the cheerful face of Lindy's mother Pearl smiling down upon him. She waved emphatically and left the window (assumedly to inform her daughter of the chariot's arrival).

In short order, Lindy was standing at the top of her steps. Excitedly, Gabe hopped up a few steps to her and put his hands around her waist, still standing two steps below whereupon Lindy leaned forward and kissed his forehead. He smiled up at her, and she wiped a smudge of lipstick off his face. He couldn't care less about a little smudge.

"You look tired. Let's get a bit of rest on the train ride?" she offered.

"Perhaps, but it's quite a view most of the way North... and even tuckered-out I'd be hard-pressed to choose between lookin' at you or the inside of my lids!" he joked as he pulled her closer.

Lindy, arms draped over his, squeezed his biceps and cleared her throat asking, "Well, if you want to make the train, we should get going, and I've packed light enough that I can get my bags just fine!"

She grabbed her small suitcases and trotted down the steps as Gabe opened the trunk of the cab once again. The driver was reading a paper, paying little attention. Gabe helped Lindy into the back of the car and took his seat, and then the driver returned to minding his customers as he headed for the train station.

The cab alighted them to Grand Central Terminal in good time and for reasonably few coins, but Gabe tipped too generously considering the lazy driver. In the massive and luxuriously marbled-and-gilded station, a brief pause was made to check their travel tickets with an agent and receive their proper train tickets in yet another set of stunningly decorated bifold envelopes. A stamp on the ticket and a staple in the edge binding it to the cardstock envelope were perfectly placed as the agent clearly had done these swift motions thousands of times before. Lindy shook Gabe's arm a bit and smiled like a cherub; she was genuinely excited.

It was just early enough that they had time for a quick bite. In the station, there was a lunch counter manned by smartly bow-tied and clean-cut gentlemen, their aprons nearly as clean as the spotless granite counter. Lindy ordered breakfast for them both and paid, against Gabe's insistence.

"You're old-fashioned, Gabe. I like taking care of you sometimes!' she chided him, as she shoved a piping hot breakfast sandwich into his hand, 'now eat, and we'll get a coffee on the train. I'd love to own a little deli or lunch counter someday, you know that?"

"I'll be a lousy cook, Lindy, but I'll wash the dishes better than anyone!" he smiled back, knowing she was serious about having her own business.

"You're better at making dirty dishes than washing them, I'd bet!"

He patted his stomach and laughed, "You would know!" They teased each other as they ate, finishing the food while leaning against a massive marble column. After they ate, they picked up their bags and slowly meandered through the cavernous train station on their way to the platform where their train was to depart in about thirty minutes.

"I think we're the slowest moving folks here!' Lindy exclaimed, 'Looks like everybody is in such a rush!"

Gabe nodded toward the far wall, where a couple of senior men in wool suits ambled along like two dapper turtles. They could be overheard passionately debating Roosevelt's economic policies.

"Not *quite* everyone." Gabe joked.

"Now that's not fair, Gabe... I'm sure they could outrun the both of us if they saw fit!"

They people-watched and bantered the rest of the way. There were a thousand people in that station, and each one was unique despite their plain-clothing theme of Sunday best, dark suits, or slick hair under dashing hats.

As they reached the train platform, Gabe looked toward the end of the train. He wondered if the observation tail car he'd been servicing recently might somehow be in this train. The railroad had at least a dozen such cars, so it would be a nice coincidence. Gabe remembered a rusty patch on the door frame and promised himself he'd check later to confirm his hopes.

At the train, a wiry uniformed lad loaded their two bags onto a larger cart and made sure they each kept their carry-on bags; the boy joked that they were under-packed compared to most folks before hustling off to the next group of travelers. Both of them chuckled, and Gabe was pleased that his lady might be a bit less fussy than some; he saw people boarding with three and four bags each for a nine-hour train, and he laughed to himself at the idea, wondering *how many coats could they need from those bags for such a short trip? Bible salesmen, I'd wager!* He declined to share his amusement with Lindy, for worry that she should think him cruel for mocking those folks. Little did he know, Lindy was thinking much the same thing to herself.

As they boarded the center coach, Gabe's attention was to the loading of the cafe car some dozen yards away. Three uniformed Porters, all looking sharp and perhaps in their thirties, swiftly loaded crates and bags of food up into the car. He asked Lindy to wait for a spell while he went and said 'hello.'

"Fellas, how's the day going?"

Two of the three stopped, taken aback by someone stopping to address them. That must have been unusual, he gathered by their reaction.

"Sir, it's a mighty fine morning, so far anyways. How can we help? There's a Red Cap just down the walk there..." the tallest of the three responded.

"No boys, I wanted to say hello to you! I work car restoration down in the dockside yard, other side of the Bowery. You boys know the yard?" He pulled out his wallet and showed them his New York Central Railroad Employee ID card.

They all paused from working now and nodded and grunted to indicate that they knew the yard. The shortest of the men gave a good thumbs-up and said, "My cousin Fredo works down there!"

"Well, that's great. I know Fredo! Hard worker. Loves talking sports, right? Heck, I'm just excited to take the train and wanted to wish you all a great day! The café car men who get scuttled in my yard for service are some great fellas, a real pleasure to work with."

His words ingratiated him with the trio, and the tall one smiled a beaming smile.

"Glad to hear it, sir! Where are you headed, all the way up the line?"

"We're going up to the falls, in fact. Taking a short vacation. Nothing too fancy, I suppose, but I sure am looking forward to it."

A hand extended toward his, clasping over Gabe's mitt like he were Harry. The man was a tower.

"I'm Mike; I run the kitchen up on this train. I live up near that way; it's gonna be a fine trip. November's the best month for views the upstate has to offer, you'll see. Been to the falls every year since I was a schoolboy."

Gabriel took his grip heartily and shook it like an old friend.

"Thank you and take care, gents. I'll see you on the train!" he waved goodbye, and the men waved in kind.

Gabe returned down the walkway toward the shimmering beauty that awaited him. She was standing with toes and heels touching, hands clasped in front of her demurely. She looked to him like a pastel sketch from an art-deco theater advertisement, or perhaps some spokesmodel for a cigarette brand lithely sweeping across the screen on the news hour's fast-talking advertisements. It was a sight, to be sure. Still, he knew she was no demure thing; she was a whip-smart, formidable personality, and he loved that more than her looks.

Lindy took his arm as they walked toward the loading car. "Making friends already?"

"Kindred spirits, you could say. Those boys work harder than I do!"

Smiling broadly, Lindy squeezed his arm tighter. "You're the sweetest, Gab." She was enamored at how kind Gabriel was to everyone he met, no matter what color or creed.

As pressure valves under the cars chuffed little blasts of air that teased the ankles of passersby, Gabe helped his love up onto the coach steps. He then proceeded behind her, holding her hand, with two bags under his broad arm.

Gabe's hat dropped off his head as he struggled around the sharp corner in the car's vestibule. Lindy caught the hat in mid-fall, the top of the hat in her open hand. Gabe stopped and smirked in embarrassment. She put the soft black hat on her head, tilted the brim to one side, and on her tip-toes, she leaned in and kissed him squarely on the cheek. With both hands, she grabbed the two bags from under Gabe's arm, and with a nod of her head in the direction of the car's far end, she led the way to the baggage rack. He almost blushed.

As he looked out the window, he saw another Red Cap (the railroad's famous ambassadors) coming onboard the far end of the car. While Lindy loaded her bags on the luggage racks near the vestibule, Gabe flagged down the Red Cap as the man stepped onboard.

"Good morning, pal! Can you direct me and this lovely lady to our seats?"

The man nodded and took the tickets Gabe was now holding out. After a glance, he gestured toward their seats.

"Sir, you're already in the correct car. One car back is the lounge car, a coach after that, and then the observation car."

Lindy's eyes widened; she reached out and clasped the man's hand.

"Sir, I'd be much happier seated between the observation and the lounge. I know the big lug would prefer to be closer to the bar as well. Do you think there might be a couple of good seats left on the last coach?"

The Red Cap reached into his pocket and withdrew a lovely silver pocket watch. After checking the time and glancing out at the platform, he drew a smile and clasped his hand on top of hers.

"Ma'am, er, Miss, I believe at this hour there should be at least enough seats for the pair of you."

Looking past her and up to Gabriel, the red cap added, "Maybe two seats for you, sir!" The three of them laughed at Gabe's expense, their joy echoing in the metal luggage vestibule.

"C'mon folks, just this way." Their guide walked them two cars back with a swiftness that had Gabe dancing around knees and elbows in the aisle.

The duo passed through the lounge car entirely, a few older men in a collection of gray suits and flannels sat sipping black coffee from decorated mugs, though a pair of them already had stiff drinks in shimmering crystal glasses. The sofas in that car were square yet plump, and Lindy made a mental note that she might wish to return later to investigate their comfort level.

In no time, the couple sat in a pair of well-worn but surprisingly comfortable coach seats, something like theater lounge chairs but a bit narrower. The stainless arms and sides had no real adornment save for one button, which Gabe promptly activated and found himself laid back into a nicely reclined position.

"You know Gab, for such a lovely train they sure could spruce up the insides of these things,' she pouted, 'my seat has a hole in the cushion!"

"Lindy, wait until you see the observation car. Honest, they saved all the decorations and fine crystal for the ones worth riding. Say, maybe we just relocate to a nice lounge chair there and let these seats rest for a while!"

"Maybe shortly, if you think they'll let us, sweetheart? I'd sure love a bigger view, and the fall colors are going to be quite a sight! Not to mention I don't want you to ruin some poor soul's knees with that reclining chair..."

He winked at Lindy and snickered a bit, nodding over his shoulder to the shawl-clad septuagenarian knitting in the seat behind him. He received only a dour, judging staredown in response.

Some folks have no sense of humor.

The train left the station as the pair watched the city outside begin to roll by. Lindy's eyes were wide at the scenery, and Gabe's hand clasped hers warmly as he watched with her.

"Never left the city by train before?" he asked, softly so as not to embarrass her.

"I haven't... Gabriel, I haven't left the city once since grade school. Isn't it shameful?"

"Not at all, Babydoll. Just enjoy the view, and I might get a little shuteye in the meantime." He knew he wouldn't sleep, but he leaned his head back and watched her watching the world go by.

After half an hour out of the city, neither of them broke a calm, happy silence. A conductor came through the car and punched their tickets. With a bit of banter, he assured them the view was worth a spell in the observation car, and their coach seats were no match. Gabe palmed the man two dollars, to which he responded with a gracious tip of his red cap.

Lindy's eyes were fixated on a cluster of orchards they were passing. Gabe stood up, stretching his legs a bit as he went.

"Babydoll, say we go back and see what all the fuss is about in the tail car?"

"Gabe, these seats are so surprisingly comfortable I'd totally lost track of time! Maybe it's a comfort hole..." she mockingly poked at the tear along the seat cushion upholstery.

"All right, trouble, maybe I'll fix it myself next week in the yard!" he winked and squeezed her hand before helping her stand as the train rocked.

Gathering their coats and hats, he led her back through the vestibule doors and to the observation car. As they entered the observation car, the view out the side door window came just in time to see the train fording a river on a brightly painted steel-beam bridge, its glossy shine reflecting the midmorning sun.

Nearing the end of the car, the streamlined shape of its hull became clear from inside. Two straight walls gently swept inward, with a narrow door in the rear center. The windows were nearly knee-to-ceiling, indeed why they named this the observation car. Its furnishings were decidedly art deco, and the small chattering chandeliers gave it an extra touch of finery that paled their coach car in comparison. They reached a small open space that served as the car's social lounge.

The train was moving at quite a pace, leaving the dizzying stripe of track in its wake. The mainline was almost hypnotic in its undulation and the never-ending stream of wooden cross-ties holding each band of iron rail precisely close together. As Gabe found open seats on a rear-facing sofa, Lindy just stood there swaying a bit with the train car, entranced. Gabe grasped her shoulders in a firm and loving embrace. She seemed so enthralled, Gabe silently chuckled at the thought that if they'd jumped off the train right here, it would have been enough for her. Yet, as he kissed her temple and led her to a red sofa, he could see in her face that she knew this was barely the beginning of their little getaway.

A short few minutes later, the pair had fully settled into the quiet, relatively tranquil sofa at the end of the car, facing away from the sun. Gabe had retrieved drinks and now held a highball in his hand; she had orange juice with a splash of grenadine. Their tumbler glasses rested on a small round table in front of the sofa, and the train rocked back and forth, slowly stirring their drinks. His ice clinked just a bit in the glass, quietly melodic.

With each curving sweep the train made to the West, Lindy would look out toward the head of the train and see this immense black mammoth of a locomotive chuffing out steam to a steady rhythm, a constant shaft of heat and smoke rising from its front stack. Then, her attention turned back to their observation windows. She pointed out the clouds of heating steam which the end-of-train car released, the white tufts trailed back a dozen yards hanging in the cold damp air outside like a lost spirit.

"I've never been on such a nice train, Gabe. I hate the subway. I'm not too fond of the L-trains either. Perhaps I should run a lunch counter on a train instead, we could travel all over! Would they let us live on a train, do you think?" She was half-serious judging by her countenance.

"I think if you love trains, I'll plan us a few good trips. Maybe Washington, definitely Oregon. Montana... just for a day. Oh, Wisconsin! Now *that* looks like a lovely place, and the Milwaukee Road has some damn pretty streamliners if you've ever seen those ads..."

Lindy clutched Gabe's hand tightly and reflected on a short story she had read in school some decade prior, a piece about the parallels between animals and machines. "It was like poetry, Gabe!" she insisted. With that, she recounted it for Gabe, as much as she could recall. She paraphrased, but he got the idea.

The article had made an objection to people referring, as they do, to locomotives as iron horses. The narrative was convincing, questioning the notion that such a massive, brutish machination that huffed loudly and announced its every maneuver with thunderous roar should be reflected in such a graceful, tame, and predictable animal as a horse simply because we once made use of them for similar labor.

No, the writer of that article had sternly argued, the modern and colossal steam locomotive at speed was far more akin to a bull. A raging, red-eyed, snorting, and hoof-stomping animal that was unpredictable to those unfamiliar with its ways whilst continuously assaulting headlong some tunnel, hill, or horizon. A blind man unfamiliar with the locomotive, the author had penned, would hear that commotion and the chuffs and all of the clanking groaning tonnes, and more likely believe he had walked into a bullfight rather than a pony stable.

She told him all of this, considering he might disagree or tell her she's talking silly.

"Why Lindy, I'm surprised you don't want to come work in the yard with me! Quite a convincing argument."

The car's gait matched the undulation of the rails and roadbed underneath, yawing side to side as it held its footing. The buildings and bridges gave way to a parkway and sparse trees; the bull raged on. The trees became more plentiful, and the skyline transitioned from jagged stone towers of man to rolling hills of amber and gold leaves, the bull raged on. The gently unfurling land became more rural as farms swept by faster than the eye could divide them. A howling whistle cry fading into the distance signaled that there were no more walls to echo its wail; the countryside of upstate New York became a palette of harvest colors and seasonal change. The bull raged on.

Mulling over the truth, this daisy of a girl sat and looked down at her bull's hoof. His nails were hard, his palms gritted like a working animal, and there was his stare. There was often a profound and burning passion in his eyes. He didn't speak much this day; in fact, there was a comfortable silence between them for much of the trip. Gabriel was tired, but looking in his eyes, Lindy appreciated that her bull was simply content and still.

Alpine

Hours passed, miles passed. Dozens of folks aiming to catch a good view had come and stood in the end of the observation car for a good look. For a while, there was a sweet-faced little girl in a lovely purple coat who sat on the arm of the sofa next to Lindy, and they discussed the trees, the foliage. The little girl had a sweet obsession with the owls that must live in those trees. She loved the sound they made, and she mimicked it sweetly. As the train continued its lolling stroll northward, Lindy gazed out to countless passing vistas and charming small towns framed by the railcar's broad, green-tinted glass. Hills became mountains, rails forded streams and rivers over iron railroad trestles that looked like bones of ancient things, herculean black skeletons lying still against the blue-purple sunset. The atmosphere on the train was relaxed, thanks to the ever-present Pullman Porters and their doting attendance to passengers' every need.

Eventually, a porter came round and organized dinner seating for Gabe, Lindy, and the few folks at the tail car bar stools. Dinner was a few cars up, so they gave the sofa to a kind older English chap smoking a meerschaum pipe and dutifully clutching a well-worn hardcover copy of 'The Iliad'.

Seated across from each other at a small table for dinner, Lindy caught Gabe spending more time watching her than the scenery outside, which he'd touted as being so worth attention. They'd both had the salmon, at the recommendation of their server, and enjoyed the meal with gusto.

"What do you think? Maybe half as good as Art's?" he asked, offering a mint from the little tray on the table, which a Porter had just delivered.

"I think those men you met earlier must have put some extra time into the seasoning just for us, Gabe. That was the best fish I have had in ages!"

"If you had your own place, A restaurant, I mean, would you serve something like that? All the garnish and such?"

She waved off the thought.

"Oh, you big silly man. I don't think I'll ever have my own place, and there are a thousand delis and diners in New York City. Too much competition! It would break Art's heart, anyway."

"That's true, but none of them have that one special thing that'd have the counter packed every day, Babydoll."

He pinched her cheek, and she knew he was talking about her.

"I'm just thinking, Lindy. About what you said earlier, opening a little place. Thinking about the future."

"My future?" She asked, with a curiosity in her eye that told Gabe she was thinking exactly what he was thinking.

"Our future, Lindy. Mine and yours, sure, but *ours*. I've been thinking about it a lot. Daydreaming, even. Harry told me there's promotion opportunity coming up soon at the yard, and your father gave me some words of encouragement-"

She had been unwrapping a mint from the little foil twist; interrupting him, she popped it into his mouth.

"Now don't you go trying to sweet-talk me, you big lug. You've gotten further than any man trying to make his way into my life, but I'm in no rush, and you don't have to make any promises. Let's just enjoy this time, and let the pieces fall into place."

Lifting his glass of white wine and toasting hers with gentle *tink*, swaying as the train rocked on its undulating roadbed, he winked at her and sipped the last of it.

"To the puzzle pieces, sure. I can work with that."

~~~

Under dark skies dashed with silvery clouds, the train came to rest alongside the depot at Niagara Falls New York for a solid half-hour, allowing time for its bleary-eyed patrons to make their way off the cars. Gabe held Lindy's hand as they found their way from the platform into the cozy New York Central train station, nowhere as impressive as Grand Central Station in Manhattan but charming
~~~

nonetheless. Its northern atmosphere was delightfully 'woodsy'. Fittingly, a few wool-cap hunters were in the station with their rifle bags.

It was the cusp of winter, and the weather was ideal for throwing on a plaid coat and venturing out to see the changing colors of the trees or feel the icy sting of the misty falls. A line of taxicabs awaited the disembarking train passengers.

The cab ride out of the city center was lovely. After narrow streets lined with pizzerias and clothing stores, a few strings of twinkling lights dangling over the restaurant canopies, the glowing little city opened up its narrow streets to offer its parkways to these weary travelers.

During the short jaunt to the Chalet Niagara, it struck Gabe that this was a clean and quiet little city, reminding him of much of the Midwest with its safe and folksy charm. That nasty business back in the Bowery was entirely put out of his mind for the weekend, and it felt pretty nice not to look over one's shoulder between street lamps.

The roadways were often one-way on either side, straddling swaths of lovely green lawns and benches, rows of thickly branched trees wearing the fiery and exciting colors of fall. Crisp leaves were scattered about, and benches were arranged along some of the parkways. Though they were empty, the amber light cast upon them by the nearby lampposts made it a genuinely inviting scene.

A short drive later, their taxi came to a puttering rest in front of the Chalet Niagara. A sweeping cobblestone driveway directed guests toward a covered curbside entrance. The Chalet's steeply slanted Alpine roof stood high against the shrubbery and its smaller, equally Alpine-inspired surrounding buildings. Lindy was in immediate awe; she had never traveled and never seen such a place, save in the occasional cinema date. Gabe, however, had seen buildings such as this on nearly the other side of the world. His treks across parts of Europe had enriched his appreciation for more romantic and historic architecture than most of the comparatively young American cities afforded. Now he stood before this Swiss-inspired lodge, and he was a bit impressed at the authenticity of it.

A cheerful desk attendant greeted them, swiftly checking them in and handing over the itinerary. Two more helpful bellhops offered their assistance in some local restaurants and amenities as idle chatter. This was the lap of luxury, to be sure. The desk manager came out from behind the oak countertop and greeted the couple as he handed them their room key, thanking them for their patronage.

"You're set for the night, folks. It's one of our finest suites, quite the view... perhaps not tonight, just a few city lights, but come tomorrow morning, the sunrise should take your breath away, miss!" His Canadian accent was warm and very welcoming.

After a snap of the fingers, the friendly Canadian called a bellhop over to lead them in stride upstairs via a sweeping red-and-gold carpeted stairway. The glossy burlwood rails were smooth as glass and gave a perfect glint in the light of the polished wall sconces. The bellhop opened the door to their room, turned on the light switch, and waved them in with a flourish. The crisply uniformed boy dropped their suitcases off and withdrew from the room like a shadow after earning his generous tip of a dollar.

They were alone now, in a toasty room that smelled of cedar and lavender. Two sconces' soft golden glow projected across the room.

Gabe sat down on the edge of the satin-covered bedspread, taking Lindy's hands in his and kissing them gently as she stood in front of him.

"Quite the trip... was it worth it Babydoll?"

"That's the silliest thing you've asked me to this very day, Gabriel. Don't think I would traipse across the state with just any scoundrel!"

"I guess I'm a lucky scoundrel!"

Gabe smiled up at her, and she kissed him on the forehead.

"You get yourself comfortable, big guy, I'm drawing a bath. That train was light on travelers, heavy on cigarette smoke!"

Gabe stood up and gently turned her to face him so the bed was behind her. He looked down at her sweet face, her hands still clasped in his.

"Cigar smoke, too. I'm sorry for that!" He apologized for smoking a stogie on the trip after dinner, offered by the Porter in the little bar of the observation car.

Lindy shook her hands free and poked him in the ribs.

"I don't mind in the least. I'm making a bath for us. You need it as much as I do!"

Gabe took her chin in his cupped palm, reassuring her, "We'll get to the bath, I promise."

Lindy stepped into Gabe's embrace, leaning into a kiss that endured so many minutes that neither of them cared to count. Lindy giggled nervously, interrupting the kiss but locking her gaze in his. Still embracing her around the waist, Gabe reached out toward the wall and extinguished those dim lights. Their night had only just begun.

Niagara Falls

Saturday, November 2nd

On Saturday morning, dawn had risen with ice-blue skies, and birds were happily chirping. A sound relatively unfamiliar to city dwellers, the shrill songs woke Lindy well before they rousted Gabe. She'd not heard birds very often in her neighborhood in New York, as trees were not so common, and where no trees grow, few birds nest. Dirty city pigeons don't chirp.

The sun snuck in around the curtains' edge at the balcony window, casting through the room and becoming a rainbow in the crystal water decanter on the side table. Lindy had put on the delightfully plush robe she'd found tied with a ribbon around the waist, hanging in the closet. The second robe was two sizes too small for Gabe, as he'd tried to put it on after the bath the prior evening and nearly ripped a seam in the attempt.

Her silhouette cut crisp in the bright morning sun as she opened the curtain, Lindy's shadow cast across her lover's face. He was sound asleep half-clutching a pillow that was tucked in the nook of his chin, the spot where Lindy had been nestled most of the night. His stubble was dark but graying, and she loved it. She loved how it made him look a bit like Clark Gable, his ordinarily soft cheekbones being accentuated by the start of a beard. She knew he'd think that was a silly comparison; she didn't care.

She slid the balcony door open just enough for her to step outside. The fresh air had been let into their cozy suite, and a bit of chill was biting her toes. Just as she spun on her heel to tiptoe back to the warm carpet of the room, the sleeping giant awoke and let out a yawn that could catch a thousand flies. He rubbed the sands of sleep from his eyes and turned to see her standing there in a halo of morning sun rays. He smiled and rubbed his eyes a bit more, almost aggressively. Lindy stepped back into the room, kneading her chilly toes into the plush carpet as she held onto the frame of the sliding balcony door. He tossed a pillow at her.

"I can see you shivering from here! You must be silly, Lindy. This bed is plenty warm."

"Oh, I don't mind. It's so lovely outside I had to see the sunrise! I haven't seen a sunrise like that in more years than I could count. I haven't left the city in years."

"That so? Can't believe you *never* mentioned that, Babydoll!" he said with a sarcastic wink.

"You know darn well I've wanted to come here since I was just a little girl, I told you that over an omelet!" she pouted, as he stood up and walked a few paces towards her.

Embracing her with both arms like a bear hugging its cub, Gabe whispered, "You're still little, aren't you?" and she blushed, though he was looking out the balcony glass and didn't see it.

Her arms uncrossed, and she wrapped them tightly around his waist. They stood there for minutes in comfortable silence.

Room service was arranged the night prior on a card they had hung on the doorknob. The breakfast was delightful—toast with honey and jam, both housemate and served in tiny glass jars. Eggs Benedict on a bed of cross-sliced potatoes, it was smothered with tart hollandaise sauce and fresh-ground pepper. The coffee on the cart was piping hot in its carafe; the juice was pulpy but not offensively so. Both of them ate with gusto, hardly talking. They shared a love of great food. This was a treat, to be sure.

"The toast is amazing!" Gabe commented.

"Fresh baked, I could bake you some just like this... oh, but that honey!" She exclaimed.

"Promises, promises! Coffee?"

After the meal, their day of adventure was to begin. Lindy wore a silken blue dress and a soft grey sweater topped with a silver-blue scarf, and Gabe wore a grey suit and a navy vest with a bright blue paisley tie cutting a line down his crisp white shirt. Their somewhat matching was wholly unintentional, and neither said a word about it. As they set off out of that lovely suite, Lindy commented cheerfully about the accommodations.

"That was most certainly the most comfortable night of

sleep I've had in quite some time. I'll say, Gabriel Marshall, you certainly are quite the cozy pillow,' she kissed him on the cheek, 'of course, after that evening I coulda slept on a pile of rocks and loved it!"

She patted him on his backside. He chuckled a bit then returned the favor with a subtle pinch of her behind.

"Babydoll, Chalet or no Chalet, I'd sleep happy with you anytime anyplace. But I've never been called a pile of rocks before!"

She smiled sheepishly at the insinuation as they descended the sweeping staircase hand-in-hand. On their way out the Chalet's front doors, Gabe opened one of the travel guides the hotel had furnished on their nightstand. He unfurled its map and started scanning.

"Gabe, what are you looking for?"

"That lovely little downtown. It's nearby, sure, but we don't want to go the wrong way and end up in Canada!"

"Oh, that wouldn't be so bad, would it?"

"Lindy, you must not have had much French food."

She swatted his arm.

"See here,' as he pointed to a spot on the map, 'It's exactly a short walk that-a-way. What say we go find a bit more coffee and maybe see some of those little shops you pointed out?"

The walk was refreshing and not too far. The morning mist subsided as they made their jaunt to town, but the grass along the parkways was still damp with dew.

Gabe spotted a coffee shop, and Lindy knew he was excited for another cup of joe; his strides lengthened as her heels clicked markedly faster on the paved sidewalk. As they approached the cafe, the first shop in the long line of canopied brick storefronts, Lindy finally tugged his hand.

"Gabriel, if you're going to walk so fast, I'm going to need a softer pair of shoes! That, or you'll have to simply fling me over your shoulder like a caveman and carry me. So, which will it be?"

He turned and leaned in close and whispered in her ear.

"If I carry you anywhere, it'll be directly back to bed..."

Lindy smirked through reddened cheeks.

They arrived at the shop with a casual stroll as Lindy had insisted they should take their time. She chose a table just as a host, looking crisp in her starched shirt, came to assist. With a quick order of two coffees and one large pastry, the woman was off to oblige their order. The table sat out in the morning sun, the canopy too high to protect them from the eastern dawn. A tablecloth with a lovely embroidery was draped over the wrought-iron table, and the wooden chairs were well-worn. Gabe helped Lindy take a seat as any gentleman should. The chairs creaked, but it was otherwise cozy.

"How'd you know I wanted another coffee?" she piped up.

"I didn't! I just figured I best fuel you up so you can move those lovely legs fast enough to keep up!"

"Well, say I have two cups and leave you in my dust like a bum!"

"Oh, you could try. I've got a secret, Babydoll."

"You do? What might that be?"

Gabe drew a brass key from his pocket.

"If you ever want to know what this key opens up, you'll have to stick around for a while. Can't leave me behind!"

He set the key on the table.

She reached across the table and placed her fingers over the key, but she did not pick it up. She lifted her gaze to his, and he was already staring into hers like a puppy.

"Gabe, you're not...' she paused as he clasped his big hand over hers. 'You're not teasing me now, are you?"

"No, dear girl, I'd never do that! But sometimes a secret can be fun..."

A mischievous grin crept across his stubbly face.

"O-kay, Gabriel, I'll play along. Shall I hold onto this for now?"

She lifted the key and held it in the air, the round end glinting in the morning sun.

"I'd say so. Now, no guesses, okay?" He chided her lovingly.

"Not even a hint? Oh, the suspense!" She leaned forward and kissed his forehead.

The coffee cups were empty in no time, the morning's chilly air nudging them to drink the hot beverages faster than they did lying in their warm bed. Gabe paid the check, and being well caffeinated, they nearly skipped to the nearest corner to find a cab resting there.

"Sir, we'd like a ride to the falls. Are you in service?" Gabe inquired.

"Sure am, buddy! Our side or across the border?"

Gabe patted the roof, offering "Say, let's keep it simple and stay stateside, thanks!"

"Well the radio's busted, but the heat works. One sec, I'll get your door."

The heavyish driver folded his newspaper and tossed it through the open window onto the front seat. Swinging the rear door wide, he offered a hand, and Lindy climbed in first. Gabe stepped in crouching, but they found the backseat surprisingly spacious. Within a moment, the driver had fired up the flathead engine, and they alighted back around the parkway before heading toward the falls. Lindy was fidgeting with excitement, Gabe was squeezing her hand and thinking about how he should have grabbed one more of those pastries before they left.

As the taxi rattled up the road, Gabe removed his pocketwatch from his breast pocket. He'd worn it properly today, clipped through a buttonhole in his vest. He lifted the watch to check the time and inspect its case. Lindy was leaning over to take in the view, a ray of sunlight reflecting off the watch face and across her shoulder through her sunny hair. The fleck of light caught her eye.

"Your father's watch?" She inquired, turning in the broad seat to face him.

Wistfully, he nodded, "yeah, and Robert's... sorry I get sentimental, Lindy."

She patted his thigh and took the watch into her hand, poring over its facets and details.

Gabe knew better than to linger on sad things on such a perfect day. He directed her attention to a flower stand on the roadside, which was exploding with colors from every shelf and vase. As she turned her attention, he tucked the watch away.

"I should have brought a camera!" Lindy exclaimed, eyes fixed out the window.

Gabe patted her leg, acknowledging, and now he knew just what to get her for the holidays.

The taxi stopped at the driveway near the tourist center at the falls. Silvery spray from the waterfall hung in the air, and Lindy remarked how sunlight was glinting in the mist. The driver came around and opened the curbside door, and Gabe climbed out. He turned and offered Lindy both hands to delicately help her out of the narrow car door and to the curb. She giggled and pushed his hands away.

"Gabe, you're too sweet. I've got this!" Lindy sprang from the car with grace. She took Gabe's hand, and they headed for the falls. The walkways were smoothly paved, the lawns neatly manicured. Folding signboards with arrows and tourist maps dotted the sidewalks.

Nearing the top of a slight incline, walking toward the sound of rushing water, Lindy was now tugging Gabe's hand to keep up. Her excitement was palpable and childlike, innocent. She moved with grace and sweeping body language, and Gabe's heavy feet plodded along carrying his burly frame. *We must make quite a sight...* Gabe kept the thought to himself. Within view of the railing, Lindy slowed down a bit.

"Gabe, we're here... I'm so excited!"

She was so enthused about the waterfall she was nearly overcoming Gabe's pace. A few more steps and they rounded a corner in the pathway. The view opened up to a broad horizon; the mist was pervasive in the air now, and it settled on their faces, tiny dewdrops collecting in Gabe's beard and eyebrows. Lindy blinked away the mist, and they walked hand-in-hand to the railing. Lindy grasped the shiny black with one hand, her other hand clutching his tightly. Coming close to the falls, Gabe bellied up to the railing while Lindy leaned against it, standing on her toes for the best view. Together, they looked out over the magnificent sprawling waterway, the morning light reflecting off the shimmering waters below the falls was crystalline in clarity and dancing with the ripples.

The waterfall had a distinct crescent shape, and one could see the falls sweeping around to the Canadian side. Their vista was beside the falls, not far from it. The foamy, wild base of the falls spilled countless tons of water dashing on the black, glistening rock. A small ferry boat chugged toward the falls, filled to the railings with passengers wearing ridiculous rubberized raincoats. Some folks held umbrellas; the mist was chilly and permeating. There in the morning sun, more glistening dew collecting on the shoulders and sleeves of their coats, Gabriel and Lindy held the railing and watched in quiet splendor for quite some time.

Across the falls, families were waving down to the boat and cheering, shouting to hear their echo above the din of the crashing waterfall. By some stroke of luck, the vista Gabe and Lindy occupied was nearly empty. A few people were at the far end of the vista point with cameras and tripods, but the pair was alone on this stretch of the railings. It was quiet, save for the sound of the falls and a few birds chirping nearby.

Gabe turned to Lindy and took her chin gently with his thumb, now having her undivided attention. "Lindy, you look like a kid in a candy store. I know you've wanted to see the falls for ages."

"It certainly feels that way, Gabriel... it was worth the wait. Isn't it lovely?' she asked, leaning her head on his shoulder briefly, 'I'm glad I waited to see them with *you*. Is it everything you thought it might be?"

Her cheerful smile was sweet, and Gabe saw a tiny teardrop forming at the corner of her eye. She was clutching both of his hands tightly.

"Lindy, I'm not much for words, you know that... yet, at this moment, I know I am *precisely* where I am meant to be. Just watching the world pass by with you, in this beautiful place."

The pair's hairs glistened with water droplets from the constant mist. He raised a hand and brushed her hair away from her eyes.

"Say, where's that key? Better not lose it..."

Lindy looked down and withdrew the key from the small pocket at her waistline. With an inquisitive look in her eyes, she held the key in her outstretched palm for him. Gabe clasped her hand back over the key. Gabe kissed her gently and took one step back.

He put his left knee down onto the cool, damp cement.

"Babydoll, I'd like to ask... I need to ask. Would you take my hand, could you grow old with me? I'm saying... ah..."

He deftly pulled a small object out of his breast pocket, bringing it up in front of her. It glinted in the sunlight. The little ring was a brilliantly clear stone in a slender gold band, and it looked so diminutive, held between his fingers. He almost grimaced, trying to bring up the words.

"See, this is just... I have a nicer ring for you; it's back home locked away at the bank, but... suppose you could call this little band a good start... if you were to..."

Lindy put her finger over his lips to shush him.

"Mister Marshall, yes. My answer is yes, it's been yes since we... I never *really* knew you would ask..." She paused and looked down at the key in her hand, then the ring in his hand. The lump in her throat took her words away for a moment. Gabe stayed on his knee, watching the mist collect over her as she brushed her eyes dry with her thumbs. She was smiling, and her face was taut in a joyous expression.

He breathed deep and squeezed her hand as she stammered a bit before finding her words.

"I am certainly going to need this key, aren't I?" she mused.

Gabriel stood up, taking her free hand and slipping the ring on her left-hand finger with a delicate touch. Grasping her shoulders and squeezing them reassuringly, he looked to Lindy in her bright and tearful eyes and spoke softly, like the gentle whoosh of the waterfall itself.

"I've got a key just like it, and a thousand miles from here, there's a much more deserving ring waiting for your hand. That will be the next train we take."

He drew her in close, her arms now wrapped around his waist. They kissed a deep and passionate kiss, tears running down her cheeks and onto the lapel of his coat. They kissed for ages while the music of the crashing waterfalls roiled on. The embrace relaxed only as they both needed a breath, and Lindy was blinking away happy tears. Gabe was misty-eyed as well, but he paid no mind. He produced a fresh white handkerchief, and he used it to dry the tears from her eyes. He leaned down a bit and kissed her cheeks one by one, diminishing the remainder of tears and warming them on this cool fall morning. Lindy said nothing, though she was trying to clear her throat. Gabe whispered again in her ear, his warm hands now cupped against her soft cheeks.

"You haven't the slightest idea how happy you make me, wonderful girl. I am your man, I'll be your husband, you'll be my wife, and we can grow old and fat together," he reached his left hand down and placed it around her small hand firmly clutching her key, "and this? This is just the start of it all, Lindy Marshall."

He kissed her on the neck just below her ear and placed his arm around her shoulder. Then, they both turned to watch the waterfall for a while longer in happy, stunned silence. She took the handkerchief from his hand and used it a few more times as they stood there in that delicate, ever-present mist.

The New Digs

Sunday, November 3rd

The following day, their suite was a bustle of packing, bathing, and affection. They'd returned to the suite shortly after the falls and found no reason to leave the room for the remainder of the day. The night was longer than the one before it, though for the sake of propriety, they said nothing of it this morning.

Gabriel felt a very tangible warmth from Lindy, and he knew she was pleased to be in his company—today, even moreso than ever before. The thought struck him that up until this little getaway, he hadn't been able to spend any significant amount of time with her outside of family dinners and mornings at the diner, but none of that mattered. He knew there was nothing she could do nor say that might sour him on his plans. He watched her morning routine, the way she poured their coffee and spent as much time as she could cuddling up against him in that bed, which felt so vast compared to where he was used to laying his head. They joked about the privacy of the chalet, and Gabe expressed how thankful he was to get her all to himself without worrying about who was going to knock on the door or overhear them.

Jokingly scowling toward the imaginary people huddled outside their room, Lindy shook her fist and grumbled, "So what? Serves them right for listening, we are adults and we are doing exactly what we should be doing." She sounded almost indignant about it.

"Yeah, what do they know anyway? It's not like your parents are down the hall!" He teased.

"Gabe, you have no idea how bad they can be! There's no privacy in an apartment; I'm thankful we've got our place to look

231

forward to; we can do whatever we want without being teased or judged over it."

"Well, we'll still have neighbors, but maybe if we don't introduce ourselves, we won't feel as guilty for being a little rowdy..."

She shrugged and turned to him, cuddling closer as she rubbed his chest.

"You must know by now that I appreciate you lacking the crude sense of humor most men have at your age. You're quite the gentleman, you know."

Gabe was a bit surprised that this would matter to her, being a tough and very willful gal, but he was pleased that she appreciated his ways.

"Babydoll, I'm no stranger to Blue words, and I can be a crude bastard if you put a little whiskey in me and the company is appropriate. I don't think I could have lasted in the army if I wasn't a little rough around the edges. But for you? I can change my filthy ways!"

She smirked at him and nuzzled under his even more stubbled chin.

"Don't change much, you big scoundrel. I like you a little rough."

They sat there and chatted through a few cups of coffee. As the coffee carafe dwindled, Lindy made time to watch over the dawn once again from the fantastic balcony. This time, Gabriel joined her; it was only half after six in the morning and they had finished the breakfast that room service had delivered nearly an hour before, swigging the last of the stiff black brew he trudged out of bed and went to the balcony to be with her, to keep her warm for the few minutes she wanted to stand there and enjoy the morning light, the crisp air. Both stood there embracing while the birds in the nearby trees sang their sweet melody.

After a little while enjoying the morning air, her toes had again started to freeze, and she dragged a half-awake Gabriel back into the suite for what she implored would only be 'just a few more minutes' in bed. By the time they were able to pry themselves out of that warm and cozy bed, it was after seven!

They shared the shower, and Lindy readied for the day in only a handful of minutes more than it took Gabe. Gabe had seen frontline soldiers take longer to bathe under a water bag than this girl;

he saw clearly that when Lindy was motivated, she was incomparable.

Arriving at precisely eight a.m. at the NYCRR Station, they grabbed their bags swiftly from the taxicab's trunk and hustled toward the platform. Gabe had tickets in hand, clutched against one of Lindy's suitcases. The leather exterior of Lindy's suitcases became slightly slick in Gabe's sweating palms, which caused him to constantly shift and try to fix his grip as they walked hurriedly, and by the time the duo arrived at trackside, they were both out of breath. A porter came to them with an amused look on his face.

"What's the hurry, folks?"

Gabe wheezed, "Trying to make the eight o'clock train!" and the porter shook his head, chuckling.

"Folks, this train has been, and will forever be, the eight-fifteen. Glad you're here, though! Let me help you onboard!"

Gabe gave two of the bags to the porter and carried one onboard himself after Lindy stepped up into the car. It was sparsely seated, with hardly any folks on the train this time. Now with a free hand, Gabe glanced at the tickets in the ticket book.

He whistled in relief and remarked, "Well I feel foolish, now, don't I? Right here in print, seven-fifteen in black-and-white."

Lindy was chipper about the scene, chiming in, "Well then we get the best seats, big guy!"

He nodded with a smile and helped her find a coach seat that would be out of the Eastern sun for the duration. Their seats were the last set in the row and had a bit more legroom due to the table between them and their facing seats. He knew these were business seats, usually, but on a Sunday, it was fair game for all riders.

They settled in with the morning paper Gabe had swiped from the Chalet lobby. Not another soul entered the car by the time their train departed. It was quiet and pleasant, and Gabe made a silent wish for there to be no loud families or city folk coming onto the car for the duration: a futile plea to be sure, but a plea made into the ether nonetheless.

Thankfully, the trip was both quiet and comfortable, with Lindy only briefly wanting to visit the observation car. Their stops at the various small towns dotting upstate New York were swift and unannounced on the intercom, as to not disturb weary early-risers. The conductors knew each passenger's destination, so with Gabe and Lindy headed to essentially the end of the line, it was a much quieter journey than the ride upstate two days prior. Late in the afternoon,

Lindy was asleep in her chair under the setting sun as the train pounded the rails toward New York City. Gabe ran his fingers through her hair gingerly so as not to wake her.

Returning to the city, his thoughts turned to those damn dirty case files of Mullally's despite his recent promise to leave it be.

I refuse to feel guilty about giving a damn. Hell, Cam could probably think of something to do, a way to help without digging myself back in the shit. He knows near as much about all this as I do. Maybe he could help suss out a killer from their hiding spot better than I could. Maybe I'm too close to it all. Maybe I've got to stay outta the bottle... it would be nice to get all this behind me, for her.

He was sure his old friend could help... maybe lend some more perspective or fresh understanding to this case. The idea of seeing Cam brought Gabe a warm smile, and he assured himself that Cam would be the man to help crack this case wide open. He thought about how he'd promised himself to distance from it, to stay away; he had someone else in his life now, he'd given his hand and in that moment become more than just a single man able to risk everything for the cause.

Doubt if I can find anything to help them without getting back out there, pounding the pavement. Mullally told me to steer clear and stay home, so maybe having another set of boots on the ground could open some doors. Cam wanted to visit, and I bet I can convince him to dig his heels in and help me do some good. I've gotta worry about homesteading for now, anyway. Besides, Cam's a natural at this detective stuff... And he must love it if he's thinking about taking cold cases for Billy Bigsby again. He can't have any worse luck than me.

For now, Gabe knew owed this small and fantastic woman the respect of staying clear of that mess, at least far enough to guarantee his own safety... but he could lend his ideas, his mind to catch this bastard and help ensure her safety and the lives of everyone in that neighborhood. It felt right, his decision to try and help close the case. Gabe was confident they could bring it to a close if they worked together. He kissed Lindy atop her head as she napped and felt no guilt about his position.

Arriving at Union Station in the evening, Gabe snagged them a cab and packed their bags into the trunk. After Lindy got into the car, Gabe gave the driver directions, but she nearly forgot that they planned to visit the new abode. On their cab ride back from the station, she started to ask aloud, "Where are we going? Oh, right, that's the plan!" and she grinned the rest of the trip as they chatted about their favorite views from the train.

The driver approached a small green city park and lapped around it. The cab came to rest when Gabe tapped the driver on the shoulder.

"This'll do nicely, pal. Thank you."

The driver helped them unload in front of the park and left with a wave out the window. Gabe took Lindy's hand and said, "Guess!"

She looked up at him, then around, then socked him in the arm. "Gabriel Marshall, I've been enduring you for two days without a peep about our new home, and you say '*guess*'? You should be ashamed!" Her feigned anger was amusing as it didn't hide her eager anticipation due to the grin she wore.

"Babydoll, I'm sorry. You're right; that is a cruel thing. Let's go see it, I'm sorry!"

She accepted his apology and picked up a bag, leaving the remaining three for him to lug.

"Across the street, see that white doorway?" He motioned with his head.

After saluting in a silly fashion, her fingers all askew, she grunted, "Yes, sir, on the double!"

He chuckled at her silliness. She looked over their new building with a nod, hoisted her bags, and started across the street. They reached the stoop together, bags in arms.

"That key you've got, it works for the door here *and* the door above."

"What's the unit number?" she asked.

"The third floor. The first unit, close to the stairs. Three-A."

He was perspiring again from wearing his coat in the warm taxi and a bit from enjoying a couple of scotch-and-sodas on the train. They made their way up to their new front door. Lindy dropped her bag and eagerly keyed open the door. She swung it wide and stood there in silence for only a moment.

"Damn!" she exclaimed.

"Everything okay, Babydoll?" he asked as he set down their bags in the hall.

"Gabriel, you big lug. Is this *really* ours?"

Her arms were outstretched, palms raised in exasperation,

and she turned slowly, poring over all the lovely details: the fireplace, the balcony, the bay window in the kitchen, the oak sideboard and armoire, and the little table near the telephone.

"This place is so wonderful... can we afford this?"

"Sure we can, Babydoll. Sure. I got a deal by promising we'd be kind, considerate tenants. Maybe he gave me the army discount, too."

She kicked off her shoes and skipped over to him, embracing him tightly by the doorway.

"Gabe, it's marvelous. It's so pretty and clean! And that little park!"

She motioned toward the well-maintained park across from the balcony, though it was looking a bit weatherbeaten with all the reddening leaves strewn about. Gabe, I'm so happy! Tell me, when can we move in?"

"Lindy, we can move in as soon as you'd like. The owner is just swell; he gave us some freedom to plan all that for ourselves. Of course, I told him it was a sure thing. Would have been a bit embarrassing if you'd said no!" He took her hand and kissed her knuckles softly.

"Gabe, never in a million years. You're my man now, and that'll never change, okay? In fact, if you'd waited any longer, I might have proposed myself!" She patted his bum lovingly and took off to investigate the rest of the apartment.

Turning to the phone on the wall, Gabe reached into his pocket and took out his wallet. He then withdrew a small slip of paper and dialed Cameron Mason's number. After two short rings, a familiar voice answered a bit raspy, "...*hello*?"

"Cam, Gabe here. Sorry for calling so late. I hope it's not a bad time."

"Oh hell, Gabe, there's never a bad time to chat with you. Well, maybe *one* bad time... anyway, I was just thinking about you. How's your world spinning?"

"Mighty well, I'd say. Might-tee-well. Been a great week to be me. Seeing as I'm standing in the new place and I can almost hear Lindy's smile from the next room, seems she likes the place! I made my move. Did you ask your lady what you were fixing to ask?"

"Glad to hear, Gabe! Virginia and I, we... I suppose we're through. She split, got a job out in Twin Cities."

"Damn, that's a shame. You'll lock one down soon, for

sure."

"Might stay loose, see what the women in New York are looking like. How's that sound?"

"We have a spare room; just leave your old boots at the door."

"Kind of you, Gabe. Mighty kind. How is... how's that other situation?"

"Took a turn, not sure where the road ends on that one."

"Gabriel, I thought Mullally told you to get off that track, didn't he? What happened?" The tone of disapproval in Cam's voice was clear as day from three thousand miles away.

"I'll tell you about it another time, Cam. Mullally doesn't know it all, but I think he's right. Had a bad run-in last week, and I'm still reeling a bit. This city is wicked. I need to step back, maybe steer clear for a while. Wondered if you might want to help."

"A *while*. Right. You just can't let this shit go, can you?"

The line was quiet for a moment, as Gabe watched Lindy tiptoe down the hallway from the bedroom to the guest room. Her silhouette was distracting, to say the least.

"I know, I know. I'm not a soldier anymore. Oughta thank you for that, I'd still be a single man if you'd let me stay in."

"You're not a private eye neither, and not for lack of trying, Gabe. Shut that shit down."

Gabe now desperately wanted to change the subject, and Lindy was now nearby in the kitchen looking through drawers.

"You're a wise man, Cam. I hear ya. Say, did you get that postcard last week with our new address?"

"Yessir. I have it right here by the telephone. I'll send you a nice housewarming, you and Lindy."

"Not necessary, but it's certainly welcome! We've got a lot of planning and decorating to do. And just as importantly, you and I have got a lot more catching up to do, don't we?"

"Sure do, Gabe. Suuuure do. Be seein' ya."

The line went quiet with a soft click. Just then, Lindy came out of the kitchen absolutely beaming. While Gabe had been conversing with Cameron, she had been cheerfully poking about the new place, taking time in each of the little rooms and closets, cupboards, and corners. With her bare feet, she stood in the doorway of the kitchen looking perfectly at home like she had been there for ages, cozy and content.

"Gabriel, I love it. It's so... it's plenty spacious, the walls are nice and bright, and so many windows! You've found the perfect home for us. I'm really just at a loss for words!' She threw her arms around his neck and kissed him sweetly, 'And you know, it's going to be lovely for entertaining. Do you know how many apartments in this city are missing a good dining room?'

"Oh? How many is that?" He humored her question.

"*So* many, Gabriel! Too many! But not our place, no sir! It's perfect! Oh, I can practically see us here right now. It's going to be such a fine home... we could put a clock there on the mantle! Say, what time is it?" She was stammering in excitement.

Gabe smiled and held up his watch. Lindy cupped it in her hand to read the time. She set to a frown immediately.

"Oh, I'm sorry, it's gotten late! I know you've got work early in the morning; how thoughtless of me!"

He chuckled and pinched her cheek sweetly.

"Babydoll, everything is dandy! We both slept a while on the train, remember? I'll be fine for work. But the same goes for you, shouldn't we get you home? I made a promise to Art, y'know..."

She nodded in agreement and collected her coat, her wide eyes still taking in the details of the new digs. Gabe dialed up the local cab company line and ordered a taxi. In a short minute, they had collected their luggage from the hallway and made their way downstairs. Lindy had been sure to lock the door and afterward hold her key up for Gabriel with a wink.

The car arrived minutes later as the duo were discussing the furnishings and decoration. Lindy talked over some excellent ideas about what they might want in each room. Curtains, tables, even the lamps. It was as though she had been planning for this moment for years. During the ride, as they talked about linens, Gabriel came to the amusing realization that she had probably been preparing for this her whole life. Most folks think about this stuff. He never really did until lately. Not until he met her.

As they talked, he thought about how absolutely ingrained in the life of all young girls, the ideation of home-making was in American culture. It amused him, as he had seen how different the standards were overseas. He remembered seeing Moroccan men arguing over doilies and lampshades in a bazaar. He recalled how one young soldier in his unit, a thickly-accented southerner, would never shut up about furniture. It was as though the man cared more about armoires and end tables than the damn war they were fighting! 'Arm-wires', he'd called them with a twang. The memory brought Gabe a deep smile, and when Lindy inquired about it, he dared not admit to his straying attention span. Instead, he responded with 'Oh, just happy you're excited about the place, little lady," and kissed her soft cheek. She leaned into it, turning to kiss him on the lips.

"I can see us making a fine little home there, Gabe. My parents are going to be so sad to see me go!"

"Oh, is that so?" He asked honestly.

"Absolutely not! They'll probably celebrate! I might get them a goodbye cake, Gabe. Mother would find that hilarious. It's my father who might find the nest a bit empty; he's so doting!"

"What a modern family..." Gabe teased, and they laughed and discussed how to break the news softly.

After taking her home and kissing her goodnight at the stoop, then making sure that she got inside, Gabe took the taxi home to the old cathouse. He couldn't wait to be out of that dusty place. Arriving in his room and kicking his shoes off, he ran a sink and filled up the small steel tub he had hardly used, intended for soaking ones' feet. After adding a bit of Epsom salts and throwing his damp socks across the room into the old wicker basket sagging against the wall, he slid his feet into the piping hot water and instantly found himself in heaven up to his ankles. For a large fellow, three days in dress shoes meant he'd be paying for it for just as many days. At this moment, he thought how silly it was that he should be forced to dress nicely when he should be relaxing.

Oh hell, I'll let 'em rest this week. Maybe buy some better boots if there's money left once we furnish the new place. Harry can't be too mad if I do my work sittin' on a stool, so long as I work!

Revelations

Monday, November 4th

The workday was the usual business of grinding, hammering, and painting. When it was over, Gabe felt like the day had rushed past like a racehorse leaving him in a trail wearing dusty coveralls. After he rode the ferry home, Gabe made a quick call to Lindy to let her know he'd be doing some moving that evening, and then he took a cold shower to get his blood moving for the work ahead. He was determined to get moved and settled, sleep be damned.

The least I can do is start collecting things here.

Still toweling off his damp hair, Gabe stood in the middle of his cramped room looking around the space at all of the little things he had collected in his time there. The day he had arrived, he'd had nothing with him but a suitcase and the cheap suit he'd bought on a layover in Buffalo before his last tour of duty, which he'd mailed to Robert for safekeeping. He'd chosen to abandon his footlocker when he left the service, though many young men insisted they'd be keeping theirs for some reason. When he'd been recovering in the base hospital, he had given Cam the go-ahead to throw away anything that wasn't in his suitcase the day he showed up. The old pocket watch, the dinged-up but still admirably ticking alarm clock, civilian clothes, and a few sundries. He'd taken nearly nothing with him from Oakdale when he left for the Army, and he preferred traveling light.

At this moment, he thought about maybe stuffing everything into a few trash bags and donating it to the local halfway house, really starting fresh this time—everything, save clothes and the little fruit crate with his urns.

No, Gabe, that's silly. Save your money and don't be a lazy cus;

240

just pack up your stuff and get the job done. Still gotta buy a better bed for the place, maybe take a trip to Sears Roebuck tomorrow... nice of the old man to leave that little foldaway with the rest of the furniture. Oh god, I hope that mattress isn't musty.

Changing into denim pants and his athletic shoes was refreshing after a long workday, and the shoes felt great. They were nearly new as they weren't rugged enough for work nor waterproof enough for the commute, and he wasn't the sort to jog, *especially* not in New York City. The athletic clubs were all uptown, anyway. Gabe slipped on a knit sweater over his white cotton shirt and begun tossing everything from his drawers into two milk crates which he'd snatched from the common room downstairs, hoping nobody would miss them for a day or two. The board games stacked inside hardly saw use, and he stuffed those in a corner under the card table. He planned to load those crates up and take a cab to the new place, intent on sweeping and making a list of things he'd need to buy before moving in completely.

Just the extra stuff, he thought as he surveyed his armoire, *anything I don't need for the week.*

Hands on his hips, he let out a low whistle at the row of shirts hanging in front of him.

A knock at his room door broke his concentration.

Who the hell would be coming around at half-past seven?

Opening the door a few inches, he looked into the hallway to see a face he hadn't expected in the least.

"CAM!"

Cameron Mason stood there, hands in his pockets, offering a shrug.

"Yeah, last I checked. You decent?"

"I don't sit around in the buff, Cam. That's more *your* style, isn't it?" Gabe teased, opening the door wide.

With a chuckle, Cam nodded and walked into the little room, leaning up against the short dresser behind the door. Gabe set upon him with a bear hug, an embrace he only had for family. Cam was a brother to him, and Gabe was choked up seeing Cam for the first time since he'd left the service.

Cam hugged him back tightly, ending the embrace with a pat on the back.

"They wouldn't let me on the plane in my birthday suit anyway, I asked. Stewardess might not've minded, but that's another story, ain't it?"

Gabe laughed heartily but was near speechless at the surprise visit.

"I know I said we should catch up, Cam, but... I mean to say... did you just hop on a redeye plane to come visit? Not that I mind..."

Cam shrugged again, cool as always.

"I'm drawing off my savings a bit while I figure out work."

Gabe clapped his hands in excitement.

"Gonna take that job from Billy like you told me about a while back?"

Cam nodded, looking around the room.

"Think so, yeah. He's got a nice new office up in that old Smith Tower in Seattle. Hell of a view, and from what Shamus said Billy's back on his feet..."

"His feet? He was in a... uh... you know..." Gabe hesitated to mention Billy's condition, which had the sharp-minded and handsome private detective William Bigsby set in a wheelchair for what doctors insisted would be the rest of his days.

"Well, you know what I mean. Hell, he's out of the bottle and takin' cases again, so... you know you can't keep that man down. Best private dick I ever met. He's hiring out again, he's got Shamus on the hook and even that knucklehead John Talbot if you can believe that!"

Gabe smiled warmly at the thought of Cam taking up work with old friends.

"Guess you gotta sell that little cottage in Richmond and haul your behind up to Seattle! But... New York ain't so bad, Cam. The city is even growing on me!"

Cam poked Gabe in the stomach.

"That's not all that's growin' on you, Gabe. She cooks?"

"Oh hell, I guess so. Mostly it's that damn diner food, but I was bigger a few months ago. This honest work thing is keeping me healthy! I'm half a size smaller than a year ago, can't let myself go, you know?"

Cam looked over to the bottle of cheap bourbon resting on the nightstand.

"Gotta try harder, Gabe. You and me both!"

"Well, I was going to pack and move some things to the

new place, but..."

His guest interrupted him, exclaiming, "I'd love to see it, Gabe! Let's head over there. C'mon!"

Gabe looked over the empty crates and decided not to bother with them; he just wanted to catch up with Cam.

"Sure, Cam. It's a plan! I know a great little Chinese restaurant not far from there. It's not Chinatown authentic, but it's good. I'm famished as it is."

Cam stepped into the hallway and nodded, ready to leave. Gabe grabbed his trench coat, put it on, and shut the door behind them.

"Gabe, listen... It's probably gonna be a late night. Why don't you call off sick to work tomorrow? I'm sure they'd understand."

With a grin, Gabe estimated wisely how this night was going to end. As they left the building, Gabe made the call to the yard office with a faked grumble in his throat and then called Lindy to wish her a good night, letting her know he wouldn't be coming by Art's in the morning as they had planned.

"See, Cam just happened to get off a plane in New York, and who am I to turn away a pal?

She gasped when she heard Cam had flown across the whole country to visit, offering, "I know how much you missed him. Call me tomorrow, and take two aspirin before bed!"

"Just might, Babydoll. We just might. I miss you already."

"Stay out of trouble, and I'll bake you boys something from Betty Crocker, but find out what sort of sweet tooth Cam has!"

She was so understanding, being excited for Gabe to see Cam after so long. Gabe wished her the sweetest of dreams and was ready for the night out.

The men stopped at the drug store kitty-corner from the cathouse and bought a bottle of Bourbon, tucking it in the deep inside-breast pocket of Gabe's trench coat.

Two blocks down, as they chatted about Cam's recent lady troubles, Cam withdrew a flask from his stylish leather coat, which had nice big square pockets on the front and a belt around the waist. Cam took a swig and talked through what happened back in Richmond, passing the flask to Gabe, who asked after Virginia.

"How'd it end, Cam? What sent her packing?"

"It's like she knew what she wanted, and when she found out about my family before, about my life... my baby girl. I think she didn't want to be second to that, you know?"

Gabe nodded, sipping the stiff, smoky scotch whisky from the flask, savoring it as they walked.

"Cam, you can't make someone feel different than they do, not really. She had every right to want something you couldn't offer her, and you have a right to find someone who'll understand you have a history. Your wife, she had her reasons for leaving too. You know that. Christ, Cam, I know I met you in your second go-round at life, but... your daughter, I'm sorry about all of that. Nobody deserves that."

"Life is hurt, Gabe. Just a mix of the good kind and the bad kind, but it's all *hurt*. Life don't care about you and me, the accident of humankind. The world ain't here for us; we're just borrowing it."

They walked for a while in silence as Gabe considered what his friend had said. He mulled over the hurt of his youth, and part of him knew he was damaged in a way that few people would understand.

Cameron understands.

During several blocks of swigging whisky and walking together in silence, Cam slowed his pace a bit and asked Gabe a question, which Gabe hoped he wouldn't.

"Do you remember what happened to you before you got laid up for a while in that field hospital? Do you really remember being a prisoner to those goose-steppin' sons-of-bitches, Gabe?"

Reaching for a good answer, Gabe swilled down the last drops of the whisky in the flask.

"I remember enough, Cam. I remember it was a hard choice, me or the unit, and getting caught bought you boys enough time to get out of there. I remember the little... the room they kept me in."

They sauntered now, taking time to nurse the flask. Gabe felt like his legs got heavier the moment Cam mentioned that hellhole.

"You remember how long you were held captive, Gabe?"

"Suppose it was a few weeks. I never...' he thought about it for a moment before answering, honestly trying hard to remember, 'I never really counted the days. Hard to do that when they feed you all those pills, no sunlight."

"Gabe, we lost you for two months. Two months and three days, exactly. Do you know how terrible me an' the boys all felt knowing what you might be going through? How *helpless* we all felt? I don't mean to diminish what you been through, but... just sayin' how important you were to us. Hell, Shamus didn't drink for the whole time. Not a god-damned sip. He was *beside* himself."

"I know all that well enough, Cam, and I know what you risked to come and spring me. I can't repay that."

They walked another half two blocks in silence. Cam lit a small spiced cigar as they walked, and in short order, they'd arrived at the Marshall's rental.

Cam walked with a scowl on his face, and Gabe wasn't sure where Cam was headed by dredging up all these memories. Cam stood there under the old streetlamp glow, smoking that cigar with his hands stuffed in his pockets. Gabe stared up at his new balcony listlessly.

"Damn near cost me my pension, that little mission. That, and what you went and did afterward... cost Shamus, too. Suppose I'm lucky they let me leave with my scraps. And do you know what, Gabe?"

Gabe looked to him and saw the most honest flash of love in his dearest friend's sad eyes.

"I would do it again. A hundred got-damned times.' He pointed to the buildings looking over the city like owls in a sycamore, 'I'd step off that Empire State if you fell first. I owe you that for the times you saved my old leathery ass, and I owe you that as a brother."

Gabe stared into the sky as he responded.

"I thought, after a while, that I'd be... that I was forgotten about. Just a lost soul. They started in with all those little mind games, and... I lost myself for a while, you know. I'm mighty grateful, Cam. I could never repay you for coming in and saving me from that purgatory."

His friend sighed, sounding exasperated.

"Yeah, you said that. And you've got nothing to repay, goddammit. What I'm saying Gabe, is that you're back in the shit again. You're *lost*, brother, and you need a friend right now. So let's go upstairs, show me this little palace you found for Lindy, and let's hash it out, Gabe. I'm fuckin' *cold*."

Shrugging against the chilly air nipping at his neck, Gabe nodded in agreement and waved Cam to follow him. It was after eight, and Gabe had promised to be a quiet tenant, so they trudged upstairs without conversation.

Shuffling quietly into the dark apartment, the men removed their coats and hung them on the coat rack beside the front door. Tension was in the air.

I hate all this reminiscing about my fuck-ups, Cam. You know that. Can't we just drink and talk about women? Cars? The damned New York Yankees?

He didn't have the guts to try and tell Cameron what-for. Gabe set the bottle of bourbon in the middle of the small, square oak dining table the prior tenant had left behind. It was stained from years of spills, edges worn through the varnish. This table had extra leaves under the top at some point for expanding the table for when company comes around, but those were long gone. Now it just wobbled pathetically.

Grabbing two small glasses from the sink, Gabe went to the table while Cam looked out the balcony window, down at the street.

"Nice view, right?" Gabe asked.

Cam turned around, distracted. "Huh?"

"It's a nice view, isn't it?"

"Oh yeah, it's quite a sight. Just a lot different than home, I suppose. You chose a good place here, under the circumstances."

"Circumstances?" Gabe inquired.

"Bein' in this big ugly city, Gabe. It's not like you fit in, am I right?"

"Well, it's my home now, and I aim to make every minute between these walls mean something, Cam. Come and sit with me."

Gabe took a seat in one of the two chairs, and Cam closed the balcony door to join him. Before his cheeks hit the chair, two glasses of bourbon were in front of them. Gabe smiled pensively.

Cam swallowed the generous pour in a gulp, and Gabe followed in kind. After a burp into his fist, Gabe filled the glasses again.

"Listen, I feel bad dredging all of this up, Gabe. I do, honest. I just... I can't help thinking that what happened to you out there, those German wackos messing with your head and drugging you all to hell, I can't help but see some shadows of what happened... after. Do you remember what happened after? Can we talk on it?"

Gabe placed his hand over his drink but didn't pick it up. He blinked furiously, fighting to focus on the present as visions of dead men wavered in the darkness, waiting to come alive if he closed his eyes. This was a familiar fear Gabe had fought off for a long time now. The drinking was a distraction, and worse yet, enough drink was a door right back to it.

"I remember a little, I s'pose."

"Say it. Speak some *truth* to what you remember, Gabe."

"I don't want to, Cam. I don't wanna say it. You sound like one of those doctors in the shock ward, poking and prodding. I thought you came here to help?"

"So let me help, Gabe. Just say it, put it out in the world. Like your mother used to say, right? You told me she made you say what you did, say what you felt. Honesty, you said she taught you *honesty*. So just do that, Gabe."

"I did an evil thing. You know I did."

Cam sat back in his chair, taking a sip of the golden liquor and waiting.

"I went out on my own. I wanted to... I wanted to get *even*. I shouldn't have done that."

"No, Gabriel, you shouldn't have. Especially after you promised me you'd stay laid up on base and get your head right. Those doctors were takin' good care of you, I saw to it."

"I should've done that. I should have *listened*. I'm sorry, Cam."

"So what did you do, Gabe? I know too damn well, but what do you remember?"

"I went out and got some licks on them, that's all. I got a little... a little revenge, all right?"

Cam clucked his tongue, disappointed at Gabe's reluctance.

"If you're gonna lie to me, fine. Your choice. But stop lyin' to yourself, Gabriel Marshall. Take a shot, stop bullshittin' and own up to it, Gabe."

"Or what"? Gabe's response came across as more combative than he had intended.

"Or I wasted a red-eye flight across the whole goddamned country."

Wasted. Like seeing your best pal could be a waste of time. Fuck you, Cam. Gabe held back a sneer. The liquor was opening doors he didn't want open.

Gabe snatched up the bourbon, slamming it back and swallowing what felt like a quarter bottle in just a gulp. The fire swirled down to the pit of his soul, the burn in his throat a welcome reprieve to the lump which had formed there. He closed his eyes, leaned his head back, and let out every bit of breath in his body.

He fell into the black pit in the back of his mind. Those ghosts he had locked away for too many nights flooded back like icy cold water rushing from a faucet, sterile and painful at once. He winced as his eyes shut tight, tired from drinking and stinging with tears.

Alone, Gabriel stood in the middle of a cramped stone building... his hands weak but desperately gripping a rifle whose barrel was searing hot, glowing in the dim light. There was stillness. A welcome silence. Ringing in the ears. His breath was baited, only to keep out the stench of copper and hot seared flesh, of voided bowels. The wetness of the slain bodies leeched into his pants. He dropped the rifle to the floor. It landed with a sickly thump, finding no hard floor; it landed on the chest of a dead man. The bodies strewn about Gabriel's feet would be hard to count, as the uniforms were all the same gray. The pooling blood, the exploded flesh and bone peeking from holes in the grey wool were an abstract painting, somehow coarse and refreshing across that dull palette.

Men lay in piles of their fluids and death; the faces of those landing on their backs were wrought with surprise and anger. Some faces mangled and torn open, some drawn tight in sheer panic. Shattered beer steins refracted lamplight like stars strewn among the warm husks of freshly dead men and boys. Overturned tables indeed hid more corpses, but this thorough and well-trained American soldier had made sure there were no survivors.

Gabe dropped that gun, scanning the room and pressing his palms to his eyes, trying to clear them of the gritty smoke and bloody spray that covered his face. He could taste this death.

The shout of his Commanding Officer bursting through the tavern doors, the same voice that now echoed in his home. "Goddammit, Marshall."

"Say it, Gabriel." Cam implored him.

That tang in his mouth, in his from across the world. It reminded him of something. Sense memory. That foul, coppery taste... the rainwater sloughing off elevated train tracks. The spatter of gore on his face in a distant life. The steam from the sewer grates outside. The smoke from his red-hot barrel.

"I did... a terrible thing, Cam. I... I went off. Those soldiers... just children. They were barely men. I followed them, and I slaughtered them—every one of the bastards. I wasn't myself... I didn't plan to do..."

Tears streamed down his face, but he sat still as a stone. The burn of salt in his eyes and the clench of his jaw were familiar pain, and he longed to feel *anything* else. Opening his eyes, he saw his home. The little dining room, the empty flower pot on the mantle. The old friend sitting across from him. He couldn't face his brother; he stared down at his glass.

The glass of bourbon which Cam had just filled for him.

"It's me, Gabe. Don't lose yourself in it. Don't get lost in your head again. Just... take a drink, and take a few breaths. We ain't done talking this out."

Gabe was breathing hard, but he gripped the glass and drank it half down. He spilled some down his chin, not caring to wipe it up.

"I don't deserve this place, Cam. They shoulda locked me up when you took me back... I don't deserve you, and I don't deserve Lindy. I'm a mess... I'm a souse. I'm a *killer*." His chest heaved as he fought his sobbing back.

"Hey! Don't get lost in it, not again. You just need to *remember*. They fought me, Gabe. They fought me tryin' to put you through a court-martial; they wanted to put you away. I put the brakes on all that, and I don't regret it. Not one bit. Fuck them top brass and their rules, never saw combat like we did. Nobody *understood.* Someone had to pull you outta the shit."

Cam's voice was calm, soothing, and trusting. To Gabe, it was like a mooring in the storm of hurt he felt.

Gabe relented. "But, you gave up your career, maybe even stripes... just to save me. I wasn't worth that, Cam. I'm not worth it. Jesus Christ, what would Lindy say? She'd leave me. Maybe I should juss tell her, she c'n leave me. I'd understand..."

Gabe's speech had begun to slur, and Cam leaned forward across the table and grasped Gabe's forearm. Gabe sipped down the rest of his glass, hoping to wash down the lump catching in his throat. That didn't help; it just burned deeper into his gut.

"Gabriel, I didn't come here to break you down. I came here to help, and that's what this is. You gotta own up to that devil inside you. You gotta face this thing, or it'll eat you alive."

Cam slammed his bourbon then poured another half-glass for himself and Gabe, who knocked it right back. The bottle was nearly depleted.

"You gotta come with me tonight, Gabe. See Mullally. We're gonna get all this ironed out, I promise. I talked to him, and he's on your side. He's a good cop, and if we don't end this, it's just gonna spiral outta control. It's gonna be the end of you, Gabe."

Gabe looked up, confusedly. His vision was beginning to blur. "...Mullally?"

"Yeah, Gabe. We're gonna go see the Sarge. He's gonna help you figure this all out."

Cam raised his half-glass to Gabe, who obliged by wiggling his drink on the tabletop. Cam drank his glass, Gabe leaned forward and sloppily drank in return.

"Do you remember the pins, Gabe?"

"Pins?"

"The pins... You pulled them off an officer who killed Parker, Gabe. Those rank pins."

"I have them... they're... ah... I think I'm a little rolled over, Cam. I'm soused."

"Goddammit, Gabe. Focus. They found one of 'em. In a place they really should not have been."

Drunkenly, Gabe chortled. "...been a *lot* of places I shouldn'a been."

Cam shrugged and poured the last of the golden poison for both of them. He shook the bottle to send the final droplets into Gabe's glass. The empty bottle looked out of place on the table. They were silent for a few minutes as Gabe caught his breath and dried his face with his sleeve.

"We ain't perfect, Gabe. Nobody is. You gotta do the right thing, and maybe I do too. I couldn't let you go through all this alone, no way. You're my brother, you know. Since the day you saved me from eating that pineapple grenade in a ditch, and every goddamn day after that."

Gabe smiled at the thought. "To brotherss!" and he drank the last of his bourbon. Cam sipped his slowly, looking toward the window.

"Cam, can... can I assk you something, jusst one thing?"

He was slurring nearly every word now and listing to one side in his chair.

"Anything, Gabe. Of course."

"Justt... explain it to Lindy, tell her I hadda go away... don't tell her all the thingss I did, 'kay?"

He squeezed his eyes tight, trying to escape images of contorted and wasted men piled high, leaking and hissing with steam from white-hot piercing munitions.

Cam nodded and stood to help Gabe to his feet. Gabe was unsteady but went along as Cam helped him up.

"I'll tell her all she needs to know, man. Let's get goin'; there's a car waiting out there for us. We're gonna go see Mullally."

"O-kay, Cam, sar-gint Mason, yesshir."

Gabe stumbled and leaned on the doorframe by the phone. He murmured to himself,

"Sh... should I call her? Nah she'll be asleep, tomorrow... yeah, tomorrow."

"Get your coat, Gabe." Cam implored.

"Nah, iss okay... I'm sweatin'!" Gabe replied, patting Cam on the back as they departed.

Gabe didn't even think to lock the door.

Wednesday, November 27th

Lindy stood firm on her side of the counter, slamming her fist on the clerk's book in front of her. She scowled at the old man, her furrowed brow and the red in her cheeks letting this man know she was serious.

"I'm going to speak to Mullally, and I don't care if he's tucked in a Murphy bed with Hedy Lamarr. You walk your wrinkled keister back there, and you find him for me, old man, or I will rip the badge off that dusty uniform of yours and shove it somewhere dark and *uncomfortable.*"

In absolute shock at the language the woman was using, the gray-haired old cop recoiled at the idea of having his badge anywhere but on his left lapel. With a defeated shrug, he shuffled off to find the Sergeant.

Impatiently, Lindy spun around and leaned back against the desk of the precinct. She folded her arms and tapped her foot in a huff, a scowl firmly set. She watched the hanging electric clock and nothing else, confident that her new angle of attack would give Mullally no choice but to see her.

"What's this I hear about one of my officers needing a proctologist?"

Mullally was kind, even disarming when he wanted to be. Still, Lindy held her ground as she swiveled toward him and poked a finger into his chest.

"Three weeks, it's been three damned weeks you've been avoiding my calls like a coward! I thought you old cops were supposed to be tough! You're afraid to be held accountable by one little woman?" She said, jabbing her finger into the meat of his chest again for emphasis.

"I'm sorry you believe that I've been avoiding you, ma'am. The truth is, I had other matters on my desk that needed attending to."

Lindy was off-put, as though there was anything more important than finding out what happened to her missing fiancé. She decided that an even more direct approach might be the solution.

"As far as I can see, you and your men are the reason that the love of my life has vanished from the face of this earth, with nothing but the shirt on his back in the shoes on his feet. You're going to give me some answers today, right here and now, or I'm going to send this story to every single newspaper in town, and it will take you until the *spring* to get the egg off of your face!"

She was livid, and rightly so. Out of the blue, Gabriel Marshall had vanished. His little room at the old cathouse was untouched, gathering dust and a deathly chill; nobody was there to turn on the steam heater. Nobody knew a thing, not his neighbors nor his coworkers down at the rail yard. It was as though he had simply jumped off the Manhattan Bridge and disappeared in the murky depths below, but Lindy knew Gabriel would never do something so asinine. She was convinced she would find her answers here.

Mullally, unaccustomed to being confronted in such a manner in the lobby of his precinct, recognized the need to mitigate the situation. With one hand on her shoulder and the other open in an acquiescing manner, he offered, "Sure, we can talk. But not here; it's just not proper. I've got a room for this sort of thing. Follow me please, ma'am?"

Begrudgingly, she nodded in the affirmative but shook her shoulder to get his hand off her. As far as body language could be construed, she was cursing like a sailor at this old man.

She followed Mullally into what she realized was an interrogation room. He held out her seat, sliding it in politely as she sat down. As he rounded the table to sit down himself, he pulled out a small cigar and struck a zippo to its end, lighting it with a puckered face.

"Gabriel, er, Mister Marshall told me about you some time ago. He sure seemed keen on you. I can see why... that boy was a glutton for trouble."

Lindy glared at him, eyes like daggers, retorting, "Do you

really think this is the time for *jokes*, Sergeant?"

Shrugging his shoulders and shaking his head, with a sigh, he replied, "I suppose not, please forgive me. I joke when I shouldn't, that's all. Didn't mean to be insulting. It's a bad habit that sometimes carries me over the rough roads."

"Well, now that we understand each other, why don't you tell me exactly what you know? I'm not moving from this seat until you do, and I have a powerful horse-puckey detector, so please don't waste my time. That fib you gave Cameron Mason to shill, that Gabe was killed in a mugging? It's so transparent it's *insulting*."

His eyebrows raised, Mullally was taken aback. He wasn't offended, far from it. He admired the woman sitting across from him, her arms folded crossly and her toe-tapping on the floor. He could tell a lot from the way a person carried themselves in a dirty police interrogation room, and this woman was not to be trifled with.

"You've got to understand, I didn't have a lot of options. We didn't have a lot of options. Gabriel was a troubled young man. From what I hear, from several sources, he spent a good stretch in the observation ward of an Army hospital before they sent him home with a discharge that was... less than ideal. Gabe's commanding officer told me how he was subject to some pretty rough treatment over there, and it's no laughing matter being a prisoner of war. It changes you as a man. Gabriel carried a lot of those troubles with him. He did some things that we can't say were justified. Some things that usually land a man behind bars for the rest of his days."

He figured that Lindy had not known about that, and by her shoulders relaxing and the pallor washing over her face, the sharp old man could see that he guessed right. As he expected, though, it didn't take her long to recover from the shock of it.

"*If* what you're saying is true, what could that possibly mean here in New York City, on the other side of the world? You don't know him like I do."

"I know him well enough to know that he's a good man, he has a good heart. But, he carries a lot of weight from what happened over there. I think that's why he came in here, trying to help. He had a bit of duality, you could say. The good side, and the bad."

Lindy uncrossed her arms and leaned forward on the table, staring into the man's tired eyes.

"That's debatable, Sergeant. What I want to know is where he is now. If it's bad news, I can take it. If he got caught up in this, if he was..." She paused to take a calming breath, wiping the tears forming at the corners of her eyes on the back of her hands.

"If Gabriel was killed, I just need proof. I just need some damn *closure!*" She hammered her fist on the table, rattling the zippo resting in front of the Sergeant.

Mullally sat back into his chair, puffing on his cigar and counting his words before responding.

"Lindy, I'm going to share some facts with you in confidentiality. Only a handful of other people in this world outside this room know what I am about to tell you, and I need you to understand that if it leaves our confidentiality, I will disavow all knowledge of the situation. You may be subject to real and tangible punishment. That isn't a threat, just the way things would unfold. Mayor O'Dwyer would see to it. Do we have an understanding?"

Frustrated, Lindy nodded in agreement again. She didn't want to speak yet, but she could feel the lump in her throat, ready to make her voice crack.

"Gabriel is alive, and he's being taken care of. He wasn't maimed, nor killed. Unfortunately, that's the only good news in this story. I assume you know about all those terrible attacks in the Bowery? Those muggings and murders?"

Finding her voice, she snarled back. "I know that was a *fabrication*, Sergeant. I know there was one killer, and you've been hunting him like a dog."

"Until we found him."

It took Lindy a few breaths to realize precisely what Mullally was implying. She could sense that the old man was being honest with her, but she wasn't so sure that he was being honest with himself.

"Until you *pinned it* on my fiancé, you mean to say? Ruined our lives for a closed case?"

Exasperated, the Sergeant tamped out his cigar on the edge of the table.

"Ma'am, I didn't want that to be the answer. It simply is. Hell, one of his commanding officers came all the way out here from California to help me bring Gabriel in. We had evidence, and even Gabriel himself didn't deny it when he came to me that night. He's not *well*, Lindy. We took him someplace where he can get treatment, get his head back on straight. You should be thanking me for not plastering the newspapers with his face. The comm- ...ah, my boss decided to let this one go down quietly. For right now, that's really all I can tell you."

Lindy jumped up from the table, her chair falling over behind her. She shook her fist at Mullally emphatically, "Some favor, Sergeant. You might have your theories, but I know better. When I get to the bottom of this, you're going to have some apologies to make." With that, Lindy stormed out of the room and found her way out of the station.

No hell nor high water could stop this woman now.

Come Back

Saturday, November 30th

The sun shone brightly, and happy birds chirped their songs joyously. Somewhere nearby, a lawnmower was cutting away, the metallic *shink-shink* of its curved blades echoed off the small cement block-constructed houses just a few miles from the Pacific ocean.

Inside, in stale air swirling gray with cigar smoke, a white phone rang once before it was snatched off the wall.

"Mason residence?" A gruff voice answered.

There was a brief silence, followed by the clacking sound of a very long-distance phone call being patched through. The static quickly died, and the connection was clear.

"Cameron Mason?"

A leaden pit sank into his stomach. He knew that voice, and it sounded sharp. Angry.

"Ah. Lindy. Hey there."

"We need to talk, Cam."

"Of course, I've got time. Just listening to the radio, not much to do...' he rambled in his unease, 'what did you want to talk about?"

"I just want to hear the truth. Not the lies that crooked old police tried to sell me, I want the damn *truth*. And I've been trying to call you for weeks, Cameron. Weeks!"

"You spoke with Mullally?" Cam didn't want to volunteer anything.

"Suppose I did."

"Well, what did he have to say then?"

"Nothing that changes how I feel. Nothing that lets you off the hook, Cam."

"Am I being lambasted for helping? I'm sorry, Lindy, I wasn't-"

"I know that you didn't really try to help Gabriel; you just sauntered out here and put him in the hands of those dim-witted detectives. You helped them take my fiancé and lock him up. Lambasted? How about held to *account*, mister Mason?"

"Gabe needed help, Lindy. I don't think he realized it, and sure maybe you were in the dark, but he needed guidance to do the right thing. I didn't think you should be burdened with all those gory details. Isn't that a kindness?"

He could hear Lindy's breath heaving on the other end; she sounded furious, but she was trying hard to keep her calm.

"Gabriel looked to you as a *brother*, Cameron. When he talked about you, it was like you grew up together. He loves you, Cam, like family. Gabe is a good, honest man. Maybe he wasn't perfect, but somehow you think he was some sort of lunatic? You've got another thing coming, mister."

"I'm sorry you feel that way, Lindy. What can we do? Gabe was really troubled. He was fighting his devils. The man is safe now, and that's the truth. I pulled that boy out of the shit in more countries than I care to count, kept him out of harm's way. Army wanted to lock him up, but I kept him safe from that! And here in a new life, he's fighting those same demons... I saw it in his eyes, Lindy. He told me as much. Not to mention the proof Mullally was holdin', he showed me everything... I don't even think Mullally wanted it to be Gabe, but that's where the facts took him."

Lindy nearly shouted back into the receiver, her voice cut through him like a knife. "Proof!? Do you want facts? I have proof that it *couldn't* have been Gabriel, and if you had thought to do a little legwork before you sent my fiancé up the river, we wouldn't be in this mess."

"What have you got, Lindy? I mean, those detectives had enough to take him in... and Gabe's troubled waters run deep, no disrespect intended..."

"Perhaps he had some trouble the past, but the man you and Sergeant Mullally imagine is not the Gabriel Marshall I know. One of these newspapers Gabe has been hoarding says they found a body on the morning of Saturday the twenty-sixth."

"...Okay, but what's the proof?"

"That Friday night, Gabe was... it was our first night. The *whole* night, Cameron. He took a taxi home the next day, and I would bet the taxi company keeps records on that. *Witnesses*, Cameron, at least several."

Cam sat down to the floor, his legs splayed out. He felt like someone had knocked all the wind out of him. He knew, just at that moment, that he had done wrong by a man who had been his best friend.

"You *sure* about this, Lindy?"

"It's the truth—cold, hard facts. And I am certain I can find more witnesses... more proof than that, Cam. He is innocent."

She waited for him to respond, hoping Cam would make the right choice.

Cam swallowed deep past the lump of guilt in his throat, "Oh, hell. You've got my attention. I'm catching a flight, Lindy. I don't know if I messed things up, but if I did, then maybe you can help me fix what I broke."

Lindy took a deep breath and let out a sigh of relief.

"Find me at Gabriel's old room. I've been staying here most nights, it's...' she trailed off for a bit, trying to find the words to explain how badly she missed him, but she decided against trying, 'just get on that plane and come help *fix* this."

Still heated, Lindy slammed the receiver down. She didn't care if she had hurt Cameron's feelings; if he redeemed himself, there would be time to make up later. Right now, she had bigger concerns.

She looked around the lobby of Gabriel's building. Realizing that she just made enough of a scene that the pair of grey-haired men near the window had stopped playing chess to observe, Lindy took a deep breath and brushed her hair out of her face before returning upstairs. Storming into the small room, her temper got the best of her. Gabe's tin lunchbox was peeking out from under the bed; she kicked that box, sending it bouncing off the wall under the window. Old, dry cracker crumbs and a few wadded-up napkins now littered the floor in an arc. It looked like a modernist painting on that faded rug.

Stupid lunchbox. Stupid damned cops.

Feeling nearly defeated and deeply frustrated, Lindy sat down on the creaky Murphy bed. For a moment, she found herself staring off at nothing and mindlessly watching the dust swirl around in the beam of sunlight coming through the musty old curtains, settling down with the crumbs. On the bed next to her was a stack of newspapers Gabriel had been collecting and annotating in his spare time.

Lindy still clutched that one newspaper, an afternoon edition more than a month old, its bold black headline trumpeting a story about a recent victim who had been found bludgeoned and robbed, left to die in an abandoned warehouse just on the northeast edge of the Bowery. It was the article that incensed her and gave her cause to call Cameron. Once again, she read over the article detailing what had actually happened to that particular victim.

"Patron of O'Reilly's bar two blocks north... bartender states left with his bearings, Well-liked regular... Found at dawn prone/face down... condemned building, signs of strangulation with implement... heavy spatter, major trauma... deceased between six and no more than eight hours..."

The article was brief but descriptive enough to impress gore and brutality. That one word, *spatter*, sent a chill up her spine. She folded the newspaper over on itself, looking down at the big block lettering spanning the front page. More specifically, the day and date just underneath. Gabriel had not circled nor highlighted it; he'd had no reason to. Now, Lindy took the pencil off the spindly three-legged nightstand next to the bed and drew a slow, lapping circle around the date.

That was the morning Gabriel had woken up bleary-eyed on the recliner in her living room, sharing a mug of coffee with Lindy well after seven o'clock wearing his slacks and her father's borrowed loafers. 'A little tight, but they'll keep my toes warm!' He had said. No blood, no spatter, no midnight murders. Nothing but two adults intertwined for a night.

She wasn't going to let some bumbling badges tell her otherwise; Gabriel was *innocent*.

Lindy was no slouch. She very well knew that even with corroborating statements from some taxi company or a neighbor, Mullally likely wouldn't buy into her story. Regardless, she was never one for lying, and the timing of that one murder gave her an honest reason to say she had proof. She knew that once Cameron arrived, she could convince him to help her find something more tangible. It sounded to her as though Cam was already regretting his decision to get Gabriel locked up.

I'll tread lightly dealing with Mullally, don't want to make an enemy of the man... just as long as he understands that I'm not going to let this go.

For now, a more pressing concern was finding Gabriel by the time Cameron arrived. She knew that her fiancé would likely be within city limits and more likely held in a ward for mentally unwell people.

There are more than half a dozen hospitals in New York City, at least four of them have wards that might take such a patient... I don't know what state he was in when they took him, but there's no way he'd willingly let me think him dead.

Frustrated and wound up like a tin toy robot, she took a swig of the cheap liquor out of the bottle from the nightstand, then laid back to think it over. A fitful sleep quickly overtook her.

An hour later, she awoke with beads of sweat on her furrowed brow. A nightmare of being lost in an unfamiliar concrete maze and bemoaning passersby had her chest tight as she sat up. A half-open window and blustery, cool breeze were quite the relief now.

The evening was cold and cloudy, the moon backlighting some of those silver clouds in a profoundly sad way. Lindy had no interest in trying to settle in for the night. She'd packed a few bags at home and relocated herself into Gabriel's old room the week prior. While it was a bit longer to walk to work from home, being there long his things helped her feel a bit closer to Gabe.

She winced as she looked at the wallpaper, wondering what secrets those cheap, faded prints held from their past tenants' misdeeds. Missing Gabe dearly and feeling very alone, Lindy supposed the best way to clear her head would be to take a walk and do some searching.

I've got work to do, and the clock is ticking on Cameron's arrival.

Nearing the door, she remembered that it was cold enough out that she would need a better coat. She hadn't brought anything from home that would fight off the nipping wind outside, but she wanted to take that walk. On the floor next to the door was a box she had picked up from the new home, which she had been forced to relinquish, as Gabriel never returned and she could not afford it alone. Luckily, the owner had collected everything left behind and called on Lindy to collect it.

Lindy remembered seeing Gabriel's trenchcoat wadded up in the box. She knew it would be just the thing to fend off the brisk weather. She grabbed the box and dumped its contents onto the floor, two empty bottles and the oversized coat resting there. She snagged the coat by the loop of its collar and picked it up; as it unfurled, she felt a weight drop like an anchor at the bottom of the coat.

Did he leave another bottle in this damn coat?

Over her dress, she slipped on Gabe's long trench coat. The collar smelled like his aftershave. Despite her fingers barely peeking out of the sleeves, she felt oddly comfortable and safe in this moment. It was as though Gabriel himself were holding her, enveloping her with love and warmth. She made a quiet promise to herself as she inhaled deeply in the fabric.

You're going to find Gabe. He's got to be here, somewhere, and he wouldn't quit for you. Find him, and damn the consequences.

Her hands slipped into the broad front pockets, and one hand grazed something cold, mechanical. As she wrapped her hand around the metal, Lindy realized what it was. Gingerly, she withdrew the heavy German revolver. Being no fool, she kept her finger away from the trigger as she grasped the stock of it tightly. In the dim light of the room, the barrel gleamed. The brass bullet casings shone in the back of the revolving cylinder. She could see a few of them had hammer strikes. A voice in the back of her mind told her to *keep it*, and that's just what she did.

The Hunt

A misty rain had fallen earlier in the evening. Only a handful of people were out and about, save for the few inebriated patrons of the local bars, as was Bowery custom. Holiday music was emanating from a few homes and at least a few bars as Lindy made her way past. Little strings of lights and cheap flickering electric candle decorations adorned plenty of windows. Thanksgiving passed generally unnoticed by Lindy, but strings of colorful lights made it unforgettable that Christmas soon approached.

It was after 8 o'clock. Lindy thought about how a bit more liquor might warm her as she walked. She knew it would do her little good, and so she kept on walking right past the very tempting bars. This woman was far too clever to try and drink down her feelings. She wondered now, though, if that's really what had Gabriel so keen on a bottle. He had always insisted he 'just enjoyed a good whisky'.

I wonder if the alcohol helped him forget all those things Mullally was talking about. Just a few years ago, my Gabe was a prisoner of war. A soldier. A killer, even if it was for just cause... the weight of it all...

Still walking that damp street, she thought about her history with the drink. About how her parents allowed her to do nearly anything she'd wanted at any time, so long as it was a *responsible* thing to do regardless of their feelings on the subject. She'd been drinking wine with dinner on occasion since her teenage years. Some of her more sheltered and perhaps more Catholic friends were not so lucky.

She wondered if Gabriel's parents had been so relaxed with him during his childhood. Then she thought about how it was almost a grace that they weren't around to see their only child being treated so poorly, locked up for no good reason.

I suppose they would be spinning in the grave knowing their son was dealt such a lousy hand.

The limp excuse Cam had given her some weeks prior, and now the story about the ordeal Gabe had been through and how it left him damaged goods, she knew Gabriel deserved better treatment than whatever he'd gotten at the hands of the clowns running the local police. Framed for murders he had no part of! That injustice cut her to the quick. Her jaw clenched. The anger she felt right now far outweighed the sadness. That rage she'd been trying to quell for nearly a month was haunting her. Unable to sleep, hardly able to eat, and the reason she was strolling down a rough city block right now with two pounds of German steel in her pocket.

Damned foolish policemen aren't going to ruin our future for the sake of a closed case, some bullshit merit badge, or promotion. It's like they don't care to do the right thing; they just want to do the easy thing. I'm not going to let them.

Lindy walked intently past countless walk-up buildings, retail shops stocked to the ceiling lights out and closed. She passed two churches, the second also housing a nunnery. From inside, she could hear conversation, laughter, and music. Someone was quietly playing a string instrument. Not all of the city was so rough and tumble as the Bowery; these streets still had little hideaways from the filth... havens of calm, bastions of peace and quiet.

I'd bet they wouldn't be celebrating if they knew a killer was still out here lurking.

More people walked the streets now than in past months. It felt as though the neighborhood had settled down a tangible amount now that a month had passed since the last grisly murder, and even though the police claimed they were simply robberies, many of the citizens knew better. Lindy knew plenty of chatty locals from her job, and people were still talking about it. Even with its dirty roots, the Bowery had never had such shock, people being dragged into alleys and abandoned spaces and losing their life over a few dollars in their pocket. Sure, the official line sounded nice in letterhead on the papers, but some citizens here were keener than that... they whispered about it over coffee or in hallways with their neighbors. So although it felt a weight had been lifted from the neighborhoods, Lindy knew the *real* truth. She knew Gabriel was no murderer, and therefore she knew the real killer could strike at any time. Anyone could be a victim, but not Lindy herself. She was ready, not to mention she felt far safer knowing that deadly implement was nestled in the pocket of her trenchcoat.

Having already walked halfway to the closest public Hospital, intent on checking their ward for her handsome though troubled fiancé, Lindy's inner voice was a growl.

If he isn't there, I'm not stopping. I'm going to check every hospital in the city, and then the damned state if need be!

Determined as ever and mad as hell, she fought the cold lifting the collars of that oversized coat as she hurried her pace, chin down and a fire in her belly.

Planning and grumbling carried her the rest of the way, and she found herself on the steps of a large and venerated hospital. A church-sponsored charity hospital, but a facility that was known to provide excellent care. She remembered several women during her brief career as a nurse who had fought tooth and nail for jobs here.

Any luck, and someone will let me plead my case.

Making her way into the lobby reception area, Lindy found a primly dressed and very friendly young woman at the desk. She returned the smile she had received upon entry and approached the desk, not really knowing where to begin. Luckily, the young lady offered help before she needed to ask for it.

"Good evening, ma'am. Are you here as a visitor?"

"Possibly, yes."

The young lady raised her eyebrows, clearly curious as to the meaning of such a statement.

"I don't quite understand. You either *are* a visitor, or you aren't? I'm happy to help if you can give me the name of whomever you intend to visit."

In a sheepish tone, Lindy responded honestly.

"Well, I'm looking for a Gabriel Marshall. That's definitely who I would like to visit, but he may not be under your care here. I wish I could say for certain..."

Her face still revealing a bit of confusion, the young woman turned and thumbed through the logbooks hanging on the wall behind her. After a search, quickly completed due to the alphabetical nature of logbooks, the lady turned back with a dour look.

"I'm sorry, no Gabriels nor Marshall's supposing it was transposed, we do *not* have a Gabriel Marshall under care, miss."

Lindy removed her handbag from under the coat. Thumbing through the purse, she produced an outdated photograph of Gabriel, which she had found in his room drawer. She slid the picture across the counter to the receptionist.

"Well, you see, he may not be registered under that name. He would be here for, I suppose, long-term care and evaluation?"

Receiving more confused eyeing, Lindy realized that a bit of guilt might curry favor here.

"He's had a bit of trouble since he returned from the service, you see. He's a dear man, and I just want to make sure he's all right."

The young woman started the photo for a moment like it was foreign to her, but she was clearly curious as she offered, "You know, I haven't seen more than half the patients here; I really only work down here at this desk. Perhaps I can ask somebody who may know better than me?"

Picking up the phone on her desk, she made a brief call assumedly to another part of the hospital and requested assistance. She smiled back and sat there, waiting with Lindy in silence. Not two minutes later, a scholarly-looking gentleman with a very significant beard came plodding up one of the stairwells. His brow was wet with sweat, and Lindy supposed stairs were a bit of a challenge for the man. She felt guilty for taking this man away from whatever he was doing but silently reminded herself that she was on a mission.

Gabriel is a priority. His work can wait a few minutes.

"Ladies, I should've used the elevator,' he offered with a genial smile. 'It's late, and I'm old, but I'm here."

He winked toward the receptionist. Turning to Lindy, he inquired, "How can I be of assistance, ma'am?"

Lindy repeated her unusual request and made sure to mention that Gabe was a veteran, hoping that he might understand and help her by looking over the photo. He did just that, peering over the rim of his round bifocals. He peered at the image for plenty of time to give her an answer. Handing it back to Lindy, he shook his head and apologized.

"Sorry young lady, no such patient here. We have seen plenty of these shell-shocked young men, under my care of course, but that *particular* man has never found his way into one of my beds. Looks like a strong lad!"

"I sure hope so. It's hard to be alone at Christmas, you know," she remarked.

Thanking the doctor, Lindy departed quickly. It was late,

and she had no time for anything but the search. A bit tired at this point, she caught a bus heading up the Boulevard. She knew that particular bus route was close to the nearest hospital equipped with a wing for long-term care.

Many of the people on the bus appeared to be third-shift workers heading to work. They were wearing various uniforms and carrying lunch pails.

This damn city doesn't sleep, does it?

As the brightly painted and chrome-striped GM bus lurched to a stop on a busy corner, she checked the street signs and made sure she was in the right place. Seeing that she was only three blocks from the hospital, she hopped off the bus and thanked the driver as any polite person should.

The walk was brief and perhaps a bit less lonely than the streets of the Bowery. Looming in nearby blocks were some of the new high-rises and many modern buildings. This block felt untouched, and a large signboard carrying a medical cross hung out over the street on wooden beams. As she looked upward, she saw aging masonry that was black against the warmly lit clouds in the sky. There were arched and stained glass windows, peaked roofs that looked as though they belonged on a church. This was a city hospital with no particular religious affiliation.

Lindy had quit nursing before the city took over this facility. She hoped they might be as friendly and helpful as the last. She ignored her sore feet, having worked the day shift and now having walked a notable portion of the city that night. Reaching the top step, she turned the doorknob, but the door did not open. Trying the knob on the adjacent door, it did not budge.

...not even ten o'clock; there must be someone here.

Insistently, Lindy pounded her fist on that oak door as she peered through the paned glass. She could see a light in the hallway, then shadows. After a few moments, she saw the outline of a person coming to the door. Stepping back just as the door swung open, Lindy prepared her smile again. Standing in front of her without a greeting was a rather sizable and very perturbed-looking woman not much older than herself.

"You don't look sick." The woman sneered.

"I'm a visitor. I need to see someone."

Stepping back and folding her arms, the woman held the door open with her toe as she stood blocking the doorway.

"Visiting hours end at seven. There are rules, you know. Come back tomorrow." She hiked her thumb toward a placard on the outer wall, which stated those visiting hours.

With that, the gruff woman turned to leave, but Lindy reached out and grabbed the sleeve of her shirt... gently, but just enough to stop her.

"I'm so sorry, but I'm not exactly a regular visitor. I'm looking for a missing person, and I believe he may be here."

The woman spun around, arms folded, but now she was somehow even crasser.

"Who *cares* what you believe? I wouldn't care if you were looking for Theodore Roosevelt; nobody comes in after seven unless they are sick or wounded. Missing persons is police business, anyway."

Lindy released her sleeve but held out the photo.

"You have got to understand, ma'am, it's my fiancé. He has been missing for weeks, and if I don't find him, I really don't know what I'll do. Police have been utterly useless. I'm at my wits' end, can't you see? What might you do in my position?"

The sneer on the woman's lip subsided, in her shoulders relaxed a bit. She stared down at the photo for a moment before taking it from Lindy's hand. Sighing, she relented.

"I suppose I can ask the physician on rounds to take a look. But you've got to wait here. I already put away the sign-in logs. Stay here."

Lindy sighed a breath of relief and sat down on the short brick wall that made up the sides of the steps. She felt the cold leaching into her from the damp brick, but she didn't care. She waited there, and it felt like ages had passed. All she could feel was pensive hope; the anger had faded a bit now that she felt some measure of progress being made. Twenty minutes, perhaps even thirty, passed. Lindy reminded herself to have faith that the woman would return; she didn't believe being impatient would benefit her with such a bully of a warden.

Maybe I interrupted her nap! Nobody's that surly all the time...

As she sat in the cold, Lindy withdrew Gabe's pocketwatch from her purse. Looking down at the face of it, she realized that she had not taken it out of her purse since the day that Cameron had handed it to her before walking away. It hadn't been wound since, and so it held no time. No ticks to be heard. Still, she stared at its beautiful pearlescent face under that glass.

Lindy hadn't even noticed her tears falling as the woman returned to the door with the photo in hand.

"Oh, thank you so much. Was there any news?" Lindy asked with bated breath.

"No, sorry. Doc didn't recognize him, and I assume the name on the back of the photo is your husband?"

"Fiancé, he is my fiancé!"

"Sorry, fiancé, sure. Whomever he is, there's no Gabriel Marshall here, and there never was."

Lindy felt a crushing disappointment overtake her excitement.

"Sorry to bother you, thank you for trying."

"You got it, kiddo, the woman said with a nod, 'I hope you find him. I had a husband, lost him before we could start a family. Pearl Harbor. Foolish men and their wars."

Lindy, bleary-eyed, caught the woman's gaze and saw a possible future for her younger self. She was lonely and angry.

"God-damned war," Lindy whispered back as she wiped the tears off her cheeks and descended the stairs.

It would be midnight before she reached her final destination, the Catholic Hospital in which she used to work. She'd thought about calling instead of making the trek to the North end of town, but she hadn't set foot in that hospital in almost ten years. At this point, she was exhausted. She felt bedraggled, run-down. She didn't have the energy to walk anywhere else, nor did she have the time to spare; she'd have to wait an hour for the next bus as it was. That simply wouldn't *do*. She thought about her options, and they were few. She was on the wrong side of town, and it was the wrong side of bedtime. Opening her pocketbook, she saw she only had thirty-five cents and not a single bill. She hadn't prepared for this, and nobody honest takes promises at this hour.

"Oh hell, at least try..." Lindy grumbled to herself as she stepped to the curb and put out her thumb.

A few minutes passed, as did several taxi cabs already occupied, but now she saw a very welcoming sight. A bright yellow lamp-lit sign on top of a taxi, and it was headed her way. As it got closer, she could see the little orange bulbs on the sides of the roof sign advertising that the taxi was open for a fare. The old cab rumbled to a stop; she stepped up to the passenger window. The driver, a nicely dressed man in his fifties, leaned back in his seat in surprise at her coming to the front door. She knocked on the passenger door glass, so he slid across the seat and rolled down the window.

"Do you need a ride, miss? You can just get in the back!" he motioned with a nod.

"So sorry, I don't want to waste your time. I'm twenty blocks from where I need to be, I haven't any money. I work down at Art's diner near the old neighborhood; I was hoping perhaps I could meet you tomorrow and pay you for the fare from tonight? Plus gratuity? I'm so sorry, it's just that..."

He raised his hand and shook his head.

"Ma'am, it's nearly midnight and it's damn cold out there. My mother would be looking down on me in shame if I left a lady out here stranded. Get on in that backseat; no fare for you tonight. Let me take you where you need to go."

Lindy felt a lump in her throat from emotion. She didn't want to cause a scene, but she realized she must look like a mess, so she resolved to keep her composure. Taking a breath, she thanked the driver.

"Your mother would be proud, sir. What's your name, may I ask?"

She was still standing at the passenger door, and he was still leaning over in the seat.

"Wallace, ma'am. Wallace Pritchett. Says so here on my drivers' registration. Had my cab in this city for some 20 years."

He proudly tapped the placard on his dashboard. She reached into the window and clasped his hand, elated at his kindness.

"Nice to meet you. I'm Lindy Eklund. As I said, I work at Art's on the other side of the Bowery, and perhaps I can repay you with proper fare and a good meal sometime."

He met her firm handshake with his own and waved her into the cab with a broad smile. She climbed in the back seat, settled into the worn vinyl, and caught her breath.

"Where are we headed then?"

"West on the avenues, Mister Pritchett, to the old Memorial hospital. I'm trying to find..." she paused, wondering if she should burden this man with her problems.

"Just Wallace! Wally, if you're in a hurry. Lost someone?" Wallace inquired.

Nodding, she looked down at the photograph in her palm

and replied, "I *hope* not, but I have yet to find him... My fiancé, Gabriel. He's a bit... under the weather."

"Wherever you need to go, ma'am, I will get you there. Slow night anyway; the least I can do is help! A proper *demoiselle en détresse*... damsel in distress! Recently tied to any railroad tracks? Slunk over medieval parapets?"

She chuckled and smiled at him through the rearview mirror. He smiled back, his eyes full of kindness and crows' feet.

"Thank you Wallace, I'll try not to be a burden. I don't speak French, but I'll try to keep up?"

"Oh, I read a good bit when there's no fares. Can't bother with the radio, too many damn opinions! Mostly sales pitches anyway, and I hate wastin' a dime."

She smiled and relaxed further into the squeaky seat.

A short while later, the white Chevrolet stopped across the street from exactly where she needed to be. They hadn't spoken for a bit, but Wallace knew precisely where she needed to go, and Lindy rested her eyes for much of the ride.

"Looks like the place, Lindy! I'll sit tight?"

Yawning, Lindy stepped out of the back of the cab. She leaned again into the open passenger window. "Wallace, I might be a bit of time. You don't have to wait."

He shrugged and put his palms up in mock defeat. "I'll give you thirty minutes, maybe even forty. Got a sandwich to eat and half the newspaper to read, but any longer than that and I'll just see you some other day at Art's diner. Ain't much for fares out this way this late, anyway."

She patted the doorframe in acknowledgment, gave him a wave before turning to head into the hospital. She hadn't set foot in this place in years, but it still felt natural. Of course, the nurses rarely used the front door as there was a side entry for staff, but it was all so *very* familiar.

She arrived at the desk clutching her purse, warm in her coat despite the chilling night air. There was nobody in the lobby, so she rang the little bell. In two beats, she heard some shuffling from a door a few yards away, likely a break room or perhaps a janitor closet.

The door opened, and out walked the best news she'd had yet on this dreary night. The face smiling back at her was Gerald Kinsolving, a former coworker and kind man. Brushing crumbs off his shirt, he looked up and met her eyes and recognized her immediately.

"Lindy, little girl! It's been too long! Where have you been hiding? I suppose I should be thankful I haven't seen you back. This is a hospital after all!"

She laughed and ran over, throwing her arms around Gerald with an excited hug. He hadn't finished brushing the crumbs off his shirt, but he returned her hug in kind. After a long embrace, they stepped apart, and he squeezed her by the shoulders.

"Honestly, I've missed you; we all have. Five, even six years, I'd say? What in the world are you doing in my lobby at midnight? Oh my word, is everything all right?"

She handed him the photograph and began to cry as she formed a response. She felt overwhelmed by a mixture of the joy in seeing an old friend and the weight of her mission.

"My fiancé... Gabriel. He's been missing. The police recommended I start here..." It was a lie, but she didn't want to speak the whole crazy truth of things just yet.

Gerald looked over the photo as Lindy stood back and remembered how much affection she had for the kind, gentle soul standing in front of her.

"Fiancé? Well now, that's serious business. What's his name?"

Still wiping away tears, Lindy reached for the photo in his hands and flipped it over, showing her friend where Gabe's full name was scrawled in pencil.

"His name is Gabriel Marshall. He's not long back from the service, and I'm worried that he may not be fully well right now; he might not even be admitted under that name. Please, could you check your logs and perhaps have one of the people from the shock ward or invalid care look at the photo?"

"Oh my... the shock ward? We don't call it that anymore, as befitting as it may be."

Gerald stepped closer and patted her on the back, still looking at the photo.

"But you know what I mean, Gerry... and I'm just terrified I won't find him."

As Gerald tucked the photo in his shirt pocket, he promised her a solution.

"I'm going to go take a look for myself. You sit in that chair and help yourself to some of the coffee over there in my thermos. I'll be back in a jiffy, or even sooner!"

He winked at her as the elevator doors closed in front of him, and in exhaustion, she slumped into his chair behind the desk. Taking him up on his offer, she took one of the paper dixie cups off a little stack and poured out some of the piping hot brew. She had only taken two dainty sips before she heard the doors open behind her. A young doctor, a man looking to be of East Indian descent, walked into the lobby and stopped in his tracks.

"I haven't seen you here before?" the man inquired, folding his arms.

He clearly implied that she might work there, and quickly, Lindy stood up away from the desk, realizing that she must have looked like she was on staff.

"I'm sorry, I'm actually here visiting, I'm looking for someone. Gerry, ah... Gerald, he's stepped away for a moment to take a look. I was a nurse here some time ago, I'm sorry... I shouldn't sit behind the desk."

The doctor relaxed his stance and waved the clipboard in a broad gesture.

"It's a ghost town in here, no harm. Take a seat if you need, and I see you got a bit of Gerald's coffee. That man keeps us going some nights, to be honest!"

Lindy nodded and set her coffee on the counter. For a heartbeat, she almost felt at home in this place once again.

"He certainly does; he's a bright bulb in a very dim hallway. That's what Dr. Marks used to say about him, anyway."

The look of surprise on the doctor's face was a pleasant one.

"Oh, you know Percy Marks? He's a good man. Retired last year, in fact. Eyesight, darn shame to lose such a deft surgeon."

Lindy nodded along, replying, "About time, he hardly left the building for the while I worked here! I remember he slept on that old brown sofa in his office most nights."

"Yes, that's him. Now on his *long vacation*, he called it. He said he was heading to Canada, something about all the blue lakes... well as it is, a pleasure to meet you, miss...?"

He held out his hand, the clipboard tucked under his arm.

"Lindy Eklund, Lindy Marshall, if we can get past all this..."

"Ace Javeera, nice to meet you."

"Ace?" she asked timidly, not meaning to pry. He

chuckled and answered with a smile.

"Easier than the whole thing, I promise. Everyone on staff knows *Ace*! My father wanted me to be a pilot in the Royal Navy, and he loved calling me that."

Just then, a bell signaled an elevator's arrival in the lobby. Gerald came bounding out, a file in his hand. He was sliding across the polished granite floor in his hard-soled shoes.

"Ace! Lindy! Lindy, he's here! Your fiancé, he's HERE!"

Lindy leaped out of her chair in excitement.

"Oh my! You found him!" she exclaimed, wringing her hands together.

Gerald was clutching the photo, waving in the air.

"It's not Gabriel, not in the file anyway... come take a look!"

He set the thin folder down open on the desk, and Lindy and Ace looked over it shoulder-to-shoulder. There was a photo there, clipped to the top of a standard intake form. The picture was Gabriel, all right. The same man in the photo she handed Gerald, the same man she had fallen in love with, and the same man who was unjustly being held prisoner somewhere in the bowels of this hospital. In black, bold letters on the enclosed pages, this man's name was William Hardy.

Lindy stepped back, catching her breath as she fought to contain herself.

"I've got to see him! That's not his name. You saw the photograph I have... I've simply *got* to see him!"

Gerald looked to Ace, who had a deeply furrowed brow as he read through the file. He leaned in close and mumbled something about the file 'not being complete'.

Ace stood up and cradled the file, saying, "Something's not right here, miss. I understand your excitement, but please take a breath and give me a moment. This patient is in our mental health ward. The file clearly states that he shall have no visitors per the inpatient documentation and the Governor's order. Unless you can provide proof that you are next of kin to this patient, Mister Hardy, there is simply no possibility I could let you in to see him without board approval.

Lindy became immediately incensed at the doctor's terrible news. That fire rose in the pit of her stomach again; she was about to let him have it. As Lindy balled up her fist and put it in front of her, she was interrupted by Gerald stepping between them.

Gerald clasped his gentle hand around her fist and slowly lowered it as he put his other arm around her shoulder and drew her in close. He whispered, "Relax, we can figure it all out. I promise. You trust me?"

She nodded her head to say *yes*, but her eyes did not leave their place burning holes through the doctor who just said she would not see her betrothed.

Turning to Ace, Gerald clasped his own hands together in a very pleading manner.

"Doctor Javeera, you know me. I've been here longer than your longest attendant, longer than just about anyone. Do you trust me, you know, professionally?"

Ace tapped his fingers on his clipboard and chewed on his lower lip a bit before responding.

"Gerald, I know what this work means to you and what you mean to our hospital. I've never had any reason to doubt your administrative capability. *But* rules are rules, and they exist for the safety of everyone. I can't just go letting anybody into a closed ward, at midnight, with absolutely no approving documentation to visit a dangerous patient."

Gerald nodded, still standing in front of Lindy. She couldn't see it, but a wry smile came over his face. He had thought of a solution.

"Well, he's under strict observation, but he will be in the sunroom or the panopticon at some point tomorrow, right?"

Ace nodded, replying, "Well, certainly. Every patient gets time in the panopticon if they're not bedridden or acting out..."

The devilish grin crept further across Gerald's face.

"Great! On a completely unrelated request, my lady friend here sure does miss the job. It might be nice if, say, tomorrow morning, Miss Lindy came back to take a general tour of her old workplace. I hear she's been considering a return to nursing..."

With a sardonic wink, Gerald made his case. It was clear to Ace just what Gerald's plan was. Ace breathed a sigh and let slip a silly snorting chuckle.

"You know, Gerald, I think that would be lovely. But you work nights? It just so happens, I'm doubling back, scheduled for attending tomorrow starting at eleven-hundred hours.' Looking over Gerald's shoulder, he spoke to Lindy. 'Young lady, I would love to give you a *personal* tour of the facilities tomorrow, regardless of whoever might be out and about. How do you feel about that?"

He smiled warmly at her, and the rage welling in her subsided swiftly. She felt a rush of relief as she composed herself and smoothed her sweaty palms down her thighs, took a deep breath, and stepped past Gerald. She extended her hand to Doctor Javeera, ever-so-slightly shaking with adrenaline.

"Quite a generous offer of your time, sir. I can't wait to see what you all have been up to since I left! I should get home, but tomorrow... Yes, tomorrow. I'll see you tomorrow, Doctor. Ace. Thank you!"

She rambled in nervous excitement, her hands trembling.

"Good night, Miss Lindy." Ace waved over his shoulder as he walked back through the hallway from which he came.

Gerald handed her photograph back, kissed her on the cheek, and she squeezed his hand tightly. Lindy left without saying another word; there was no need. Gerald's kind face said it all. Now, Lindy felt not just relieved but joyous. She had not only found her fiancé, sleuthed out his whereabouts, but the elation that she would be able to see him in a matter of hours was overwhelming. Her only concern now was waiting.

How am I going to sleep a wink tonight?

She asked herself this as she walked out the lobby doors. Exhaustion was a small problem, a small price to pay. No longer feeling so tired, she bounded back down the stairs and out to the street. A familiar sight set in front of her, the Chevrolet taxi and its driver munching away at what looked like a very generous rye bread sandwich. She ran to the window and poked her head inside once again, grinning from ear to ear.

"Wallace! Wally, it's great news! I found him! Well, I can't see him tonight, but I've found him all the same! May I burden you with a ride home? That is, of course, once you finish your sandwich?"

With his mouth full, Wallace nodded to her and waved her back into the cab. She slid into the backseat, bouncing on its old springs in excitement. He gulped from his thermos and looked back through the rearview mirror.

"Little lady, consider me your chauffeur for tonight. Just tell me where to go!"

She gave him the address of the old cathouse, knowing that she needed to collect a few things before she went to visit Gabriel in the morning. A few blocks down the drive, Wallace broke off a good portion of his sandwich and offered it to Lindy, who gladly accepted.

"My wife, bless her, she always makes me too much food. I'm not complaining, no ma'am, but I think she wants me fat. I'm pretty sure she wants to see me with a big Santa Claus belly! Not today, no sir!"

Lindy ate the sandwich with gusto, while Wallace shared a few more stories of his wife to help this time pass on the drive. They'd been working on reading the works of Shakespeare, and Wallace joked that she'd started teasing him with a feigned peasant accent too often around the house, and he was ready to donate the whole book collection to the local primary school.

"She doth insist I wash the dishes! It's *maddening*, Lindy!"

It wasn't far, perhaps twenty minutes, though Wallace drove slowly and cautiously. He listened as Lindy told him of her struggles to find Gabe and how she would hopefully see him the following morning. Wallace minded the road but paid attention like he was listening to an enthralling murder mystery on a late radio hour.

"You never know what you're going to encounter this time of night; it's after midnight, and these streets are full of crazy! 'Least we got some good news, little lady. *Mighty* good news for you." he had insisted.

They rumbled up to the cathouse, and Wallace let out a whistle. "This place has history, little miss. You'd better find a new spot soon as you're able!"

"Just temporary, I promise!" she replied as she leaped out of the cab and met Wallace at his window.

Grasping and shaking his hand, she thanked him profusely for his help and guaranteed him the most enormous breakfast he had ever seen on whatever day he happened by Art's. "More than you can eat, your wife will appreciate it!" she promised, and he had a long laugh at that one.

"I'll be seein' you, but now just remember to temper those expectations, you'll get through it! No point in worrying; just see what you can see. Wish your husband well for me!"

They parted ways as Wally drove off into the misty rain that had begun to fall again.

The rest of the night was a blur. Lindy went up to the room and used a few rags to dust and clean the place. It had been neglected for too long, and she chided herself. *Can't have Gabriel coming home to a mess!* It helped her relax a bit as well, and it was three in the morning before she finally felt tired enough to fall asleep.

She had been thoughtful enough to call Art from the downstairs lobby phone the hour she arrived, letting him know she wouldn't be to work the next day. She didn't inform him the reason, supposing it was too long of a tale for a call after you woke an old man up past midnight, but Art gave her the day free and wished her well with 'whatever it was that she was so excited about'.

She truly loved that old man; he was family as much as any boss could be.

Unison

Sunday, December 1ˢᵗ

The chiding tone of Gabriel's little wind-up bedside alarm clock woke Lindy just past eight.

Five hours of sleep ought to do, sure. She lied to herself. She'd barely slept three of those hours.

Lindy took her time getting ready, as she wanted to be at her best when she saw Gabriel. She shared the group bathroom with a pair of lovely older ladies, who chatted about nothing as they took turns at the sinks and showers. "So strange to see a beautiful young lass in this rundown place!" one of them had teased. Lindy had almost grown to like the building, but she knew that as soon as she got Gabriel home, she would need to find them another proper home. That would, of course, depend on how quickly Gabe recovered and perhaps returned to work.

Wonder what state he'll be in? Oh, I could wring his neck for not reaching out! What in the world would drive a man just to lay down and accept such a fate? Are they barring him from contacting me? He must be so horribly lonely.

Her imagination hounded her over what could have happened, what they said or did to convince Gabe to go along with such a scheme.

Did they convince him he's some sort of crazy? Is he too doped-up to say anything? For Pete's sake, Lindy, just go see the man. You'll get him out soon enough, and then you'll have your answers.

Shortly after nine, she made her way down to the lobby where the owner was seated at the desk, mindlessly reading a copy of Life Magazine.

"Are there any messages today, sir?" she politely inquired. She did this as a routine every time she came and went if someone was seated at the desk.

"Sure is, ma'am, just one, but it seemed important. A nice man called me here at the desk a few hours back and told me to let you know, he caught a... a 'hopper flight'? And that he should be arriving this afternoon. Said you should wait here, and he was pretty firm about it."

The old man returned to his magazine, and Lindy saw no reason to continue the conversation except to say, "Thank you!"

She strolled out the front door with a spring in her step. She had a smile drawn tightly across her face, as she knew she did not have to wait long until she saw her love again. Her heartbeat was fluttering with excitement. A short walk ended at her bank that was three blocks east in the neighborhood, certainly on a better street than Gabriel's building. She withdrew twenty dollars from her account with hopes to treat Cameron to a decent meal and, with any luck, pay for a cab to bring her fiancé home.

As she walked from her bank to the bus that would take her to the hospital, she took a moment to remind herself of the reality of the situation.

I may not be able to release Gabriel without a fight, so Cameron had better be useful.

The emotional part of her desperately ached to bring Gabe home as soon as she saw him. However, Lindy knew that wasn't how things worked when somebody had been committed, especially against their will, which she knew was likely the case.

She also figured, logically, that Gabe would need to be released to a family member or guardian. She was hoping that Cameron might be able to pull some strings, perhaps get the Army involved. Not knowing what to expect, she pushed those thoughts aside and got onto the bus, finding a seat and trying to stay calm as ten o'clock passed. Sitting there in the damp GM coach watching the lively streets pass by in the window, she pulled out Gabriel's pocket watch and glanced at it. She wished now that she'd wound it, fidgeting with excitement while she pondered if it was unusual for a lady to be carrying a pocket watch.

The bus took her far uptown, and the trip seemed to take ages. Growing impatience took over as she counted the blocks, but eventually, she arrived safe and sound with time to spare.

Standing on the hospital steps and looking up at those gothic spires, Lindy could feel a tightness in her throat and a churning in her stomach. She clenched her hands tightly and resolved to herself on the steps: She wasn't going to be emotional. This was a terribly difficult situation, but she knew she had the gumption to get through it.

Just be smart, stay level-headed as can be, and don't make a scene. You've got this.

As Lindy walked into the lobby at quarter-to-eleven, she stood away from the lobby desk and near the seating area. She was rocking a bit back-and-forth on for heels; it felt like ages as the minutes ticked by on the electric lock hanging on the wall. She watched that slowly sweeping red hand make over a dozen passes before she felt a tap on her shoulder.

"Miss Lindy, mighty nice to see you again. I take it you are ready for a tour?" Ace's smiling face was there, his white coat nearly blinding in the fluorescent lights.

"Oh, you have no idea, Ace! I don't know if I've ever been this excited about anything! I'm fretting and probably a bundle of nerves... and now I'm rambling, I'm sorry!"

Ace took her by the hand and led her to the elevator.

"*Remember*, Lindy, this is just a brief tour. I've put you on the guest registry as *my* guest. You didn't happen to bring that old photo along with you?"

"Of course I carry it *everywhere*, Ace..." Lindy nodded and went to draw it out, but Ace put up his hand in protest.

"That's sensible, though you don't need it at the moment. I believe we should pass by the cafeteria for a coffee before we continue to tour to the more interesting places, such as our modernized care ward's beautiful, sunny panopticon. It will give us a moment to prepare ourselves. Is that all right, Lindy?" He asked, receiving an enthusiastic nod from her.

They made their way to the cafeteria, where each filled a ceramic mug with black coffee. They found a seat near a window that looked out over the busy streets below.

She could tell he was stalling, but she wasn't sure why. He answered that question without her asking.

"Have a bit of coffee, and let me tell you what you can expect. Certain patients, you see, have certain personality characteristics that we need to help subdue. It's commonplace, and I am certain you've seen it in your time as a nurse. You must understand that it's the only way to help these people truly progress in their treatment. I'm sure you agree?"

"You're saying he's going to be full of dope. Maybe a bit out of his head?" she replied dryly, not intending to sound curt.

Ace nodded as he sipped. "Looking at a particular resident's chart, I could see that they were receiving treatment for numerous psychoses and violent tendencies. To be honest, I was surprised. That doesn't sound like the regimen appropriate for somebody's fiancé, nor someone who I hear was escorted in the door without manacles. Records sealed the mandate in the file, so I could only posit a theory as to why a man might need to be so medicated. Not all doctors in this hospital are generous in sharing their patent care regimens."

"It's a case of mistaken identity, that's all. Gabri... ah, said *patient* is probably a wonderful man and has never done anything to warrant such treatment.' She hushed her voice and leaned in close so as not to be overheard by the other patrons of the cafeteria, 'I know that I won't be able to do much today, but I just need to see him. I just need to hold his hand. I know we can work on getting him released soon, but today all I ask is that you let me see him."

"Finish your coffee, and let's get this perfectly professional tour started," Ace said with a wry smile.

In short order, he had walked her past a few exam rooms and clerical offices, care wards, nothing interesting. Half-past eleven, they had made their way to the last wing of the hospital, facing south so sunshine could enter the panopticon year round. Due diligence did not take long; Ace simply signed the two of them in at the podium of a towering, surly man clearly handling security for the ward. He then directed them to follow a narrow hallway, stark white and freshly mopped with the odor of bleach still tainting the air. A person could nearly see their reflection on the speckled-tan linoleum floor.

When she reached the swinging double doors at the end, Ace paused, placed her hand on her shoulder, and spoke in a low tone.

"Just remember, let's keep this brief and avoid anything unseemly. One would have quite a bit of paperwork to do before the hospital could officially consider a person next of kin."

She nodded, clutching her purse tightly in one hand and holding a handkerchief in the other. She took a deep breath in the air of that sterile hallway.

Ace opened the door and let her into the observation room known as a panopticon. It was a large and very spacious octagonal shape, the broad paned-glass windows peering out over a lush green courtyard. In the center of the massive room was a security booth that had the same eight-sided design. Inside, two nurses were taking turns between glancing up at their various patients and looking down at whatever it was they were writing. They paid little mind to Ace and his visitor.

There were seven separate alcoves on each side of the room, separated by half-height barrier walls. Each had a game table, bookshelf, or stacks of magazines for the patients to enjoy. One alcove had a television for the patient seated there. Static crackled on the screen between channels, but no sound emanated.

Ace walked Lindy around clockwise as she scanned the room. He was idly chatting about the room's design, but she wasn't paying attention. Blood rushed to her head, and she could hear her heartbeat in her ears. She strolled with her guide, but it was all she could do not to break into a sprint to find Gabriel.

They had walked around the perimeter of the room and passed five patients, all of whom were seated either in reclining chairs or wicker wheelchairs and generally staring off into nothing. Her wracked nerves had her shaking in anticipation. As they reached the second-to-last alcove, they came across an old man hunched over, gazing out the window as the record player nearby scratched out a tranquil but brassy tune.

She recognized the silhouette, but it was somehow... soft. It seemed almost unfamiliar, but she knew with absolute certainty that Gabriel was seated in front of her. Taking another deep breath, Lindy squeezed Ace's arm, signaling that they were in the right place. Ace paused his stride and nodded knowingly toward Gabe before he stood back to read something from the chart he had been toting around.

With slow steps, Lindy made her way to the wicker wheelchair. It was facing away, though she could see just enough of the man's jaw and cheek to know immediately that it was most certainly Gabriel Marshall. She drew closer slowly as her heart screamed out for her to run and leap to embrace him. It was terrifying and elating all at once. She dropped her purse on the floor and made the last few steps toward him.

I just can't believe it... They've had him here this entire time...

As she got close enough to touch the man, she placed her

hand on his shoulder. He didn't move. Her heart sank as she realized this was going to be hard. *Damned* hard.

She stepped around in front of Gabe and knelt, coming face to face with the love of her life who was now bobbing his head trying to meet her gaze. She whispered, "Gabriel? It's me, it's Lindy... it's your fiancée..." She placed one hand on his cheek and lifted his head, looking into his bleary eyes. She wiped dried saliva from his chin onto her cuff.

He stared back, almost looking past her. Like she was a stranger. His eyes couldn't focus. His brow furrowed just a bit, and he opened his mouth to speak, but she could see by the white at the corners of his mouth that he was parched. She looked around and saw a glass of water on a nearby table. The cup was filthy, but right now, she didn't care. Lindy gently brought the glass to his lips, and he very gingerly took a sip, smacking his lips together.

The corners of his mouth turned up, and she retrieved the handkerchief from her purse to wipe his face. She dabbed the bit of water that dribbled out of his mouth away, as she still cradled his cheeks.

"Gab...?"

With a raspy voice, he scratched out cheerfully, "I'm... William. They call... me William. Hellooo." His head lolled again, but his eyes started to focus and meet her gaze, noses nearly touching now.

Her voice was a hush, a whisper. It crackled with emotion.

"Gabriel Marshall, it's Lindy. You've got to see that? You're not William; that name belongs to someone else. Look at me, just remember?" She drew his hand into hers and clasped his cold fingers tightly.

His eyebrows rose slowly and subtly. He lifted his other hand and rested it limply on top of hers, looking down at their hands together in his lap for a moment. Then, she kissed him gently on the forehead.

His head lifted, and she could feel him trying to squeeze her hand, but his grasp was weak.

"...Lindy?"

His mouth hung open a bit, but he mustered a shy smile.

Tears streamed down Lindy's face as she sprang forward and embraced him, right there in the creaking wicker wheelchair. The ache in her chest and the cold of his skin caused her to wince, but she knew at that very moment that she would stop at nothing to bring him back; she would seize him out of this sterile prison.

"Gabe, you've been lost... I found you... Those bastards locked you away!" She growled, but his gaze told her Gabe could likely not understand her words as his eyes fought to focus, drifting in and out.

She held onto him for what felt like ages, and her tears soaked into the collar of his linen shirt. Then, she felt a hand calmly placed on her arm. She opened her eyes, and Ace crouched behind the wheelchair, locking eyes with her. In a hushed voice and with the most intense look on his face, he implored her to get up.

"It would be best if we don't cause a scene, my friend. I've got some ideas, but for now, we need to leave him be."

Knowing that she was already treading on thin ice, Lindy nodded in agreement. Fighting down every emotion, she clenched her fists and dug her nails into her palm. The pain helped her refocus her feelings, and she exhaled a deep sigh.

She stood up, quickly kissed Gabriel on his cheek, and smoothed out her blouse before joining Ace as he walked back out of the double doors and into the hallway. Just as she caught up with him, he stopped and turned to her.

"What are we going to do now?" She whispered. He took her elbow and walked her further down the hallway before replying.

"Right now, you will jot down a phone number and address where I can reach you, and then you will go home and collect yourself. While I cannot share any specifics with you, we have a complex problem."

She swallowed the lump in her throat.

"Complex?"

"Lindy, this man... *William*... surrendered himself for psychiatric evaluation and was remitted to us by the New York City Police Department. That, the Governor's order, and there is also a letter of advisement from a city attorney here which I simply cannot ignore. Understand that if I were holding *proper* documentation on this man, we wouldn't be standing here; you would be fighting in the courts."

"I would do whatever I had to..." she interrupted.

"*But*, this file on Mister Hardy is far too thin for that man to be on the medicinal regimen he's on, and I cannot stand by and ignore my Hippocratic oath in the face of this oversight. I've got some research to do, so please be *patient*. Perhaps be thankful that proper procedures were not followed in mister Hardy's case. A lobotomy had been prescribed but delayed for reasons I do not know."

"How *monstrous!*" she grumbled, as Ace led her off down the hall.

Lindy was fuming and distraught but bit her lip and held her composure as she joined the doctor in his office for a moment to leave her contact information. He assured her he had her best interest in mind, and she thanked him before swiftly departing.

Finding herself standing outside in the cold winter sun and far more upset than she had expected, she did just as Ace advised and took a taxi back to the old cathouse.

The taxi driver she waved down curbside was not Wallace, and that made her doubly sad.

Reconnaissance

It was nearly 2 p.m. as she dragged her weary bones into the lobby of that old cathouse. She made her way past the lobby, not bothering to acknowledge the old man at his cluttered desk. She started to take off her coat and stopped caring halfway through, one arm still in a sleeve. She unlocked the door and stepped into the room. A voice startled her out of her exhaustion.

"Lindy? I..."

In surprise and panic, Lindy dropped her purse onto the floor and swung a hand out wildly, clocking Cameron Mason across the jaw. Mid-swing, she had lost her balance slipping on the newspapers still strewn about, and while she had sent Cam reeling back onto the little bed, she ended up landing on her backside on the floor next to the bed.

She started to stand up but was too tired and defeated to do it.

"For Pete's sake, Cameron." she huffed from the floor.

"Dammit, Lindy!" Cam shouted, "That hurt like hell!" He rubbed his jaw where she'd smacked him squarely.

Sitting there among the scattered contents of her purse, she glared at him and growled back, "You deserve worse than that! You put my fiancé in the nuthouse! He's a vegetable, Cameron. Doped out of his *MIND*!" she shrieked. Tears of rage welled in her eyes.

Cam stood up, palms upward as if to surrender.

"I am so sorry, and you're right, you're right... Lindy, you got to understand. We thought we were doing the right thing. Gabriel believes it himself; he signed himself in. Mullally was there, and some cat from the Governor's office... I was there making sure it all went down clean!"

She looked up at him through glaring eyes and wanted so badly to fight him, to share her pain.

"What makes you think he was in his right mind to do something like that?"

"He *wasn't* really, Lindy. That was the point. I've known that man a lot of years, and he has had his troubles. Troubles you don't know about. It's not my place to tell you everything here and now, but I can tell you it's not his first time in a hospital bed."

She scrambled to her feet, fists balled up. "You're going to tell me *everything*, or I'm going to toss you out of this room through the god-damned *window!*"

Cam put up his hands in protest. "Okay, okay. Take a seat, and I will, but just calm down, okay?"

Begrudgingly, she sat down in the little corner chair and crossed her arms. She was furious, but she had resolved that she wouldn't kill Cameron as long as he helped get Gabriel out of this mess.

"You know when I came to visit, just after you two got back from Niagara Falls? I came because Gabe was hung up on this mess. Mullally told me what was going on. He told me about everything, Gabriel's involvement. The coincidences. The evidence, it was found on another mangled body."

"Pfft. Evidence. I say it's a ruse! Bullshit!" she retorted.

"Do you know they found one of Gabriel's keepsakes on one of the victims? A little pin, a Nazi uniform pin. I was there the day he pulled the pair of them off the SS sonofabitch Gabe had just... Gabe killed 'em in a firefight."

At that moment, Cam declined to tell her about Gabe's revenge, nor about Parker's last moments, where the pin had come from. Lindy was listening, but her eyes gave away that she doubted his every word.

"Lindy, I was sure of it. When they told me what those bastards did to him while he was captive, I was so sure that he had finally gone off the rails. They tortured him, Lindy. They held him for months, and they hurt him. Hurt his mind... they cut him up, they put sticks under his fingernails and toenails to get him to talk. Cigarette burned his ba-... I mean, they messed him up *bad*, Lindy."

Lindy scoffed at the idea that Gabe was a crazy person. "I could have set you straight, Cameron. You never thought to tell me about it? Any of it? And a terrible ordeal doesn't necessarily break a man that is *so* narrow-minded! He showed me some of his scars. That doesn't mean a damn thing!"

"Gabriel didn't want you hurt. Just before I came and saw you? I mean, he wanted me to tell you that he'd be okay, but... the cops and that attorney made me sign some papers and told me I'd be in the shit if I told anyone *anything* besides the official City Hall line that Gabe got killed in a mugging. Well, I'm doin' it now. Damn the consequences."

Lindy realized that Cam probably was putting himself at risk helping her and felt poorly about it.

He might have kept those dirty cops from harming Gabe. What if they'd come for Gabe without Cameron intervening to arrange things? Oh, I hate to think...

Settling her nerves, she said, "Well you're here, and you're going to help me right these wrongs. They've got Gabe looking like a cadaver in that damned place, Cam! He's barely holding on!" She leaned forward toward Cam, looking ready to pounce.

Cam knew he was on thin ice with Lindy.

"Listen, ever since I left New York, I knew that wasn't going to be the end of it. None of this felt right, and now you say you've got proof he *couldn't* be the killer. Okay, here I am. Ready to right that wrong. But, you better be *damn* sure about it because we can only surprise them once. Tell me, I need to hear about your evidence?"

She pointed to the corner of the room near the door where the stack of newspapers sat collecting dust.

"There's no doubt he involved himself in this mess. But the last victim, the body they found the week before? Gabriel was in my bed that night. The papers said it all; someone found the body at a time we were still asleep. I hadn't served him coffee yet! It's so *obvious* it can't be Gabriel!"

"Well, that wasn't the last body they found, Lindy."

She was indignant. "Well, the last victim in Gabe's stack of papers, but it doesn't matter. He couldn't possibly have killed *that* man, so that tells me he couldn't have done any of it."

"So you have eyewitnesses? You have people who can corroborate?"

"I made him toast and eggs, and the taxi driver got to talking with us before he took Gabe home. I'd bet he can corroborate!"

"It's thin. I believe you, but it's paper thin."

"You mean it's not enough to get him out." She sneered in

retort.

"I don't know. Mullally said this case is closed, and he's not the only person we've got to convince. They involved the District Attorney to get a mandate for his indefinite committal. Used a fake name and everything. I suppose they took it off a stiff that nobody claimed, so we are in *deep* on this. There's no easy out."

She folded her hands on her lap and sat there for a while, ruminating. Eventually, rubbing her temples, she stood up and beckoned Cam to come along.

"We need to go see him, and we need to go speak with Ace. The man who helped me... Doctor Javeera. I believe he's on my side. I hope. Maybe you can help me move this process along." She knelt and began throwing her belongings back into her purse as Cameron stood up and looked around the cramped, tired old room and fixtures.

"I can try. The only thing that Gabe cared about in this world was you, and I'm sorry. I should have brought you into the fold, but this felt like soldier business. Now... well, now I'm going to do whatever I can to get him home."

He stood up and glanced around the small room at the old splitting furniture.

"Well, maybe not *here*," he joked cynically, as Lindy stood in the doorway, ready to leave.

"I know it's crummy, Cam, but we can find another apartment. I'd live under a bridge with that man. Now, let's get going!" She was in no mood for jokes.

"I've got the cab fare," he offered as they left.

~~~

"I thought I told you to go home and rest? That was doctor's orders!" Ace chided as Lindy stood in front of his desk. Cameron had his arms folded and was leaning against the doorframe to Ace's private office in the lowest wing of the hospital.

"I had a visitor I didn't expect so soon. I wanted you to meet him."

She leaned over his desk as Ace rocked back in his chair a bit.

"I don't need your help yet, Lindy. I just need your patience, please!" Ace implored.
~~~

Cameron sauntered into the room and reached across the desk, and shook Ace's hand.

"Cam Mason, sir. Ah, Doc. Doctor. A longtime pal of Gabriel's, we served together. I was his Commanding Officer for a while, if it matters."

Ace motioned for the two of them to sit at the chairs in front of the desk.

"That would explain the man's Army tattoo, considering that Mister Hardy's file states no military record." He'd made quotation marks with his fingers when he said 'Mister Hardy'. That made Lindy a notch more confident.

Cam spoke gently, "I was here when Gabriel, I mean *William*, surrendered himself. He wasn't in a good way at the time, but this is excessive. He doesn't deserve to be in here. He didn't do what they locked him up for."

Ace clasped his hands over his lap, the stern look on his face subsiding a bit as he replied.

"That has been argued for a multitude of patients over the years, but people who commit themselves are considered to be the best judges of such drastic measures. Of course, I've already made maneuvers to reduce his drug schedule, and the nurses in the ward agree that he is charming and docile. Perhaps, soon, he will be of sound mind, and we can reassess this unfortunate situation. It might take a bit of time to make those changes, so again, I just need patience here."

Cameron chewed on his lip a bit before responding. Lindy had started to speak up, but Cameron had raised his hand indicating for her to hold the thought.

"Okay, you've got it, Doc. We can be patient. Everyone who knew Gabriel Marshall has been told he died in a mugging gone south; we could use the time to figure out a good story. Say, is there any chance that we can see him?"

Ace leaned forward in his chair and rapt his knuckles on the desk toward Lindy.

"This young lady has already had the pleasure."

"Sure, I know. It's just that I really miss the poor sap, and I just want to see that he's okay with my own eyes. I promise I won't take long. Please?" Cam was polite in his pleading, perhaps even charming, so Lindy decided to let him lead the show; she was still mighty perturbed about the situation and didn't wish to agitate things.

Ace stood up from his chair and shrugged with a sigh. "I suppose we can give you a brief tour of the ward and panopticon, and on the slim chance that we recognize a patient in there? Please be *brief.*"

He led the two of them back out of the administration wing and toward the ward where Gabriel was captive. Lindy could feel her heartbeat in her throat; all she could think about was seeing her love once more, however briefly.

Within minutes, the three of them were standing behind Gabriel, and Gabriel was sitting in exactly the same place. This made Lindy terribly sad, so she grasped Cam's hand for support. Cam's hand was clammy, and he looked shaken.

Lindy stood back while Cameron spoke a few words to Gabriel. She loved to see him, yet she felt weak in the knees. As Cam spoke, Gabe responded with a bobbing head and a half-grin. His eyes were closed most of the time, and Cameron quickly realized that talking with Gabe was a lost cause for now.

"Doc, I've seen enough. Thank you for the tour. I think it's time for Lindy and me to hit the bricks." Lindy reached out and grasped Gabriel's shoulder, but she was fighting her emotions and forcing a smile, pretending that everything was just fine.

Ace knocked on the little half-wall divider between them and the next patient. "All right, you two, I'm glad for that. Let's leave these nice folks in peace."

Ace led them toward the double doors to leave the panopticon, but they paused to let a rosy-cheeked nurse pass by with a very gray, decrepit old man in an ancient wooden wheelchair. As they passed, one of the wheels squeaked its song, and the stench of bodily fluids reeked in the air. The nurse stopped in front of them.

Nodding to greet the visitors, the nurse smiled and remarked, "It's a beautiful room, isn't it? Some of these poor souls, it's the only beauty they have. Those trees outside the window breathe life into them. I can see it in their eyes."

Lindy looked down at the poor old sap, wispy hair, and significant scars along the top of his head. His body was frail, just skin and bones. Then, she saw something that really caught her eye. "Oh, his tattoo. That symbol on his arm, that's... interesting. I believe I've seen it before. Do you know what it means?"

The nurse looked down at the old man and shook her head. "I doubt you've seen that before, sweetheart. That's no sailor's tattoo." She carefully wheeled the man through the double doors and down the hallway.

Ace's 'let's go' signal came from behind as he knocked his knuckles on the clipboard he was carrying. He said, "Well, we had better be going. I have your information, Lindy, and I will be in touch soon."

He beckoned for the two of them to join him down the hallway, but Lindy folded her arms and cocked her head to one side.

"Certainly, but... that old man. Can you tell me anything about him?"

Ace seemed surprised at her curiosity. "Oh, that's Mr. Krieger. Vegetative state, poor sod. He was a prisoner of war. During an escape attempt, he was shot in the head. Likely you noticed all the scarring. There's a saying that I don't particularly appreciate, but it fits here: 'The lights are on, but nobody is home'. A sad end, regardless."

Suddenly, Cameron felt a hand clutch his arm, digging into his bicep like a steel vice. He turned to look, and it was Lindy. She looked as though she had seen a ghost. Cam knew something was amiss but didn't address it. Instead, he turned to Ace.

"Doctor, thank you for the tour. This has been a long day for the little lady. I think we can show ourselves. Thank you again for all of your help."

With that, he took Lindy by the hand and swiftly walked her down the hall, out of the building. When they reached the sidewalk, he turned to her and saw that she still appeared shaken.

"Lindy, what-"

She interrupted him, "I can *prove* Gabriel is innocent. I mean it, real proof."

"Okay, care to share?" Cam asked.

"Sure, but first we've got a party to plan."

Cam didn't dare ask, but he wondered, *what the hell does that mean?*

She bounded to the street corner, raising her hand to hail a taxi. Cam's jaw hung open in his confusion, but Lindy paid no mind.

Company

Cameron stood in the kitchen drinking a can of beer as Lindy's father, Philip, stirred the red sauce simmering on the stove. Lindy was in the next room, delicately placing silverware on linen napkins around the table. The kitchen was adjacent to the front door, and a lovely cottage table sat in the middle of the dining room.

Cam leaned on the doorframe of the kitchen, chatting with Philip idly.

"You have quite a formidable daughter, sir; she's really a strong character. I know Gabriel was lucky to meet her; I'm lucky to call her a friend. She sure looked out for Gabe, and that means a lot."

Mindlessly stirring the sauce with a long wooden spoon, Mr. Eklund turned to Cameron with a very melancholy smile.

"He was a good man. Wish I had known him better, a damn shame what happened. He was too young. I appreciate you coming and visiting. My little girl needs all the friends she can muster right now."

Cameron nodded to her father and raised his beer in cheers. "The least I can do sir, help her go through his room and clear out some of his things. All I need is the memories, he saved my butt more times than I can count! Left me with a story or three."

Lindy and Cameron hadn't told her parents exactly what they were planning; they knew it was best this way. Everyone believed Gabe had met his end in a robbery gone bad, and Lindy had upheld that fabrication with her family for so many weeks despite her knowing it was all a lie. She hadn't wanted them to worry about her, recognizing she might have been obsessing over it all, and now the big lie suited her cause.

"Thank you for coming, young man."

Pearl was in the kitchen behind Cameron, placing her hand on his shoulder.

"Thank you, ma'am. Hard times, all we have is family."

"We do the best we can for our children. Have you got any little ones running around, Mister Mason?"

Cameron looked down at the crooked tab on the top of his beer can. "No ma'am, no children. That time in my life is long past. And you may call me Cam or Cameron, ma'am."

"Oh, you never know what the world has in store for a person. And if you keep calling me ma'am, I might make you salute! When you're in my house, Cam, you are welcome to call me *Mom.*"

"And I'm Pop, and that's final!" Philip chimed in with a grin, clinking Cameron's bottle with his own.

Cameron smiled genuinely. They had no idea he was nearly their age! This diminutive woman was clearly where Lindy had gotten her fire. He could see a gentle soul in Lindy's father. He felt the pain behind their cheerfulness, hiding in every word, and he understood.

"Sorry, ma- ... *mom,* old habits and all... Say, I really appreciate you having me here for dinner. I brought an apple pie from the market, and it's warming in the oven."

She peeked in the oven and with a broad smile turned to her husband, poking him in the chest.

"When's the last time someone has brought me a dessert? I don't think you've stepped foot into a market in a decade!"

Philip chuckled and wagged a finger toward Cameron as Pearl shuffled out of the kitchen with plates and glasses.

"You better be careful, or she might ask you to stick around for a while, Cam!" He lifted his beer and clinked it against Cameron's just as there was a knock at the door.

"I'll get it!" Lindy exclaimed as she strode to the door and opened it to find Harry standing there with a bottle of wine in his hand.

"Mister Harold Burton! You found the place okay? I'm so glad you could come!"

Harry took off his hat and handed the bottle to Lindy, hanging his coat and hat on the rack near the door next to the rest of the coats.

"Lindy, you look lovely! Nice seeing you again. What a wonderful place. Sure, I found it just fine. I haven't been to a family dinner in... well, too long. I really appreciate the invitation. Even if it's under such dark circumstances."

Lindy placed her hand on his arm, offering a comforting smile. "There's not a lot of fairness in this world."

"I didn't know about Gabriel, sad to hear that he passed. Until you called, I figured he had simply found a new job or left the city like he had said more than a couple times. I'm so sorry. He was a real pal."

Lindy took Harry's coat and sat him at the table, introducing him to her mother, who was in the living room placing a big-band instrumental record on the turntable.

"Sauce is ready!" Philip shouted, loud enough for the neighbors to hear. He poured the sauce into a lidded serving dish and handed it to Cameron, who came out of the kitchen facing Harry. Harry popped the cork on the wine, waved, and smiled at Cam.

"Harold Burton! Howdy!"

Cam set the pot on the lazy Susan and shook Harry's hand.

"Cam Mason, old friend of Gabe's. New friend of Lindy's. And mom, and pop." He nodded toward them each.

"I've heard of you, I think. Gabe had a lot of fine stories of your adventures."

Harry smiled and returned to pouring a modest glass of wine for each of the five table places. There was one empty place at the table, kept open perhaps in remembrance. In no time, everybody had sat down at the table, and Pearl was serving a heaping pile of angel hair pasta onto each plate. Philip had the honor of spooning out the sauce while Lindy grated fresh cheese over each dish. It was a bountiful meal, and everybody was ready to eat.

"Does anybody mind if I say a prayer?" Lindy offered. The rest of the table took each other's hands and closed their eyes, bowing their heads in observance.

"Lord, I thank you for this opportunity to be with truly good and kind people. I thank you for the providence and all of the good that we have in our lives. I would like to ask that you take all who are gone into your arms and let them look down upon us, knowing that they left the world a better place. This meal is in honor of my love, Gabriel. Amen."

Everybody was quiet for a few moments, and Lindy wiped tears from her cheeks with her stiff white napkin. Her mother was misty-eyed and staring off away from the table.

"Swell place, really cozy. Have you folks lived here long?" Harry inquired as he buttered his bread before passing the basket down.

Pearl took a short swig of the sweet red wine and patted her husband on the shoulder. "We've been here a good twenty-five years, or just about. Raised that beautiful girl here with plenty of wonderful memories." She motioned toward Lindy, who was buttering her bread.

"Nothing but the best memories, that's true. You know, Gabriel had found us a place..." Lindy paused and took a deep breath before changing the subject, "But yes, so many good memories here. I used to play with dolls out there on the balcony when the weather was nice. Perhaps someday I'll have a place like this all my own..."

Cameron interjected, raising his glass. "A toast to all the wonderful people we have ever known, and all the wonderful people we have yet to know." His toast was met with resounding agreement and the clinking of glasses over the table.

Harry stood up. "I'm so sorry. May I use the washroom? It was quite a trip over here."

Lindy waved him toward the hallway. "Second door on the left, our home is yours!"

Harry walked down the hallway and found the door ajar. As he reached for the knob, he heard some shuffling in the room behind the first door, but didn't make much of it. He used the washroom and returned to dinner, where he found that everybody was nearly done with their pasta.

"Looks like I've got catching up to do!" Harry joked.

The family talked for a while about the passing fall and the beautiful colors in the park. They also discussed the fear of heavy snowfall, which wreaked havoc on the city virtually every year. Lindy's father had a friend who ran the horse-drawn carriages at Central Park, and they all agreed that it would be wonderful if they could get together sometime soon for a ride through the park before the snow *really* set in.

Cameron talked a bit about his travels, how his good friend in Seattle was imploring him to come and take a job up there, and how he would likely sell his little house in Richmond. He chortled as he spoke;

"Now Billy Bigsby is quite a character. This man insisted he climb up some damn mountain in the far east Orient, and took up a plane to someplace I can't pronounce. In no time, Billy got himself stuck in a blizzard. His climbing partners lost him and all their gear under a small avalanche, so by the time Billy climbed down to the bottom of the mountain, he had frostbite on both of his legs. You know I never heard the man say a cross word about it? Says he had a 'great vacation', if you can believe that!"

Philip raised a glass and chimed in, "Don't suppose I ever met such a man, but I don't think I'd forget him if I had!"

"You've got to see it, I've never seen somebody so motivated. Honest, he's one of those adventurer types. Maybe in a past life, he discovered the pyramids or something historic!"

Pearl remarked that "man must have a strong spirit to match all that will."

Lindy shared that she was considering returning to hospital work. As she put it, "I can't simply be a waitress forever, no matter how much I love working at Art's. It's hell on my feet, and I don't feel as though I'm really *helping* anyone, you know?"

Philip retorted, "It's nice getting the family discount at Art's; it helps me plenty!" Pearl jokingly chided him for being so shallow.

"You could stand to skip a few big breakfasts, my dear... your sweaters are all threadbare just in the middle!"

"I could use some of *that*!" Harry joked about his lean build.

It was a delicious dinner, and Pearl produced a second bottle of wine just as "this one seems to have evaporated," she joked. Soon after, Cameron retrieved the pie from the oven and implored Lindy to help him serve the five little dishes of piping-hot apple pie.

Over dessert, they asked Harry about his work and what life was like in the railyard. He shared a few anecdotes about people who were not cautious around the heavy equipment and ended up limping home or worse.

"It's hard work, takes a strong guy to do it. Someone with a good head on their shoulders. You know, like Gabe. He was a great worker. Oh, I don't mean to... anyway..." changing the subject, Harry told them about one of the quirky ladies in the office who had a terrible habit of wearing too much perfume. "She's trying to fumigate us, I swear. I'd rather smell the Hudson River on a summer afternoon. Heck, some days I open my office window and do just that!"

Not to be outdone, Cam told them the story about the fish he caught by hand. "No fibbing, that fish was the size of my thigh! Coulda eaten it for weeks! Instead all I got was to *smell* it for three weeks on my damn cot..."

The dishes rattled with the laughter of happy people. Hearts set to warm after the long chill of love lost.

After dessert plates were cleared of all traces of that piping hot apple pie, and they had all taken to the living room to let their meal settle, Lindy clinked her glass with a spoon to gather everyone's attention. She took a deep breath and spoke with great emphasis.

"So, my family and my friends, I have an announcement to make. I just wanted to have a nice meal before I shocked anyone with our revelation."

Mom and Pop were seated together on the couch, and Cam and Harry were each in a wing chair adjacent. Lindy was standing in the center of the room.

Harry chimed in, "Well, I sure like good news, even if it's a surprise..."

"Oh, this is excellent news, Harry. Perhaps the best news I've ever heard. My love, my fiancé Gabriel, is *alive*."

The collective gasp seemed to suck the air out of the room. Her mother dropped her wineglass on the rug, sweet red vino soaking into the fibers and Pearl not even glancing down at it.

"Lindy... how could... Gabriel is *alive*? How could you know? Where *is* he?" Mom asked in near-panic.

Pop clutched his arms around Pearl, grimacing. "Lindy, what in the world are you on about?"

"Mother, I have seen him, and he's perfectly alive and well and being cared for by some very skilled people."

Harry sat forward on the edge of his seat. "Where is he? What do you mean cared for?"

Cam stood up, and wrapped his arm around Lindy's shoulder before he explained; "Folks, your daughter here is one damn fine detective. Smart as a whip. She took to searching for Gabe in the only place where the world could forget him; he's in a hospital ward on the north side of town. He's recovering and coming to as we speak."

In shock, Philip sat back into his seat and clutched his loving wife tightly. "Well how could he go damn near a month without saying a word? Without letting us all know he's alive, and the police said he was *killed*? This has got to be some joke..."

"Father, I can assure you it's not. He couldn't contact me, but now that I've found him, he'll be released soon!"

Her mother gasped, covering her mouth in excitement.

Harry's leg was shaking like a small dog, nervous and energized. "Then how are you getting him released? What's he there for?"

Cam sat Lindy down, and he explained to the group exactly what had happened.

"Come to find out, Gabe was framed for some terrible crimes. They locked him away and doped him up, and he had no mind to get himself free. But Lindy here, she figured it out. She knows who *really* did those terrible things, and once we catch that bastard, they'll have no choice but to let Gabe loose. In fact..."

He paused for them, and the air was thick with anticipation.

"In fact, the *real* killer that's been terrorizing the streets is going to be here any time now, and you all are going to help me and Lindy catch him." Cam had a devious smile on his face.

Harry stood up and looked pekid. "Jeez, this is all... this is a lot to take in, you two. I mean, Gabe and I were best pals, but... some *killer*? A nuthouse? This is all too much..."

Lindy walked to Harry, wrapping her arm around his shoulders and embracing him reassuringly.

"Harry, we need folks who knew Gabe and cared for him. And in this city, that's a short list. Listen, let's go get you a glass of water, okay?"

Harry shrugged, wavering, and leaned into Lindy as they walked to the kitchen with her arm around his shoulder.

Standing there sipping a cool glass of water over the sink, Harry started to come around.

"Lindy, I sure appreciate you bringing me for dinner and the big announcement. If there's anything I can do to help Gabe, I'm all in."

Lindy smiled and rubbed his back, remarking, "Wonderful! Say, before all that, would you help me wash and dry some dishes?"

Harry set his glass down and turned to the sink, saying, "I'd love to help, whatever way I'm able!" He then rolled up his sleeves to wash plates and silverware.

Lindy reached over and tied a short apron around his waist, giving him a warm smile. "Just dishes, for now. Don't want you getting your clothes mussed up! That's my apron from Art's. Don't think it's ever been worn by anyone but me until now."

Harry chuckled and shrugged, "What an honor, it's a decent fit too. Maybe my next career!"

Lindy left Harry in the kitchen, returning to her parents to console them.

Her father had a mildly perplexed look on his face, seated with Pearl on his lap and holding her around the waist. "Lindy, I'm not much of a man of action, so I suppose... what are we to do when this person arrives?"

Lindy rested her hand on the back of his neck and, in the most reassuring voice, said, "Don't worry, pop. Cam and I have it under control; you'll see."

Harry chimed in from the kitchen, "Say, I'm not much for action either... but should I do anything special?"

Lindy walked over to the doorway near the coat rack and said to Harry, "Just reach in the pocket of that apron!"

Harry, looking confused, flung the soap foam off his hands into the sink and reached into the apron. He fumbled around a bit, withdrew his soapy hand clutched around something small.

"Lindy... is this a goof or...?"

She folded her arms, a scowl now furrowed into her brow.

"You know it isn't. And you know why I gave it to you."

Harry looked into his wet palm, and a gleaming little gold Nazi pin shined back at him, now gleaming and sudsy.

Cameron stood near her parents as they watched the scene unfold through the serving window between the kitchen and dining room. Pearl started to speak, but Cam softly placed his hand on her shoulder. She looked up at Cam, who had his index finger pressed to his lips.

Harry stepped back from the sink and held out the pin for Lindy. "I have no *idea* why you would give me this. I know it belonged to Gabe..."

"It isn't the pin that sold you out, Harry."

He looked out into the dining room, to Cam and her

parents, and then back to Lindy, his expression even more confused.

"It's your arm, Harry. Your tattoo. I saw it at the diner, but now I know what it *is*."

Harry looked at his forearm, and in a flash, his demeanor reconstructed from wine-blushed cheeks to a gaunt, icy grey. His flesh exposed below cuffed-up sleeves, bearing an arcane norse-patterned tattoo that was unique to one small group of people; High-ranking Nazi commanders and their elite soldiers, and in Harry's case, the mourning brother of a dead nazi SS specialist officer. The symbology was unimportant; Harry's tattoos were identical to the arm of that brain-dead prisoner-of-war Lindy saw wasting away in the hospital.

Sneering, Harry finished drying his hands on his apron and then threw the pin toward Lindy; it bounced across the floor.

"I usually wear *sleeves*, you see..."

Lindy stood there, giving an icy glare to the sonofabitch standing in her kitchen. Harry leaned back on the kitchen counter, threw his head back, and let out a growling sigh. It echoed in the tiny home; it was animalistic and tinged with frustration.

"I was hoping for some more of that *pie*, but things have taken a turn, haven't they?"

"Harry, why in the world would you do such a terrible thing?" Lindy asked, in a tone that belied her anger with him. She did not move.

Harry shook his hands dry, stood up tall, and untied the apron, dropping it around his ankles. He responded, but it was like hearing a different person speak. His voice was lower by an octave, and his tongue now hissed out a distinct German accent.

"Your... love? YOUR LOVE?! That *bastard*, he killed my brethren, my countrymen, you stupid *cow*. Probably even murdered my *brothers* Sigmund and Heinrich... and in ze strangest twist of fate, he was brought to my stoop for recompense. For retribution. For ze meting out of God's justice. I have been killing you American *garbage* for years. Hiding amongst you dolts like a wolf in sheep's attire. It was so *easy*."

He turned to the dish rack and withdrew a ten-inch-long, serrated bread knife. Lindy steeled her resolve as Harold spun the knife in his hand, twirled it around as its polished blade glimmered under the kitchen light.

He turned back to her, not advancing but now raising his shoulders like a cougar on the verge of attack. "You know I cannot let zis pass, I have much invested in zis life here. Perhaps your *soldier* will prevail,' he growled as he looked to Cameron, then turned back to Lindy with fury in his eyes 'but at least I have ze footing to open you up and spill your life out, *harlot!*"

"Put the knife down, give it up!" a new voice boomed from the hallway. Mullally emerged from the spare bedroom, gun drawn and raised toward the ceiling, as he paced toward the kitchen. He was nowhere near a clear shot at Harold. He was old, slow. Lindy reached to her left, where a trench coat hung limply on the coat rack.

"*BASTARDSSS!*" Harry screamed maniacally as he lunged toward Lindy, only a dozen feet between them.

Cam flinched to react, but he was too far away. He shouted "LIND-!" but his shout was overcast by the explosive sound of a single gunshot.

BANG

Through ringing in their ears, everyone heard the sound of a body collapsing on the floor. Mullally rounded the hallway corner into the kitchen and saw the scene in vivid color, blood sprayed across the cabinets. The body of Harold Burton lay face-down on the cold tile floor, a hole through his torso the size of a fist.

Mullally raised a hand to stop Lindy's parents from coming to see; Philip and Pearl stood embracing each other tightly near the dinner table, breathless and panicked.

Lindy stood a pillar in the kitchen doorway, calm and unmoving, clutching a revolver that still spilled oily, hot smoke out of its barrel. As she lowered the weapon, her hands trembled slightly. Cam rushed over to her, wrapping his arms around her and clasping her hands. She let go of the German pistol, and he let it fall to the carpet with a thud.

"Christ, Lindy, what a *SHOT!*" Mullally exclaimed as he turned the body over. Harry was lying in a pool of his blood while a gurgling noise escaped his chest; the slug of the powerful German revolver had blown through his ribcage and lodged in the doorframe behind where the villain stood.

Lindy turned to Cam, pressing her face into the collar of his shirt.

"Is it over?" her voice trembling, muffled by his shoulder.

Mullally used his revolver poking Harold in the chest adjacent to the wound. Harold's eyes rolled back into his head, almost as if to catch a final glimpse of the indomitable woman who ruined his schemes.

"Ffffuckkking... cowardsss," the villain hissed with his final breath, spitting blood onto Mullally's coat.

Cam held Lindy tightly and whispered, "It's over, Lindy. We're safe."

She stepped back and locked eyes with Cam; he reached for his handkerchief but saw no tears on her face.

"Gabriel isn't safe, not yet. That's all that matters *now*." She grasped Cam's hands and squeezed tightly, turning to look back and survey the reality of what she had just done.

Mullally stepped over the fresh corpse in the kitchen and went to Cam and Lindy with a grim face.

"Lindy, I... ah, it's hard to say. I feel like this is my fault, and I even let your plan put you in danger. That being said, Gabriel is-"

Lindy's eyes narrowed as she interrupted him. "Gabriel is coming *home*, Sergeant. No damned excuses!"

"Ma'am, I was *trying* to say, Gabriel is already in a recovery room under guard by my best officers. He'll be released to you; we can see him in the morning."

Lindy looked down at the body lying nearby on the floor and to her parents still standing there tightly embraced. She turned back to Mullally, and with ice in her veins and hellfire in her eyes, she grasped Mullally by the forearm.

"No, Sergeant. Not tomorrow. *Now*."

Lurching back, Mullally holstered his weapon and raised his hands in defeat.

"He's all yours, I'll see to it." He went to the phone and dialed out for backup.

Lindy turned to Cam and hugged him tightly. "Thank you for trusting me."

Cam didn't need to respond. He hugged her back then wrapped the trench coat around her shoulders.

~~~

The clock in the hallway ticked by, echoing off cold glass and hard flooring. One flickering light cast into the corner of the room over a lonely soul. The rustling of hurried footsteps came out into the hall and drowned out the ticking entirely. The jangle of a ring of keys, a clipboard clattering to the floor.
~~~

Hushed voices carried down hallways in stale air.

That's Room seventeen...   He's intravenous right now. you can't yet!...

    ...paging the doctor...

With a whoosh, the steel door swung open and slammed into the wall so hard that its handle embedded itself in the plaster. At the doorway stood several figures, all dark-clad and silent, pensive.

Dry, slow eyes of the room's sole occupant struggled to adjust.

"Hel... hello?" his gravely and timid voice asked into the darkness, into these three faceless forms.

They moved slowly into the room. With a squint, their features could be distinguished under the light of a five-watt pull-cord lamp dangling from the ceiling.

"...t-told me to sleep..." that weak voice whispered again.

Now, the shape of many stepped into the cast of light. They became a very distinct three.

One old, sturdy. One young, dark and dashing, A friendly face.

Then, the most diminutive of the three. A kind face, a familiar face.

The voice crackled, coughed, and rasped out to that soft and smiling visage.

"...you're... back?" the question drifted faintly into the air.

It was met with a sharp exhale, then hurried footsteps. The sound of someone falling to their knees, the sound of gentle sobbing.

"I'm here, Gabriel. I'm here for *you*." The girl's countenance contorted in exquisite joy as fingers fumbled and gave a trembling grasp, a soft hand pressed into a cold hand.

There was silence for a moment while the occupant's diluted mind worked to recall. Then came a warm reply.

"...Babydoll... I... I had the *strangest* dream..."

~

www.ingramcontent.com/pod-product-compliance
Lightning Source LLC
Chambersburg PA
CBHW030121010826
48973CB00002B/364